The

LONDON
BOOKSHOP
AFFAIR

Also by Louise Fein

The Hidden Child
Daughter of the Reich

The
LONDON
BOOKSHOP
AFFAIR

A Novel of the Cold War

LOUISE FEIN

wm

WILLIAM MORROW
An Imprint of HarperCollins*Publishers*

HarperCollins books may be purchased for educational, business, or sales promotional use. For information, please email the Special Markets Department at SPsales@harpercollins.com.

FIRST EDITION

Designed by Diahann Sturge-Campbell

Title page and part opener illustrations © Gasper Gomes Costa; Alvaro Cabrera Jimenez/Shutterstock

Library of Congress Cataloging-in-Publication Data

Names: Fein, Louise, author.
Title: The London bookshop affair : a novel of the Cold War / Louise Fein.
Description: First edition. | New York : William Morrow, 2024.
Identifiers: LCCN 2023018767 | ISBN 9780063304840 (print) | ISBN 9780063304857 (digital)
Subjects: LCSH: Cold War—Fiction. | London (England)—Fiction. | LCGFT: Historical fiction. | Spy fiction. | Novels.
Classification: LCC PR6106.E385 L66 2024 | DDC 823/.92—dc23/eng/20230501
LC record available at https://lccn.loc.gov/2023018767

ISBN 978-0-06-330484-0 (paperback)
ISBN 978-0-06-335971-0 (hardcover library edition)

23 24 25 26 27 LBC 5 4 3 2 1

To Julian, my island in stormy seas

Any fool can start a war, and once he's done so,
even the wisest of men are helpless to stop it—
especially if it's a nuclear war.

—NIKITA KHRUSHCHEV

The
LONDON
BOOKSHOP
AFFAIR

Prologue

Jeannie

London
February 1942

The air was choking, thick with a heady mix of cologne, sweat, liquor, and smoke from a hundred Lucky Strikes. So many couples were packed onto the dance floor of Feldman's Swing Club, jiggling, swaying to the big band, it was impossible not to collide with one another. Who cared? Not Jeannie, cheeks aching from so much smiling in one evening, toes clamped into the viselike grip of her too-tight dancing shoes, skirt flying as she swept around the floor.

How many hours had she been on that dance floor? She'd lost track. But even after a ten-hour shift in the café, she wasn't ready for the night to be over. She never wanted it to end. The gleam of trumpets, saxophone, clarinet under the low lights, the heat, the illicit feel of the place—but most of all, the proximity to Harry. A wave of dizziness as the band segued into a new, slower beat and Jeannie drew closer into Harry's arms, intoxicated by the smell of him. The rough feel of his uniform against her cheek, the brush of his chin on her hair. She closed her eyes. The bold, bright sound of the music throbbed through her, spoke to something primitive deep inside. She was lost to him.

She'd met him only two weeks ago. But in times of war, when every minute of every day was precious and stretched out for as

2 ~ Louise Fein

long as it could be; when they wished they never slept, it had to be enough. In five days, Harry would be gone. Back to USAAF Station 1101, Daws Hill, Buckinghamshire, although it might as well have been the moon, it felt so far from Oxford Street, this club, and Jeannie's life. Her life, which had been turned upside down by this GI's arrival. It was as though she'd been asleep for all her nineteen years until Harry Marshall marched in with his wide smile, his deep, dark eyes, and his captivating soul and woke her. Nothing, not Mother or work or sensible thought, would keep her from him until the very last moment when he had to return to his squadron.

The music paused and Harry released her. He cupped her chin with one gentle hand.

"You hungry, sweetheart? Not sure how much longer I can stay upright without food."

"Now you mention it, yes, and my feet are killing me. What I'd give to sit down . . ."

"C'mon. I know a place."

With an arm slung around Jeannie's shoulders, he led her outside into a frigid February night. They walked toward Piccadilly, bodies in sync. Somewhere a clock struck the half hour. Jeannie hoped Mother hadn't waited up.

"You ever tasted American waffles?" Harry asked.

Jeannie stole a glimpse of his profile in the semidarkness. The moon was full and the night clear. Her heart tilted.

"Not yet."

"Then you're in for a treat."

The recreation rooms at Rainbow Corner were a little slice of America. A home away from home for the troops. Pinball, juke-boxes, Coca-Cola, slouchy sofas, Yankee voices filling the space between the walls. How she loved them. All of them, here, in their vital, high-octane, high-energy wholesomeness, come to save them from the Nazis. And the Rainbow Corner! It was young and vibrant. Jeannie wanted so much to be a part of it. This bright, bright place, a world away from ground-down London, her parents' stuffy, hard-backed furniture, dark wallpaper, coal fires, oil lamps, and hardship.

Harry steered Jeannie to a table with a checked tablecloth and went to fetch the food. Glenn Miller was playing on the jukebox. Jeannie crossed her legs and tapped her foot to the rhythm, staring around the laughter-filled room, trying to look as though she belonged.

"What time does this place close?" she asked when Harry returned. "It must be nearly midnight."

"Never." Harry smiled. "It's open twenty-four hours, seven days a week. Just like New York." He laughed and thrust a hamburger at her. "Here, your first taste of the US of A." There was a plate of waffles to share after, and Coca-Cola in glass bottles full of bubbles that went up her nose, making her cough and splutter. Such plenty here, in a land of rationing and shortage.

"God bless America!" Jeannie said, laughing, savoring the sweetness of the waffles on her tongue. She looked at Harry smiling at her, the warmth in his eyes. Hope blossomed, like spring. "It will all be different now that you're here. We—I mean England—are so happy, so grateful." She swallowed. "*I'm* so happy . . . Harry, you are the best thing that's ever happened to me."

Harry gazed back at her, eyes gleaming in the lamplight. Then, suddenly, he looked serious. "Marry me, Jeannie," he said.

"What?" Jeannie dropped her fork. A piece of syrupy waffle flew off and landed with a squelch on the table between them.

"I mean it, baby," Harry said, ignoring the waffle. "I've never

4 ~ Louise Fein

felt this way before. Never. And I know you feel it too. When this shit show is over, I'll take you back to New York. We'll live in style, up in a high-rise, and have babies, and, well, you can do whatever you want. I promise. I'll make you happy. Just say yes, little darlin', just say yes."

He looked scared suddenly, vulnerable, like a small boy. Waiting for one three-letter word from her that would determine his future. Jeannie wondered for a moment if he'd left anyone special behind. If this was just a ruse to get her into bed. She knew it happened. Father had warned her about men who seduced young women more times than she'd had hot dinners. She'd gotten so used to it, she barely even heard him anymore. But staring into Harry's eyes, she wondered, a tantalizing, until now unimaginable new life shimmering before her. She hesitated, just for a moment, then breathed deeply, because there never really was any doubt.

Jeannie smiled wider than she ever had before. "Oh, Harry! Yes, yes, yes!"

Later, smuggled into his digs, she melted naked into his arms, his fingers tracing patterns down her skin, a breath of wind on silk. She closed her mind to Father's warning: *Be careful.*

They were going to be married. It would all be fine.

The next day, after Jeannie's shift in the café, Harry gave her some cheap thing he picked up from a pawn shop. He promised her something better. He would save up, give her the ring she deserved.

Jeannie told herself she didn't care. She twirled the piece of metal, too loose, around her finger. Pewter, she reckoned, deciding to tell her parents about the engagement when Harry was back, when she had the ring he'd promised.

For now, this was enough.

Jeannie barely went home for the rest of the week. She threw excuse after excuse at Mother. Working extra shifts. Helping a friend. Something for the war effort. When she wasn't at work, she was in his arms, or in his bed, or huddled together for warmth on a bench under a tree in Hyde Park, watching the ducks and the pigeons.

"Useful birds, pigeons," Harry said, leaning back, head tilted, eyes trained on their bobbing heads. "They carry messages undetected—you know that? Very reliable too. Long as the enemy don't shoot 'em down."

But they tried not to talk of the war, only their joint future. Their new life, afterward. They even had their photographs taken, so they could each have something of the other to hold close to their hearts while they were apart.

The day Harry had to return to his USAAF station in Buckinghamshire, they said good-bye on the station platform, clinging to each other, ignoring the shouts, the footsteps, the slamming of train doors, the steam and whistles, the clunk and chug of the trains. It was just Harry, his breath warm on her skin as he murmured in her ear.

"Till next time, my love," he said, twisting Jeannie's hair around his fingers. "And while I'm away, steer clear of those darned American GIs. They can be very persuasive when it comes to pretty young things."

"Oh, I'm quite immune," Jeannie said, smiling up at him. His face shimmered and blurred as tears filled her eyes. "There is only one airman who will ever capture my heart."

He kissed her then, long, hard, urgent.

"Next time," she said, even then knowing she would nudge the cheap ring from her finger into her pocket when he had gone, "you must meet my parents."

"Of course. Next time."

The whistle blew.

Harry bounded on board, then reappeared in a window as the train heaved itself through a cloud of smoke out of the station. With a sad smile and a wave, Harry was gone.

THE NEWS CAME one warm afternoon in late May. A narrow-faced, sandy-haired chap, tall and lanky, wearing the same uniform as Harry. He hovered outside Lyons Corner House for a while, peering through the window now and then as though unsure whether to come in. Jeannie put down the tray of dirty crockery she was carrying and went to the door, wiping her hands on her apron. Perhaps Harry was here too. But the blood froze in her veins all the same, because somehow, she already knew.

"Name's Nat. Good friend of Harry's," the man said, thrusting out his hand. They stood for a moment in awkward silence, staring at each other, he on the doorstep, Jeannie, feeling as though life itself was draining out of her, clutching at the open door.

"I—err . . . Is there somewhere we can talk?"

Jeannie turned and called to the woman behind the counter, "Okay if I go on my break just now, Margot?" She didn't wait for a reply.

In the alleyway next to Lyons, Nat broke the news. Jeannie heard only *His bomber went down* and *Lost in action*, and the rest was white noise as she slumped against the wall, as if her bones had all disintegrated at the impact of his words. With shaking hands, she took a drag on the cigarette Nat pushed at her and coughed her guts up as he spoke of his promise to Harry that he would tell her in person if the worst happened. How Harry talked of her all the time, how he, Nat, knew how much Jeannie meant to him. How she was the love of his life and how sorry he was. Just so sorry.

"Thank you, Nat," she managed. "You've been kind to come all this way to tell me. I appreciate it. Really."

Then he was gone too, shoulders sagging as he walked away. And she was all alone, a mess of tears and snot, rage and despair. She had only just found him. The love of *her* life, too, and he'd already been wrenched away. Visions of him plummeting to his death in a burning aircraft flashed in her mind. She retched her meager lunch into the gutter.

Jeannie sat there in the alleyway for as long as she could get away with, wondering what on earth she was going to do now. Wondering why she hadn't told her mother about him weeks ago. Hadn't told a single soul. She had never felt more alone.

She balled her fists and willed herself to stop crying. Dried her eyes, blew her nose. She stood and heaved three ragged, deep breaths.

She would find a way to cope. What choice did she have?

Jeannie pushed herself off the wall and, holding her head high, walked back into the café to finish her shift.

Part I

Chapter 1

Celia

April 1962

Adventurous girls of the nineties went on the stage.
Between the wars they turned to the film studios. Now
it is the turn of television, the lodestar of dreamy-eyed
youngsters who see themselves after six months as Polly
Elwes or Nan Winton, or a purposeful floor manager
striding about the studio with earphones and plenty of
authority . . .

—*Good Housekeeping*'s "2nd Annual Careers
Guide for Girls," November 1961

Television. Well, wouldn't that be the thing? Celia pictures
herself in a smart checked suit—Mary Quant, obviously—
clipboard in hand, queen of all she surveys in the recording
studio at Television Centre. *Dim the lighting*, she commands.
*Camera one, ready? Camera two, stand by. Actors, in position,
please. Cue music and*—

"Celia, for heaven's sake, get your nose out of that magazine
and eat your breakfast if you don't want to be late for work."
Mother thumps a plate of bacon and eggs in front of her. "If it's
not a book, it's a bloomin' magazine . . . It's a wonder you're not
boss-eyed, the hours you spend with your nose buried in print."

Mother tuts, then pats Celia on the head as though to take the sting out of her words.

Celia sighs and puts down the magazine, still open at the careers page. A career sounds so . . . *appealing*. Celia, the Career Girl. An Independent Woman, thanks to her *career*. She mulls the prospect over in her mind. The money, the independence—they'd be nice. Especially if it came with some glamour. She could get away from Southwark: the home of the Elephant and Castle, the Shot Tower, fish and chips, and the original hooligan, with its down-to-earth pubs, street markets, and gambling shops. She could live up West with other girls—Jean Shrimpton look-alikes in a groovy flat. They'd throw impromptu parties for their cool workmates, play music, *dance*. It's the 1960s after all. Girls, according to the *Good Housekeeping* careers guide, can do all sorts of jobs. From science to business to travel to television. Working in a bookshop has *seemed* fine for the last three years; she's enjoyed it. But just lately she's been thinking it's time for a change.

It's time for Celia to move up in the world.

But Mother, well-meaning though she is, is a walking relic from the last century and doesn't believe in bettering oneself. Working class and proud of it. Stay true to your Southwark roots and all that. What would you want to go mixing with anyone north of the river for? She will never understand what it is to be young and modern.

Mother was born pious, rigid, and middle-aged. She must have been. It's quite impossible to ever imagine a person so opposed to anything fun or a little bit thrilling, or to ever have been nineteen, the age Celia is now. *No* is her reflex response to everything. *You might get hurt, in trouble, lost, taken advantage of.* Even as a child Mother must have been a smaller version of the woman she is now, dressed in a dull, loose day dress, apron wrapped around her waist, graying hair wound into a tight bun. Fewer wrinkles, maybe, but otherwise the same.

Celia scoops scrambled egg onto her fork and surreptitiously scans the rest of the article. *Possibilities of a career in production for girls are limited* (likely impossible). *There is keen competition for the rare production secretary. Secretaries are usually recruited at about twenty-one to twenty-five years of age* . . . Still time, then, if only Mother and Father would agree to secretarial college. *With first-class secretarial experience, initiative, energy, intelligence, mobility, and almost unlimited stamina.* Well, the lack of experience rules her out, even if she would fulfill the other requirements. *Costume supervisors and assistants, a field happily dominated by women* . . . Hmm, costumes. Daphne, Celia's dear friend, certainly has a keener eye for fashion, but—

"Celia Duchesne!" Father barks from his position of authority as Head of the (kitchen) Table. "Put that magazine *away* and do as your mother asks!" Father, equally Victorian in outlook but instinctively suspicious of religious piety, was in 1914 a penniless Belgian refugee who arrived in Margate, England, at the age of twelve. He never left his adoptive home country and is now a well-respected chef of tip-top French cuisine at the Strand Palace Hotel. Prone to morbidity of nature and an overindulgence in home-brewed beer and gooseberry wine, the two conditions very possibly linked. He and Mother rarely agree on anything, the exception being the curtailing of Celia's spirited nature.

Mother disappears for a moment into the larder, and Father leans toward her, reading spectacles balanced on his nose. "Can't you see you're upsetting your mother having that rag at the table?"

Celia eyes his open copy of *The Times* folded at the football results page, propped up against the milk jug beside his plate.

"Then why are *you* allowed to read the newspaper? What's the difference?"

Father swells. "The difference is . . ." He pauses, his bushy eyebrows drawing closer together. "The *difference* is newspapers are for news. It's important I know what's going on in the world."

Celia cranes her neck to read the article on the side of the paper half-hidden by the jug. *Nuclear Blackmail: Without her own nuclear deterrent, Britain could not resist the threat of a Russian nuclear attack and would have to surrender to . . . Possession of the deterrent was an essential element in preserving peace . . . the Lord Chancellor, Viscount . . . response to the protestors against the nuclear bomb at the Aldermaston march over the Easter weekend . . .*

"I think you're reading the wrong side of the newspaper, Father," Celia points out. "The football results are hardly—"

Father darts her a stern glare and mutters, "Less of your cheek," as Mother emerges from the larder with a bottle of HP Sauce.

"Found it," Mother says, waving the bottle and taking her place at the table.

Arguing back is frowned upon at Number 13 Copperfield Street. But Celia can't help herself.

"This *is* important," she blunders on, stubbornly tapping *Good Housekeeping* with her fork. "I'm researching my future career. That is, assuming we aren't all obliterated first by a nuclear bomb." She inclines her head toward the discarded newspaper.

Mother and Father stare at her.

"Why," Father says, a perplexed note in his voice, and ignoring the pointed remark about the nuclear threat, "would you be looking for jobs when you have a perfectly good one already?"

"I thought you loved working in that shop?" Mother's forehead creases. "You've only been there three years. I've been at the deli nearly twenty-five."

"I don't want to be a shopgirl forever. It's not a *career.*"

"Ambition isn't an attractive quality in a girl," Mother says eventually, jutting her chin and sawing through a rasher of bacon. "And besides, you'll have to give it all up when you get married. Careers aren't for the likes of us, Celia. It won't make you *happy.* Only family, God, and knowing one's place does that." She pauses, chews, swallows. "You should quit your dreaming. Too much reading, that's what. Fills your head with silly ideas." She sighs as though Celia is a troublesome un-trained dog that is still adorable nonetheless.

"And what would Mr. and Mrs. Blythe say if they lost their shopgirl?" Father remarks, removing his glasses and pushing the folded newspaper away. He looks at Celia, at the magazine, and back at Celia again.

Celia slaps the magazine shut with a huff and shunts the warm body of Bartholomew, her orange tabby cat, off her lap.

"Sorry, fella." She gives him an apologetic stroke, and his large amber eyes regard her with disdain. He flicks his tail and makes a dignified exit through the open kitchen window. "That's just it, Father. They've gone. I thought I told you?" Father looks blank. "The Blythes have retired and sold the shop. The bookshop has changed hands, and today, in fact, is the first day the new owner will be there. She might not even want me. And even if she does, it won't be the same without the Blythes. I can't imagine the place without them. Now seems the right time to look for something better."

"*She?*"

"Yes, Father. Lone women are allowed to own shops in the twentieth century."

Celia turns her attention back to breakfast. But her stomach is now a tight knot, and she has lost her appetite. The stark truth is, she doesn't have many options. She has no connections or particular skills, and without qualifications, the odds of her moving up in the world are about as good as a three-legged donkey winning the derby. If her mother has her way, at twenty-one she will marry someone like Sam Bancroft from next door. Her mother has dropped enough hints about him lately, now that he's stopped seeing that Tessa who works at the sweet shop. She imagines a future with him in a modern, new flat, likely no more than three streets away, where Celia will raise a clutch of children and Sam will work long hours for the gas board. She will see Mother every day, and to please her, she will dress the children nicely for church every Sunday. She and Sam will take the family in his gas board van to Littlehampton every summer to play on the beach for a long weekend. A vision of herself in forty years' time, stout and stooped, worn down and gray-haired, slowly dying inside from dreary boredom, hovers ominously before her.

There is nothing wrong with Sam. He moved in next door when Celia was thirteen, he fourteen, and Mother quickly struck up a friendship with his mother, the then recently widowed Mrs. Bancroft, who'd lost her husband, Leo, in a freak lightning-strike accident when he was out fishing. Celia was charged with trudging all the way to school with Sam, making sure he knew where to go. Mother instructed her to *introduce him to the right kids*, whoever they were. It was an excruciating experience for them both. Back then, Sam was awkward, grumpy— undoubtedly grieving his father—and answered her questions in monosyllables. That first morning, they had run out of conversation well before they reached the end of the street. Over time she got to know him better. He shrugged off his shy discomfort, grew into himself. He even turned out to be rather charming. So much so, the girls at school quite fancied him. Especially Tessa. They'd been together almost three years. Broke it off because he failed to pop the question, according to Mother. She had looked mighty pleased about that.

But to Celia he's just Sam, the boy from next door, who volunteers every Sunday at the animal sanctuary off the Old Kent Road. He is as much a part of her life on Copperfield Street as coddled eggs and hot tea in the morning, the ringing bell and call of the rag-and-bone man doing his rounds every week, or the cheery whistling of the milkman and clink of bottles on the doorstep in the still-dark hours of the early morning. She's as likely to marry him as she is her old pair of slippers.

Besides, while he seems content with his status quo, she longs to get away from Southwark, the dog-end of South London, with the remnants of its run-down slums and back-to-back terraces now terrifyingly dwarfed by swiftly rising concrete tower blocks—the government's answer to overcrowding, poverty, and deprivation.

Lying on the marshy south bank of the Thames, Southwark has experienced grinding poverty for hundreds of years. Dickens wandered these streets, both as a child and an adult, finding inspiration for the likes of Oliver Twist, Pip, William Dorrit, and Nicholas Nickleby. There has always been a pervading stench from the dockyards, where the working classes labor day and night, helping Britain's burgeoning empire and filling its bellies with the fish cured and eels chopped in its backyards and narrow alleyways.

But to the locals, many of whom have lived here for generations, Southwark has been a thriving community, a different country from affluent London across the river. Southwark has long been a place of fascination for journalists, writers, and aristocratic do-gooders, from Charlie Chaplin to Jessica Mitford to George Orwell, who, like Dickens, descended upon it for inspiration and for firsthand experience of the urban working class. But what none of them have ever really captured is the strength of the community, the we're-all-in-this-together-ness, and the sense of pride that binds them.

That's what Mother bangs on about as she tuts at the council's plans to sweep away the little Victorian back-to-backs, like those remaining on Copperfield Street, and replace them with tall concrete blocks, several of which already rear up above the neat terraces like glowering, multi-eyed spaceships.

Mother's aversion to progress is equal and opposite to Father's support of it. The more he wants change, the harder she fights it. *She's driven me to drink*, Father complains whenever there is a disagreement (often). He *is* a foreigner, so that has been a bad mark for him from the get-go. But there is more to it than that. There's a broiling resentment between them, rumbling somewhere beneath the surface; its source, a mystery. Perhaps, after all the years they've been together, they are simply fed up with each other.

After living with her parents for the past nineteen years, Celia is, unsurprisingly, a marriage cynic. All fairy tales, she realized long ago, end at the point of marriage. Once the prince has secured his bride and the children arrive, the romance will be long gone. The beautiful princess, in all likelihood, will have nothing more than domestic drudgery to look forward to.

"Celia . . ." Mother brings her back to the present.

"Yes, Mother?"

Mother is peering at her. "Is that cardigan covered in cat hairs?"

Celia looks down at herself, hastily brushing evidence of Bartholomew from her clothes.

Father clears his throat. "Do we think that to be a suitable garment for her to wear, Maggie?"

"It is a bit tight." Mother frowns.

"And red," adds Father. "Perhaps not the best thing to impress the new owners."

"What's wrong with it?"

"Tight, red spells *tarty*. Hardly suitable for a bookshop, is it?" he says.

"Secondhand bookshop." Mother sniffs.

"It's *antiquarian*." Mother gives Celia a blank look. "We sell valuable books, rare first editions."

"Makes no difference to what you should and shouldn't wear," Mother says, straightening her bony shoulders.

"The point is," Father adds, "whatever you got away with before with Mr. and Mrs. Blythe, the new owner might be a different kettle of fish. *She* will surely want a serious, sensible girl. She doesn't *have* to keep you on, does she?"

Celia swallows a mouthful of scrambled egg, her stomach clenching in protest. She takes a long, slow breath.

"I'm well aware of that. Which is why I was looking at the career guide. May I go and change now? I don't want to be late." She waits for Mother to say something about wasting food and wasting time reading pointless magazines about pointless careers, but in the end she simply nods.

Celia dashes upstairs before either of them has time to say more.

Chapter 2

Celia

Celia steps off the double-decker bus outside Somerset House just as she has done every workday morning for the past three years, wondering if this is to be her last. It was all left so up in the air last week as she said her good-byes to the elderly Mr. and Mrs. Blythe. They were upset to be leaving their beloved shop after forty years, but in the past year, Mr. Blythe's health has deteriorated, and Mrs. Blythe can no longer care for him and the shop. *We have to accept his lungs are not going to get better*, a moist-eyed Mrs. Blythe had said as they finished packing up. Celia couldn't bring herself to ask what it meant for her. She hopes if she simply turns up, the new owner might be glad of her help.

Celia is bowled along the Strand by a fast-paced tide of commuters streaming toward Fleet Street and the City of London. Besuited men in black, the odd splash of color bobbing among them: evidence of a woman in their midst. Newspapermen most likely. The neater, better-dressed ones will be solicitors and barristers, or possibly men of finance, bound for the banks and financial institutions of the Square Mile, the City of London, farther east. Whatever their vocation, they bear deadpan, unsmiling expressions.

Perhaps Mother is right. Careers don't appear to make people happy.

Celia arrives at H. J. Potts, Booksellers, est. 1843, a few

minutes before nine o'clock. It's easy to miss the tiny book-shop, squeezed as it is between two more grandiose shops. The one on the right selling barrister's apparel, wigs, gowns, and such; the other, bespoke handmade business suits. She wonders how many of these commuters, passing the shop every day for years, have even noticed its existence. From the usual lack of footfall through its doors, she suspects barely any of them.

She pauses at the door, anxious, recalling the very first time she came upon the shop. Recently out of school and on the lookout for a job better than the monotonous part-time work in the launderette, she had been sent on an errand by her mother. Her father, rushing to get to work in the hotel kitchens, had left his reading spectacles on the kitchen table. Mother had been certain he would dice his fingers along with the carrots, and then where would they be without his money coming in? Celia had been dispatched to chase after him. Jogging from the bus stop along the Strand toward the Strand Palace Hotel, she'd spotted the sign H. J. POTTS, BOOKSELLERS, EST. 1843, for the first time.

What had caught her eye, and her breath, were the books. Specifically, the stunning, first-edition copies of all three volumes of Mary Shelley's *Frankenstein: or, The Modern Prometheus*, which had been displayed in pride of place at the center of the bay window, their brown spines a little bent at the edges, their blue covers mottled with age. There is still something about old books that makes Celia's spine tingle. Arranged around the Shelley volumes were other gems—Virginia Woolf, James Joyce, even a Lord Byron poetry collection. The sight of them had knocked all thought of impending risk to her father's fingers from her mind, and the spectacles case remained unconsciously clasped in her left hand as she'd been drawn inexorably inside.

The interior was a dark, dusty treasure trove, packed floor to ceiling with old books. It smelled of dust, leather, and beeswax.

Celia had naïvely inquired about the Mary Shelleys. She'd prattled, overcome with the excitement of her discovery of this shop. Reading was something she had always loved, finding it an escape from her drab homelife.

"I love old books . . ." Celia had beamed at Mrs. Blythe. "Well, any books, really. But nineteenth-century fiction is a favorite of mine. The Brontë sisters, especially, and I'm a big fan of *Frankenstein*. Terrifying, of course, but imagine her writing that book when she was only eighteen? I've never read anything like it, before or since, I mean . . ."

Mrs. Blythe had looked Celia up and down.

"Now, my dear. I don't want to make any assumptions about customers, but you don't look more than eighteen yourself—"

"Sixteen, actually."

"Well, then. Exactly. Now, I can tell you are a big reader, but unless I've got you all wrong, I'm quite sure *Frankenstein* will be out of your price range. In fact, we are sending that one to the auction houses next week. It's for display only, you see, to show the sort of quality items we carry here." She waved a hand vaguely at the books that lay in piles everywhere and were on bookshelves that covered the walls. "But I must say, you have good taste." She granted Celia a smile and a sharp look.

"The Shelley is a first edition, one of only five hundred printed. We expect it to fetch a fine price at auction," Mrs. Blythe said.

Celia had rapidly concluded that there wouldn't be a single page let alone a whole book in this shop she would be able to afford. She began to shuffle closer to the door, suddenly remembering the glasses in her hand and wondering guiltily if Father's fingers were already severed on a chopping board. But, most of all, she wanted to escape and avoid the humiliation of being directed to WH Smith, where she would find a cheap paperback she might have a hope of paying for.

"In fact," Mrs. Blythe continued, without seeming to notice Celia's sidle toward the exit, "if we make a decent amount from the Shelley sale, we're hoping to hire a shop assistant. Mr. Blythe and I are getting on a bit in years, and with Mr. Blythe's weak lungs . . . Well, some help would be nice—"

"I could do it," Celia blurted out before she could stop herself. "I am awfully good at organizing, I love books, and, as it happens, I'm just in the market for a job."

The rest, as they say, is history.

Now Celia hovers outside H. J. Potts. She tugs at the sedate beige cardigan, swapped for the racy red one, sliding it down over her hips. She takes a deep breath and, possibly for the final time, reaches for the door handle.

Eyes adjusting to the darkness of the interior after the bright daylight outside, Celia glances around the familiar surroundings. Nothing seems to have been altered, and relief sweeps through her. At the back is the old-fashioned glass-topped counter dominated by a large cash till. The art deco lamp, too, is still here, throwing multicolored patterns through its beveled glass shade onto the walls and ceiling. Celia remembers how delighted Mrs. Blythe had been to have found it, *an absolute gem*, on the Portobello Road. The same shelves of books run floor to ceiling around the outside walls, with the ladder propped just as it has always been against the upper shelves. On one side, the locked glass cabinets, containing the most valuable stock. In the center, two rows of open stacked shelves. Even the trolley, half-filled with books, is still here, pushed against the counter. Everything is exactly as before, even the smell—old leather, wood polish, and the acerbic hint of musty mold. For a dizzying moment, Celia wonders if perhaps the Blythes changed their minds, and they are just out back, in the stockroom, or making their stiff way downstairs from the flat above the shop.

"Hello?" Celia calls. "Mrs. Denton?" She remembers the name of the lady who purchased the shop. *Nice woman*, Mrs. Blythe had told her. *American . . . They have deep pockets, you see. Offered over the odds for it, if you ask me. More money than sense that lot, but still . . . We're grateful.*

Silence.

Nothing moves and there is no sign of anybody. The place is as lively as a morgue.

Then, the sound of shuffling behind the door that leads to the flat above, and it swings open. A petite middle-aged lady with tightly curled hair coiled high on the top of her head, reminding Celia of a sprightly poodle, stands on the threshold. Permanently waved, Celia thinks, her coiffed mop adding at least three inches to her height. She carries a look of bewildered surprise, as though seeing another person in her shop is the very last thing she might expect.

"Can I help you?" The woman approaches the counter, regarding Celia through the thick lenses of a pair of tortoiseshell-framed glasses, far too big for her small face. A string of iridescent river pearls hang around her neck, catching the light from the lamp on the counter as they swing backward and forward. There's a waft of Lily of the Valley scent.

"Hello, yes, I'm Miss Duchesne. Celia . . . I'm not sure if Mr. and Mrs. Blythe mentioned me. I'm the shopgirl here. Or at least, I was—"

The woman starts. "Oh!" she exclaims, eyes widening. She

clutches the counter as though Celia is the ghost of Miss Havisham herself.

"I—I'm sorry," Celia stutters. "Perhaps you don't need—only . . . Well, never mind. I'll just go then, shall I?"

"Wait!" Mrs. Denton exclaims as Celia turns to leave. "You're the girl who's been working here? The previous owners *did* tell me about you. Of course I shall need you. I'm very glad you dropped by." Mrs. Denton's words have a soft twang of an American accent. Celia recalls Mr. Blythe saying she was from California. What a very peculiar move. Who, in their right mind, would choose to leave *California*, the home of Hollywood stars and golden beaches, for London, the home of beer-swilling old men and the London Underground? Though the market for old books is likely better over here. People in California must be too busy enjoying themselves to have time for reading.

"I apologize." Mrs. Denton lets out a tinkle of laughter. "It's just been a little crazy with the move and all . . . So much to organize and it is just me here. Mr. Denton, in case you were wondering, walked out on me a year ago for a . . . young lady, let's just say to be polite, and I thought to myself, 'Vera, what you need is a fresh start.' After a little court battle, and the realization I was far better off without the cad, I had some money in my pocket, and I fancied an adventure. I have *always* wanted to visit London, and so I thought, why not? But I couldn't just float about like a tourist, and the money wouldn't last forever. When I saw this place advertised for sale, I thought, now that's the opportunity I've been looking for. So, here I am, and here you are, and we'll be a team, won't we?"

She beams at Celia, who blushes at such intimate personal information, coming from someone she only just met.

"Now, you man the shop, or should I say *woman* the shop, while I finish sorting out the flat. Then you can show me the ropes. How does that sound?" Mrs. Denton pats her hair.

"Well . . . I . . ." Celia isn't too sure what to make of Mrs. Denton's entrusting the running of her brand-new empire to her. Mr. and Mrs. Blythe almost never left her alone in the shop. There are priceless books here, after all, and important decisions to be made about value and authentications and a myriad of other things she shouldn't have to worry about. Or so Mrs. Blythe would say.

The woman frowns at Celia's hesitation.

"Oh, I'm sorry, Celia—it's okay that I call you that? You're wondering about the salary, aren't you?"

Celia blushes even more furiously and freezes. Nobody in England would dare to mention such a dirty thing as money up front like that.

"What did they pay you before?" Mrs. Denton presses, apparently quite unaware of Celia's discomfort.

Celia clears her throat and looks at her shoes. "Six pounds, ten pence a week, for five and a half days' work. They kindly gave me Saturday afternoons off, but if you—"

"Is that all? That doesn't sound enough for all the responsibility of running this shop. Listen, I'll pay you eight. No, let's make it ten. Ten pounds a week, how does that sound? Don't want to lose you, do I?"

Celia's head snaps up and she opens her mouth to speak, but no sound comes out.

"Will that be enough to entice you to stay?" Mrs. Denton repeats, and Celia nods, dazed. She'd probably have stayed on for nothing if Mrs. Denton had asked nicely enough.

"Excellent. I'm glad that's all settled, and we can get on with the business of the day." She rubs her hands together. "I'll be back once I've sorted this flat out some." And then she's gone, the door shut firmly behind her, leaving Celia staring after her in astonishment. Footsteps sound on the wooden stairs rising up to the flat above, and a few moments later, bangs of hammer on nail. Mrs. Denton must be putting pictures up on the walls to make the place homey. A woman doing home improvements *and* owning her own business. There is much about Mrs. Denton to admire.

Celia tiptoes around the empty shop, running her eyes across book spines to check all her favorites are still here. Austen, Brontë, Chaucer, Dickens, Eliot, James, Joyce. All present and correct. She stares out the dusty window onto the Strand at the passing traffic and the seemingly endless column of commuters.

A warm glow spreads from Celia's midriff right up to her reddened cheeks. This changes everything.

The raise, which Celia will keep to herself, means she will have a good deal of money left each week after handing all her wages, bar a little pocket money, over to her mother, just as she always does.

And secret money for herself means opportunity.

Chapter 3

Celia

Four days later, at five thirty on the dot, Celia is waiting on the corner of Aldwych and Kingsway. A light drizzle is falling, and she stands well back from the curb to avoid the gritty spray thrown up by the heavy wheels of passing double-decker buses. The steady stream of dark suits and black umbrellas is traveling in reverse direction from that of the morning, now bearing down the Kingsway toward her, likely heading to Aldwych tube station or over the bridge to Waterloo, the suburbs, smiling wives in flower-printed aprons, scrubbed-clean children, and their homecooked teas.

And here, among them, like a solitary splash of color in a black-and-white film, comes Daphne, her lemon sherbet cloak swinging. With matching hat and gloves, light tan shoes paired with bag, natch, and her striking blond hair curled just so at the bottom, she looks as though she should be on the catwalk in Paris rather than a soggy London pavement.

Celia knew she would be best friends with Daphne on her first day at St. Thomas's Elementary School. She first spied the young Daphne, with her wide blue eyes and halo of golden hair, in the sandpit beating Billy the bully on his square behind with her spade for daring to pick on Rudy until Billy had yelped.

She'd thought their friendship would end when Daphne sat for the eleven-plus exam to get into grammar school. Celia hadn't been allowed. *What would you want to go to that highfalutin place for?* Mother had cried. *All those stuck-up boys and girls. You'd hate every minute of it, Celia. Besides, the uniform, the books, and what-not, it'd cost us an arm and a leg.*

Perhaps Mother had only wished to save her from the shame of not passing, like Daphne, who'd failed by a hair's breadth and carried the burden of that all the way through secondary school like a boulder on her back.

Celia had, selfishly, been secretly pleased when her best friend hadn't gotten into the grammar school and the two could stay together. Daphne was uncommonly clever, but somehow Celia had managed to stay in her class and not get streamed with the dunces. She just wished her parents had let her go to secretarial college, too, like Daphne, when they'd left school, instead of urging her to go straight out to work.

Secretarial college is the epitome of success for the ambitious girl leaving secondary modern, pronounced the careers guide in *Good Housekeeping, university being the preserve of only grammar-school graduates. A good secretary can have a wonderfully satisfying career.*

And so, here is Daphne, a legal secretary no less, with a top job at Thompson, Parker & Edgely, one of the many firms of solicitors in High Holborn, just ten minutes' walk from H. J. Potts.

"What ghastly weather!" Daphne greets Celia with a kiss on both cheeks. "Hope you've not been waiting long."

Daphne threads her arm through Celia's and they enter the welcome dry, beer-scented warmth of the Wellington. Daphne removes the yellow cloak, revealing an elegant seal-gray fitted work dress, and drapes the cloak over the back of a chair.

"C'mon, I'll get these. To celebrate," Daphne offers, which is lucky, as Celia hasn't even two bob to rub together until she gets paid.

"What are we celebrating?" Celia asks, shrugging off her damp, seen-better-days, utilitarian taupe raincoat.

"It's Friday. Do we need another reason?"

"Won't say no then." Celia smiles, then blows into her hands to warm them up. Who would believe this is April? "Ginger beer, please."

"*Ginger beer?* Really? Your mother isn't here, you know, Celia. I'll get you a Cherry B." Daphne winks one bright blue eye before elbowing her way to the bar.

Daphne's right. Mother isn't here, but if she was, she wouldn't approve of Celia drinking alcohol. Not unless it's the half a glass of red she is permitted on a Sunday with her dinner after church. According to Mother, alcohol is the path to ruination and damnation. She never mentions Father, of course, when delivering her lectures on the dangers of drink, but this would be unnecessary, since Celia can witness this fact for herself.

I am nineteen years old. I'm a Strong Independent Woman. Mother need not approve of everything I do. She repeats the words a few times to herself as she watches Daphne, so relaxed, so at ease with herself, jostling through a sea of men at the bar. She needs to be more like Daphne.

She watches her friend ooze sophistication, the men parting to let her through, practically salivating at the sight of her. Before today, a flicker of something hot and ugly might have risen in her belly, knowing her friend is going up in the world while she, Celia, vegetates and fossilizes, her only escape from reality between the covers of a good book. But not anymore. Not now that she has this chance. Daphne waves two brown bottles of cherry wine in one hand, two glasses in the other, and Celia is unable to suppress her smile.

"So?" Daphne fills the glasses and pushes one across the table, raising her voice above the hubbub. "Spill the beans. What are you so happy about?"

"Am I normally that miserable?" Celia takes a sip of the sweet, syrupy cherry wine. Then another. And another.

"Often." Daphne laughs and wrinkles her nose, nudging Celia's knees beneath the table. "But today you look like the cat that's got the cream."

Celia laughs, too, lighter always in the orbit of Daphne's positive aura. Or perhaps it's already the effects of the Cherry B.

"The new owner started at the bookshop this week," Celia explains.

"Ah," says Daphne, sipping her wine as Celia tells her the circumstances surrounding Mrs. Denton's arrival in London.

"I really admire her. A lone woman, moving halfway around the world, running her own business. And she's really very nice. I thought I'd hate the shop without the Blythes, but she's giving me free rein to run it how I think best. Like I'm the flipping shop manager! Fancy that, eh?"

"Quite right too. Cheers!" Daphne drains her glass.

"I just hope I'm up to it."

"'Course you are!"

"Anyway, how are things at the firm?"

"Busy. Mr. Edgely is preparing for a trial starting in two months, so I'll probably have to start working overtime. I don't mind, not really. The extra money will come in handy. And guess what?" Daphne's cheeks grow pink. "That articled clerk, you know the one I told you about . . ."

"Graham Drayton?"

"Oh no, not him." She rolls her eyes. "All wandering hands, that one. Only interested in getting past first base. No, I mean Thomas Fitzpatrick. He is *much* more upmarket. Sort of looks like a young Gregory Peck. He's asked me out on a date tomorrow!"

"Lucky you." Daphne has an ongoing and enviable succession of boyfriends whom she tosses aside every few weeks as the novelty wears off, or just around the time they are keen to get serious. While Daphne is on the hunt for Mr. Right, the boys she dates seem to be after one thing only, and, she says, that's the one thing they won't get without a ring on her finger.

"Yes. Lucky me. But what are we going to do with you, Celia Duchesne? You are never going to meet Clint Eastwood in that dusty old shop, however nice Mrs. Denton is."

"Oh, don't worry about me."

"What—you're content with just reading books?"

"I love my books, Daph . . ."

"I know, but you can love books *and* boys."

"Not interested in bothering with boys." Celia sighs, just imagining how her parents would react to her introducing a boyfriend, the prospect of which makes her perspire. "But I *do* want a career. Look, I've had an idea." She searches her handbag and pulls out a leaflet. She shoves it at Daphne, bursting with the secret she's been keeping all week. Daphne will be the only one to know. "See, the Pitman's College offers night-school courses in shorthand and typing. I've signed up for a six-month course. I start next week." That bubble of excitement again, this time nothing to do with the Cherry B. "I know it's not secretarial school, but it'll be enough to join a typing pool. I can work my way up. BBC, here I come!"

Daphne scans the leaflet and looks up at Celia. "But . . . how will you afford the fees? I thought you had to give all your wages to your mother. You barely have enough each week for the bus fare and all the bloomin' books you're always buying."

"I know. But Mrs. Denton thought I wasn't being paid enough. She almost doubled my wages, just like that!"

"Seriously?" Daphne's mouth drops open. "Why?"

"I've no idea. Well, I have. I think she was terrified I'd leave, and she wouldn't know how to run the shop without me."

"That's wonderful, Celia, but don't you think—?"

"Thing is, I won't tell Mother or Father. I'll carry on giving them the five pounds I always have, and they'll never know. They'll think I'm still keeping just the one pound, ten pence. So we'll all be happy."

"How will you explain your absence in the evenings?"

"Overtime, to help Mrs. Denton, seeing as she's all on her own. It's two hours on Tuesday and Thursday evenings, five thirty to seven thirty. I'll have to leave work sharpish at five, but Mrs. Denton was fine about it when I told her. I'll feel a bit bad for Mrs. Denton when I eventually leave, but I think, being a businesswoman herself, she'll understand. And I'll help her find a replacement. I could have a new, fancy job *in television* before Christmas, Daph, what do you think of that?"

"I think it's positively marvelous." Daphne's face is all soft warmth, her eyes glinting as though reflecting Celia's excitement. "I bloody love you; you know that?"

"I do, and I you. Now let's drink to us both being Strong Independent Women of the 1960s!"

They clink glasses and do just that.

CELIA HAS LIVED at Number 13 Copperfield Street all her life. A terraced Victorian workman's cottage in a stunted row of identical dwellings, humble, down-to-earth, and functional. Like their occupants, one by one they have been, to varying degrees, dragged into the twentieth century. Since the Second World War, modern conveniences have been added—fitted kitchens, central heating, indoor toilets, electricity. Anderson shelters hastily constructed during the war years dismantled and replaced with flower beds or vegetable patches. Fireplaces have been bricked up, and in their place stand gas or electric fires, ugly but healthier, to satisfy the Clean Air Act of 1956.

This is development. Advancement. Human Progression gathering speed toward a better, more comfortable future. That is what Father pontificates upon on Sunday as he sits in his position as Head of the Dining Table. Celia knows better than to offer any contrary point of view to her father. But what she *wants* to discuss is why Human Progression seems to have skirted around the fact that humans consider themselves to be becoming ever more civilized when really, their nature hasn't changed a jot since prehistoric times. They are still the same bundle of instincts, ready to fight for life and territory and resources. It's simply their tools have gotten more useful, their weapons more lethal. So much so, it's quite likely, if one believes the swelling numbers of peace protestors, that the two superpowers may well destroy the entire planet if relations between them get any worse.

But she keeps quiet, stirs her steak-and-kidney pudding in its sea of gravy around her plate, and listens to her father's ridiculous justification for installing a television into the front room. *We can watch the news rather than listen to it on the radio. Such modern technology will soon see the demise of the radio altogether, and then where will we be?* They all know it is really so he can watch the football World Cup this year from the comfort of his own living room. He will do what he wants anyway. For he who earns the money holds the power.

That simple equation has slowly dawned on Celia over the years. She never thought twice about it until Mrs. Ursula Bancroft moved in next door after she lost her husband. Leo, it turned out, unusually among the male population of Southwark, did not drink, gamble, or smoke away his earnings, but he squirreled them, leaving his wife enough money to afford a relatively comfortable house and without the need to find a replacement husband, which, she informed anyone who would listen, was a blessing, because what on earth would she ever want another husband for?

The concept of a woman without a man to support her had been a revelation to Celia. It stirred in her the beginnings of ambition. An ambition to be self-sufficient. And now there is Mrs. Denton to add to her growing dossier of evidence of what is possible for a Modern Woman to be. She hugs the secret of her Pitman's course, her kernel of hope, quietly inside, like a fragile, unhatched egg.

"You'll come to see," Father is telling Mother, mopping up the last of the gravy on his plate with a hunk of bread, "that television will bring enjoyment to your life."

"It isn't *me* who needs enjoyment," Mother says, voice sharp as needles.

"That's what you think." Father downs two-thirds of his glass of wine, then refills it.

Celia sighs. In her humble opinion, they are both as miserable as each other. So they sit, in stony-faced silence, until it's time to clear the lunch things away. Afterward, Celia settles herself onto the sofa in the front room to read her latest novel, *Catch-22*. She is trying to broaden her reading and quizzed Mrs. Denton about American authors. Mrs. Denton was oddly evasive. She admitted to a love of the Russian greats—Dostoevsky, Tolstoy,

Chekhov, Nabokov—and the French masters—Victor Hugo and Alexandre Dumas. But then she'd laughed and said she finds very little time for reading these days. Which at first Celia thought odd for the owner of a bookshop, but then, the poor woman has had quite the year and is now singlehandedly running her own business.

There is a bang on the front door.

She sighs, laying her book on the coffee table, barely a page read.

Sam, tall and lean in his overalls, is standing on the doorstep, a wild-eyed Bartholomew in his arms. His smart new cream-and-red van, *Clean Heat—Modern Gas* emblazoned in big letters on its side, is parked in the street. For a moment she thinks he is going to ask her if she fancies going for a spin in the van the gas board gave him last month—it wouldn't be the first time. She knows he is awfully proud of it, but frankly she'd rather be reading than sitting in the London traffic.

Sam holds the cat out toward her like an offering. "I found the little chap up on the main road. Terrified, of course. Think he might have been chased by a dog. I managed to grab the poor mite. He's had a ride home in my van. Can't say he was too impressed . . ."

"Oh, Sam!" Celia takes the cat, stiff with fright, and nestles him into her arms. His body softens against hers as she rubs his head. "How can I thank you? That's so kind, and sorry for all the bother." What other lad would stop all the traffic on Southwark Bridge Road to rescue a cat, let alone even notice an animal in distress? Her heart melts a little. Next time he offers her a ride, she will say yes.

"Don't be daft. You don't need to thank me." He grins and

reaches out, tickling Mew's cheek. "I'd do it for any animal. You know that."

"I do." Celia plants a kiss on the cat's head and releases him into the house, pulling the door closed behind him. She turns back to Sam. "Do you want to come in for a cuppa? I just made a pot of tea."

"You're all right, Celia." He looks down at his overalls. "Your mother'd have a fit if I sat on her clean sofa like this, all covered in grease. Just finished my shift, see, so I need to wash. Besides, my mother will have my dinner waiting."

"I didn't know they had you working Sundays too."

"Sure they do." He smiles at her again, the skin at the corners of his eyes crinkling. "People need gas twenty-four-seven, so the gas board works round the clock too. No rest for the wicked, eh? I'll see you around, yeah?"

"All right, well, thanks again for saving Bartholomew."

He steps across into his own tiny front garden, neat and already blooming in full glory under the magical green fingers of Mrs. Ursula Bancroft. For one crazy moment Celia wonders if Mother might just be right about Sam being the perfect match for her. Then she laughs at the ridiculousness of the idea.

Just because he rescued her cat.

And besides, unlike poor Elizabeth Bennet, she will find a way never to be financially reliant on any man, even Mr. Darcy, if she were to be lucky enough to happen upon him.

Chapter 4

Septimus

Septimus Nelson is a horribly pretentious name.

It makes him stand out, whereas his inclination is to blend in. Still, he supposes notability has its benefits, especially now that he lives in a new country, a new city, where he knows almost no one.

And finally, last night, the name Mother and Father Nelson chose for Septimus the day he was born in Canada proved its value.

Septimus smiles at the memory as he walks from his flat in Paddington across the expanse of Hyde Park to the American embassy in Grosvenor Square. It's going to be a glorious day. The first warmth from the sun since he arrived in this gray city four months ago in early January. Until today, London has been almost permanently swathed beneath leaden clouds, damp rising up from the sidewalks and out of the very fabric of the buildings as much as it falls in fat drops or fine mist from the sky. Even the people here are solemn in their demeanor and pallid with their sun-starved skin. An adolescence in California has made him yearn for light, bright days. Now May has arrived, and with it the sun, in perfect sync with the levity of his mood.

And, weather aside, he must still pinch himself at what he has already achieved in his twenty-six years of life. This job, this place. He takes a long, deep breath of relatively fresh park air. Septimus has always relished fresh air, wide-open spaces, the countryside. It reminds him of home. Although, to be fair, Hyde Park is hardly the wilderness, but, for the middle of the sprawling metropolis of London, it is not at all bad.

He stares up into the surprisingly cloudless sky, washed the palest blue by overnight rain. London summers, he presumes, will never reach the intense heat, nor the shocking cold of winters, of home. Home. It jolts him to think of it, still, that way.

The home he hasn't seen since childhood.

Septimus is a nomad. It's the most natural state of human existence. To stay somewhere awhile, reap its benefits, then move on to pastures new. It's the way the ancients lived. Sadly, a form of freedom nowadays enjoyed by so few. He is lucky to have no ties, to be able to depart on the spur of the moment, leaving no trace of his ever having been somewhere. Of adapting and molding. Of only having to worry about himself.

Although, in reality, the decision of where he goes next is not his at all, but down to the will and whim of his bosses. Still, he isn't going to worry about moving on yet.

Septimus gives himself permission to allow his mind to wander wherever it chooses for as long as he is in the park. Once he is out of the gate and walking the up-market streets of Mayfair, he will bring his focus, fully and completely, onto the tasks ahead. *Always be governed by intellect, never emotion.* Absolute self-discipline, preparation, intellectual focus. It's what's gotten him to where he is today. He drifts back to last night's cocktail party. The surprise of David Bruce, the American ambassador, also known as the Big B, placing a large and heavy hand on his shoulder.

"Septimus Nelson, isn't it?" he'd said, peering down at Septimus. Despite his advanced years, Bruce remains a tall, broad-shouldered, impressive man who looks down on most people, physically as well as metaphorically. Up close, Septimus had noted how perfectly trimmed and slicked back his white hair had been, how expensive and well-fitting his suit looked. The man was the picture of elegance. As aristocratic as any American could be.

"Yes, sir," Septimus had replied, nervous suddenly to be addressed directly for the first time by the ambassador.

"I've been hearing great things about you, Septimus," the Big B had continued, with a crooked smile, sending a thrill through Septimus's body. "Hadley is really impressed. And let me tell you, impressing Hadley is no mean feat."

"Listen," he'd gone on, waving a glass of something at Septimus. "Come see me in the morning. I have a proposition to discuss with you."

Septimus had barely been able to contain his excitement. His hard work and dedication were paying off. Hadley *had* noticed. Had appreciated all the extra hours, the volunteering, the careful note-taking, and the keenness to learn.

Septimus had watched Bruce wander away to talk to Lord Home and someone important from the Israeli embassy about the bedeviled Soblen case. That was when he'd noticed the woman watching him. Women's ages are always tricky, but he'd put this one at around thirty. He often catches women giving him *the look*. Septimus isn't a vain man, but he knows he cuts an imposing figure. His height, his build, his striking looks. He ignores most female attention, but there had been something about this woman. Her eyes perhaps. Large, sloping hazel ones, full of boredom and desire for attention. A flash of memory of her gleaming brown hair caressing her bare shoulder. Long slender legs. He'd met her type before. She was the perfect form of female company. No ties. Just a mutual longing for a few precious hours of company and love.

It was what they both needed. The sort of encounter that left him glowing and happy for a couple of days, then increasingly hollow in those which followed.

AT 7:45 A.M., SEPTIMUS announces his arrival to Mr. Bruce's secretary, stationed outside his office door. He only waits five minutes before being invited in.

"I'll cut to the chase," the Big B says, after the opening talk about the weather, roadworks, and how bad English coffee is. "I need a special sort of assistant. An aide-de-camp, if you like. And Hadley thinks you could be just the man. I know you've not been in the job long, but I've taken a look at your background, your qualifications, and the fact that you had a flawless reference from your time at the embassy in Ottawa." He leans back and observes Septimus with shrewd eyes. "I think you would be ideal. What do you say?"

This was not at all what he'd been expecting—nothing so utterly perfect, anyway—and he is momentarily lost for words.

"I expect you want to know more about the role, eh?" David Bruce fills the silence. People always do. "Well, to be honest, it's a new one, so we will have to make it up as we go along. I've got far too much on my plate. Of course, I have assistants, I have Hadley, but he has a huge workload of his own, and I have a secretary for the administrative stuff." He waves a hand at the door and the distant clatter of her typewriter. "But I need someone . . . someone who can be much more than that. A sort of right-hand man I can rely on, who is quick to learn. Who won't mind doing some low-level, boring jobs like taking notes or organizing logistics. But someone sharp I can take along to meetings as an extra pair of ears and eyes. I think we could be a good team. My experience and age, your youth, hunger, and energy." He nods to himself. "Does that sound like something you might be interested in?"

Septimus finally finds his voice. "Absolutely, sir! Thank you for the opportunity. You won't regret it, I promise you that."

"Excellent," he says, tapping his pen on his notebook. "We will have to start with a trial period. I'll get a contract drawn up and have Shauna organize a desk for you in the office next door. It will be hard work, long hours. You prepared for that?"

Septimus finds he is grinning. "I relish hard work, sir. Hadley surely told you that. I'm not embarrassed to admit it, sir, but I'm ambitious. I want to succeed. I will give it my best shot."

"Great," says Bruce, his shoulders visibly relaxing. "Then we are both on the same page. Welcome to my team, Septimus Nelson."

Chapter 5

Celia

The first Tuesday in May, Celia leaves the shop at 5:00 P.M. on the dot and walks briskly up the Kingsway. Her breath is shallow, and the walk makes her hot and bothered despite a sharp breeze. What if she can't remember what all the squiggles and dashes of shorthand mean? What if she is the slowest typist to ever darken the famous doors first opened by Sir Isaac Pitman himself in 1870? She will be an embarrassment to the women's rights movement, that's what.

Pull yourself together, girl. Daphne's voice floats into her head. *I can do this.*

She takes a deep breath and steps through the imposing entrance of the Pitman's College on Southampton Row, climbing the stone steps to the reception area.

"Here for the rapid course?" A woman with a clipboard accosts her before she is fully through the door. "Name?"

"Celia Duchesne."

The woman gives her a sharp look. "French?"

"I beg your pardon? I thought the course was in English?"

"*Of course* we teach in English. I meant your *name*." She runs her pen down the list of names, crossing out Celia's when she comes to it.

"It's Belgian," Celia explains, feeling a blush creep up her neck.

"Ah." The woman grants her a fleeting smile. "Excellent,

excellent. Languages are *so* valued in a good secretary these days. And if we are *ever* accepted by the French into the European Community—well! You will find yourself very much in demand."

"Oh, but I don't speak French. Sadly, my father . . ."

But Clipboard Woman is no longer listening, attending to the next girl who comes through the door behind Celia. "Do join the other girls in the waiting room," she calls over her shoulder. "I'll take you through to the classroom shortly."

Never spoke to me in French, Celia finishes her sentence in her head. Regret and long-buried anger rise in Celia's chest at Father for having failed to grant her the gift of bilingual language ability when she was a small child. It would have made her stand out. She could have been good at *something* that would have given her advantages in the job market. She supposes he never saw the point and wonders, for the thousandth time, if it would have been different had she been born a boy.

Around fifteen girls chat in huddles of twos and threes around the room. All are smartly dressed, studious-looking types, ranging in age, Celia guesses, from sixteen to early twenties. She sidles up to the closest group, introducing herself, and finds out the names of the others—Marjorie, Betsy, and Ellen—who are chatting quietly about nerves, self-improvement, and what they hope to do after the course.

Clipboard Lady soon joins them, clapping her hands for silence as she stands to attention at the front of the room.

"Welcome to our world-famous Pitman's school. I am Miss Anderson, the administrator here. By taking our rapid touch-typing and shorthand course, you are gifting yourself something unmeasurable in financial terms. You will be acquiring an education and skills that will make you much sought-after in the workplace. Now, every girl will work at her own pace, some advancing quicker than others, but we shall all get there in the end. And what I mean by *that* is, we aim for you to leave here with typing speeds of at least sixty to ninety words per minute, and shorthand speeds of a minimum one hundred words per minute, ideally one hundred and thirty, both with ninety-eight percent accuracy. Employers will be snapping you up. Shorthand is a vital skill for many professions: journalists, stenographers, et cetera. And let's not forget, a good typist, a good secretary, is worth her weight in gold to her boss. But I'm sure you already know that, my dears, as here you all are." She beams and holds her hands aloft as though she is a preacher addressing her flock. "Now, how will you achieve these enviable results? One word: *practice*. Daily practice is crucial if you want to succeed." Celia's heart sinks. Who has a typewriter at home to practice on?

"As a student at our school," Miss Anderson continues, as though hearing Celia's thoughts, "you are welcome to use our typewriters in our practice suite anytime. You simply book a slot with reception."

Lunchtime, Celia thinks with a gasp. *There is time for half an hour's practice every day.*

"Now follow me, and I will show you around, then I'll take you up to Miss Cutter for your first typing class."

The Pitman's building is huge, spread over six floors. It accommodates fifteen hundred students and is the leading training institution in the United Kingdom. Miss Anderson is puffy as a peacock with pride. After the building tour, they file into the typing classroom. The room is grand, high-ceilinged, with tall windows overlooking Southampton Row. Lines of desks fill the room, each with a large typewriter on it. Celia takes her place between Marjorie and Ellen, with Betsy at the far end of the row. All eyes are fixed on Miss Cutter.

"Good evening, girls." She smiles at them. "We will begin with how to correctly set up the paper and carbon for the copies into the paper rest."

They learn the functions of the knobs and levers and how to change the ribbon when the ink is low.

"Excellent," Miss Cutter declares, clapping her hands. "Now we can make a start on the home keys before you leave for the evening." She points to the chalkboard behind her where the letters *a, s, d, f, g, h, j, k, l* are printed. She slowly walks around the room, showing them how to place their fingers and feel their way around the keyboard. The room is soon filled with the discordant clattering and stamping of keys and the swing and bang of carriage returns.

Every now and again, Celia exchanges a glance and a nervous smile with Marjorie or Ellen. Gossiping between students is banned during class, Miss Cutter tells them, as concentration is key, and good work habits should be built from day one. Speaking in any case, Celia thinks, would be difficult above the noise of the typing.

At the end of class, they say their good-byes. Celia runs down the steps and out onto the pavement with a soaring sense of achievement at having successfully navigated her first clandestine lesson. Her mother didn't query the mention of two late nights of working each week. She approves of hard work. Working, in her mother's opinion, is second in terms of merit only to time spent in church and very far above the degenerate activities of watching television, reading, dancing, or having any form of fun.

Walking toward the bus stop, Celia smiles to herself.

Her journey of self-improvement has begun.

ON FRIDAY, DAPHNE is free to meet for lunch, and Celia decides that in her lunchtime typing practice this week she has fully mastered the home keys and so deserves a day off. They sit at a small table in the cramped space of Jack's Café. The air is thick, warm and fuggy with hot breath, scalding tea, and the smell of deep-fried chips.

"How's it going with Thomas?" Celia asks, remembering the first date Daphne had with him last Saturday, swiftly followed by two more during the past week.

"Ah. Not so dishy, as it turns out. Terrible kisser and sweaty palms." Daphne wrinkles her nose. "In fact, I've come to a momentous decision . . . It is 1962 and I've no need for a boyfriend. I am going to be more like you. I am a Strong Independent Woman, and I am expunging the male sex from my life."

"*You?*"

"Don't sound so surprised, Celia. There are more important things out there in the world to worry about than boys."

"Really? Like what?"

The waitress arrives with their drinks, tea sloshing out of the spout of the cheap brown teapot.

"Nuclear Armageddon," Daphne whispers. "We are all just carrying on, heads in the sand, ignoring the fact that if we don't *do* something, the whole world will be blown up, and us with it!"

"I know, Daph. It's truly terrifying." Celia lets out a helpless laugh. "Like we can do anything about it."

"But that's just it." Daphne leans forward, her eyes growing larger. "We *can* do something about it. We can get informed. We can protest. If all of us, the entire country, make a noise, they can't ignore us, can they?"

"All right. Maybe that's true, if it were even possible to get enough people to make a noise, but we are just little old England. Our empire is gone. We don't hold much sway in the world anymore. America isn't going to care what we think. Nor the USSR, and they are the ones who need convincing."

Daphne shakes her head. "We can't think like that, not anymore. We sleepwalked into the last war, and we are in danger of sleepwalking into another one. And this one, the world may *never* recover from."

"That's all very worthy, Daphne, but I still think it's beyond us. We're just, well, ordinary girls. Besides, exactly how is the sudden shunning of boyfriends in favor of saving the world going to help?" Celia pours a cup of tea, frowning at the pale color of it. Stingy with the quality and quantity of leaves, she reckons. "Can't you have both?"

"I'm serious, Celia. I've been reading things, at night, before I go to sleep."

"I've read about it, too, but really, Daphne, I don't think there's much—"

"I don't just mean the mainstream newspapers," Daphne interrupts. "What gets in there is probably censured by the government or something." Her eyes grow wider. "I mean more in-depth stuff. I'm talking about specialized articles and editorials written by anti-nuclear experts. And truly, Celia, it's terrifying. Shocking *and* terrifying, the stuff our government is getting away with under our very noses."

"Such as?"

"Such as the Tsar Bomba, the most terrifying nuclear weapon ever detonated. One thousand five hundred times more powerful than the combined effects of the bombs dropped on Hiroshima and Nagasaki. The shock wave circled the globe *three times*. Houses were flattened up to a hundred miles away, and third-degree burns caused over sixty miles away. The explosion could be seen six hundred miles away. All this testing has to stop."

"But I thought it was the Soviets who did that test?"

"It *was*, but does it really matter which idiot side did it? Our side is just as bad. The Americans, with our pathetic government doing whatever they ask of us, are carrying out more and more tests, so they can beat the Soviets by having ever-bigger, more powerful nuclear weapons. I've been reading Bertrand Russell on this. He might be old, but I tell you, that one man has more brainpower than all our stupid politicians put together."

"Since when did you become so political?"

"Since Thomas introduced me to it."

"What, the terrible kisser with sweaty palms?"

"Yes, him. He's a member of the CND. The Campaign for Nuclear Disarmament. He's not a looker, but he is interesting. He opened my mind."

"Fast work . . . Perhaps you shouldn't have dumped him, then?"

"He was still a terrible kisser . . . Anyway, the point is, each side," Daphne continues, "I mean Kennedy and Khrushchev, is trying to outdo the other, little boys flexing their muscles in the playground, showing off that they have the best toy. They are ridiculous. Dangerous, stupid, *and* ridiculous." Color rises in Daphne's cheeks.

She is right. Celia hasn't been able to ignore the headlines about more and more weapons testing by the Soviet Union and America. For months now, it seems there's always another—in deserts, out at sea, underground, even up in space. The fallout from the tests alone will likely be enough to kill them all, without war to finish off the earth for good.

"It's a wonder you're getting any sleep if you're reading that sort of stuff at bedtime." Celia gives the tea a vigorous stir. "Honestly, I recommend novels. Georgette Heyer, Ann Stafford, Elizabeth Hoy. Mills & Boon even, if you are into that sort of thing—give it a try. Much more relaxing."

Daphne ignores her. "The point is, I'm dedicating myself to the cause. I'm going on a protest march, Celia, and you're coming with me."

Chapter 6

Celia

It's been a slower-than-usual morning. Just one customer since 9:00 A.M. He had a browse, then asked Celia for their French section. The man was middle-aged, dressed in casual slacks and a leather jacket, and Celia knew in an instant he wasn't a buyer. They get a lot of those. She has, over the years, developed a good sense of buying types and the plain nosy.

"We have a small selection here." Celia led him to the relevant shelf and paused. "A mixture of original French and some in translation . . ." She passed her eyes over the book spines. Proust, Sartre, de Beauvoir, Zola, a couple of poetry collections. "Was it something for you, or a friend?"

"Nope. Just seeing what you have," the man said, confirming his intention not to purchase. He was also standing just a little too close. He smelt strongly of tobacco, and she caught the whiff of whisky on his breath. She'd have to keep a close eye on this one in case he slipped a small volume of something into his pocket.

"Well, then," she said, taking a step away. "I'll leave you to browse."

He'd smiled at her, and she'd gotten a good look at his face. Just in case she needed to report him to the police. He might once have been a handsome man, with almost black hair, turning gray at the temples, and deeply hooded dark eyes. He bore a noble roman nose and chiseled cheekbones. But the dented red line of a scar marred one side of his forehead, running diagonally across his eyebrow toward the outer corner of his eye. Celia tried not to stare. A man who had lived a life, and she wondered about the story behind the wound. An accident, a fight, or perhaps some heroic action during the war? Or something altogether more sinister? She shuddered and retreated behind her counter.

"I notice you have a translation of *Crime and Punishment*. Have you read it?" he asked, approaching the counter.

"No, not yet," Celia said. "It's a big, heavy book. I'm not sure I have the time at the moment. But I will, someday."

"You should. An excellent novel," the man said. Then he slipped a sealed envelope out of his jacket pocket and handed it to Celia. "This is for Mrs. Denton. Please make sure she gets it, will you?"

She hesitated in surprise, then took it.

"Yes, of course."

He thanked her and walked out of the shop. Since then, her eyes have been drawn repeatedly to the scratchy handwriting on the envelope: *Mrs. Vera Denton. Private.* She can't imagine what's in it. An invitation, perhaps? Maybe there is more to Mrs. D than meets the eye. Perhaps she plans to take full advantage of her new life without a husband and have men friends. There is absolutely nothing wrong with that. And if you ignore the whisky breath, and stale tobacco smoke, and the scar, the man isn't bad-looking. But still. She wouldn't have thought he was Mrs. D's type. Too rough, surely.

She wonders about Mrs. D's divorce. *Divorce.* Such a dirty word. One she has only ever heard whispered, like *sex* or *death*. Mrs. Denton is a revelation. There is not an ounce of shame or regret about the woman. Could Mother be happier if she wasn't with Father, divorced like Mrs. D? Her parents have never shown any affection toward each other, not so much as a squeeze of a hand or an arm around shoulders that Celia can remember. But however much a couple might loathe each other, where Celia comes from, divorce is as unthinkable as walking on the moon.

The jangle of the shop's doorbell makes Celia jump. Peering around the side of the till, she is hopeful for a proper customer in need of assistance. She is beginning to worry about how quiet the shop is. It's always been like this, relying on the odd sale of a really valuable book to keep afloat. But there haven't been any of those lately, and Mrs. Denton must be concerned about her income. Besides, while the lack of customers is good for giving Celia time to study her shorthand and read the novels on the shop's bookshelves, it does make for monotonous days.

It turns out not to be a customer, but Mrs. Denton herself, returned from a morning browsing the shops of Regent and Oxford Streets, bringing with her a gust of exhaust-scented air from the Strand. Her fancy high-heeled shoes make a fast *click-click-click* across the wooden floorboards.

"Thank you, dear, for keeping an eye on the place." She drops her many shopping bags on the floor and pats her hair. "It's sure windy out there this morning. Truly ruined my hair."

Celia can't see a single strand out of place. Mrs. D wears so much hairspray even a gale-force wind wouldn't dislodge it.

"It looks as good as if you came straight from the hairdressers."

"Oh, you!" Mrs. D tinkles with laughter.

"Buy anything nice?"

"I did." She riffles through the bags and pulls out a tailored dress the color of pea soup from Selfridges, patent-leather shoes from Jones's, and a beautiful, sparkling Dior handbag. The whole lot must have cost her a fortune. Mrs. D clearly has no money worries if she can buy like this on a whim. She must have done very well in her divorce settlement. But to Celia it all seems so frivolous. When one is used to counting every penny, these shopping sprees can make one feel distinctly queasy.

"Now," Mrs. Denton says, replacing the items in their bags, "I'll just go and pop these upstairs if you wouldn't mind being on your own for a little longer?" The string of pearls she habitually wears over a variety of pastel roll-neck sweaters swings and sways as she bends and straightens to scoop up the bags.

"Yes, of course. And, oh, Mrs. Denton, a man in a leather jacket came in and left this for you." Celia picks up the envelope and hands it over.

Mrs. D's eyebrows knit together in confusion.

"I thought maybe you have an admirer?" Celia prompts with a smile.

"Oh!" Mrs. Denton's features unfold. "Of course. It must have been Alfred Humphries. He's, err . . . Yes, he's a friend. I'm sure he'll be back again soon. It's good to have men as friends as well as women, don't you think, dear?" She gives Celia a little nudge with her elbow.

Celia listens to her footsteps clicking up the stairs behind the closed door to the flat. She squeezes her eyes shut, visualizing the page of dashes, dots, and squiggles she's been studying in her handbook, *Pitman's Shorthand Rapid Course: Complete Edition with Supplementary Exercises.* The book claims to be an easy-to-follow, rule-by-rule guide, but after two hours of trying to memorize the write-by-sound rather than longhand spellings, her brain is feeling distinctly befuddled. She shuts the book and rubs her eyes to erase the images of dancing black lines that are now imprinted on her retinas.

Pitman's, though hard work, is a blast. Miss Cutter has told

Celia that she has an aptitude for shorthand and is moving her on faster than some of her fellow students. Fancy that. An *aptitude*. She's never been told she has an aptitude for anything before.

The jangle of the doorbell jerks Celia once again from her reverie. This time it really is a customer. A tall man in a suit and hat, his body silhouetted against the light outside. He nods a hello and begins to browse the shelves. After a few moments, he selects a slim volume and strolls toward the counter.

"Hello, can I help you?" Celia asks, climbing down from her perch on the stool.

"I hope so. Is Mrs. Denton here?" The man has an American accent. Surely not another of her man friends. This one seems too young. Crikey, Mrs. Denton has only been in the country a few weeks and already she's acquired more friends and acquaintances than Celia has in three years.

"She's busy out the back, I'm afraid. I can fetch her, or perhaps I can help you?"

"Do you work here?" the man asks with a frown.

It seems an odd question, seeing as she is standing behind the counter.

"Yes, I've been here longer than Mrs. Denton. Is there something in particular you are looking for?"

He stares at her with his mouth half open. He shuts it, opens it as though he is about to say something, then seems to have second thoughts and closes it again.

"Look," she says, becoming faintly irritated. "Would you like to buy that or not?"

"What?"

She points to the book in his hand. "That," she says, wondering if there is something wrong with the man's brain.

"Ah." He looks down at the book as though he is surprised to see it there. Then his face livens with a hopeful smile. "Is it any good?" He thrusts the book toward her. *Sons and Lovers* by D. H. Lawrence.

Celia looks at him properly. He is a good deal younger than most of the other customers who wander in. Perhaps he's a lost tourist and has mistaken this for an ordinary bookshop selling cheap paperbacks. She should probably direct him elsewhere. But she finds she doesn't want to let him go, not just yet.

"Between you and me, I find Lawrence a little depressing."

The man removes his hat, revealing hair the color of freshly brewed tea. He seems to have recovered his senses and rearranges his face into a smile. "An honest shopkeeper. Well, fancy that. What can you recommend instead?" Celia stares into the man's startling tawny eyes. Midtwenties, she reckons. In addition to excellent bone structure, he has something almost *leonine* about him. The coloring, the build. Definitely the unusual eyes.

He is quite magnificent.

She tucks her hair behind her ears. "Are you particularly interested in English classics? We have a large international section too. Perhaps you are looking for yourself, or is it a present for someone special? We have many collectibles here—first editions, some signed by the author, and such like."

"Err . . ." His eyes dart around the shop. "Do you have any American novels here?"

"Of course!" She slips out from behind the counter and leads him to the American section.

"I'm looking for something for my boss. It's his birthday. He's a cultured man, and I don't want to resort to a bottle of whisky. I'd like to get him something a little different."

"What a thoughtful idea." She runs her fingers along the

spines until she finds it. "This is in excellent condition, a very powerful novel." She hands him the copy of *The Grapes of Wrath* that she just finished reading. It would make a wonderful gift for a discerning recipient. "I'm sure you are familiar with it, seeing as you are American . . ."

He laughs. "I was born in Canada, as it happens, but I grew up in California. Trust me, I've not lived long enough to have read all the books published in America. I'll take it." He runs a palm across the cover with a pale, manicured hand.

"Is that how you know Mrs. Denton, from California?"

"Yes, that's right. An acquaintance of my mother's."

"Oh, I see. So . . . are you here on holiday?" she asks, keen to keep him talking a little longer. She wraps the book in brown paper.

"I work at the American embassy. I've been here since January."

"How exciting! And are you enjoying London?"

"Very much so. Bar the weather."

"It must be awful after all that sun in California."

"Exactly," he says with a chuckle. "But, in fact, I was at the embassy in Ottawa for two years before coming here. The name is Septimus. Septimus Nelson." He holds out a hand to shake hers.

"*Septimus Nelson.*" A bubble of irrepressible laughter rises before she can stop it. Nerves. They always make her laugh with borderline hysteria.

"I know, I know," he says, bowing his head as though he has heard it a thousand times before. "What were my parents thinking . . . ?"

"I'm sorry," she splutters. "You must think me awfully rude. Celia Duchesne." She grasps his warm, firm hand. "Nice to meet you."

"It's a pleasure to meet you, too, Miss Duchesne," he says, holding her eyes just a little longer than necessary, making her skin tingle.

She finishes the wrapping, taps the price into the till, takes his money, and hands back the change.

"Thanks," Septimus says, waving the wrapped book at her. "I'm sure my boss will be very pleased. Do pass my best wishes to Vera—Mrs. Denton. I just wondered how she is getting along."

"Of course."

"And tell her that I'll pop back another time."

Celia leans on the counter staring at the empty space he left as he shuts the door firmly behind him.

Septimus Nelson is coming back, she thinks, unable to suppress a smile.

OVER THE LAST couple of days, the temperature has climbed, a miasma of heat shimmering over the city, softening its edges, its pace dwindling like a slow-moving river. Celia steps off the sweltering bus, thankful to be in the relative fresh air of Southwark Bridge Road. She is still thinking about Septimus. Those tawny eyes. She has a sudden urge to tell Daphne about him. She hopes he is as good as his word and returns to the shop. Only to admire from a distance, of course. He is far too well-bred for the likes of Celia.

"Hey, Celia."

"Sam!"

He's leaning against the bus shelter, out of his overalls, wearing a gray-and-white-checked short-sleeved shirt tucked into neat, gray slacks. He's looking dapper. She hooks her bag onto her shoulder, wondering if he is waiting for someone. Sam pushes himself off the bus shelter and comes to her side.

"Mind if I walk with you?"

"Don't tell me you were hanging around for me." She flaps a hand in front of her face in a vain attempt to cool down.

"'Course not! I just . . . you know."

". . . Finished work?"

"Hours ago, actually."

Celia looks at him. His eyes are fixed on his shoes.

"Been on earlies this week. Start at four, finish at two. Just needed to get a few things from the shops."

Celia glances at his empty hands. So, he *had* been hanging around waiting for her. Could it be possible Mother put him up to this?

They set off in the direction of Copperfield Street.

"Four in the morning? You must be exhausted."

"As I said, gas board never sleeps, Celia."

"Glad the same can't be said for bookshops."

"D'you fancy a choc ice?" he asks as they pass the newsagents.

"Ooh, yes, but a strawberry Mivvi for me."

He grins and runs inside, returning a couple minutes later with the ice creams. They walk slowly. The Mivvi is cold, tangy strawberry and buttery ice cream.

"I was wondering," Sam says, through a mouthful of choc ice, "if you'd like to see *Bon Voyage!* at the flicks on Saturday night? I'll be off earlies by then."

Celia takes another bite of her ice cream.

"It's a comedy," Sam adds. "I thought you might like it . . . Only if you are at a loose end, that is."

She can feel his eyes on her, and an unexpected flush of heat flows up her neck to her face.

Celia is mute. It's not like they haven't been to the pictures or out in the evening together before. They are friends. That's what friends do. It's just . . . something about the way he asked her, it feels different. She gives herself a metaphorical shake. She's being ridiculous, putting meaning where there is none, just because he's no longer with Tessa . . . Nothing has changed. Nothing at all.

"Of course I will." She grins at him, and he looks relieved. "You know me, always at a loose end!"

Chapter 7

Celia

The aged Bertrand Russell takes his position at the microphone and looks up to face the people, of which there are many, crammed into every square inch of Trafalgar Square, spilling out into the surrounding streets, leaning out of open windows, and hanging off statues for a better view.

"Friends," he begins. The crowd falls still and silent. Daphne's hand floats up to her chest as she sucks in a breath of reverence. "The dropping of the A-bombs on Hiroshima ushered in the atomic age by the slaughter of over one hundred thousand civilians of a nation already willing to surrender. The H-bomb is a thousand times more powerful. Both Russia and America have very large stores of H-bombs. Each has boasted recently of the power to destroy the other. But each side is willing to start the massacre ignoring what its own side would suffer. All the inhabitants of Britain would perish—in fact, no country would secure anything it desires by means of a nuclear war. While the countries of East and West proclaim their readiness for negotiations, they continue unabated their preparations for war. In America and probably in Russia, public opinion is incited to a hysterical degree in which sacrifices are represented as heroic and not insane. In this country, the authorities are playing down the threat and keeping the population ignorant until the last astonishing moment of universal death."

There is a collective horrified inhale.

"See?" Daphne says, turning to Celia. "Nobody has any idea what danger we're in."

"Well, I think they might now." Celia looks around at the television reporters with their cameras trained on Bertrand and the crowd. Now, that *would* be a fascinating job. The power of those lenses, the snap decisions about what to capture and transmit to millions. The shaping of public opinion hinging on the angle taken and then simultaneously sent around the globe.

"We who are now present," Russell continues, "are calling upon the British public and the public of other countries to wake up to the threat to the human population. We urge the Berlin question—and any other question—be solved through negotiation at a conference, if necessary, with the friendly help of neutrals. If negotiations fail, the likely outcome will be war, and that war will be nuclear. In nuclear war, not only will Britain and Western Europe cease to exist, not only will Russia and America cease to exist as ordered communities, but all that men"—*and women*, Celia mentally adds—"have built up over the centuries by way of civilization will cease to exist. There is only one way to arrest this march to the abyss—by a vast, mass protest."

Or maybe, Celia thinks, put some women in charge for a change. Perhaps they wouldn't make such an almighty hash of it all?

"The danger is imminent and far greater than the British public is allowed to know. Each one of you can do something. If you act now, you may win such a victory for humanity as will resound through all the ages to come."

An enormous cheer rises up like a roar. A current, the collective force of the will and desire to live, urgent and strong, passes through the crowd, carrying them forward, or so it feels, to some sort of common and desired destiny. A single individual can, as

Russell has proclaimed, be ignored, but this *thing*, this move-ment, is so great, it cannot. Together, they really can change the world. This is what *power* feels like. Celia waves her sign— BAN THE BOMB!—with renewed enthusiasm alongside Daphne's BAN NUCLEAR TESTS NOW! as the refrains "Ban the bomb" and "Action not reaction" rise around them.

Celia resolves in that moment to become better educated about this whole issue. For the first time, she feels a sense of taking control, not only over her own trajectory through life, but in doing something for the greater good. And, she thinks with a little dart of fear, if the danger really is as great as that spoken of today, then there is no choice. She *must* do something if she wants to have any future at all.

That evening, Celia and Sam head to the cinema to watch *Bon Voyage!* She'd been nervous, after the hunch she had that day at the bus stop, that Sam had been asking her on a date. But the film, a rather silly one about Americans causing pandemo-nium on holiday in Paris, is light relief after the serious nature of her day, and it brightens her spirits. Afterward, they share a portion of chips, wrapped in newspaper and liberally sprinkled with salt and vinegar, as they sit side by side on a bench on the South Bank, the dark, wide strip of the Thames before them, lights from the Embankment blinking in the distance.

"Do you support nuclear disarmament, Sam?" she asks, after telling him about the march and her determination to join the fight.

Sam considers the question for a moment, his forehead wrinkled in thought. "I'm not sure," he says finally. "Of course nobody wants nuclear war, but if we get rid of our weapons, who could be certain other countries wouldn't secretly keep theirs? I mean, it's never simple, is it?"

Celia shakes her head, helps herself to another chip.

"But, hey, you can do all your doom-mongering talk with Daphne. I invited you out for a cheery film and a bit of fun, so no talk of apocalypse tonight, okay?"

She smiles her agreement, and he tells her, happily, about a stray litter of puppies he managed to find homes for at the animal sanctuary last week. The atmosphere between them is easy, the talk comfortable, and she wonders if the awkwardness she remembers in Sam when he suggested this evening out was simply a figment of her imagination.

THE FOLLOWING DAY, once Mother has left for church, Celia and Father settle into a well-worn Sunday routine. Father is more generous of heart and chirpy of nature before midday when he allows himself his first pint. After that, he spirals downward until the day ends with morose introspection. Fortunately for them all, Father's drinking habits don't result in the violent mood swings Celia knows afflict some other heavy-drinking men. But for now, before his first drink, in the absence of Mother, there is a convivial, relaxed atmosphere between them. When the three Duchesnes are together, there is a charge in the air, like static electricity before a storm, putting them all on edge.

Seated at a table by the window of the Tea Rooms, Father has a copy of *The Times* tucked under his arm and Celia has come with her own more serious reading instead of the usual Agatha Christie or Jane Austen.

"What's that you're reading?" Father asks, an eyebrow raised in surprise.

"Just a newsletter," Celia replies, lifting it for him to see.

"*Weekly Journal of the Socialist Labour League* . . . 'On the

March Against the Tories, Aldermaston 1962,'" he reads. "What's this—you turning socialist?"

"No, but I've joined the CND—the Campaign for Nuclear Disarmament."

"I know what it stands for, Celia. I'm not stupid. But why? You should steer clear. The CND is full of communists and revolutionaries touting their dangerous ideas. It's hardly suitable . . ."

"It's about taking action against the nuclear arms race, which frankly we should *all* be interested in, regardless of our political leanings. If we don't, whatever our politics, none of it may matter at all if war breaks out. We'll all be dead, or if we aren't, we soon will be."

"It won't."

"How can you be so sure?"

"Because there is a balance of nuclear power between the superpowers, and neither will dare attack the other, for fear of the consequences."

"Don't you think that is a rather risky assessment? I mean, what if there isn't *really* a balance of power? What if there is a miscalculation, or a mistake or an accident? It only takes one finger on one button. Look, it says here, in the event of war breaking out . . . 'initial striking power will be decisive: it is essential to get in the first blow on the enemy's towns, launching sites, and warning systems. A first strike and the fallout effect of a nuclear attack on Britain might leave just nine to twelve million people alive, and they will face a slow death from famine, radiation sickness, and the complete breakdown of society into barbarism . . .'"

"Propaganda," says Father. "Fearmongering. You do realize, don't you, that it's the communists behind that CND organization? Wouldn't it play perfectly into the hands of the Soviets if we unilaterally disarmed, like many of that lot want us to do, so that they are left with ultimate superiority? Where would we be then, eh?"

Celia shakes her head, takes a sip of tea. "I don't know," she says, staring out onto the street. "I don't know what the answer is, but I want to do something. It's my future at stake, and I want to protect it. I don't really know how, or the best way. And it's probably silly, but protesting and joining CND is all I can think to do at the moment."

Father gives her a long steady look. There is something unreadable in his dark eyes. A sadness, or pain of some sort. Perhaps he is remembering his own experiences of fighting in North Africa during the war. He never speaks about that time.

"I don't think women should meddle in politics," he says finally, dropping his gaze.

Celia splutters, half choking on her tea.

"Father, you do know women have had the vote for some years now?"

He shuffles uncomfortably in his seat. He opens his mouth, then snaps it shut, as though thinking better of saying whatever it was on his mind.

"Fine," he says, resignation in his voice. "Just don't tell your mother anything about it. That's my advice, for what it's worth."

Chapter 8

Celia

Later that afternoon, after the Sunday roast has been shared with Mrs. Bancroft and Sam (thank goodness for Sam, who always manages to lighten the atmosphere), Celia makes her excuses to visit Daphne. She lives, like Celia, in the same house she has lived in since they first met at elementary school, two streets away from Copperfield Street. But Daphne's house is the flip side of Celia's. Completely modernized, filled with noise and people and laughter.

"Come up to my room," Daphne urges, the moment she steps inside. "I need to show you something." She pulls Celia by the hand, past the racket of Daphne's two younger brothers playing a wrestling game in the front room.

Clothes, newspapers, and magazines are strewn across Daphne's bed and floor, makeup paraphernalia covers her dressing table, and half-built BAN THE BOMB signs are propped up around the room. Daphne's walls are covered in huge posters of all her heartthrobs: Elvis, Marlon Brando, Paul Newman, James Dean, Gregory Peck. Celia would never be allowed to keep her room in such a state, or to desecrate her own pristine walls with boys staring at her with their come-to-bed eyes. How Daphne sleeps between them all is quite a wonder. Celia picks up a discarded *Vogue* magazine and begins to flick through. "Four Famously Well-Dressed Women Discuss Their Own Rare Clothes Mistakes." Daphne paces the floor, chewing on a nail.

"What on earth is going on, Daph?" Celia asks. "What did you want to show me?" Unflappable Daphne has been very much flapped by something this afternoon.

Celia shuts the magazine and taps the bed beside her. Daphne sinks down with a sigh. "Celia . . ." Daphne takes a sharp breath, as though psyching herself up for running the one-hundred-yard sprint. She turns to face Celia, clears her throat. "Well, you see, on Friday, Mr. Edgely had a pretrial hearing, and so I was on my own all day. Most of the work I had to do was done, and I was twiddling my thumbs a bit, so Mr. Parker decided I could make good use of the time by getting on with some archiving. Well, there really isn't a more boring job. Up and down those bloomin' stairs to the basement. Anyway, he asked me to go through this ancient filing cabinet that used to belong to old Mr. Thompson and nobody has bothered with in years. Everything in there was for archive, but right at the back, I found a thin file."

"Right," Celia says, only half listening. She picks up the *Vogue* again and reopens it.

"Celia, are you even listening?"

"Yes. You were archiving. Up and down the bloomin' stairs . . ."

"This is serious, Celia!"

"Okay, okay. I'm sorry!"

"It concerns *you*."

"What concerns me?"

"The file. I knew you weren't listening."

"*Me!* How on earth could it be anything to do with me?"

"Well, not you, exactly. Your parents."

"My parents have never set foot in a solicitor's office. They're not the type. What could *they* possibly want to discuss with a solicitor?"

Daphne shrugs. "I don't know. I didn't look inside. I just slipped it straight into my bag before anyone saw what I was doing."

"You *stole* a file?"

"I know. A sackable offence. The things I risk for you. But I don't think anyone will ever find out. It was going to be archived anyway."

"Daph! I'm sure there must be some mistake. You'll have to take it back. But, well, go on, then, show me."

Daphne pulls from under her bed a thin buff file and places it unopened on Celia's lap. Celia stares down at the printed label in disbelief.

FILE OPENED: February 1946
PARTNER: Reginald Thompson
CLIENT: Mr. and Mrs. André Duchesne
RE: Miss Duchesne—Code Name Anya, deceased
   July 1944
MATTER: Compensation Claim—War Office
FILE CLOSED: April 1948

Miss Duchesne . . . Deceased . . . Something thumps hard inside. Celia's mind does a quick calculation. She would have been three years old when the file was opened, five when it was closed. She doesn't know about any other Miss Duchesne. Her father was an only child, and his parents went back to Belgium after the First World War, leaving him in England as a young man alone to complete his apprenticeship to become a chef. Both of her grandparents are now dead. And what could *Code Name Anya* mean? Could there be another André Duchesne in London? Was that too much of a coincidence?

From outside, somewhere in the far distance, comes the low rumble of thunder. Inside, the air sits thick and sticky.

Daphne breaks the silence. "Shall I leave you alone while you open it?"

"Please stay . . ." Celia gingerly opens the cover.

The first thing she sees is a black-and-white photograph of a smiling young woman—a girl, really. She is sitting on a picnic blanket in a park, a wide circle of skirt spread out across the blanket at her feet. A cardigan is thrown over her shoulders, and it must have been a windy day because a lock of her dark hair, swept up, 1940s style, has escaped from the pins and floats up and away in the breeze. The girl is laughing, staring straight at the photographer with dancing eyes, head thrown back a little. Celia imagines the photographer saying something to make the girl laugh, to relax her, so she smiles as he clicks the shutter.

"What a pretty girl," Daphne murmurs.

There are two more photographs beneath, lying on top of a few sheets of correspondence. The second photo, stuck onto a thick cardboard backing, is a square formal headshot of the same girl. Here, she has the barest hint of a smile on her face. Daphne is right. Those large, dark, serious eyes, her face chiseled with high cheekbones and a sharp chin, a touch of Vivien Leigh about her.

"She's very beautiful," Celia agrees.

"She looks like you."

Celia gives Daphne a sharp look. "Don't be daft."

"I'm not. It's true."

Daphne picks up the second photograph to take a closer look, revealing the final one. The sight of it sends a bolt through

Celia, puncturing her lungs, all breath rushing from her body. The girl again, this time flanked either side by a younger version of Mother and Father. They stand together, close and relaxed as only a family can, their bodies leaning into one another. She stares at the picture as one might a mirage, not believing the image she is seeing before her.

Daphne leans over Celia's shoulder, letting out a whoosh of breath.

"But who is this?" Celia finally whispers, as though Daphne, or the universe, may have the answer.

"Read the letters," Daphne urges.

Celia hands the photographs to her friend. She flicks through the correspondence. There are three letters in the file and a handwritten note of a telephone conversation between Mr. R. Thompson and Mr. A. Duchesne dated March 23, 1948. Nothing else. She turns first to the letters.

July 1946

Dear Mr. and Mrs. Duchesne,

I trust that you are well.
    Further to our recent meeting, as I conveyed to you then, I'm afraid my suspicions have been borne out and I can now confirm, with no further doubt, that your daughter, Jeannette, code name Anya, is dead.

Celia gasps.

"What?" Daphne leans over as Celia points to the text. They read on together.

I'm truly sorry that I am only able to bring you this distressing news after some considerable delay, but as you can imagine, in the confusion and disarray of Germany after the cessation of hostilities, it has not been easy to ascertain the exact whereabouts of all our agents. However, there is no longer any doubt that your daughter was among those SOE agents captured by the Nazis in Paris in late 1943. She was held at Fresnes Prison near Paris for some months. In early summer 1944, she was taken to Karlsruhe prison in Baden-Württemberg, Germany. For reasons I don't yet understand, in July 1944, your daughter was transferred to Natzweiler-Struthof concentration camp in France, where she was, shortly after arrival, executed.

Please be assured that her death was both swift and brave. She was in the company of other British agents, from whom each would have gained great comfort, and I have this on good authority, not only from survivors but also from the perpetrators of this heinous crime themselves. These men will be brought swiftly to justice, I can assure you of that too.

Jeannette was a young woman in possession of immense courage, presence of mind, and fortitude, who in the face of extreme personal danger acted with the greatest of honor in the name of her country. I shall ensure your daughter's name is put forward for the highest award of valor of which she will be more than worthy.

Yours sincerely,
Miss Muriel E. Clarke

"Bloody hell, Celia, you've got a sister!"

"Had a sister."

"Yes, sorry. Don't you remember her?"

Celia shakes her head. "I was only tiny when she was captured. I don't remember a single thing."

"This is crazy!" Daphne says, staring at Celia with wild eyes. "Not only did you have a *sister*, but she was a bloody *secret agent*!"

Celia is devoid of speech. Outside, the growl of thunder comes again, closer this time.

"But why don't your parents ever speak of her? Are you *sure* they've never told you?"

"Never!"

"What else is there?" Daphne nods at the rest of the papers. "Maybe the answers are in here?"

Celia turns to the next letter, again from Muriel Clarke. This one is much shorter and dated December 1946. It explains that since her last letter, Miss Clarke has had more information regarding Jeannie's death and that the writer felt it best to convey that information in person, rather than by letter. She suggests a time and a place for the meeting, hoping it will be acceptable for Celia's parents. The third letter is an official one, dated 1947, from the War Office. It refers to Jeannette's name being mentioned in dispatches and apparently contained the oak leaf device she had earned for her valor. That item is not in the file. The note of the telephone conversation between Mr. Thompson and André Duchesne, as far as she can decipher from Mr. Thompson's slanted and spidery handwriting, confirms the view that no pension or compensation would be available to Jeannie's next of kin due to her civilian status and that, really, there was nothing more he could do.

Celia is frozen, numb with incomprehension. Fat raindrops hit the window. Celia watches as they trail down the glass, blurring the view of the houses, the street, the outside world.

"Daphne, do you think I could hang on to this for a bit?" Celia finally asks, closing the file and smoothing her fingers down the front.

"Of course. It's listed as archived now. Nobody is going to go down and unseal the boxes to check it's there."

"Thank you," Celia whispers.

"What a shock . . . You've always wanted a sister. Well, it seems you have one, after all."

"Had," Celia corrects again.

A sister. She *had* a sister. What was an ordinary girl, just like Celia, from *Southwark*, doing in France being captured by Nazis? It sounds so preposterous; Celia has the urge to laugh out loud. But here it is, in black and white. Her *sister* was a brave and dashing heroine, albeit an executed one. Shouldn't her parents have celebrated her sacrifice and shouted about her from the rooftops? Shouldn't there be photographs and tributes and the sharing of fond memories, despite the grief and sadness of it all?

Who exactly was this sister, *Jeannette, code name Anya*?

WHEN CELIA LEAVES Daphne's, the file tucked safely inside her bag, rain is bouncing off the pavement as fast and furious as fingers on a typewriter. Celia huddles beneath a borrowed umbrella and hurries back to Copperfield Street. She racks her brain for ways to find out more of this story without asking her parents directly—there must be a reason they have kept this from her, and she has a feeling asking questions will open up a Pandora's box. But other than writing to the War Office, who presumably have records relating to Jeannette, she can't think of any other way. She has a right to know about her sister, doesn't she? Perhaps she might be able to track down the Miss Clarke who wrote those letters. But the file was closed fourteen years ago, and is about matters that happened several years before that. Miss Muriel Clarke could well be dead. But in the absence of any other options, it must be worth a try.

When she gets in, her skirt soaked through, Father has gone to have a pint in the Horse's Head to celebrate some success in the football pools this week, and Mother is in the kitchen with a pot of tea and a chicken sandwich, listening to the dulcet tones of Alistair Cooke in *Letter from America*.

"Oh, love, you're drenched!" Mother exclaims. "What a night! Still, we need this storm to clear the air. Go and put on some dry clothes, and I'll fix you something to eat."

Back in the kitchen, they chat about banalities. Mrs. Bancroft's plans for her garden. The roadworks on the bridge. Old Mrs. Cooper's gammy leg. Does Celia have any old clothes or books for the church charity sale on Thursday next week? Finally, Celia announces with a yawn she will go to her room to read.

But, tucked up in bed, Bartholomew curled beside her, Celia is unable to focus on the pages of *A Room with a View*. She can't bury the burning desire to know more about her sister. She puts the book down, and, very slowly and carefully, she goes through the buff folder once again, making sure there was nothing she missed. She reads it all three times over.

She climbs out of bed and, at her dressing table, begins to write.

Dear Miss Clarke,

I do hope, if this letter finds you at all, that you are well. I believe at one time you knew a Miss Jeannette Duchesne,

*who was killed in a concentration camp, Natzweiler–Struthof,
sometime in 1944.*

*I would like the opportunity, if it is possible, to ask a few
questions about her. I would be most grateful if you would
be so good as to reply to me, C/O the address at the top of this
letter.*

Thank you in advance.

Yours sincerely,
Celia Duchesne (Miss)

Celia adds the address of H. J. Potts rather than her own.
She can't risk Mother or Father finding out.

It's a long shot, and she doubts she will receive a reply. But
still, she'll post the letter in the morning. She absentmindedly
strokes Bartholomew and lets her mind form images of that girl
in the photographs.

Jeannette. Jeannie. Her sister.

Chapter 9

Septimus

They say that knowledge is power, that information is king.

They, whoever they are, Septimus thinks as he finally switches off his desk lamp after eight o'clock one Thursday evening in June, knew a thing or two. And Septimus needs to gain both, fast. Since he began his new position last month, it feels as though he has been dropped into a gladiator pit, armed with merely his wits. Staying on top of it all is exhausting. Being elevated to such an illustrious position as the American ambassador's aide-de-camp, over the heads of those undoubtedly more experienced and better qualified than him, has not only raised a few bushy white eyebrows, but has set him right in the sights of the pit's circling lions. If they can see he will be useful to them, they'll accept him as one of their own. But if he wrong-foots it, they'll eat him alive.

What Septimus had *not* been expecting was to be plunged so quickly, so completely, into the most urgent matter of American foreign policy.

The Cold War.

Where, in place of the gladiator pit, the two great powers, America and the Soviet Union, face each other, ready to fight to the death. A standoff between ideologies: capitalism and communism. The American eagle versus the Russian bear. But instead of claws and talons and teeth, the threat of victory by annihilation is nuclear war, the ramifications of which would spread far and wide outside the pit. A threat where, indeed, there can be no winners, so here they stand, facing off against each other.

As the ambassador, the Big B, has impressed on Septimus at every given opportunity, with the stakes so impossibly high, what matters most is *intelligence*.

"We need to know not only what our enemy is doing, planning, intending. We need to know what he is *thinking*. We need to get inside his mind," the Big B had told Septimus on his very first day on the job. "But that is only part of it. The other part, because for sure the enemy will be seeking just the same—we must assume he has eyes and ears *everywhere*—is that we must sow a complicated web of *dis*information. We must spread false news to obscure the truth."

Whatever *truth* really is.

David Bruce's eyes had twinkled beneath the lamplight. "My background, you may or may not know, is intelligence," he informed Septimus. "Indeed, I was in London during the war gathering intelligence to assist the allies. Back then I worked for the Office of Strategic Services, the OSS—the precursor to the CIA. It was useful training. And let me tell you, Septimus, the battle for intelligence has never been more important, as you will quickly learn."

Real power, Septimus muses as he leaves the building now, comes with the innate ability to interpret, to hold one's nerve, to have vision through the chaos, and to control the subversive forces in your *own* camp, as well as in theirs.

Outside, rain is falling. He hails a black cab on Grosvenor Square, thanking his good fortune not to have to wait for one. He shakes the rain off his jacket. "Winfield House, Regent's

Park," he tells the driver. As he leans back, he reminds himself
that this *is* what he has always wanted, what he has worked so
hard for, for so long. The cab speeds up through the rain-soaked
streets, the lights of London becoming a wet blur.

"Come over for a drink this evening," the ambassador had
said jovially that morning. "You can meet Evangeline, my wife.
Oh, and there is someone else I'd like you to meet."

This will be his first visit to the private home of David Bruce.
He takes several deep breaths. He can act the part of sophisticated, confident, commanding Septimus. The archetypal, well-
brought-up, going-places young American. These are challenging,
interesting times. He wonders what the Big B has in mind for
him. Nothing he does is merely for social niceties. There will be
a plan. And Septimus feels his blood fizz with the thought that
this could be an opportunity to make a real difference, to gain
further promotion and respect, to shape world events. What he
does over the coming months *could* even change the course of
history. It *could* help push the world toward war or steer a course
away from it.

But at the sight of Winfield House, he begins to sweat. It isn't a
house at all. It's a mansion. An actual mansion. The responsibility
of it all sets his stomach churning.

Septimus shoves too many bills at the taxi driver and steels
himself. Mind control. He can do this.

He is shown by a liveried young man, who doesn't meet his
eye, into a large, sumptuous sitting room, lit with many lamps
and dripping in wealth and history. He accepts the offer of a
drink—"Whisky, on the rocks, thank you." As he waits, drink in
hand, his eyes wander, taking in the colonial, imperial grandeur
around him.

"Ah! There you are, Nelson," says the Big B as he enters the room. "Evangeline is on her way. Welcome to my humble abode."

Septimus almost spits out his mouthful of fine Scottish single malt.

"Well, thank you for the invitation," he manages, swallowing hard. "It sure is a beautiful place you have here."

The Big B looks around him with satisfaction in his eyes. "It serves a purpose," he says. "It's a family home. A slice of America. A place to entertain our guests." The door creaks as an elegant middle-aged woman, presumably the Big B's wife, and a short, stocky figure enter the room. Septimus's pulse surges when he recognizes the man. He takes a long, deep breath.

"Nelson, this is Evangeline and my good friend Sir Reginald Fox-Andrews. He and I go way back to my time in London before, like I told you, during the war. Fox-Andrews is in intelligence. As you know, Britain is our closest ally, and as such, we share all our intelligence with each other. Vitally important if we are to keep the Western Hemisphere safe from the ever-present threat of communist infiltration."

"Delighted to meet you, sir," Septimus says, with a small bow. He turns to Evangeline. "And you, Mrs. Bruce."

"As you are aware"—the Big B claps Fox-Andrews on the shoulder—"Nelson here is my new aide-de-camp. He's security cleared. He is already doing an excellent job and making himself quite indispensable. I thought an introduction over dinner would be a nice, informal way to meet. You will be spending a fair bit of time in each other's company."

"I shall look forward to getting to know you, young man," Fox-Andrews says, stepping forward and shaking Septimus's hand vigorously. He doesn't blink, doesn't miss a beat.

THE FOLLOWING DAY is relatively quiet, as days at the embassy go. The quiet days, Septimus is finding, are rather few. He takes advantage of the full lunch hour to go back to the little bookstore on the Strand, H. J. Potts, to see if Vera is actually there this time. With a girl to manage the store, it seems she has it nicely organized so that she can enjoy all the freedoms and luxuries London has to offer. There is a certain irony in that.

Last night's rainstorm has washed the city clean. The air is fresh and cool, and, like a drowning man, Septimus takes several deep lungfuls.

H. J. Potts is absurdly old-fashioned. It's all wonky beams, dusty books, and dark corners. He sees the girl behind the counter, head bent low over an open book. Vera must be out again, and a swell of irritation rises in his chest. It's not always easy for him to get here.

He approaches the counter, and the girl glances up. Seeing him, she drops her book and springs from the stool as though stung by a bee.

"Good afternoon to you, Miss . . ."

"Duchesne," she breathes. "It's Miss Duchesne. We met before."

"Of course. I remember." He studies her. He did remember her. He never, ever forgets a pretty face. And hers is, he must admit, uncommonly pretty.

"So, did it go down well?" she asks with a shy smile.

"I'm sorry?"

"*The Grapes of Wrath.* The present for your boss. Did he like it?"

"He did indeed. An inspired present." He beams his most charming smile at her.

"That is good news!"

"Always good to be on the right side of one's employer."

"Quite."

"My boss has a strong social conscience, so a book like that . . . It hit the spot, so to speak." She nods vigorously, her face full of anticipation for more. "Such a book is still relevant, don't you think? We—as a society, I mean—have much to learn about exploitation, the destruction of nature. The treatment of ordinary people. The suffering of the poor . . ." He rests an elbow on the counter, taking her in.

"I do." She grants him a dazzling smile. She looks suddenly very young, very sweet, and his heart cracks open, just a little. She isn't like the other women he has encountered so far in London. They are all sophistication and skeptical knowing. She is fresh, raw, honest. Distracting.

Never be distracted.

"I came to see if Mrs. Denton is here," he says softly, "and since I've come quite a distance, I don't wish to leave without seeing her for a second time. Is she in?"

"Yes, of course. I'll fetch her from the back room—she's just attending to some paperwork. I won't be a moment." Miss Duchesne throws a glance around the empty shop.

"It's okay," Septimus whispers, leaning toward her across the counter. "I'll keep an eye on the place." He winks at her and notices the bloom of color on her cheeks as she turns to leave through the door that divides the flat from the shop.

Moments later, Miss Duchesne returns, Vera close on her heels.

"Septimus! How lovely to see you at last!" She opens her arms and plants a kiss on each of his cheeks. "Now come on out the back and have a coffee with me. We've lots of catching up to do."

"I've enjoyed chatting with you, Miss Duchesne," Septimus says as he follows Vera into the flat. "Let's do it again sometime."

Her cheeks once more flush red, making everything around her, just for a moment, recede.

Part II

Chapter 10

Jeannie

England
December 1942

Y ou've broken his heart, you know that?" Mother let the bucket clatter onto the tiled floor to make her point.

"Yes. I know. You tell me every day." Jeannie held the needle up to the weak winter light, threading the end of the cotton through the eye, and then began to sew the first of six tortoise-shell buttons onto the front of the soft cream baby's jacket, her feet resting on a chair. Jeannie's ankles were swollen, her back hurt, and her large, hard belly permanently pressed uncomfortably on her bladder, sending her to the freezing outside toilet more often than she could bear. But she didn't complain. She didn't dare. She had no right, having only herself to blame for being in this awful mess.

"Your poor father. Fighting for this country, stuck out there in the hellish heat of North Africa." Mother dipped her scrubbing brush into the bucket, her hands blotched with chilblains, and got down onto her hands and knees to scrub the already-clean floor with enough vigor to make her point.

"It's where he wants to be, fighting for his beloved country . . . He'd rather be there than stuck here, with us."

The brush paused. "Don't be churlish." She dipped the brush again, shook it, continued.

But it was true. There was nobody in England more passionate about defending the country that took him in as a child. *This,* he had told Jeannie as she watched him pack and ready himself to leave the moment war broke out three years ago, *is not merely a duty, but an honor, and one I take on gladly.* His patriotic devotion reminded her of the lost age of chivalry.

From her position on her hands and knees, Mother spoke to the floor. "I had a reply from André to my letter." Her tone was quieter, gentler. "I needn't tell it all. But the gist is, what you want is out of the question. There is no alternative, Jeannie. This child will have to be put up for adoption."

Jeannie stabbed her thumb with the needle. "You know I don't want that." She swallowed hard against the lump in her throat.

"This is the best solution all round. Besides, it's what we agreed before we came down here to this cottage in the middle of nowhere."

"But I've changed my mind."

"For heaven's sake, Jeannie. You should have thought of all that before climbing so freely into his *bed.*" Mother spat out the words. Her face was long and thin. In that moment, with her cheeks sucked in, her brow furrowed, the disgust in her eyes was clear. It made Jeannie feel dirty. Ashamed. She looked away, hating what she'd done to her mother. Hating what her mother was doing to her.

The baby shifted, and Jeannie laid a hand softly on her belly. The idea of getting rid of it hadn't seemed too bad at first. But when she finally blurted out her problem at five months, she was too far gone. Adoption, then, seemed like the only option. However, as the weeks rolled on, as she felt the baby kick inside her, an alternative idea took hold. Perhaps she could find a way to keep it. This baby she and Harry had made together, out of love. All her deepest instincts were screaming at her. Protect. Nurture. Never let go.

"There are plenty of war widows," she spoke into the silence, "or engaged mothers-to-be, who will keep their babies, and there will be no shame for them. They'll be given sympathy and help from their families. It wasn't like Harry was a fly-by-night. We were going to marry, you know that. He gave me a ring!" Jeannie cried, unable to keep the emotion out of her voice.

Mother sat up on her haunches, breathing fast. She wiped a hand across her brow.

"Any rogue can give a girl a cheap piece of metal and throw empty promises at her. You should've known better than to fall for it. Thought I'd brought you up to know right from wrong. To respect God's laws. Fact is, there was nothing official, and you barely knew him. He was probably already married and took you for a fool. If you don't give this baby up, your father will disown you. Throw you out. Is that what you want? To be out on the streets with nothing? Not be much of a fit mother then, would you?"

Jeannie threw the jacket onto the side table. Heaved herself out of the chair and stormed out the back door of the cottage. She couldn't bear to be in the same room as Mother a moment longer. Her with her disdain, her disapproval, the shame that hovered between them, an ever-present bad smell.

Outside, the morning was raw. A low mist hung over the cottage garden, moisture dripping from the surrounding trees and shrubs. The flower beds had been dug over for vegetables. In place of delphiniums, chrysanthemums, rose bushes were the higgledy mess of potato plants, cabbages, carrots, and winter greens. The chickens chattered and preened, gathering at the edge of the coop as they heard her step. Out the back gate, Jeannie stood and shivered, feet wet from the thick grass in the cow field, the hillside rolling away into more fields. Among them were scattered farm cottages, like theirs, smoke curling from chimneys into the frigid winter air.

How far away from London it felt to be here, escaping the bombs, the nights spent in shelters. And the real reason she and her mother ran away. To escape the gossip, the disapproval, the disgrace of the new fatherless life inside her. How could she make them understand? That this child was all Jeannie had left of Harry. Harry who filled her dreams each night and Harry who left her hollow and bereft and wanting all the long days.

Time was running out. Mother had arranged it, on Father's instructions. The baby would be sent to an orphanage to be cared for until some family unable to have a child of their own would be given Jeannie's instead. He or she would, eventually, have a good home and legitimacy. Much better than bearing the lifetime burden and blame that came from being the child of a loose woman.

JEANNIE KEPT QUIET about the labor pains that started in the early evening as they both sat sewing next to the range for warmth, oil lamps bathing the kitchen in an amber glow, the radio playing in the background. The pains didn't get bad until the longest, darkest hours of the night, when Jeannie sweated and paced and bit her lip to stop herself from crying out and waking Mother. Some part of her brain thought if she could just do this alone, without anyone interfering, she could stop the inevitable separation. Mother took one look at Jeannie when she rose at six and ran to fetch Mr. Binden, the farmer from whom she had rented the cottage, so that he could drive them to the maternity home, which he kindly did, anxiously glancing at Jeannie's writhing, sweating body and accelerating, not minding the bumps and potholes in the road.

The maternity home was a prefabricated building hastily erected on the grounds of the closest hospital in the town of Dorking, five miles from the cottage. It was overflowing with evacuated women from London due to give birth.

"That's the one I told you about," the ward sister said, once Jeannie had been ushered through. She wrinkled her nose at Jeannie as though she had dog shit on her shoes. "Can you organize the moral welfare worker to be advised, Nurse Campbell?" Her lip was curled with distaste. "Put her in the side room so she doesn't go about upsetting the others."

The room was tiny, just space for the iron-headed bed and for someone to walk sideways around it. The walls were thin and not soundproof, the air filled with guttural groans and shouts of laboring women, the shuffle and scrape of shoes on the linoleum outside the room, cries of "Nurse, help here, please!"

Jeannie began to shiver, consumed with terror about what was to come. But it didn't take long. She was so far gone already, the baby arrived within a matter of a couple of hours.

A healthy little girl.

A midwife took her away to clean her up and to hand her over to the moral welfare lady when she arrived. Jeannie didn't even see her face. Just the glimpse of a dark, wet head and one tiny foot dangling as she was carried away.

"I want to see her," Jeannie called after the midwife. "I want to see her face. To hold her. Please. Just for a moment." But the footsteps receded into the distance until Jeannie couldn't hear them anymore.

The nurse came to stitch Jeannie up, indifferent to the pain she caused. Jeannie fought against her in the only way she could think of. By not giving her the satisfaction of wincing or crying out at the prod and tear of her needle. Nor did she let her see a single tear shed. Instead, Jeannie willed herself to stay silent throughout the ordeal. But inside she was screaming, and her arms ached with emptiness.

After she finished, Jeannie rolled over, curled into a ball, and faced the beige wall, too exhausted to wipe away a tear that managed to escape. She had no idea how much time had passed. Perhaps she dozed for a while, because she didn't hear the door open and close. The presence of someone in the room filtered through, and, suddenly alert, she looked around. A tall, thickset woman loomed over her, a clipboard in her hand.

"Good morning. I'm Miss Jones, the moral welfare officer. Sit up, please. I need you to sign here"—she lowered the clipboard and jabbed a finger at an official-looking form—"and here."

Jeannie read the words *Released for Adoption* at the top of the form, and the tears flowed freely.

"But I haven't seen her . . . Won't I even get to see her?"

"Now, buck up and stop crying. Tears won't solve a thing. The best outcome from all this mess is that your little problem is sent away. Eventually—although heaven knows when, the orphanages are stuffed full of mistakes like yours—a loving couple who need a baby will get one. At least that will, in some part, help you overcome your shame."

Jeannie picked up the pen and signed her name.

They would expect her to pretend it never happened. Her baby would be forever brushed under the carpet and forgotten, like unwelcome filth. But not in her mind. She would always be with Jeannie, wherever she was, whatever she did.

Her daughter needed a name.

"I'm naming my daughter," she announced to her wretched-faced mother when she arrived to collect her. "Celia. It means heavenly."

Chapter 11

Celia

O ne Saturday morning in June, Father leaves for work and Mother for her job at the deli. Mrs. Denton had kindly granted Celia a whole day off, and now she is alone in the house, apart from Bartholomew, who trots upstairs after Celia, a low purr rumbling in his throat.

It's been more than two weeks since Celia learned she wasn't an only child. Two weeks for curiosity about her sister to grow into an insatiable appetite to know more. Daphne thought it perfectly understandable when the two caught up with each other the previous night at the Wellington.

Celia had sipped at a pint of cider, ignoring the mental tutting from Mother. She needed this, and she felt certain Jeannie would approve. Anyone who headed off alone, or practically so, to face the Nazis would not worry about their mother's disapproval of an alcoholic beverage.

"Perhaps there is something in the house that might give you some clues about her," Daphne suggested.

"Not that I've ever seen. They must have got rid of everything."

"I bet some of her things are squirreled away somewhere. The attic, or under your parents' bed."

It takes two attempts to turn the handle of her parents' bedroom door with palms slick with sweat. She stands on the threshold of the sanctity of their room, ears straining, nerves on edge. The room is simple. A double bed against the wall next to the door. A wardrobe and chest of drawers against the opposite wall. A dressing table sits in the curve of the bay window, her mother's jewelry box, hairbrush, and comb laid neatly on top in front of the mirror. On each side of the bed is a nightstand, a lamp on each. On Father's side lies *A Manual of Fly-Fishing*, a folded newspaper with a half-finished crossword, and a pair of his reading glasses perched on top. On Mother's side, a pocket-size Bible and a folded handkerchief. Celia looks around the room in despair. Nothing.

She wanders over to the disused fireplace to look at the framed photographs arranged on the mantelpiece. She's seen them before, but maybe there is something she's missed. There is a photo of her parents looking young: smiling and happy in the doorway of a church on their wedding day. Another of Mother's parents, Celia's grandparents, with a clutch of children standing barefoot on the beach. Celia picks out Mother, reckons she looks around eight. She turns the fading picture over and reads, *Littlehampton, July 1913.*

Celia knows Mother was nearly forty when she gave birth to Celia. Awfully old to be a new mother. Perhaps she was an unintended surprise. It's an uncomfortable thought, one she's had before. She pulls out the drawers of the dressing table. Searches the wardrobe, checks the shelf at the top where an empty old suitcase sits. She looks under the mattress and the bed. Nothing. Inside the drawer of Mother's nightstand, a pot of Vicks VapoRub, a box of matches, a glasses case, a stack of hankies. That's it. Not a secret in sight.

Celia searches the rest of the house—backs of cupboards, through bookcases, even in the drawers of the kitchen dresser. There is nothing of Jeannie anywhere.

The last place to look is the loft space. Checking the kitchen clock, she reckons she still has an hour. She fetches the big flashlight from the pantry and runs back upstairs, grabs the pole from the airing cupboard, and fits the hook into the loft door. A layer of dust and old leaves float down as the door creaks open. The loft space is not large, and she can only stand right in the center at the highest pitch of the tiled roof above her head. Celia crawls past an abandoned pile of Father's fishing tackle and an ancient set of golf clubs. There is even a pair of skis up here, a neatly packed tent, and, in a neighboring box, camping equipment, a stove, two folding chairs. Everything a keen camper might like. Father must have been quite the adventurer in his youth. Another side of her parents' lives she knows nothing about.

She moves on to scan a stack of boxes layered in dust and debris. Some books, an old sewing machine perhaps belonging to her grandmother. Finally, a small box containing baby clothes. She pulls out a pair of knitted booties and a pale pink cardigan. Hers or Jeannie's? At the bottom of the same box, she finds a woman's blue cardigan that has been eaten by moths, and a silk scarf. The scarf is wrapped around a slim journal. It's old with tattered edges. Celia squats down between the boxes and, propping the flashlight on a box so she can see, carefully opens it and flicks through. Three-quarters of the journal is empty, but the first part has been written in, in Mother's scratchy handwriting. Celia's pulse thumps in her ears. This feels significant. A thin blue envelope flutters out. It's addressed to Mother, and the postmark is stamped Chelsea, London. Inside is a short, handwritten note dated October 7, 1943. The bottom half of the note has been torn off. She checks the envelope; there is nothing else there.

64 Baker Street
London
W1

Dear Mrs. Duchesne,

*Following our brief meeting last Thursday, I'm writing to let
you know that you may contact me at the above address and
telephone number anytime, should you have any questions or
concerns. I can assure you that your daughter is in safe hands,
and all is going marvelously. We are most grateful to have her.
I am sorry that we cannot be more specific about her whereabouts.
Please do not worry, and as explained to you on Thursday, she is
really very well. Discretion here is absolutely vital.*

The rest of the note has been torn away.

There is a bang from downstairs. Celia freezes, the note in
one hand, the journal in the other.

"Celia? I'm home . . . He let me go early . . . very quiet . . ."
Her mother's voice, faint from the hallway.

Nausea pumps in Celia's guts. She fumbles to fold the note,
shoving it back between the pages of the journal. She throws
the journal in the box, grabs the flashlight, and stumbles toward
the hatch. She leans over the edge and calls, "I'll be down in a
moment! I'll pop the kettle on!"

Celia trips over a box in her haste to get back to the ladder
and bangs her knee, dropping the flashlight with a clatter. She
swears under her breath and scrabbles to retrieve it.

"Celia?" Her mother's voice, disembodied and strained at the
bottom of the ladder. "What on earth are you doing up there?"

Damn. Her mind stubbornly refuses to come up with a reason for her presence in the loft, a place she has never ventured before. She is rooted to the spot, staring down at the top of her mother's head below the loft hatch. Mother looks up and their eyes meet.

"I was just . . ." Should she confess the truth? Confront her mother? But the words stick in her throat.

"Celia?"

"I'm coming down." She turns and climbs backward down the ladder on trembling limbs, thinking of the torn letter. *I can assure you that your daughter is in safe hands, and all is going marvelously. We are most grateful to have her.*

"I asked what you were doing in the loft." Mother's voice is hard with suspicion.

In the hallway, she turns to face her mother, her heart leaping like a demented frog, banging against her rib cage, the desire to know the full, unfettered story too much to bear.

"Who was Jeannette?" she asks, the words out before she has a chance to stop them.

Mother freezes, color draining from her face.

"What did you say?" She lists like a stricken ship and leans against the wall.

"I asked," Celia says, her own voice wavering—but it's too late now, Mother heard exactly what she said—"who Jeannette was."

Mother says nothing. Her face is sickly gray, and her eyes seem to have sunk deeper in their sockets. "Where did you hear that name?" she asks finally.

"Does it matter?"

"Yes."

They head to the kitchen, and Mother leans on the table as though she can no longer support her own weight. The room is heavy with silence.

Celia fills the kettle, takes a deep breath. "All right. It was Daphne. She found something at work. A file, with your names and the name Jeannette Duchesne, code name Anya, on the front. But you can't be angry at her. She just asked if I knew anything about it."

"Did she read the file?"

"No! Of course not. She was doing some archiving, and it was one of the files being sent for archive. She just read the label on the front." She decides not to mention the stealing, the later reading of it, and the fact it is now right here, hidden in her bedroom.

"What did she tell you *exactly*?"

"Just that. It was your names, the date the file was opened, and that it concerned a Miss Jeannette Duchesne, *deceased*."

Mother's mouth flaps open and shut, like a fish drowning in air, but no words come out. She stares down at her own hands, clasped together on the kitchen table.

"I thought perhaps there might be something in the loft about who *Miss Jeannette Duchesne* was."

"Did you find anything?"

"No," Celia lies. Mother should tell her the truth, voluntarily, not because she's been caught out. "I just found layers of dust and boxes of old fishing tackle and camping stuff."

Mother releases a breath and looks away. The clock ticks loudly behind her head. Celia watches the small, shiny gold pendulum swing back and forth as though emerging from each of her mother's ears. Wisps of hair escape from her bun; her cheeks are sucked in tight. Celia suddenly thinks she looks older, a reduced version of herself.

"Surely there are rules against this. It's a breach of client confidentiality. She had no right to tell you about any file," Mother says as the kettle begins to hum.

Celia's mouth goes dry. Mother is going to complain to Thompson, Parker & Edgely about Daphne. They'll find out about the missing file, and Daphne will get the sack. It will be all Celia's fault.

"Please, Mother, it wasn't Daphne's fault! Don't tell on her. She'll lose her job and—"

"She should have thought about *that* before she said anything, shouldn't she!"

"But she didn't know there was some family secret . . . Was Jeannette my sister?" Celia needs to keep Mother's attention on the main issue.

Mother gives Celia a sharp look. "She really didn't look in that file?"

"No. I promise you, Mother, she didn't open the file at work. She was archiving, like I said."

"I didn't even know it was still there." Mother's voice is tremulous. "I suppose they would have kept records. I should have the file returned to me." Celia mentally calculates how she can get the file back to Daphne to return to its rightful place before Mother calls up on Monday morning.

"Please tell me who Jeannette was. I have a right to know, don't I?"

Mother gasps, as though she can't quite remember how to breathe. She avoids Celia's eyes as she begins to speak. "I can't . . . I won't . . ."

"*Please . . .*"

Mother shakes her head. Bites her lip.

"All right," Celia says, trying hard to stay calm. To not give in to the urge to shake the words out of her mother. "Well, I'll tell you what I think. That Jeannette, code name Anya, was my sister and that she was somehow involved in a covert operation during the war and she lost her life." Mother is silent. "If you won't tell me, I'm sure there is another way I can find out—"

"Jeannette was murdered in a concentration camp in northern France," Mother interrupts, her voice flat, robotic. "She was just twenty-one years old when she died. It's too hard . . . When you lose a child . . . You need to understand, Celia, many, many parents lost their young sons in the war. They don't like to talk of it—it's too painful to bear. It was the same for us. We didn't want that constant reminder of the worst time of our lives, all day, every day. We didn't want it to impact you. We wanted you to grow up unfettered by grief. You were so small at the time, you would have had no memory . . . We didn't want you to live under the black shadow cast by what happened to Jeannette. For right or wrong, we kept it secret. Buried it. Moved on. That's all there is to say."

The kettle begins to whistle. Celia takes it off the heat.

"But . . . what was she doing there? In France, I mean. How was she captured?"

Mother's face sinks into her hands. When she lifts her head, her cheeks glisten with tears. "She wanted to do her bit for the war effort. She was fluent in French, thanks to your father. So, unbeknownst to us, she volunteered to join the Secret Operations Executive as a special agent. They went behind enemy lines to commit acts of sabotage, that sort of thing. Well, what business did they have sending young girls to fight the Nazis, I ask you? . . . It was utter madness, desperation. They were sending them to their deaths . . . Your father and I, we were so angry . . ." Her face reddens as old fury rises inside her. "But anyway, they did, and of course, many of them were captured. The Nazis sent them to their concentration camps. Our Jeannie was executed. She never even saw her twenty-second birthday." Tears are now streaming down her face.

"Oh, Mother . . . I'm so sorry. So very sorry." Celia reaches for her mother's hands across the table, guilt at having upset her like this crawling across her skin like an ugly rash.

Mother pulls a hankie from her pocket and blows her nose. "Yes, well. It's water under the bridge now. The file Daphne found . . . We were trying to get compensation from the War Office. Of course money can never replace a person, but it would have helped—" She stops. Breathes out heavily. "Your father . . . It broke him, losing Jeannie. You mustn't say any of this to him. He was on the edge for a long time. Promise me, Celia?"

"I promise. I won't say a thing."

"We've come to terms with it in our own way, I suppose."

But you haven't, Celia thinks, seeing the agony in her mother's face. *You've buried it, and it's eating you up from within.*

"I'm sorry I brought it up," Celia says, "but I'm glad to know I had a sister. And that she was clever and brave."

Mother says nothing, lips pressed tight, eyes brimming with tears. She squeezes Celia's hand. "I think perhaps I will leave the file just where it is. It's better archived than here, where your father might find it."

"Will you say something to Daphne?"

"No . . . She wasn't to know."

"Thank you," Celia whispers. "Thank you."

"But you must tell her this stays strictly between us all. Nobody can breathe a word, not you, not Daphne, nobody. Ever. Do you understand?" Her voice is urgent, eyes wide.

Celia nods. She wants to dig further. Why all the secrecy? Something niggles at her that there is more to all this than Mother is letting on. But the desperate look on her mother's face stops her.

"Now," Mother says with a sniff and a final wipe of her eyes before she stuffs the hankie back in her pocket, "I think I'll go up and have a nice hot bath."

"I'll bring you up a cuppa. Will you be all right, Mother?"

"Yes, love. I'll be right as rain in a bit. You'll see." She stands and walks stiffly to the door. Then she turns and says, "Everything we did after Jeannie died was for you. We both love you very much, even if we don't always show it. That's something I wish I'd managed to say to Jeannie before she went. But I never got the chance."

THAT NIGHT, CELIA can't sleep. Disparate scenes from her childhood revolve through her brain. It is all beginning to make sense. The problems in her parents' marriage. Her father's drinking. His refusal to speak to her in French. Their overprotectiveness. She can't burden her mother with more questions, and she has promised not to mention any of it to Father. Perhaps if they had done things differently, they might have worked through their grief. But she has to respect their decisions.

After all, they did it to protect her.

She must tell Daphne about the letter she found. She tries to remember it. *I can assure you your daughter is in safe hands, and all is going marvelously.* There was something about being grateful for her and then, *we cannot be more specific about her whereabouts.* It was an oddly worded letter, especially if it concerned Jeannie. *All is going marvelously. We are grateful for her.* What did that mean? Her secret operation? Why was the letter torn? Who had written it? Her mother's strange, fearful reaction to Celia's questions. There is more to this story than Mother has told her, and Celia knows one thing for sure.

She won't rest until she gets to the bottom of it all.

Chapter 12

Celia

A pyramid of post lies on the floor inside the shop door when Celia opens up on Monday morning. She sorts it into two piles on the counter: shop post and Mrs. Denton's personal post. It's been only two months since Mrs. Denton took over the shop, yet she's received more post in that time than the Blythes did in the three years Celia knew them. She seems to have an awful lot of friends and acquaintances, many of whom are frequent visitors to the shop. She spends most of the day either entertaining them behind the black door to the flat, or hoovering and cleaning in preparation for their visits, or after they have gone. Quite frankly, Celia thinks, stacking the letters into a neat pile, it must be a godsend for Mrs. D that she has inherited Celia to keep the place running smoothly. She seems to have precious little clue about antiquarian books or the running of a bookshop at all.

But, despite this, they have settled into a comfortable pattern of working together, and it seems she and Mrs. D really do make a good team. The woman treats her as an equal. Celia *has* become manager, not just an assistant anymore, and her heart swells with pride and gratitude that Mrs. Denton thinks her worthy of her trust. It's then that she sees it. A letter addressed to her, *The War Office* stamped across the top in thick black letters.

She tears open the envelope, full of nerves at the prospect of hearing from Miss Clarke and learning more about her sister.

True to her promise to Mother, she has not mentioned a word about Jeannette to anyone, and has impressed on Daphne the importance to keep the secret between the two of them.

Dear Miss Duchesne,

Thank you for your letter of May 13, addressed to Miss Muriel Clarke. I am sorry to inform you that Miss Clarke was decommissioned by the Women's Auxiliary Air Force shortly after the war. We do not retain records of forwarding addresses for more than seven years, and hence are unable to assist you in locating Miss Clarke. One of my long-serving colleagues, however, does remember Miss Clarke and tells me that she went on to work for UNESCO's education bureau as office manager.

I am sorry not to be able to assist you further.

Yours sincerely,
Miss E. Bowden
Secretary

Damn! Celia folds the letter and puts it back in the envelope. It's a disappointment, but at least Miss Clarke must be still alive and might be reachable at the UNESCO office. Buoyed by this idea, she retreats behind the counter, riffling beneath it for the Yellow Pages. She flicks to *U* and finds UNESCO's London address and phone number.

Celia takes a sheet of writing paper with H. J. Potts letterhead and resolves to type up the letter during her lunchtime practice at Pitman's.

She is just dropping the letter, paper, and an envelope into her handbag when Alfred Humphries steps through the door. He's become a regular visitor. What goes on behind the closed door of the flat when he pops in for coffee, she can only guess at.

Celia checks her watch. It's only five minutes past nine.

"You're early this morning, Mr. Humphries," she calls out brightly. "Mrs. D hasn't appeared yet, I'm afraid."

He removes his fedora and smooths back his hair. The livid line of his scar still shocking every time she encounters it.

"Oh, I'm aware of that." He gives her a crooked smile, the type that says, *I'm the cat that got the cream.* He jerks his head toward the flat door. "I spent the night here. Just popped out to get this." He taps a folded newspaper tucked beneath his arm.

Celia covers her exclamation of surprise with a cough.

"Gives us a chance to chat, Miss Duchesne," Mr. Humphries says, sauntering toward the counter. "We don't always get that, do we, eh?"

Celia feels the little hairs rise on the back of her neck. His eyes are fixed on her. There is something greedy in them, and it makes her shiver. She busies herself at the till, counting the ha'pennies, the pennies, and the shillings, putting each in a separate bag for delivering later to the bank. *Don't be silly*, she thinks, giving herself a stern talking to. *Mrs. D would not be friends with a sleazebag. He has an unfortunate manner about him, that's all.* Even so, she feels safer with the counter between the two of them.

He licks his lips, and his mouth slides into a glistening smile.

"Actually," he says, "I've been meaning to ask you, Miss Duchesne, where are *you* from? There is something a little exotic about you. The surname, of course, and the way you look. Your almost-black hair, your darker skin." He pauses. "Italian perhaps? Or Spanish?"

Nausea rises in her throat, and Celia feels the blood rush to her face. "Southwark," she says firmly. "I was born and bred in Southwark."

"I don't mean to embarrass you," Mr. Humphries says, leaning farther across the counter. "But I meant originally. Where are you from *originally*?"

Celia begins to sweat.

"I am *originally* from London, Mr. Humphries."

"Alfred, please."

"Mr. Humphries. My mother," she continues, "is English, from Southwark, just like me. My father is Belgian, but he grew up here. I'm afraid there is no hint of the exotic about me."

Alfred Humphries continues to stare as though trying to read her genealogy.

"Interesting," he says at last, eyes roving over her face. She finds she has lost count of the pound notes in her hand and has to begin again.

"You just look—"

Her insides clench. Enough is enough.

"You, Mr. Humphries," she interrupts firmly, knowing how people, especially men like this one, enjoy talking about themselves, "have a faint accent yourself . . . I can't quite place it. Where are you from?"

Alfred's jaw tightens. "I've lived all over," he says. "Spent some time in Paris. Italy. The Far East. And now here I am, back in good old Blighty."

"I see. Now if you'll excuse me, Mr. Humphries, I really need to count out this cash. Would you mind?" She gives him a glare.

"Fine." He straightens, moves away to examine the bookshelves.

Mrs. Denton appears at last, her face fully made up, her hair beautifully set. She smells of hair lacquer and her familiar Lily of the Valley scent. She is too good for Mr. Humphries, Celia thinks, as Mrs. D, pink-cheeked, invites him up for breakfast.

Celia pretends she doesn't see the wink Mr. Humphries gives her as he passes.

THE UPSTAIRS ROOM of Number 13 Goodwin Street, Finsbury Park, home of the working group of the Committee of 100, is packed, the air sticky and thick with cigarette smoke. Celia is squeezed between Daphne and Sam, who announced he wanted to come out of curiosity.

The Committee of 100 was established by Bertrand Russell a couple of years ago, separate from the CND, to take direct action for nuclear disarmament. To her right are two men discussing their Oxford University colleges in plummy tones, and to her left, a group of hawkers from Covent Garden Market. Her chest swells at the thought that a common goal—to avoid nuclear catastrophe and save their world—has brought them all together. Whatever their differences, however far apart they are across the economic and political divide, this comes before and above anything, and everything, else.

"Our aim," Bertrand Russell says from his position at the podium, "as many of you will know, is to create the maximum possible disruption by peaceful means. This will be organized by a series of sit-ins, like the successful ones we held last year outside the Ministry of Defence in Whitehall, and when we blocked Trafalgar Square last September. Despite the arrests— and as you know I chose to go to prison myself—I think we can declare these a success, with almost *fifteen thousand* people attending. And so, we need *you* now, more than ever, to be willing to come with us. To spread the word and to bring with you your friends and family."

A cheer breaks out. Above the applause Sam leans toward Daphne and asks, "Aren't you afraid of losing your job? If you were to be arrested . . ."

"It is a risk," Daphne agrees, never taking her eyes off her soon-to-be ninety-year-old hero. "But I'm willing to take it. He did. He went to prison after the sit-ins last September for a week, at his age!"

"But he doesn't need a job. Not like you or I do. He's aristocracy!"

"Does that matter? You're missing the point. Which is, I'd rather go to prison than be nuked. Wouldn't you?" She gives Sam a hard stare.

"Well, I, err . . ."

"And you?" Daphne turns to Celia. "You would, wouldn't you?"

Celia thinks of what Mother and Father would say if she were to be arrested. They would never live down the shame. But then she thinks of Jeannie. She wouldn't have thought twice. If she was willing to die for freedom, then she, Celia, should at least be willing to spend a few nights in jail.

"No question." She smiles, gives Sam a sympathetic wink, and turns back to listen to Russell.

"We are planning a demonstration on September ninth outside the Air Ministry," he is saying in closing. "Friends, if you join us, you will be doing something important to preserve your family, compatriots, and the world."

Russell sits beside the other London committee members,

and a young man takes his place at the microphone. Celia recognizes him as one of the chaps discussing his Oxford University college. He introduces himself as Bob.

"The media are becoming bored," Bob says, "the government choosing to ignore us. What we, the Spies for Peace, are proposing, is radical action. We believe our government is currently preparing for nuclear war." Bob pauses to let this sink in. "But this fact is being kept secret. Their preparations are probably better known to our foreign enemies than they are to us, the people they are supposed to protect. Right now, they are readying deep bunkers at secret locations in the countryside for government use in the event of nuclear attack. They don't want you and me to know. The Official Secrets Act, meant to protect our country against foreign spies, is instead being used against its own people. There is a media blackout. And if we report it, not only will our reports be covered up, but we will be criminally charged and gagged."

Someone a few rows in front calls out, "And what can we do about it?"

"Our plan," Bob continues, raising his voice over the mumblings in the audience, "is to produce pamphlets once we have compiled enough concrete evidence of the bunkers. It is imperative the authors are kept secret from the authorities, for fear of prosecution. Hence you will know me only as Bob. We have no funds to speak of, so we need your help. Thank you."

Bob steps away from the microphone.

"I don't like this," Sam mutters, shuffling uncomfortably in his chair. "It feels subversive. I'm all up for demonstrating, but I'm not sure about breaking the law . . ."

"If the laws are *wrong*, though. If they are endangering us . . ." Celia says, as much to herself as to the others. "I mean, who knows what the truth is? And I suppose, just because someone is in a position of authority, it doesn't make them good, or right."

"Exactly," Daphne says. "Think Hitler. Or Stalin. Anyway, I'm going to offer up my help. I can probably get them paper and envelopes and such like. You could help with typing, Celia. What do you think?"

"Maybe, as long as it doesn't stop me getting that job at the BBC . . ."

"There won't be *any* jobs at the BBC, Celia darling, if there is another war."

Chapter 13

Septimus

Septimus is rarely privy to the reasoning behind what he is asked to do. The information train, it seems, only runs in one direction. But nevertheless, the daily briefings he attends between Ambassador Bruce and Mr. President or his office, and the now regular contact with Fox-Andrews, who, perhaps, is less discreet than he should be, means he is able to piece together disparate material and gain a sketchy picture of the most important matters he needs to be paying attention to.

The good thing is that he has gained the Big B's trust. The ambassador is content to off-load onto Septimus, and Septimus, eager to learn, eager to please, is only too keen to take up the mantle.

He is early for the drink Fox-Andrews invited him to at The Red Lion, just off Jermyn Street. While he waits at the bar, he downs two neat vodkas to settle his nerves, then orders a soda water with lemon and ice.

He mulls over what he knows of the current state of things. Berlin is the desired prize both the Americans and the Soviets want. The island of capitalism that is West Berlin, one hundred miles deep in the German Democratic Republic and so hotly fought over, is now surrounded by a ninety-six-mile-long wall, like a ghetto. But this wall is not to stop people getting *out*; it's to stop people getting *in*. The bleeding of the cream of East Germany being lured to seek their fortunes in the West proved too much for Chairman Khrushchev last year. Something had to be done, he obviously decided, and in those tumultuous months toward the end of 1961, which could so easily have escalated into war, he found a practical solution. Why it's so important for the Americans to hang on to it (and, on the other hand, for the Soviets to gain it), other than for the symbolic value, to keep its allies in Western Europe happy, or simply to prevent the Soviets getting what they want, Septimus isn't sure. He is probably missing something, but to him it doesn't seem worth risking nuclear war over.

In any event, according to what Septimus has learned, the Soviets thought Kennedy *owed* Khrushchev for (in their opinion) helping him to win the election back in 1960. Chairman Khrushchev had, perhaps naïvely, although maybe understandably, expected some form of thank-you present, such as Berlin, to cement a new era of trust and good relations. But, thinks Septimus wryly, even *he* at his young age knows one should never expect people to behave in the way you think they ought to. *Never trust anyone, not even your own mother.* Sure enough, Kennedy didn't follow through, which has made Khrushchev an unhappy man. Furthermore, as the Big B has told Septimus on more than one occasion, with Mao Zedong snapping at Khrushchev's heels, vying for the position of world leader and defender of communism, he is also a man desperate to prove himself, which makes him a dangerous and volatile one.

Septimus hears Sir Reginald Fox-Andrews before he sees him, recognizing the deep-throated phlegmy cough behind his left shoulder.

"Hullo, my man," Fox-Andrews says, holding out a fat hand. A heavy gold signet ring is wedged so tightly onto his little finger the flesh bulges on either side of it, blotchy pink, like raw sausage meat. He leans his bulk across the bar and booms his beer order at the none-too-pleased-looking landlord. Once a pint of frothy-headed beer, the color of ripe plums, is balanced in his hand, he bends to take a long drink. "C'mon, let's step outside, Sep, old chap," he says, serious now. "More air out there."

Sep. It makes him sound like a sheepdog. He feels a ripple of irritation.

Outside, they lean up against the wall of the pub, beneath the foliage of a row of hanging baskets. Other pubgoers have spilled out onto the sidewalk, too, but all are deep in conversation, intent on letting off steam after a long day at the office. Nobody pays the two of them any notice at all.

"You're a lucky fellow," Fox-Andrews comments after downing a third of his pint in one gulp, leaving a thin, frothy moustache across his top lip. "Landed on your feet." He stares morosely into his glass. "At such a young age . . ."

Septimus smiles for a second time, remaining silent. *The less said, the less anyone can hold against you.* The lessons he learned long ago are branded into his brain.

"Anyway," Fox-Andrews continues, giving himself a shake, "David Bruce seems very taken with you. So, whatever you're doing, keep it up." He smiles wryly. "All you have to do in this business is keep the sharks happy." Fox-Andrews always sees it necessary to feed Septimus, the young pup, little tidbits of advice. "They leave you alone that way."

Septimus nods. Lions; sharks. Interesting how they both think of their superiors as predators.

"In fact"—Fox-Andrews is warming to the sound of his own voice—"it's the US congressional elections in just a few months. Kennedy will need all the help he can get. 'Course, it's in *our* interests to ensure he does well. What I *can* tell you is there is a top secret plan being discussed. Don't ask me what it is, I can't divulge, but the fact of the matter is, to avoid discovery of this plan, the secret one, attention needs to stay focused on Berlin. The impression needs to be maintained and enhanced that things could well escalate, possibly resulting in war before the end of the year. This will focus everyone's minds and play in Kennedy's favor. He needs to shake off that reputation of being weak. We will use all the influence we have to cement the impression of *strength*." He pauses, takes another slug of his drink. He drags the back of his hand across his top lip, wiping away the line of foam.

The man makes Septimus's stomach turn. But he pushes that aside. *Focus on the task in hand*, he reminds himself. And this intriguing plan. Septimus would love to know what that is.

"The Soviets," Fox-Andrews continues in a low voice, "are calling for the full withdrawal of American, British, and French troops from West Berlin. They say it's inconceivable that there can be any German peace agreement until the occupation by Allied troops is withdrawn. This is very dangerous, you mark my words. The Soviets are pushing themselves into a corner with this. If America refuses to withdraw, it will lead to a sudden explosion of hostilities. Neither side will want that . . ."

Fox-Andrews waves his almost-empty glass flamboyantly as though holding forth at a podium. At least he keeps his voice low. Septimus is always on the lookout for listening ears that may belong to the most innocuous-looking bystanders.

"What the Soviets want is for the occupation forces to be gone, a temporary UN force to replace them, and then, after a few years, for that to be gone, too, and for West Berlin to become a free city, independent as a political entity. This will pave the way for a German peace settlement and a nonaggression pact between NATO and the Warsaw Treaty Organization, plus better relations between the US and USSR."

"Right," Septimus says, not entirely sure what is expected of him. "Sounds like a reasonable proposal to me."

"You really are green about the gills! You think the Americans will agree?" Fox-Andrews chuckles, his belly jiggling. "A free city? Kennedy would rather eat his own head . . . But where you come in, Nelson, when this is all out in the open, is to keep your ear to the ground as to what the PM thinks of it all. France, the West Germans. Italians, too, as they will all need to be consulted. Kennedy, as you know, listens to Macmillan. We want to understand the lay of the land. The way the wind is blowing. And however which way you can, make sure the focus is kept on Berlin."

Septimus furrows his brow. The English have a hideous habit of using idioms that rarely make sense to him.

"Listen," Fox-Andrews says. "I've got to dash, I'm afraid. Will be in touch soon. And, Nelson," he adds, "whatever else you do, keep delivering the goods. There're some high expectations of you, after that spectacular promotion . . ." He sucks a noisy breath in between his teeth. "You've got yourself a rod for your own back now, what?"

"I've got this," Septimus says with a confidence he is becoming a master at displaying. "I won't let anyone down."

"Excellent, excellent . . . Well, till next time."

Septimus watches Fox-Andrews shove his bulk through the crowd before leaving himself. He strides quickly along Piccadilly toward Hyde Park. It's a nice evening, and he needs to clear his head. Relax, think. He checks behind him, across the street. Always the worry that someone is watching. It's more likely now, in this position, than ever. Didn't the Big B say as much? Eyes and ears everywhere?

What chills him more than anything is that the watcher could be from his own side or the other. The risk to him, either way, is pretty much the same.

Chapter 14

Celia

In among the Thursday morning post is a slim envelope with Celia's name on it. Pulling it open, she finds a short note on UNESCO education department stationery. It confirms that the elusive Miss Clarke *did* work there until only six months ago, when she retired. The note says that they have taken the liberty of forwarding Miss Duchesne's letter on to Miss Clarke, together with her address at the bookshop, in the event she wishes to get in touch. Celia puts a hand over her mouth to stop herself from shouting out in glee. She's getting closer!

She busies herself going through a box of books that arrived in the shop overnight. Stock sometimes arrives like this, straight from people's homes, because they have moved house or died or had a clearout. Often the quality is poor and the resale value insignificant. But occasionally a gem is found.

Celia picks through this latest selection and finds a copy of J. M. Barrie's *Peter Pan in Kensington Gardens*. Her heart beats a little faster as she opens the cover to see it's been inscribed by the author and signed by the illustrator, Arthur Rackham. This edition, from the publisher Hodder & Stoughton in 1906, is the original publication and undoubtedly worth a great deal. She is about to call out to Mrs. Denton, who is working on the monthly figures in the back room, when the doorbell jangles.

Septimus Nelson closes the door behind him, pulls off his hat, and comes toward her, a broad smile lighting up his face.

Something about him always sets the butterflies to flight in her belly.

"Miss Duchesne. What an absolute pleasure to see you again." The enthusiasm behind his words seems so genuine. It makes her flustered, unable to think of anything to say that won't sound crass or keen or stupid.

Celia jumps to her feet, placing the book on the counter before her sweaty palms damage its cream cover.

"Hello, Mr. Nelson," she finally manages. "More books already? Or are you here to see Mrs. Denton? She's just out the back . . ."

Like Mr. Humphries, Mr. Nelson has become a regular visitor to the shop. Often buying and inquiring about books. He seems to have become quite the fan of Dickens. He purchased *Bleak House* only two days ago. Besides, Mrs. Denton is always sending him on some errand or another. She has a knack for getting people to do things for her, with a girlish smile and a tilt of the head, or a self-deprecating word or two about her inability to do this or that. Within just a few moments, almost complete strangers are fixing broken lamps, looking at her boiler, fetching or carrying, helping her with paperwork. It's quite a skill, and Septimus seems as susceptible as the next man.

Mr. Nelson shakes his head and takes a step closer to the counter. He hesitates, drumming his fingers on the glass surface.

"Actually, Miss Duchesne, I came in to see you."

Celia's heart stops.

"I've been thinking for a while now," he continues, "how nice it might be if you would agree to have a coffee with me sometime?"

"Oh, I don't drink coffee, I'm afraid," Celia replies before her brain makes contact with her mouth. "It's awfully bitter, and not all that good for you—that's what my mother says, in any case . . ." *Good God, she is babbling nonsense.*

Mr. Nelson laughs. "All right, how about tea, then? Or . . ." He leans an elbow on the counter and looks up at her with devastating eyes. It is clear in that look that this is a man who is rarely, if ever, refused by a woman. "Perhaps lunch? I know a lovely little French bistro just around the corner. What do you say?"

Lunch? Her? With a chap like this? Her brain ticks over. Father's warning words in her head: *Men are only ever after one thing.* Why would a man like Mr. Nelson be interested in a girl like her? She is certain he has had a long string of girlfriends, glamorous and sophisticated, no doubt, given his looks and the circles he mixes in. Her own experience of boyfriends is, by contrast, limited to the extent of being, well, nonexistent. There were two dates with Norman from the warehouse when she worked briefly at Selfridges and a few fumbling kisses at dances, but other than that, she is a complete novice. Mother and Father implicitly discourage any notion of boyfriends, with their constant warnings of the lurking dangers of predatory men and wicked ways and ruination of girls who *get themselves into trouble.* The whole terrifying notion being enough to send Celia scuttling in the opposite direction if any boy so much as looks her way. His interest in her makes no sense. Perhaps he thinks English girls like her are easy. She can feel her face flush with shame that he might think she is a *willing* sort of girl.

"I couldn't possibly."

"Don't you eat lunch either?"

"Well, yes. I do. But I don't know you . . ."

"So . . . you only have lunch with people you know?"

"Exactly! Do you have lunch with people you don't know?"

"All the time." He laughs again. He looks lovely when he laughs. The skin beside his eyes crinkling, his teeth straight and white. She suddenly wonders what it would be like to kiss him, and the flush of heat intensifies to a furnace, spreading from her chest and up her neck, making her cheeks scorch red.

"It's part of my job, Miss Duchesne," he is saying, "in case you were thinking I habitually invite strangers to have lunch with me."

"Of course. Sorry. I sound like a fool."

"No you don't." His tone is kind, and Celia thinks that in spite of everything, she *would* rather like to have lunch with him, if only she were brave enough. Daphne, if not saving the world, would. She definitely needs to work on being more like Daphne.

"All right," he is saying, "so, how about a cup of tea, after work? I'm guessing for tea you don't need to know a person quite so well?"

"If it's just tea, I guess not."

"Great!"

"But I can't do Tuesdays or Thursdays. I go to night school after work, so not today, I'm afraid."

"Ah." He cocks his head. "Tomorrow, Friday, then?"

"Fine," she says, before she can think better of it. "Tomorrow."

IN BETWEEN DICTATION sessions later that evening, Celia can't help but discuss Septimus with the girls in the shorthand class.

"Would *tea* mean I owe him anything, well, you know . . . ?" she whispers.

"Owe him anything after a cuppa? I should bloomin' think not," Marjorie exclaims.

122 ~ Louise Fein

"Sssh!"

"To be fair," Ellen comments, head to one side, "if it's tea at the Ritz, with fancy smoked salmon sandwiches with their crusts cut off, champagne and cake, well, then . . ."

"Yeah, she's got a point," agrees Betsy.

"Right, thanks, girls. I know just where we're going then." Celia giggles. "Jack's Café shouldn't raise any expectations over a peck on the cheek."

"Quiet, girls." Miss Cutter raps the desk and frowns at the room. "I am about to begin the second dictation."

A hush descends, and Celia is forced to forget all about Septimus as she takes down the long and detailed letter Miss Cutter reads out as she paces back and forth across the room. Her words are spoken at a normal speed, neither clear nor well pronounced, and it's all Celia can do to keep up. Her notebook quickly fills with lines and dots and dashes until Miss Cutter announces dictation is over and they should leave their work on their desks for marking.

When Celia arrives home that evening, Mother is applying lipstick at the hallway mirror. She is dressed to go out in her long navy skirt and jacket.

"Ah, just in time," she says, fixing on her hat with the mother-of-pearl hatpin. "Ursula and I are helping Mrs. Fernandez organize the flowers for her daughter's wedding on Saturday. I'll only be gone a couple of hours. I've left your supper in the oven." She glances at Celia. "You look tired, dear. That bookshop really works you hard."

"I'm fine, Mother, really. Thanks for the supper, and enjoy sorting out the flowers."

Mother pulls the front door closed behind her, leaving Celia alone with an opportunity she has been itching for these last weeks.

She gives it ten minutes to make sure her mother won't come back for any forgotten items; then she gingerly climbs the ladder into the loft, armed with Father's big flashlight, her breath catching in her throat as she crawls to the abandoned box.

Shining the flashlight inside, relief floods her veins. It's still there. Thank goodness Mother didn't move it. Now that Mother's getting on a bit in years, she probably didn't want to venture up here.

Celia searches the box thoroughly for the other part of the torn letter, but it isn't there. She climbs down the ladder with the journal, the thin blue envelope and letter tucked inside, settling on her bed to read.

Her mouth is dry. With shaking fingers, Celia puts the note to one side and turns to the journal. There are no dates, but it is clear when she begins to read that the entries were written during the war years. Most of it is mundane. Day-to-day happenings, hardships, names of friends who had lost loved ones. There are some recipes and jottings about getting stains out or how to mend or fix things. But between those, Celia finds the odd sentence where, perhaps in desperation, Mother has written down her thoughts. Desperate, plaintive thoughts that send Celia's heart ticking faster.

Whatever are we going to do? If A finds out, he will go spare. I don't see there is any choice in the matter. Whether J likes it or not, it's the only solution.

Celia looks at the date of the entry. August 1942—four months before her birth. She searches her memory. She recalls her mother saying Father was in North Africa the year she was born, so far away, and that Mother had gone to live in the countryside for safety's sake. J could be Jeannie, or could J be someone else entirely? *Surely* Mother couldn't have had a lover?

She reads on. There is nothing else of note until the summer of 1943.

I know I've gone against his wishes, and he is furious with me. But what else could I do? I am certain we are doing the right thing. I have prayed so much. God approves, if only A would too. But I don't know if he will ever find it in his heart to forgive me.

Another entry a few days later reads:

Guilt is a fruitless, pointless, painful thing. Yet I will carry it around with me always, a stone around my neck.

A sudden thought strikes her. Could she, Celia, be the child of an illicit love affair? Perhaps the torn letter isn't about her sister at all. *I can assure you that your daughter is in safe hands, and all is going marvelously. We are most grateful to have her.* She picks up the letter and stares at it again. What if the daughter referred to in the letter is her? That would explain the animosity between Mother and Father. But *Mother*? She can't imagine anyone less likely to have a love affair.

She had scratched in the journal:

Is this my fault? Is it my punishment that I have to bear this loss?

Then later still:

I think perhaps I was wrong. Perhaps God disapproved of my choices. I was wrong and this is why I have been punished. I must bear this with fortitude. I will not turn away from Him, like A has. I will repent as best I can.

Or maybe it wasn't that simple.
The last entry reads:

The not knowing is suffering in itself. These past months have been torture. But it is 1944, and I must try to see this as closure. I cannot write in here anymore.

The agony Mother felt is imbibed in the ink on the page. Tears well up. Celia can't help it. For Mother, for Jeannie, for surely that last entry is about her. For the disappointment in being no clearer about the letter, or why there is this deep rift between Mother and Father. This will remain a mystery unless Celia can find a way to unravel it.

Then she remembers. There was an address at the top of the letter.

64 Baker Street
London
W1

Perhaps she will find the answer there. She'll talk to Daph about it. She always has bright ideas.

Back in the attic, she crouches on the dusty floor, rewraps the journal in the scarf again, and places it, together with the letter, back where she found it. She should go down, eat her supper. Feed the cat. She pauses for a moment, staring at the box, at all the abandoned items up here. Then she turns and makes her way back to the open loft hatch, leaving the unwanted fragments of her parents' past lives behind her.

Chapter 15

Celia

"What sort of music do you like?" Septimus asks Celia as they share a pot of tea and two slices of Battenberg cake in Jack's Café. There are undoubtedly better-quality cafés, lying somewhere between this and the Ritz, but Jack's is close to the bookshop, and it won't give him any false ideas about her or what she might be willing to do. She doubts if the well-bred, well-dressed, well-to-do Septimus has ever set foot in a greasy spoon café in his life. He winces as he drinks. He clearly doesn't think much of the tea, which, to be fair, has a distinct pond-water taste to it.

"Oh, you know. Elvis, the Everly Brothers, Ray Charles, Sam Cooke, that sort of thing."

"Pop music, then?"

"Yes. What about you?"

"Sure, all that. But I love jazz and classical too. I played the violin as a kid."

"When did you give it up?"

"At about sixteen. It was not a cool instrument. Girls liked the guitar or the saxophone. I was not a cool kid."

In spite of her jangling nerves, Celia laughs. Septimus is easier to talk to than she had imagined.

"My mother is a staunch Christian," she tells him. "I had to sing in the church choir, even though my voice is terrible. It was only when they said I was ruining the performances that she agreed I could give up."

"I'm sure that wasn't true."

"Sadly, it was. I wasn't a cool kid either, nor in possession of any talent."

"I am sure you possess lots of talent. And it's a fact, uncool kids make the grooviest of adults."

"You think?"

"Sure."

Septimus shudders as he downs his tea.

"Is it really that bad?"

"It honestly is," Septimus says, looking at his empty cup with distaste. He glances around. "What is this place, anyway?"

"I come here for lunch sometimes with my friend Daphne. She works at a solicitor's firm not far from here. I'm sorry. I expect you are used to fancy restaurants and a much better class of tea."

He shakes his head at the teapot. "I'm telling you, that is probably the worst tea I've ever drunk in my life."

Celia giggles. "You're right. It is the worst."

"Did you bring me here just to put me off?"

"Not exactly . . . Well, perhaps a little. I didn't want to give you any funny ideas about me."

Septimus raises an eyebrow. "Funny ideas?"

"About what sort of girl I am. You know . . ." She can feel her chest growing hot. The color rising to her cheeks.

Septimus laughs. "Sweetheart, I invited you for a cup of tea and a little company. Nothing more, nothing less. I'm a foreigner in your town. I never intended to make you feel uncomfortable. I get a little lonely, you see, spending so much of my life working. It doesn't leave much time for anything else." He smiles, genuine and warm.

Those eyes! Celia laughs.

"So, what exactly *is* your job, Septimus?"

"I'm aide-de-camp to the ambassador," he explains. "Sort of his right-hand man. Actually, that makes it sound far grander than it is. Truth is, I go along to meetings, take notes, pour tea and coffee, order those below me around a bit, that sort of thing. It really isn't as important as it sounds."

"Well, it sounds pretty grand to me."

"It's long hours, seven days a week, pretty much. But I'm not complaining. It was my dream to work in the diplomatic service, and I never expected this promotion—I'd only been in the job a couple of months. I just got lucky—right place, right time, that sort of thing."

"Congratulations on the promotion, then."

"Thank you . . . Hey." Septimus leans forward. "What do you say to getting out of this place with its substandard service and god-awful tea? There are some nice hotels close by we could get a much better-quality cup of tea. Just so you can get to know enough about me so I can qualify as a potential lunch companion . . ."

Celia smiles and opens her mouth to reply, *Okay, but just one as I need to get home*, even though she doesn't, not yet, but she's distracted by a cry of "There you are!" in a familiar voice.

Daphne.

"Celia, darling! I've been looking for you everywhere!"

She rushes over to their table.

"Everywhere?" Celia queries, confused by her friend's sudden arrival.

"Well, I mean at the shop. Mrs. Denton told me you'd come here, with a friend." She glances at Septimus, who is now politely on his feet, and does a double-take. "She didn't mention he was a man friend."

Daphne sticks out a hand for him to shake. "Daphne," she says. "I'm a friend of Celia's."

"Great to meet you, Daphne. I'm Septimus," he says, offering her his seat.

Daphne gives Celia a surreptitious thumbs-up before turning back to Septimus. "Thanks, but I can't stay," she breathes. "Sadly."

Septimus continues to look at Daphne and a stone settles in Celia's stomach. Now he has met glorious Daphne, he will never have eyes for *her*.

"*Actually*," Daphne says, giving Celia a pleading look, "I'm so sorry to intrude, but I'm afraid I need to steal you away." Daphne gives her large shoulder bag a little pat. "Remember, Celia, we are supposed to be making some CND banners this evening."

"We are?"

Daphne gives her a nudge beneath the table, forcing her to admit to an error of memory.

"CND?" Septimus asks, forehead wrinkled.

"The Campaign for Nuclear Disarmament," Daphne explains.

"We're both big supporters," Celia adds.

"We're planning a protest outside the American embassy. They just need to get on and sign that treaty banning testing," Daphne says. "That's just the first step, though. We want the earth to be rid of *all* of them. That's the goal."

"I see," Septimus says, winking at Celia. "And when might this protest be?"

"I have to keep it secret," Daphne is saying, missing the wink and the question. "My employers wouldn't be too impressed. They're very establishment. You know, the type who think those in favor of peace are all communists and revolutionaries."

Celia internally winces. *What must he think!*

"Um, actually, Daph, Septimus works at the American embassy," Celia says when Daphne finally stops for a breath.

"Oh!" Daphne slaps her hand over her mouth. "*Why didn't you tell me?*" She narrows her eyes at Celia.

"You didn't give me a chance!"

Septimus chuckles. "Ah, don't worry. There are *always* protests outside the embassy for one thing or another. That's sort of what it's there for, I suppose."

"You must think me such a fool."

"Why would I? There is nothing wrong with wanting peace," Septimus says. "At the end of the day, I guess it's what we all want. We just have different visions of how to get there. And besides, protesting is simply exercising your democratic rights."

"Will it make a difference?" Celia asks.

"Not a bit, I should think."

"We're going to go ahead and do it anyway," Daphne says. "It will at least get media attention, if nothing else."

"Sure, that's true. Go on, off you go," Septimus tells Celia. "I look forward to finding out more about your radical activism."

Is he being sarcastic?

"We'll do this again sometime," he adds, "but next time, I get to choose the venue."

"Okay." She smiles. "It's a deal. Have a nice weekend, Septimus. And sorry to leave you in the lurch," she adds, as Daphne grabs her by the elbow and drags her out of Jack's.

"Blimey, Celia!" Daphne says, the moment their feet hit the pavement. They walk arm in arm along the Strand toward the bus stop. "Septimus is a bit of a catch. What cheek, keeping him all to yourself!"

"I'm not keeping him to myself. He's been coming into the

shop for a while, but I'd no idea he had noticed me, not in that way, at least. He comes in to see Mrs. Denton—she was a friend of his mother's in California. I suppose she has taken him under her wing. Or perhaps it's the other way around? He's always running errands for her. In fact, she is very good at getting her friends and acquaintances to run about after her. I've no idea what her secret is. But anyway, that was the first time he invited me out for a cup of tea, and we'd only been there about ten minutes before you came in and ruined it!"

"I apologize for my terrible timing. Had I known you were on a date with such a dish, I'd have waited till the morning."

Celia sighs. "It wasn't really a date. I mean, why on earth would a man like him be interested in a girl like me? He's got a high-flying job at the American embassy. I'm sure he meets all sorts of far more fascinating people than me. And now that he knows I'm a CND supporter, that's probably that."

"Don't be silly," Daphne says, shaking Celia by the arm. "I'm sure he doesn't care what your politics are. And perhaps all those people he meets are more boring than you think. It is *possible* he just plain likes the look of you. And if you don't want him, please send him my way!"

"I thought you were expunging men from your life?"

"I might make an exception for a truly special one, even if he does have an unusual name . . ."

"So," Celia asks, shaking Daphne's arm, "tell me what's so urgent you had to steal me away?"

"I've been doing some digging. That address you mentioned to me, 64 Baker Street . . ." Daphne reaches into her bag and pulls out a handwritten note. "We keep all old copies of the Yellow Pages in one of our meeting rooms. Apparently, solicitors find that sort of thing useful. Anyway, I've looked into it for you, and the organization who occupied 64 Baker Street in 1943 was something called the Inter-Services Research Bureau. I checked each year they were there—1940 to 1946, then they were gone. I couldn't find any subsequent address for them, and I've had no time to look further."

"Inter-Services Research Bureau . . . What on earth does that mean?"

"I don't know, but I'm sure an intelligent girl like you will be able to find out."

"Oh, Daphne, I owe you. *Thank you.*"

"Bit premature for thanks, Celia. And if I get the sack for wasting my work time on personal matters, you can find me a job in that bookshop. The pay's not bad and with customers like Septi-what's-his-name, I might just be tempted . . ."

THE FOLLOWING AFTERNOON, Celia stands on Baker Street and stares up at the six-story stone building numbered 62–64 Baker Street. There are no clues here. A hardware shop on the ground floor and commercial offices on the floors above. The shop assistants stare at her blankly when she asks if they know anything about an organization called the Inter-Services Research Bureau. But then, she thinks, finding out what this mysterious organization was by coming here would have been too easy. She feels as though she has been dropped into the center of a maze with a few scarce clues. If she is to discover anything more about Jeannie Duchesne, it seems she is going to hit a few dead ends along the way.

But Celia isn't going to give up. She'll just have to find a different route.

Chapter 16

Septimus

It's Sunday. In theory, Sunday means Septimus doesn't need to be in the office. But more often than not, it is where he finds himself, for a few hours anyway. But not today. On this muggy June morning, Septimus has arranged to meet someone. That, in itself, is unusual. He is a creature of habit, of routine and order. And as much as he possibly can, he avoids meeting people on the weekends if he can avoid it. But his reach is growing, and this is unavoidable. He brews his morning coffee and settles back into bed with several newspapers spread across the covers. The smooth voice of Ray Charles crooning "I Can't Stop Loving You" from the radio is making him feel unaccountably empty.

He snatches up the newspapers and scans the front pages. Splashed across the front of the *Sunday Mirror* is a half-naked Richard Burton lying atop Elizabeth Taylor on a boat somewhere off the Italian coast, relaxing, apparently, from their busy filming schedule for *Cleopatra*. GROCERS JOIN TO FIGHT THE SUPERMARKET THREAT, he reads. FASCISTS HOPE TO ELECT CANDIDATE IN CAMBERWELL LOCAL ELECTIONS. TOUR DE FRANCE BEGINS! He couldn't care less about any of it. He stares out the window of his one-bedroom embassy-funded flat in Paddington. The sun is already high in the sky.

He has a growing sense of unease. Could it simply be his own mind refusing to accept that it can be this easy? Or should he pay attention to this unfurling dread? On the one hand, the Big B is very happy with his performance. He has passed his probation with flying colors. Further, Fox-Andrews seems to be satisfied with his help in relation to the Secret Plans, whatever they may be, which are apparently to be actioned throughout July. Septimus's brief, to assist in keeping the focus on Berlin, has not been hard. Foreign policy is *dominated* by Berlin as far as Kennedy is concerned. It isn't difficult to convince him that protecting West Berlin from the Soviet Bloc is a redline as far as America's European allies are concerned. Any attack on West Berlin is an attack on the Western Hemisphere. The consequence of *that* would be war. *Nuclear* war, and Kennedy, Septimus knows, is paralyzed by that prospect.

As, to be fair, everyone in their right mind should be.

But on the other hand, and closer to home, Septimus is becoming more and more convinced he has a tail. An extremely discreet one. If he wasn't so paranoid, Septimus figures he never would have noticed.

Or perhaps he simply *is* paranoid, and the tail is a figment of his own feverish imagination.

But his gut tells him this sense of always being watched is real. And his mother long ago taught him to follow his gut. The tail is never the same person, he thinks. But they are of a type. Nondescript besuited men who randomly happen to be on the same street as he is, alone or in a pair. Beautiful women planted to seduce him, to get him talking when he is at his most relaxed. In some semi-drunk postcoital haze where he forgets to hold his tongue. So far, he has merely given them the cold shoulder. Even if he were tempted, Septimus Nelson would never give anything away, ever. Discretion is as much part of him as his bones and sinew, and besides, his life depends on it.

"Fine," he says to the empty room. Whoever they are, whichever side they are on, from now on, he will make darned sure they have nothing on him. After today, he will keep his routine dull and predictable. Morning exercise regimen, early to work. Long working day. Evening functions several nights a week, or home to catch up on reading.

And there she is, slipping yet again into his mind. Celia Duchesne. Her quick smile and beautiful eyes. Her down-to-earthness. Her funny turns of phrase. The flush on her cheeks when she knows he is watching her. He wishes, just for a moment, he could be completely open with her. That, of course, is impossible. But perhaps this is the missing piece in the puzzle of his life. And perhaps *she* might unwittingly help him without her ever having to know why.

ALFRED HUMPHRIES IS waiting for him, as arranged, in front of the fountain in Trafalgar Square. Septimus arrived early, of course, taking a circuitous route that involved much doubling back and loitering in shops along the way. He watched Alfred's arrival, made sure he was alone before finally joining him, tossing a coin into the shallow turquoise water like any good tourist would.

Alfred would not have been Septimus's first choice. *Always surround yourself with those whom you would entrust your life.* Alfred is the type who only looks out for himself. But the man was foisted on him, and to give him his due, he is beginning to prove his worth. Septimus has thoroughly checked him out, of course, as any good professional would, and it is fair to say, Alfred's past is nefarious. But that is no surprise, Septimus supposes. His line of work attracts the misfit, the misaligned. Alfred's sole motivation is money, which is an abomination in itself, even if he ignores the man's wretched past.

"Lovely morning," Septimus comments, slipping his hands into his pockets and staring up at the plume of water driven high into the pale blue sky. Fine droplets catch the sunlight, hanging iridescent for a fraction of a second before falling into the shimmering water below.

"Indeed."

"Shall we?"

They walk across Trafalgar Square and join the line at the National Gallery, making polite conversation about the weather, soccer, and the rooms inside the gallery they plan to see.

Once inside, they stroll around, pausing here and there to admire a painting, always moving, Septimus constantly checking who is close. He imagines what the passersby will see. Two nondescript men, art lovers, in casual linen suits, spending a lazy Sunday morning indulging in their passion. Alfred's face is in shadow, his hat pulled low, his scar hidden. Nobody will remember their faces if they cannot be seen.

"Any progress?" Septimus asks finally in a low voice. "If there is nothing of value in your current department, you should ask for a transfer—"

Alfred tilts his head. "I don't think that will be necessary." He steps closer to Septimus, reaches into his breast pocket, pulls out an envelope, slips it into Septimus's jacket pocket. "I've got lucky with a secretary at AUWE. She's a gold mine," he adds, staring as though transfixed by a huge, dark painting of piles of dead pheasants and rabbits on a long table, heads and feet lolling over the table's edge.

"Excellent work. Keep it up."

Alfred smirks. "Never had a problem with that, my friend. I assure you, I've had no complaints." He chuckles to himself.

Septimus ignores the man's vulgarity. "Does she know what you do?"

"I'm not an idiot." Alfred turns to look at Septimus. "I've been around a long time. I was doing this sort of thing while you were still in nappies . . ."

Septimus bites his tongue. What he *wants* to do is tell the man exactly what he thinks of someone who sold his soul to the devil back then. Of someone who, unlike Septimus, has only his own interests, and not that of all mankind, at the heart of everything he does. But saying what one thinks is usually not a good idea. And besides, it must be hard to take orders from someone half your age.

"Good, I'm glad to hear it," he says instead. "Tell me when you have anything more, and I'll let you know when and where to meet."

He turns on his heel and leaves the gallery without a backward glance, the thin envelope tucked safely into his top pocket. It will have taken Alfred two, possibly three, hours to drive from the Isle of Portland to central London, and after a thirty-minute meeting, he will now need to make the long drive back. Too bad, Septimus thinks, running down the gallery steps. He needs to keep the man on his toes. Alfred has been a maverick for too long, and it's about time he experienced a bit of discipline.

But Alfred's words about the secretary resound in his head. He thinks of his possible tail, whom he fervently hopes he has managed to lose this morning. A girlfriend, he thinks, might not be such a bad idea. And a girlfriend who works at the bookshop would be utterly perfect.

Part III

Chapter 17

Jeannie

London
February 1943

Seventy-six days and eight hours ago, Jeannie watched her baby daughter being carried away, an image forever stamped in her brain. She never saw her face; all she had was that dangling foot, the flash of dark hair, the tiny bundle. She wondered endlessly where Celia was now, who was taking care of her. She imagined a gurgling baby smiling into another woman's eyes, believing her to be her mother, answering to a different name.

A wave of sickness swept through her.

It's for the best, her own mother had repeated too many times to count. *A child with no father has the odds stacked against her in this world. You know that.*

She did know that. But it didn't make it any easier to bear.

She somehow needed to put it all behind her. Bury it and move on. That was Mother's advice. And she was trying. She really was.

Please let her be happy and loved. Please.

Would she ever be free of this torment? She couldn't imagine that time ever coming.

"Best keep busy," Mother had told her as they packed up their things to come back to London. They couldn't stay in that awful damp cottage a day longer, with its taunting reminder of her empty stomach and empty arms. "Get out to work. Do your bit for the war effort," she'd said.

Jeannie was on an afternoon shift back at Lyon's when the two gentlemen came in. They were French and barely spoke a word of English between them.

"Bloody hell," Margot said, rolling her eyes and sweeping her forearm across her brow. "As if we aren't rushed off our feet enough without all the bloomin' foreigners coming in here, not knowing their arse from their elbow. So many of them these days! How the hell am I supposed to take their order?"

"Don't worry," Jeannie said. "I'll see to them."

"Oh, right. 'Course you will. Fluent 'n' all, I 'spect." She laughed and flapped a dismissive hand toward the table where the two middle-aged men were slumped, unshaven and quite possibly unwashed.

Jeannie made her way over.

"Bonjour, messieurs, comment allez-vous aujourd'hui? Savez-vous ce que vous aimeriez commander, ou puis-je vous aider avec le menu?" Jeannie glanced over her shoulder and smiled at Margot's open-mouthed astonishment.

The men perked up at being addressed in their native language. They ordered black tea and toasted tea cakes, then told her they were refugees and shared a gripping story of how they managed to get here; how they planned to go back and join the resistance. But Margot wasn't having any slacking, so Jeannie smiled her apologies and got on with her work. She hadn't noticed the woman sitting quietly alone at the next table reading a newspaper and smoking a cigarette until she called Jeannie over.

"L'addition s'il vous plaît." Jeannie wondered at the sudden infiltration of French speakers into the café that day but said

nothing and fetched the bill for her. The woman gave Jeannie a long, searching look. In Jeannie's experience, waitresses were generally invisible to customers, bar a certain type of man who considered it his right to study her bust rather than her face, tap her behind, and appraise her entire body as one might a racehorse or a prize cow. Jeannie shifted under the unusually penetrating gaze of this attractive woman dressed in a WAAF uniform who carried an air of significance about her. Perhaps she could tell, despite the fact that Jeannie's figure had pretty much returned to her prepregnancy shape thanks to the food shortages, that she was a fallen woman. Or perhaps she could sense Jeannie's wretched melancholy, which had burdened every cell in her body like lead weight since they had taken her daughter away.

"Your French accent is rather top-notch," the woman said casually, in equally top-notch Queen's English, peering at the bill, then opening her purse. "How did you acquire such fluency?"

"My father," Jeannie told her. "He's from a small town on the French-Belgian border. He's spoken to me in French from the day I was born."

"What a wise man." The woman was counting coins onto the small pewter plate Jeannie had brought with the bill.

"He's a chef," Jeannie added, as though this countered the idea of his being at all wise. "But he's serving in North Africa now. He drives a tank. Fighting to keep this, his dear adopted country, free." She didn't add that he was probably happy he wasn't here to experience the shame of seeing his daughter give birth to a bastard child, and he'd been far, far away when they had wrenched Celia from her and taken her to the orphanage.

"That is good to hear. Keep the change." The woman slid her

purse back into her handbag. "Have you thought about doing anything for the war effort? Language skills like yours are in short supply."

"Well . . ." Jeannie hesitated. "Not really," she said finally. "Mother needs the extra money coming in. She . . . Without Father here, well, you know how it is . . ." She trailed off. Of course, the woman didn't know, she was a complete stranger.

"Indeed. But . . . a girl like you . . ." Those appraising eyes again. "We would be extremely interested in talking to you."

"We?"

"Think about it," the woman said, rising from her chair and hooking her arm through her handbag. "Please call in at this address anytime you like. We would be pleased to talk to you." She smiled briefly again, holding out a card for Jeannie to take.

Jeannie took it, watched the tall, elegant woman weaving through the tables toward the door, and thought of Father. Father, who, at this moment was out there, somewhere in the desert, doing his bit for England. Father, who had so lovingly taught her perfect French. Father, who now despised her. What if she really were to do something important for the war effort? Something that involved her brilliant French. It just might go some way toward winning him back.

Jeannie stared down at the card in her hand. How very opaque. The woman hadn't explained anything at all.

Miss Muriel Clarke
Inter-Services Research Bureau
64 Baker Street
London

What on earth did that mean?

Jeannie was sliding the card into her apron pocket when she heard Margot yell her name. All afternoon as she took orders, served drinks, delivered tea and cake made with powdered egg and no sugar, she thought about that card. How tantalizing the idea of doing something greater than serving all day in a café. Something that *actually mattered*. Something that could blunt the pain and help her forget. She imagined telling Father about it someday and about how much the disdain with which he now considered her ate away at her.

Because although she knew it was both of them who had forced her to give up the baby, it was Mother who had been there. Mother who had seen it through. Mother, now, for whom she held a burning anger and from whom she needed to get away. Without her baby, without Harry, without Father, she had nothing left.

Ever since she could remember, she and Father had formed a little gang of two. Mother couldn't speak a word of French, so she was automatically excluded. Jeannie quickly became the son Father always wanted, accompanying him on weekend camping trips into the countryside, where she soaked up his praise for her stamina and boldness like the roots of a thirsty tree. She was his *coeur de lion*. His lionheart.

Mother would joke when they got home on Sunday evenings as she filled the tin bath in front of the range, ready to sponge away the mud and bits of leaves from their adventures, that Father was turning their Jeannie into a wild thing. *Look at her, André*, she'd say, daubing Jeannie's nose with soap. *You're turning her into a tomboy! How will she ever catch a husband?*

Good, Father would retort, with a wink to Jeannie. *We can keep her all to ourselves forever.*

They never told Mother, knowing how she'd wince, that Father had taught Jeannie to fish and trap rabbits, to erect a tent and make it secure, to tie all manner of knots, and to fix and mend. He taught her to survive on her wits, showing her how to skin and cook what they caught, and to not be squeamish about the killing part. Growing up on his parents' farm in Belgium, these things were all second nature to him.

By the time Jeannie was nine, summer expeditions extended to visiting his parents' smallholding near the pretty town of Tournai, not far from the French-Belgian border, for as long as he could escape from work, leaving Mother at home to mind the house. She had no interest in leaving England, knitting her brows at the perplexing idea of wanting to go anywhere farther than Dorking. Jeannie came to love those carefree summers, playing with the local kids, skin turning acorn brown in the sun.

Looking back now, Jeannie could see how hard it was for Father to watch his tomboy grow into a young woman. But she imagined the hardest thing for him to swallow was the idea of his daughter being with a man. The idea of her and Harry together must have torn him in two. An *American* who threatened to take his beloved girl far away. Worse still, bedding her, then going off and dying before he could make an honest woman of her.

With the last customers of the day gone, Jeannie switched the sign to Closed. She wiped the tables, swept and mopped the floor, lost in her thoughts about Father. How the letter from Mother about her growing belly, with no gallant husband to legitimize the whole sordid thing, must have driven him mad with shame and anger. Jeannie had not received a single letter from him since. She saw how it had driven an irreparable wedge between them. He, unable to forgive Jeannie for being female and flawed. Jeannie, for him turning his back and abandoning her, just when she needed him the most.

The girl he had thought was possessed of a lion's heart was merely a fallible woman after all, no better than the rest. The thought shifted something inside her. Perhaps she could prove to him she still *was* the old Jeannie, worthy of his respect and admiration.

His *coeur de lion*.

Jeannie propped the mop and bucket back in the closet and fingered the card in her apron pocket. Tomorrow she would call in on Miss Clarke at the Inter-Services Research Bureau and find out just what this place and what "we" were all about.

TWO DAYS LATER, Jeannie stood before the front desk in the small entrance hall of Orchard Court, where a receptionist spoke in hushed tones to someone on the other end of the telephone. Jeannie wondered if she'd made a terrible mistake coming here. She had, as requested, visited 64 Baker Street the previous day, asking for Miss Muriel Clarke. The receptionist had looked up and smiled and said she had been expecting Jeannie. She directed her to Orchard Court, Portman Square, at 2:30 P.M. the next day for an interview. The whole thing was so odd, so cloak-and-dagger, she wondered if she was being taken for some damn fool.

"Take a seat," instructed this receptionist. "I'll tell them you're here."

Five minutes later, in came a scruffy middle-aged man with a limp moustache, greasy hair, and the puffy, wan skin of someone who hadn't slept for several nights. He led Jeannie to a small office along the corridor and launched straight in, speaking French, asking what Jeannie knew about France and Belgium, how she felt about the Germans, who she'd lost in the war. It really was the oddest of interviews. After around half an hour, the man told her to report back to reception for the next stage.

Jeannie contemplated walking out. She had envisaged a room full of girls translating messages from French to English, but this Inter-Services Research Bureau seemed to be a most peculiar outfit. She wondered what Harry would make of it all. And she decided to stay put. She thought he would have liked the mystery and that he would have found the whole thing faintly amusing. She ached to meet him afterward, to tell him about it, to hear his guttural laugh.

The woman behind reception was on the phone when Jeannie emerged from the interview room. She smiled and indicated Jeannie should wait. After a few moments, she put a hand over the receiver and mouthed to Jeannie, "Leaving or staying?" as though that were the most natural question in the world.

"I was told to come back here for the next stage."

"Gosh, well done, you!" The woman looked impressed. "Only half get through the first round, you know," she said, then, into the telephone, "Hello. Yes. The two thirty P.M. is through. Shall I send her in?" She nodded as someone said something inaudible at the other end. "Righto." The receptionist dropped the receiver back into its cradle. "He'll see you now. Come this way."

Nobody seemed to use names in this organization, whatever it was.

Jeannie followed the woman's fast clip down a long corridor, passing closed doors on either side. They came to an abrupt halt at the second-to-last.

"Here we are," she said, then knocked and opened the door without waiting for a response from inside. As Jeannie passed her, she said, "Good luck, you."

Another middle-aged man was in the small room, standing next to the window, hands crossed behind his back. The room was almost filled with a huge mahogany desk on which lay a towering pile of manila files.

"Ah, Miss Duchesne. Do take a seat." He indicated the two chairs drawn up before the desk. Like the last one, this man didn't introduce himself. This was getting ridiculous.

"Pleased to meet you, Mr. . . ." Jeannie held out a hand for him to take. *She* wasn't prepared to surrender her manners, even if he was. He studied her for a moment with pale blue eyes. He was a short, balding man with a thin face and small, round glasses. It struck her as a kind face, well-meaning.

"Berkley," he said finally, extending his hand to take Jeannie's. "Peter Berkley." Something in the way he said it made Jeannie wonder if it really was his name, or one he had simply plucked from thin air for her.

Peter Berkley searched through the pile of manila files and pulled one out. As he opened it, Jeannie realized with a stab of fear or excitement that this file was about her. That all these files belonged to dozens of people being considered for this role, whatever it was. How the hell could they have a file on her? She'd not sent in an application, or told them anything about herself. Surely all they knew was that she was a waitress at Lyons Corner House who happened to speak French. She tried to remember if she had given Miss Clarke her name. She was pretty certain she had not.

"I hear you are keen to do your bit for the war effort, Miss Duchesne," Berkley said, looking up at her again. Tell me, why is that?" He sat back in his chair.

"Look here," Jeannie said, jutting out her chin. She wasn't going to be bamboozled into answering any more questions without asking a few herself. "I don't know what sort of outfit this is, but how on earth do you have a file on me? I didn't even apply for a job here. Now, that doesn't mean I don't want one— I may very well do—but please could you tell me what this is all about, and how you happen to have a file all about me?"

"All in good time, Miss Duchesne. I promise," the man said, in a soothing tone. "As I'm sure you will have gathered, what we do here is . . . let's say *sensitive*. Loose talk costs lives, so it's all on a need-to-know basis, for security reasons, you understand? I assure you, it's all above board. Now please just answer the question. You will have your chance to ask some in due course, should you successfully move forward through the selection process."

Jeannie closed her mouth and cleared her throat. "Okay," she agreed. "Fact is, I lost someone awfully dear to me, and—"

"Your fiancé?" He glanced down at his file. "An American airman? Harry Marshall, lost in action, wasn't it?"

Jeannie stared at him in surprise. They have been busy, this Inter-Services Research Bureau. This was no simple translating job. That much was clear.

"Yes, that's right."

"How much do you want to get back at those who took your Harry?"

How could she put into words that her blood still boiled with rage? That the Germans hadn't only stolen her love, but as a result, her child, and ruined her life. That she had nothing more now to lose. And if she could earn back her father's love and respect, well, that would at least be some compensation.

"Mr. Berkley, I will personally wring that Hitler's neck with my own bare hands if ever I get the chance."

Peter Berkley leaned back in his chair and beamed. "That's the ticket," he said. "That's just what we are looking for."

A WEEK LATER, Jeannie was on a train bound for Bournemouth. Tucked beneath her legs was a small case with enough clothes for a long weekend. Stout country gear. That was all Miss Clarke had told her to pack. She stared out the train window at the passing countryside, flickers of fear and tingles of excitement in equal measure blunting the hateful fight she'd had with Mother before she left. She'd told her she was going away to do some translation for the war effort and may be gone for some time. That now she had lost her daughter, she saw no reason to remain at home.

Mother had taken it badly, wringing her hands and wishing things had been different. That the baby had had to go for the good of everyone. How she didn't want to lose Jeannie too. But she had gone anyway. Mother, of all people, should understand that pain of separation and why she needed to get away.

Jeannie took the train to Brockenhurst, where a driver picked her up at the station. He said nothing as they drove to Beaulieu through the wide expanse of open heathland and scattered trees of the New Forest National Park. She spied small groups of shaggy-haired wild ponies grazing between clumps of flowering heather. Finally, they pulled up in front of the grandest country house Jeannie had ever seen.

After unpacking her few things, Jeannie returned to the drawing room, where six or seven guests stood drinking tea, regarding each other with a mixture of bemusement and suspicion, making polite chitchat. Jeannie crossed the room, assessing its occupants as she went. A man with one arm. Two women. An elderly gentleman, sixty at least. Two rough-looking men who looked as though they had been dragged out of prison, and a Czechoslovakian refugee, as he announced proudly to anyone who would listen. If this lot were all the country had left to defend it, she reckoned they were pretty well done for.

Jeannie helped herself to a cup of tea and a slice of shortbread, turned, and there he was. Another latecomer. Tall, dark, and handsome. She almost laughed at the stereotype. But he truly was.

He immediately caught her eye, bowed a little bow, and smiled, coming straight over to her side. He was overconfident, this one. Arrogant perhaps?

"Captain Maurice Albert," he introduced himself. "*Enchanté, mademoiselle.*"

Just in time, Jeannie remembered that, according to the instructions she had found in her room, she was, for the purposes of this weekend, to be known by another name entirely.

"Anya Moreau," she said without a moment's hesitation and with the fluency one might have with saying that name all her life. "Delighted to meet you, too."

Chapter 18

Celia

It's Saturday afternoon in mid-July, the quiet hour post-lunch, and Celia stands before a smart row of yellow-brick Georgian town houses in a quiet side street in Chelsea, West London. There is no question this is an upmarket address, and Celia experiences a sudden failure of her nerves that keeps her on the doorstep, thinking incongruously how fortune must have shined on these wealthy addresses, as the entire vicinity seems to have escaped any wartime bombing. She suddenly wishes she'd asked Daphne to accompany her.

The letter arrived from Miss Clarke exactly one week ago. It was a hastily scrawled note, sent to Celia at the bookshop. The writer had explained that UNESCO had forwarded Celia's letter asking after Jeannie Duchesne. She said that she had been expecting to hear from Celia and was only surprised it had taken her so long. She'd included an address and suggested they meet in person. And now, here Celia is, outside Miss Clarke's home.

She presses the bell. There is a sudden click and the white noise of the intercom.

"Yes?" The upper-class, English accent comes through sharp and clear in that one short word.

"Miss Clarke? It's Miss Duchesne."

"Excellent." A hint of a smile in the voice. "I'll come down."

A few moments later, there is the sound of footsteps on the stairs, the quick click of heels on a hard floor. The heavy front door swings open to reveal a tall, slender woman of indeterminate age. Celia reckons she is anywhere between fifty and early sixties, but elegant and well-preserved, as only the wealthy can be. She has the bone structure of the well-bred and her clothes the excellent cut money buys. Closed, Celia thinks. A closed face that won't reveal any more than she needs to. Miss Clarke dangles a hand in greeting.

"Celia," she says. "How very good of you to travel all this way. Do come in."

She steps to one side to let Celia through.

"I'm up on the second floor, I'm afraid, and there is no lift in the building." She leads the way, the muscles in her long calves bunching and flexing as she climbs.

In a grand drawing room, perched awkwardly on a salmon-pink sofa, Celia is handed tea in a cup and saucer made from bone china so thin she can almost see through it. A fan of vanilla cream wafers lies untouched on a matching plate on the coffee table. Celia doesn't dare disturb the pattern, although the sight of them makes her mouth water.

Miss Clarke folds herself into an armchair, crosses her legs, and regards Celia for a moment before launching into a one-way conversation about the weather and the vagaries of the public transport system. She then explains how, now that she has retired from her position at UNESCO, she has too much time on her hands and was delighted to have received Celia's letter. She says she is pleased to see her again after all this time. Celia's heart jumps.

"We've met before?"

"Yes, but you wouldn't remember me. You were tiny, only around two years old . . ."

How incredible it is to be sitting in the same room as this

woman who knew her sister. Who, perhaps, the very last time she saw her had held Celia's hands in hers.

"Now, my dear," says Miss Clarke, her voice dropping an octave and softening, as though it has been rolled in velvet, "I'm sure you have many questions, so you must ask away, anything and everything."

Celia suddenly senses this is a rehearsed speech. As though numerous such conversations have been held here before. How many parents, siblings, spouses, lovers may have sat here, on this very sofa, hanging on every word this woman utters because she is the single thread connecting them with their lost loved ones. She wonders if Mother and Father sat here, too, years before, their entire future happiness in the balance while they waited for news of their daughter. The way Miss Clarke holds herself, the directness of her eyes, leads Celia to think that although the woman is guarded, she understands and feels the weight of what she must impart very greatly indeed.

Miss Clarke falls silent while she waits for the questions. But where on earth to start? Celia is once more aware of her appraising eyes.

Celia shifts in her seat and clears her throat.

Miss Clarke breaks the silence and pushes the plate in her direction. "Do help yourself to a wafer." She smiles. "You look so like your mother. Dear Jeannie."

Celia devours the snippet like Bartholomew a morsel of fresh fish.

Then her words penetrate.

Your mother.

The room spins. Miss Clarke is speaking, but Celia doesn't hear. There is just the echo of that one word. *Mother.*

"I'm sorry." Celia interrupts the woman's flow. "You just said 'your mother.' I thought . . ." She stops. Swallows. "I thought that Jeannie was my sister."

There is static in the room. Miss Clarke's eyelids flicker. "Oh dear," she says finally. "I've let the cat out of the bag, haven't I?"

Celia begins to tremble, right from her very core to her fingertips. Her teacup rattles on its saucer, and she places them back on the coffee table for fear of dropping them.

"I . . . I didn't know. I didn't know anything about Jeannie until a month or so ago. I found something . . . A file. It had a few letters in it, a few photos. Your name. Something to do with a claim for compensation from the War Office."

"Ah yes. That never came to anything."

"I asked Mother about it . . ." *Not Mother*, her brain screams. *Maggie is not your mother!* She thinks back to that conversation with her. Had Mother-Maggie—*what is she to Celia?*—actually said "sister," or was it she, Celia, who had assumed sister, and Maggie hadn't denied it? The latter, definitely the latter. "She didn't say anything about Jeannie being my mother . . ." Her voice fades. She thinks back to that conversation. How Mother had forbidden Celia to discuss it with Father. Well, of course she did. It all begins to make sense. "It was as though they wiped Jeannie away," she says slowly. "I never knew she even existed. There's not a single photo or item of hers in the house. They hid her from me." She was *my mother*! "Why? Miss Clarke, do you know why?"

Miss Clarke stands and walks, stiff-backed, to a drinks cabinet filling the space between the wall and the hallway door. "I think," she says, "we will need something a little stronger than tea."

She pours two measures of whisky and tops them with lemonade and ice. She hands one to Celia, who takes a large gulp. It doesn't stop the shaking.

"I feel rather awkward," Miss Clarke continues, "being the one to break this to you. I don't suppose your parents—well, grandparents, to be correct—will thank me for this. But now that I've opened Pandora's box, I suppose I had better fill you in with what I know. What you do after that is up to you." She takes a sip of her own drink.

"I made it my duty to know all my agents," she says. "It was vital we knew everything about them. Their idiosyncrasies, weaknesses, trigger points in equal measure to their strengths and talents. We had to understand them inside and out to ensure their suitability for the field. They underwent weeks of intense training, without even knowing what they were training for, all under the closest of observation."

"So . . . were *you* in the Inter-Services Research Bureau? I found part of a letter . . . The address 64 Baker Street was on it. I tried to find out what it was all about, but there was no trace."

Miss Clarke smiles. "Yes, it was the incognito name of the Special Operations Executive. A secret organization set up by Winston Churchill himself that helped us win the war. And your mother was part of it. What we knew of Jeannie was that she was a twenty-year-old unmarried mother. She had been secretly engaged to an American GI, but his plane was shot down and he was killed before they could become formally engaged. He never knew he was to be a father. To be an unmarried mother was—still is—considered a terrible thing. I'm sure your grandparents did what they thought was right in the circumstances, but they forced Jeannie, as I understood it, to give you up for adoption after you were born. I came upon her by chance, just as she was at her lowest point. She gladly volunteered to do whatever she could for her country. I believe she felt she had nothing more to lose. I suppose for her, it was a way of escaping the pain of losing her child."

"But I don't understand," Celia interrupts. "If she gave me up, how come I'm here?"

"Ah." Miss Clarke offers her a wan smile. "Now that you will have to ask your grandmother. She did tell me she had brought you home some months later, but I don't know the details."

Celia slumps onto the arm of the sofa. There is so much to take in. The trembling in her body has been replaced by numbness. Each uttered word of Miss Clarke's brings a renewed sense of unreality. Mother and Father are not her parents. They are Grandmother and Grandfather. Her parents were a terrified young girl, just twenty, and a shadowy, faceless American airman. Both brave, both never knowing she had been brought back into the family. Both dead. She will never know either of them. She is adrift.

Suddenly, she has no idea who she is.

"Tell me what Jeannie did? What was the point of her going to France?"

Miss Clarke clears her throat. "The purpose of the Secret Operations Executive was to provide specially targeted sabotage and disinformation campaigns in Nazi-occupied territory. Your mother joined the French section, where we worked with local resistance groups to disrupt and weaken the enemy from within, so to speak. Our work was vital, at a time when things did not look good for Europe." A shadow passes over Miss Clarke's face. "I can tell you more of that if you like, but in answer to your earlier question, after passing her training with flying colors,

Jeannie was dispatched straight to Paris as a wireless transmitter. She sent and received messages for her network to and from London. She did this for just two months until she was caught by the Nazis. Unfortunately, it happened before she found out your grandmother adopted you."

Miss Clarke is respectfully quiet, as though understanding how hard this is for Celia to take in. Celia sips her drink, question after question rolling around in her mind.

"Why did she never know about the adoption," Celia asks at last, "if she was sending messages back and forth to London?"

Miss Clarke clears her throat. Her face bears no expression. "This was war, Celia. We couldn't transmit personal messages to agents in the field. Of course, had she been able to return, we would immediately have informed her." Miss Clarke gives her a sad half smile. "Jeannie was a fully committed SOE agent, and she was determined to complete her missions. She knew the risks, but she went anyway. She loved you, of course. And in her heart, I believe she did this *for* you."

Celia has no words.

"Your mother was special," Miss Clarke says. "I knew that right from the start. She was clever. So strong, as events were to prove."

There is cold steel about this woman beneath her smooth and polite exterior. She appears almost devoid of emotion. That's the aristocracy for you, Celia reasons. All lesser beings are disposable. Jeannie was disposable, and now she, Celia, has no mother.

She can't bear to be here any longer. Most of all, she needs to speak to Mother and Father . . . *Can I even call them that anymore?* Although, should she believe what Miss Clarke has told her? Is she trustworthy? She supposes it doesn't really matter whether she is or not. She is the sole link, other than her *grand*parents, and all the complexities that go with them, to her mother. For Miss Clarke, this is all history, so Celia supposes she has no reason not to tell the truth.

"Miss Clarke," Celia says, standing on unsteady legs, "I need to leave. I wasn't really expecting . . . I need to speak to my parents—I mean grandparents—although I'm certain I shall never get used to calling them that. I can't really think straight. I am sorry. You've been kind, and there is so much more I would like to learn about Jeannie . . . my mother . . ."

"My dear," Miss Clarke says, standing and taking Celia's hand, holding it in both of hers. "I totally understand. Your parents were never really fans of mine. They hold me responsible for the loss of their daughter. I don't suppose my little slip of the tongue will ingratiate me to them any further. But if you wish to speak to me more in the future, you are of course welcome, anytime." She gives her hand a squeeze and bestows on Celia a sad smile.

Little does she seem to realize the bomb she has just exploded in Celia's heart.

It's AFTER FIVE by the time Celia arrives home. Her feet ache from all the walking, but she needed to be calm before tackling Mother and Father. *Not* Mother and Father. She has tried to think of the right words to begin, but there are none. There is such a turmoil in her head, she no longer cares about the impact she knows the words will have. Whichever ones she chooses. Her heart batters her rib cage as she opens the front door, her breath catching in her throat.

Bartholomew is the first to greet her, running down the dark, narrow passageway from the kitchen with his tail raised and a loud mew. She bends to stroke him, gathering her courage.

Father appears at the kitchen door, cap and jacket on.

"I'm off," she hears him say over his shoulder and then Mother's muffled reply. He is a few steps along the passage before he notices her.

"Celia? When did you get in?"

She releases Bartholomew and stands, holding the wall for support. "I need to speak with you and Mother."

"Sorry, love. I'm late. I must get going."

Close up, she can smell the beer on his breath. How they don't notice at work, she has no idea. Perhaps they do. But surely, being drunk in a kitchen with gas burners and hot ovens is a hazard they could do without. Chefs are two a penny in London. He is on borrowed time.

"No. This is too important." She stands still, blocking his exit.

"What? Don't be silly, Celia. I'm sure your mother can deal with whatever it is."

"Please. Can you telephone and tell them you will be a little late?" She grabs the phone receiver and holds it toward him. "I *really* need to speak to you both."

Even in the dark, she can see the alarm in his eyes. He silently takes the receiver and begins to dial.

In the kitchen, the three of them sit with the pot of tea Mother had fortuitously already made. Father is agitated, refuses the offer of tea and nurses yet another beer. Mother won't meet Celia's eyes.

"What's this all then?" Father asks gruffly. "I can't keep being late for work—I'll get the sack."

Anger flares that in this moment, this most important of moments, he isn't prioritizing her.

"It won't be your timekeeping they'll be worried about," Celia retorts, frowning at his beer. "And don't look so shocked. It's the truth," she says, fury emboldening her. "But that's not what I wanted to talk about." She has his attention now. He opens his mouth to speak but then closes it, seeming unsure how to respond.

She takes a deep breath. "There is no easy way to say this, Mother, Father. But I know the truth. I know that you aren't them. My mother and father, I mean. I thought she was my sister—Jeannie—but now I see that was stupid, and I don't know why I didn't figure it all out sooner—"

Mother gasps. "*Celia, no!*"

"What the—?" Father drops his beer. The glass bottle lands on the table with a dull thud, frothy foam gushing over the top and pooling on the table.

"I'm sorry. I know I promised not to say anything, not to tell Father I knew, but you didn't tell me the truth, did you? Because Jeannie was my mother, wasn't she? *That* much I know now, but I want to know all of it. I want to understand why you lied to me. Why you—"

"*Maggie?*" He turns to look at his wife, the color draining from his face. "What the *hell* have you done?"

"Nothing! I—"

"Don't go blaming her!" Celia cries. "You always do that. Mother, or should I say *Grandmother*, didn't tell me anything. And I have a feeling it's *you* who has always stopped her. As it happens, I had to learn the truth from Miss Clarke—a complete stranger. But I think I deserve to know it from you."

"That *bloody* woman . . ." Mother mutters, face puce. "Bane of our lives . . ."

Her voice peters out, and for a few beats, there is stunned

silence. Then both of them begin to speak at once. Questions, accusations, harsh words, until Celia has to jump from her seat and shout at them both, tears now streaking down her face.

"*Why* do you always have to make this about you? And don't go blaming Miss Clarke. This isn't her fault—"

"It *is* her fau—"

"Stop! Please, I'm going mad with this. I just need to know the truth."

Silence again until Mother begins to speak, her voice croaky with emotion. "Whatever we did, Celia . . . the actions we took then . . . You have to understand, all of it was meant to be in your best interests. In Jeannie's. We couldn't bear you to carry the burden of being a fatherless child all your life. You'd have been bullied, ostracized. Nobody would have wanted to marry or employ you. Do you understand, Celia? We did it out of love."

"No. I don't understand. Miss Clarke said Jeannie didn't want to give me up. So why did she? Why did she do that, and then run off to France?"

Neither speak. They suddenly look old and helpless.

"Jeannie went to fight the Nazis," Father answers finally, staring at the bottle, the froth having subsided, "because she was a *coeur de lion*. She had a brave and generous heart. She fought for liberty—"

"She left because she couldn't bear to be without you," Mother interjects. She throws Father a daggerlike look. "And she knew how her getting into trouble without being married had upset her father. I imagine she thought, this way, she could win back his respect and his love."

"Miss Clarke said she left because you *made* her give me up, and she was so heartbroken, there was nothing left for her here."

Mother huffs. Father lets out a noise somewhere between a

sob and a groan. He pinches his lips and shakes his head as though trying to stop the emotion flowing out. His Adam's apple rises and falls in his throat as he swallows.

"She left because she couldn't bear the shame of what had happened to her. That man took advantage of her innocence and sweet nature . . ."

"*Le Yank*," Father says, turning to French when his emotions run high, old anger rising swift and red to his cheeks. "*C'était une grosse merde. Un fils de pute . . .*"

"André, stop."

"You should have protected her!" Father directs his vicious words at Mother, spit flying as his voice rises. "He turned our girl into a *Yankee bag* . . ."

"What's a Yankee bag?"

"A . . . You don't want to know."

"I do!"

"It's a woman who . . . a woman of loose morals. There. So, now you know the dirty truth of it, I hope you're satisfied."

And with that, he shoves back his chair and slams his way out of the room, leaving Celia and Mother staring at each other, frozen and numb.

Chapter 19

Celia

Since the Revelation by Miss Clarke a week ago, relations at the Duchesne home are strained, to say the least. Father spends as little time at home as he can, disappearing to the Horse's Head daily, returning home unsteady on his feet, vowels slurring. Mother says nothing, but her disapproval is clear in the banging of doors, the tight muscles of her jaw, and the rage in her eyes.

Celia cannot ignore the obviousness of what she now knows to be true. Her parents being so much older than those of her friends. Their inexplicable resentment toward each other. Their strict, old-fashioned attitudes. The lack of indulgences. The niggling feeling that she wasn't quite loved. Wasn't quite appreciated. Wasn't quite *right*.

On the inside, Celia's world is turned upside down, though life on the outside trundles on as it always has.

Each day, she goes to work. She stacks shelves, exchanges banalities with Mrs. Denton when her employer deigns to drop into the shop, serves customers, attends her Pitman's classes on Tuesday and Thursday. When Septimus comes into the shop looking for her, she dodges him, busying herself in the cellar, where they keep boxes of books yet to be displayed, stationery, office supplies.

At home, she feeds the cat, feeds herself, helps with the chores, has a bath each evening. She even goes to the King's

Head with Sam on Friday evening and drinks two double gin and limes while he watches her in shocked fascination. Her tongue loosened by the alcohol, she spills the whole sordid truth to him.

"Oh, Celia," he says, sympathy oozing like treacle from his dark eyes. "I'm sorry you had to find out such a thing like that." He slips off his barstool and pulls her into a warm embrace, her tears spilling onto his shoulder, a wet patch spreading across his shirt.

"I'm sorry," she says, drying her eyes and nose on the handkerchief he offers her. "I've ruined your shirt."

"This old thing? Don't be daft." He gives her a lopsided grin. "Although, you could improve the look by giving me a matching patch on the other shoulder."

She sniffs and gives him a weak smile. "Will you think less of me," she asks, "now you know the truth?"

"Celia," Sam says, taking her hands and giving them a firm shake. "'Course I don't think less of you. We none of us can be held responsible for the sins of our parents. I think that's how the saying goes, no? You're really special, you know that? Well, you always will be to me. Come 'ere."

And then she's in his arms again, spilling fresh tears of relief.

"Don't tell anyone else, though, will you?"

"Your secret is safe with me. Promise," he says, releasing her.

It helps, opening up to Sam and knowing he's there for her if she ever needs to talk about it.

Afterward, Celia does her best to avoid both her parents (grandparents!). She finds she can't bear to be in the same room with them. Every time she sees them, an anger she never knew she could feel rises inside and threatens to burst out in the form of words she knows she may live to regret. It's best to stay out of each other's way.

Now Saturday afternoon stretches bleakly in front of her. She leaves the bookshop at noon, and, needing to be out of the house, she knocks on Sam's door, but Mrs. Bancroft tells her he left for work an hour before. Deflated, she decides it's time she brought Daphne up to speed, and besides, other than Sam, there is nobody else she can think of who can cheer her up like Daphne.

"Sweetie!" Daphne flings open the front door. "You look like you haven't slept for a week! Whatever is the matter?" She holds out her arms, and Celia collapses into them.

"I've so much to tell you, Daph . . ." Her voice is muffled by the soft fine knit of her friend's shocking pink cardigan. "I don't even know where to start."

They take cheese-and-pickle sandwiches and glasses of lemonade onto the newly laid patio at the back of Daphne's house, reclining side by side on the sun loungers Daphne's mother optimistically purchased two weeks ago. A thick layer of cloud coupled with bracing gusts of wind make any hope of suntanning remote as they huddle beneath wool blankets.

"Start at the beginning," Daphne says. "I'm all ears."

Between mouthfuls, Celia fills Daphne in about who Jeannie—Anya—really was and how she found out. When she reveals how Jeannie was actually her mother, Daphne almost chokes on her sandwich, coughing until her eyes water.

"I don't know who the heck I am anymore, Daph," Celia concludes. "It's such a shock, finding out Mother and Father are actually my *grandparents*. But to be honest, it's all beginning to fall into place."

"What do you mean, fall into place?"

"Things like Mother's dogged devotion to God and the church to which she must have turned in her grief. Her strict approach to keep me on the path of righteousness. The forbidding of boy-friends, of alcohol except half a glass with Sunday dinner, of any *fun*, pretty much. Dancing in particular."

"I'm so sorry, Celia . . ."

"And then there's Father, the way he point-blank refused to speak to me in French or even help me learn, however much I begged him. I guess he didn't want to risk the same mistake he made with Jeannie. It was her fluent French that took her away from them."

"I suppose, although it was rather unlikely it could happen twice."

Celia shrugs. "There's still so much I don't really understand, and the worse thing is, they won't talk about it."

Daphne reaches out and gives her hand a squeeze. "I'm here for anything you need. And remember, tomorrow we have some demonstrating to do. That will help take your mind off it for a bit."

CELIA, EXHAUSTED AFTER the day's CND protest outside the US embassy with Daphne, drags her tired limbs down Copperfield Street.

In the kitchen, the smell of something good baking in the oven makes Celia's mouth water. She has barely eaten all day. Bartholomew greets her with a mew, and she sweeps him into her arms, burying her face into his fur, feeling the soft rumble of a purr in his throat.

"I've made a shepherd's pie," Mother says stiffly. "It'll be ready in about half an hour." She pauses and Celia feels her eyes on her turned back. "I'll put the kettle on. We've time for a cuppa before dinner."

She's trying. Making Celia's favorite dish. But there is still so much unsaid, and until it is, how can Celia even begin to forgive? How can they simply go back to the way they were, to pretending this knowledge doesn't exist?

Not speaking doesn't rid her of the nasty truth: Celia is a *bastard*.

The hateful word rises and rises in Celia's mind like bubbles in the churning, boiling water of the kettle.

She recalls that word being thrown around at school as the worst of insults, before any of them had a clue what it meant. There was the shunned George Dunbar, a snotty-nosed, skinny kid, always playing truant, *no father*. The teacher and the kids picked on him, and everyone knew why. Eventually he didn't bother to come to school at all. She wonders what happened to him. Jail, probably, that's what. Having an unmarried mother is seen as filth.

Children, she thinks, are overwhelmingly likely to become what everyone expects them to be. And she knows it's true, too, about unmarried mothers. There are mother and baby homes, places where girls who have gotten themselves into trouble are sent in disgrace. She remembers it happened to a girl in her class, Stella Johnson, who had been going steady with Tony Potter at fifteen. Her parents said she had some mysterious illness that she needed to recover from and had been sent somewhere near the seaside to get better. But everyone knew anyway, once the extra weight she was carrying couldn't be disguised any longer. She came home months later, flat-bellied and dead-eyed, without the infant who had been spirited away somewhere else.

She was disgraced. Reduced. Shunned. And nobody said a word about it. But Tony was treated just fine. It was as though he had had nothing to do with any of it. As though Stella had gotten herself into that mess all on her own.

Celia sits at the table, devoid of strength. "I don't know what to call you anymore," she says finally. "'Mother' and 'Father' no longer feels right."

Mother's eyes widen. "We *adopted* you, Celia. Of course it's right. And besides, no one can ever *know* . . ." She shudders and places a cup of tea in front of Celia.

"Miss Clarke told me I'd been taken to an orphanage, and you adopted me some months later. What happened? Did nobody want me?"

Her voice is flat. It's how she feels. Like she has been run over and her very soul squeezed out. She hugs Bartholomew tighter.

Mother shakes her head, says nothing for a full minute, her lips squeezed tight, her breath quick and shallow. Eventually, she clears her throat. "It wasn't like that, Celia . . . André doesn't want me to talk about it. He thinks it will make things worse."

"He need never know."

They stare at each other.

"All right." Mother pulls out a chair, sits. She is stiff with discomfort. "What do you want to know?"

At last.

"Everything!" She takes a deep breath to still her racing heart. "Can we start at the beginning? What you know about my father? His name, where he came from. His family—perhaps I could get in touch with them? How he died?"

"Jeannie never told us anything except that he was an American airman . . . All I know is he was one of the better paid, better dressed, confident, and charming boys who landed in Britain in early 1942. Back then, the London streets were filled with them, showering our girls with gifts and the promise of love. His name was Harry Marshall. Your mother only knew him a few weeks. I imagine he sang sweet nothings into her ear, fed her lies she fell for, and . . ." Mother stops, then continues in a spitting, angry rush. "I'm sorry to say it, Celia, but the horrible fact is, you were probably conceived up against a wall in a back alley somewhere, then off the bugger went into the sunset, leaving your mother in a fix."

Celia sinks her face into Bartholomew's neck, his purr reverberating into her chest. At least *he* doesn't judge her for what she is.

A bastard.

Mother stares at the floor. There is the heavy press of unspoken words between them.

"I'm sorry," she says suddenly. "That was harsh." Mother speaks to the teapot. "But I raised her to be more sensible. She knew sex before marriage is a sin. Yet she . . . It's not your fault. But babies like you pay the price for the rest of your lives." She shakes her head. "That's why we thought it best for you to be brought up by a family who couldn't have their own child. You would have a nice home; you would be loved. But Jeannie was so against it. She thought she could manage somehow, but what did she know? She was only nineteen when she fell pregnant. She'd had a sheltered life and knew nothing of the world."

"What made you change your mind?"

"Once you'd been born and taken away, we came back to London. The Germans weren't really bombing London after the Blitz, not until 1944 at least, so it felt safe to return. We rented a flat near King's Cross. It was cheap, and with André away, we didn't need anything fancy or big. But after a few weeks, she just

left. Said she had been given a job translating for the government. I knew there was something off, and I suspected what she
was doing was hush-hush or at least more dangerous than she
let on. That Miss Clarke wrote to me. Told me she couldn't tell
me where Jeannie had been sent, but that she was safe. 'Course,
I never believed a word of it. I was desperate to get her back,
and as it happened, I couldn't stop thinking about you either.
I wrote to the welfare officers to find out how you were, if you'd
been adopted yet."

Mother took a sip of her tea.

"They told me you were still at the orphanage. So many
unwanted babies . . . It seemed Jeannie wasn't the only one
to fall." She shook her head. "Anyway, it felt like fate. You
still there . . . I thought if André and I adopted you, perhaps
I'd entice Jeannie back home. Jeannie could have you back in
her life, you wouldn't suffer, and neither would she. It seemed
like the perfect solution. André thought it was a terrible idea,
though. Thought I would forever burden her with your presence,
a reminder of her fallen status. He forbade it, but I forged his
signature on the forms."

A cavity opens in Celia's heart. Father never wanted her.
Mother never wanted her. She was bait. Bait to bring their
darling daughter home, that was all. Ice creeps across her skin.

"André blamed me," Mother is saying, "for not keeping
Jeannie safe in the first place. It was me who allowed her out
dancing and the freedom to be with Harry. But what could I do?
She was nineteen years old when she met him. I could hardly
keep her locked up like Rapunzel in her tower, could I?" A sob
escapes, and Mother stops, screwing up her eyes and bunching
a hankie against her mouth.

They sit in silence for a few moments, Mother's words percolating through the fog in Celia's mind. Mother's cheeks are wet with tears, her eyes red-rimmed. She looks wretched. But Celia cannot think of a single thing to say.

"You have to understand," Mother finally continues, as though desperate to fill the silent void, "we did the best we could. With Jeannie gone, I moved back here, to Southwark, to my roots, and where nobody knew—seeing as we'd been gone so long— that you weren't mine all along." She takes a deep breath. "André might never have forgiven me for what I did, but once he was home for good, he came round, at least to you. He and I, well, we've done our best to be good to you." She takes a shuddering breath. "And now, well, you know the truth, but you should put it all behind you. We must carry on as we were."

Carry on as we were? It's like finding out Santa Claus isn't real. It's impossible to go back to believing that he is.

Mother carries on talking, but her words don't reach Celia.

Mother and Father had wanted a child. They'd wanted Jeannie.

It was Celia they didn't want.

Celia's chest tightens. There is no air in here.

"I'm going for a walk," she announces, standing in a rush. She hurries out of the house and stumbles straight into Sam.

"What on earth are you doing on my doorstep?" she cries, tears now uncontrollably streaking down her cheeks.

Sam stares at her in horror. "I'm sorry," he says, holding his hands in the air as though it is his fault she is in this state. "I didn't mean to startle you." He shuffles his feet. "Just popped round to see if you were okay . . . After what you told me the other night, you know . . ."

Celia blows her nose. "That's kind of you. Actually, I was just going for a walk to clear my head."

"Fancy some company?"

"I'm sorry, but I'd prefer to be on my own right now," she says, not meeting his eyes, embarrassed by the tears. "Thank you, though."

"I'm always here for you, Celia," he says simply. "I hope you know that."

"I do," she says, risking a glance at his face. "Thank you. You're a great friend, Sam."

There is a tiny pause before he says quietly, "That's what friends are for, right?"

He gives her arm a gentle squeeze. Then he is gone, back inside his own front door, leaving Celia alone with her jumbled thoughts in the gathering dusk.

Chapter 20

Septimus

Septimus climbs into a hot shower after his early run on Monday morning and thinks back to the discussion with his superiors when he found out he was to be transferred out of Ottawa.

Don't fall in love, they said before he left for England. *Have as many girlfriends as you like, just don't go getting attached to any of them.* Those instructions echo in Septimus's head as he walks briskly to H. J. Potts, Bookseller, alongside the distinct disapproval he had received from Vera when he'd mentioned his interest in Celia. *Leave the girl alone. Everything is perfect as it is without you upsetting the balance.* But he doesn't care what she or anyone else thinks. He knows what he's doing. This morning he won't be at his desk as he normally is by seven thirty. There is something he has to do first. Needs must, as they say over here. And he won't get attached. He barely knows the meaning of the word.

If he has timed it right, he will catch Celia Duchesne just as she opens up the shop. He has got the distinct impression she has been avoiding him of late. Each time he has come in, she has scurried away on some errand or another.

He pauses to cross the Strand, choked with morning traffic. The hairs prick on the back of his neck, and he forces himself not to turn and scan the crowd. He imagines whoever is watching him, their interest piqued as to his frequent visits to the quaint little shop. If, later, they witness him emerge with the pretty shopgirl, they will be satisfied. At least, that is his hope.

There is a gap in the traffic, and Septimus sprints across, slowing his pace as he approaches H. J. Potts.

To date, Septimus has been faithful to the girlfriend advice, none of them featuring longer in his life than a few weeks at most. This one is going to need to be different. He will deal with the inevitable disapproval when it comes.

Just see this as a time to have some fun, Septimus. Sow those wild oats while you build your career.

He has had fun. But even he admits that, every now and then, the constant swapping out of girls can get tiresome. Sometimes it would be a relief to let down his guard. To really relax with someone. Although that is not an option, having a longer-term girl might at least relieve the isolation. How nice it would be to wake up with the same face on his pillow every Sunday morning. Variety isn't always the spice of life.

The Open sign is already displayed, and his heart lifts at the thought of seeing Celia. As he slows to open the door, a man in a dark suit with a hat pulled low over his forehead walks briskly by, head tilted away, and a chill creeps up Septimus's back. He shakes it off, then steps inside.

"Good morning," he says cheerfully, giving her his most charming smile. "Has the world of antiquarian books become so very fascinating that you have been avoiding me in favor of Dickens, Miss Duchesne?"

"Septimus." She smiles back, not looking totally unwelcoming. He steps closer and sees that her cheeks are hollowed and her eyes puffy. "What makes you think I've been avoiding you?"

"Only that when I came into the shop twice last week looking for you, you scurried away as soon as you set eyes on me."

"I don't think so. Or if I did, it wasn't intentional," she says with a frown, although she doesn't meet his eyes. "Are you looking for Mrs. Denton? She's not up yet, I'm afraid."

Septimus leans toward her, forcing her to look straight into his eyes. "Celia, has something happened? You look tired. Perhaps a little sad . . . Is there anything I can do?" For a moment he thinks she might cry. "Is it trouble with a guy? Give me his address, and I'll go smack him around . . ."

Now she laughs, and her face momentarily lights up. Something sparks, just for a second; then it's gone.

"It's nothing to do with any fella. I'm sorry . . . I was . . . It was just a bad week."

"Was the weekend any better?" he asks.

"Worse."

"Then perhaps I can cheer you up over lunch today?"

She hesitates. "You won't be able to help with this. Nobody can. And honestly, Septimus, I'm not sure I'm very good company at the moment—"

"I don't care. Truth is, I need a friend too. Could do with a bit of help myself, if I'm honest, and I figure you are just the person who might be able to give it. We could listen to each other's troubles and come up with a fix. What do you say?"

She stares back, this time not dropping her gaze. Septimus can see an internal struggle, but she is tempted. He pauses. There's a time to push, a time to hold back.

Silence settles around them. He can almost hear her think.

"Oh, why not," she says finally with a *whoosh* of held breath. "It might be nice, although I'm warning you now, I'm neither clever nor useful. And I'll pay my way. Don't want you thinking I owe you anything in kind . . ." Her face reddens, and she looks away.

"Of course I'll pay. But look here, I'm offended *you* would think I'd have that kind of expectation. I mean, what sort of guy do you think *I* am?" He gives her a mock hurt look.

She laughs, her shoulders visibly relaxing. "All right, then. As long as it's all clear between us."

"You bet," Septimus assures her. "I'll come by for you at twelve."

AT HALF PAST twelve, they are seated at a cozy table for two at Luigi's, around the corner from Covent Garden. Septimus orders a glass of house red, Celia a glass of water. She is nervous, twitching and shifting in her seat, her hand trembling as she lifts the glass repeatedly to her lips as if she needs something to do. Septimus can see she isn't used to going on dates. She really is one of the sweet and innocents, and he wonders how old she is. Something about her stokes a memory of someone he knew long, long ago. *Rosa. Dear, sweet Rosa.* There is a melting inside, and he resolves to treat this girl like a princess.

Don't get distracted.

"So, tell me," he begins, once they have ordered, "what the trouble is?"

She takes another glug of water. "Really," she says. "I meant it when I said I can't talk about it. Why don't you tell me what you need help with instead?"

"All right. So here it is . . . Look, I'm American, and working at the embassy with little free time, I don't find much opportunity to experience *real* London. I get to see the prime minister now and again, and some pretty important wealthy political types, but I'm curious to know more of the—how can I say it?—

down-to-earth side of life here. I guess I'd like some advice about where to go, what to see."

Celia's eyes narrow. "You mean . . . you want a tourist guide?"

"Well, not exactly—"

"They sell them in WH Smith. Not expensive and, I imagine, pretty comprehensive."

"Sure, I can get a book, but I want more than just the usual tourist sights. While I'm living here, I guess I want to experience it as an ordinary Londoner might."

"So, what you are really after is a personal guide who can show you hidden London, things off the main tourist trail."

"Exactly!"

"And you want that guide to be me."

"Are you offering?"

"No, I'm not offering, Septimus, but when you said *help*, what you really meant was something entirely different."

Perhaps he was wrong about this girl. There's more to Miss Celia Duchesne than may be assumed at first appearances, including a sharp tongue. She is not looking to be the pushover Septimus thought she might be.

He holds up his hands.

"Okay, okay, you got me. All right, truth now. Fact is, I *would* like to see more of London, not as a tourist or as a diplomat. Second fact is, I rather like you, Celia Duchesne, and I'd like to get to know you a little better. All my cards on the table now."

The waiter returns with rolls still warm from the oven and tops up their glasses.

"And just how many other girls have you asked to be your personal tour guide?"

Septimus laughs at her spikiness. Her crossed arms and suspicion. In spite of her resistance, or perhaps because of it, he's rather enjoying himself.

"None! I promise. Just you."

Celia takes a roll and tears off a chunk. She keeps those deep, dark eyes fixed on him while she chews. "Well," she says eventually, "you seem to be the type of feller who would have a string of girls hanging off your arm. I'm not joining the queue. I imagine, anyway, I'm not really your type."

"How would you know what my type is? Who says I have a type?"

She screws up her nose. "Marilyn Monroe would be your type. Or Brigitte Bardot. Or maybe it's more Audrey Hepburn?"

"They'd be every man's type, sweetheart, let's be honest. But as it happens, not really what I'm looking for, and I *for sure* wouldn't be their type. Listen, if I want a pretty bird on my arm, I can go out and find one anytime, no problem."

"Modest too, huh?" He shrugs and she laughs. "You'd be my friend Daphne's type."

"Celia, I'm not interested in Daphne."

"Well, I'm not interested in having a boyfriend. My parents wouldn't allow it, and anyway"—she lifts her chin in some sort of defiance—"I'm devoting my life to the cause, like Daph. Because it's more important than anything else, since, well, if we don't have a world to live in—"

"Whoa, whoa, slow down. I'm missing something here— what *cause*?"

"CND. The Campaign for Nuclear Disarmament, remember?"

"Oh, that's right. You and your friend . . ."

"Daphne."

"Daphne, whom I'm not interested in, and you, were going off to make banners for some march."

"Well, it was Daphne, to be fair, who got me into it in the first place. But I've been doing my research. This constant, ever-growing nuclear testing being carried out by *your* country and the Soviets, it's just terrible! The tests alone are ruining lives, killing people, killing animals. Destroying nature. Just imagine if we roll into all-out nuclear war, which is perfectly possible." Celia is becoming animated, her voice growing louder. "And what's more, the threat is far greater than anyone realizes. I went to a meeting of the Committee of 100, which is sort of an off-shoot of the CND. Anyway, there is a small group called the Spies for Peace who have found out that our own government has been covering up secret war preparations, while we go about in blind ignorance! They are building RSGs—regional seats of government—in underground bunkers in secret locations, deep in the countryside. I mean, what sort of government plans to pro-tect itself and leaves the entire population of London exposed . . ."

"Come again?" Septimus leans forward in his seat. "What's this now?"

Celia blinks, and her fingers float to her mouth. "Oops, I'm not sure I was supposed to say that . . . Oh hell, why not? The more this is out in the open, the better. But still, the point *is*, if we don't *do* something, *everything* will be destroyed. We'll have no planet earth to live on, so petty problems, politics, boyfriends, nothing will matter, because we'll all be dead!"

"Wow." Septimus sits back in his chair to watch this strange, passionate creature. How quiet he thought she was. How *wrong* he was. And she is even more intriguing now that she has let slip she knows at least something of the British government's building of the secret bunkers. He'll get her to open up more about that, when the moment is right.

"Did you know," she continues, eyes wide with fury, "on July tenth your government unleashed an atmospheric hydrogen test bomb, two hundred miles up into the clear, unsullied air above the Pacific Ocean? The light from the explosion could be seen for thousands of miles around. In Hawaii, seven hundred and fifty miles away, night became day and likely nothing will be the same again. What irreparable damage has already been done to unsuspecting nature in that part of the world? What of the animals and birds, the sea creatures and the ordinary people who just want to live their lives?"

Septimus leans back in his chair. "Celia, you *are* cheery company."

"Well. I think it's best you know what you're getting if you spend time with me."

"That's fair. But I still want to. I find you rather interesting. You can't put me off so easily."

"Oh, really, I'm not so interesting, Septimus. I'm nineteen years old, I live at home with my . . . *parents*, I work in a book-shop all day, go home at night. I don't go out dancing—not much anyway—or drinking or to parties, because I'm not allowed. I *wish* I could be more, or different, or live somewhere else and be a person who thinks profound thoughts and makes a profound difference in the world. But I'm not. Truth is, I'm awfully dull, and I think you should find someone else to show you around London, because with me, you wouldn't have any fun at all. I'm sorry if you've wasted your time and your money on this lunch."

Septimus is about to laugh, but notices Celia's eyes are moist and shiny, as though she is on the verge of tears. He swallows his laughter.

"I'm just a plain, ordinary girl," she says, choking a little. "And I don't think that is really what you are looking for."

Without even thinking, Septimus sits forward, reaches across the table to take Celia's hand. She freezes, then tries to pull it away, but he hangs on.

"I don't think there is anything ordinary about you," he says. "You are passionate and interesting because you think about important things. You are also rather beautiful, even though you probably don't even know that about yourself. I *really* want to get to know you, Celia. I'd even like to find out more about this CND, because although you, like everyone else, probably think I'm the living American dream, I tell you, I'm just as full of misgivings and uncertainties, and yes, I care about the future of our planet, too, more than you could know. I am all for this nuclear test ban treaty, and if I could make it happen, then trust me, I would, but I'm *really not* that important. I'm just as ordinary as you. Remember, I'm simply the notetaker, not the note maker. Pretty much all of us are just little pawns in someone else's game of chess. I admire anyone who resists and stands up against the hand guiding the pieces."

Celia stares at him, wide-eyed, and they stay there, warm hand clasped in warm hand. The waiter arrives with their food, and Septimus finds he doesn't want to let go.

Celia picks at her food for a while, every now and then glancing at him. He stays quiet. The ability to stay silent, Septimus thinks, is an undervalued skill. It achieves more, at times, than anything one can say.

"I'm sorry," Celia finally says, putting down her cutlery. "I've been awfully rude, and ungrateful. You have been kind, and the food is delicious, and you must wonder what on earth you have done, asking me out to lunch." She looks so dejected; he has the sudden urge to take her in his arms and somehow fix the world for her.

"Seems I'm drawn to trouble," he says instead, giving her a wink.

She smiles, and her face lifts. "All right," she says. "You're on. I'll show you London. But we can never be anything more than friends. I'm as good as engaged to the boy next door, so I'm unavailable, okay?"

Her words take him by surprise. How can she be as good as engaged if she's not allowed boyfriends? He dismisses it as an unimportant detail. She's agreed, and that's all that matters.

"Absolutely understood."

"And my parents can never find out, nor Sam, so I can't bring you anywhere near Southwark."

"Also understood."

"I can do Sunday mornings for a couple of hours, that's all. My mother will be at church then, and my father, to be honest, will be happy to have time to himself."

"Perfect." Septimus breathes an inward sigh of relief. There's a slight sick feeling in his belly that could be disappointment if he didn't know himself better. More likely it's the sauce. Too much cream isn't good for his digestion. No romance is just fine. *Don't get involved. Sow your wild oats while you build your career, Septimus.* There will be no oat sowing with Celia. "And I'll say one more thing, Celia Duchesne. Why think anything is impossible? Ordinary people do extraordinary things all the time. Don't underestimate the power of the ordinary."

Celia smiles back and picks up her cutlery, this time tucking into her *piccatina al limone* with gusto.

Later, Septimus boards the Central Line tube at Holborn for the three stops back to Bond Street. He allows himself to think about Celia for the length of the journey, which is about five minutes in total. There is something about her that has burrowed right under his skin. She really does remind him of Rosa. That hint of the unobtainable. She is far from the first meek impression he had of her. He shakes his head. He also needs to find out from whom she is learning her information about the highly classified secret war planning. And soon.

But all in all, today has been a success. And he can't help but look forward to seeing her again on Sunday, hoping the days past swiftly until then.

Chapter 21

Celia

"M rs. Denton, I've been thinking," Celia says during a rare moment when they are both in the shop at the same time. For a bookshop owner, it surprises Celia that Mrs. D shows remarkably little interest in selling books. Instead, she appears to be spending a good deal of time entertaining. But it's understandable, Celia supposes, that the woman wants to make the most of her freedom from what, she can only imagine, must have been an oppressive marriage. And the bonus for *her* is that she has free rein—something she never experienced with the Blythes—to run the shop as she sees fit. Now it is time to show Mrs. Denton her faith in her has been right all along. That she, Celia, can shake it all up for the better before she moves on to her future career.

"Yes, Celia? What about?"

"I'm worried about customers."

Mrs. Denton gives her a startled look, her finger resting halfway down a page in the telephone directory. She's been looking for a carpenter to do a few little odd jobs around the flat. "What's wrong with them?"

"The lack of them."

"Oh. But was it any different under the previous owners?"

Celia sighs. "Well, not really, but this is an opportunity, isn't it? The shop is under new ownership, so you should put your stamp on it. Liven it up a bit, bring it into the 1960s. So, I was thinking, how about a little advertising? It needn't cost the earth, just a small ad in the literary journals, or upmarket magazines like *The Lady* or *Country Life*. The main thing, I think, is that people walk past this shop without even *seeing* that it's here. It looks so small and drab from the outside. There is no sign or anything to attract attention. Even the name, H. J. Potts, has faded so much you can barely read it. I bet it hasn't been painted in a hundred years! How about we at least do that?"

Mrs. Denton gazes steadily at Celia for a few moments. "Well . . ." She licks her lips. "The thing is, I rather like the old-fashioned nature of the place. It's antiquarian. We can't have it look too modern, can we?"

"Well, no, of course not. But we could still spruce it up tastefully, couldn't we? And what about the advertising? I'm happy to organize it all. If you just let me know what budget—"

"No." Mrs. D's voice is sharp. "I've no interest in advertising. Our sales are just fine as they are. If I need to advertise, I'll be sure to involve you. Now, as it's currently quiet, I need to clean the flat. I'm expecting visitors later. Can you manage here?"

"Of course," Celia replies.

And with that Mrs. Denton *click-click-clacks* on her heels into her flat, shutting the door behind her. Celia is bruised by the knock-back. Perhaps Mrs. D thinks she's overstepping? Maybe she *is* overstepping. She is just the shopgirl, after all. Heat pulses in her chest. It rises up her neck and flames her cheeks. The humiliation. Still. It will make it easier to leave when the time comes. She won't have to feel any guilt at leaving Mrs. Denton in the lurch when she moves on to bigger and better things. Perhaps when she tries out other shopgirls, Mrs. D will realize what she has lost in Celia.

From upstairs comes the distant sound of the vacuum, followed by bangs, crashes, and sounds of swooshing. She imagines the swooshing to be Mrs. Denton pulling up the rugs to vacuum underneath. Celia is mildly intrigued by the idea of stepping inside that black door dividing the shop from Mrs. D's private living quarters.

She releases a puff of air and stares around at the empty shop. There are still three hours to go until closing. She fumbles below the counter for her bag and pulls out her copy of *Pitman's Short-hand Rapid Course: Complete Edition with Supplementary Exercises*. She might as well do some practice before this evening's class.

She is just opening the book when the doorbell jangles and Septimus rushes in, a thin envelope clutched in one hand. He's breathing heavily as though he has run all the way here, beads of sweat at his hairline. He wipes his handkerchief across his brow.

"Celia, I'm glad you're here."

"Oh? Where else would I be?" She jumps off the stool behind the counter.

He shakes his head. "Of course you are here. That was a silly thing to say. We're still meeting on Sunday, aren't we?" His state of agitation is confusing. Normally he is so calm and controlled.

"Yes, absolutely."

He looks around the shop as though expecting to see someone loitering among the bookshelves. "Actually, I'm in a tearing rush. But could you give this to Mrs. Denton?" He waves the envelope at her.

"She's upstairs cleaning. I can fetch her, and you can give it to her yourself."

"Sorry, I've no time. I'm late for a meeting at the Guildhall. It's really important she gets it."

"Of course."

Vera Denton, it says on the front, *Private and Confidential*.

As if Septimus really can read her mind, he says, "Vera asked me to help her renew her passport. She needs to sign some paperwork."

"Ah." Celia takes the envelope. "I'll make sure she gets it."

Septimus is already heading for the door. "Looking forward to our rendezvous on Sunday!" He turns and winks; then he is gone.

Celia stares after him. Those tawny eyes. The pull of him. A growing longing to always take a step closer. To catch a whiff of his scent. To let him kiss her, even. Was this how Jeannie had felt when the American GI, *Harry*, seduced her? *Before* the Revelation, she might have been tempted into something more than friendship with Septimus. But not now. She has a pretty good idea what sort of man Septimus is. A seduce-and-leave kind of chap. She can't make the same mistake as her mother. Fall for someone and then get into trouble. She must resist Septimus, even if it kills her.

She notices him then, collar turned up against the rain now sloshing down the shop window, loitering on the pavement. A man in a dark gray fedora brushes past as Septimus steps outside, his body between the window and Septimus. The pause is momentary. Septimus looks at the man, and he says something, his features strained, urgent. Then he moves away and is gone. The interaction is no more than a few seconds, and Celia wonders at it. Did they know each other, or was there some sort of altercation on the street?

Her thoughts are broken by the jangle of the doorbell once more, and the man in the gray fedora enters the shop. With a jolt she realizes it's Alfred Humphries. It's been a few weeks since he last came in, and Celia had been relieved that whatever had gone on between Mr. Humphries and Mrs. Denton seemed to have fizzled out. He really isn't the best company for the flighty and possibly naïve Mrs. D to be keeping. Celia knows his type. There are plenty of them hanging about the less salubrious pubs of the Elephant and Castle and the bookies on the Old Kent Road. He's after her money, Celia is sure of it.

Mr. Humphries approaches the counter, his hat now clasped in one hand, the shiny strip of scar clearly visible on his brow. A brown leather bag, the type a person might use as an overnight bag, dangles from his other hand. He doesn't even pretend to be looking at the books. Celia's heart sinks.

"Ah. My favorite shopgirl. How are you, my dear?" His eyes rake slowly down her body, unfurling prickles like spines along her back.

How dare he.

"Are you here to buy any books, Mr. Humphries?" Celia asks crisply.

"No, I'm here to see Vera. But to encounter your pretty face first is a pleasurable diversion." He places his palms on the counter and smiles, revealing yellowed teeth. His manner is too nonchalant, blasé almost, as though he owns the place. She sees again Septimus's expression as Humphries brushed past him. He must have known who he was too. From Mrs. Denton. Perhaps he, like Celia, is worried for her welfare.

"She's not here." Despite the knock-back over the advertising, Celia makes the snap decision to protect her employer. "But I'll tell her you came by. She has your telephone number and can call you if she wishes." She grants him a tight smile, which she hopes will be enough to send him packing.

"I am not in a hurry," Mr. Humphries says. "We have plans for the evening. Indeed, for tomorrow morning too." He glances down at his bag, then looks at Celia and grins. "I'm happy to keep you company while I wait." At that moment, the sound of the vacuum starts up again. Mr. Humphries cocks his head and points skyward. "Would that be a *ghost* up there, then?"

"She must have come back from shopping and used the side door," Celia says, feeling the flush of shame at being caught. "I'll let her know you are here." She makes for the door to the flat, but Mr. Humphries moves fast around the counter and places his hand over hers as she reaches for the handle.

"It's sweet of you to look out for her," he says, his breath hot in her ear. She can feel the weight of him against her back, too close, and she tries to move away, but his hand tightens around hers, keeping her close. "But you see, *she* invited *me*. It seems she can't resist my charms." He laughs and releases Celia, slipping through the door of the flat. "Have a nice day, Miss Duchesne." She hears his laughter recede as he ascends the stairs to the flat above.

"Ugh! What is *wrong* with everyone today?" she exclaims to the empty shop.

Celia doesn't see Mrs. Denton until she returns from her lunch date with Daphne at Jack's later that afternoon. Alfred Humphries is nowhere to be seen. Celia finds her employer humming and chirpy, the long string of pearls swinging around her neck as she rakes through a delivery of books on the counter.

"Ah, there you are, Celia dear. Now would you look at this!" Triumphantly she pulls out a brown leather volume, its spine embossed in gilt decoration with marbled boards and endpapers. Even from here Celia can see this is a glorious-looking edition. She takes it from Mrs. Denton. It's a Dickens. *The Old Curiosity Shop*. Flicking carefully through the pages, she sees that the book is filled with pictures of black-and-white textual engravings. Not a first edition, this being the entire book in one volume, but with only minor cracks and worn edges, it's in good condition.

"It's beautiful," Celia mumbles, handing it back. "That will be worth a tidy sum."

"Indeed!" Mrs. D's eyes sparkle with excitement. "I knew you would like it. I found it last weekend. I took a trip out to the country with a friend. We visited the little town of Dorking—do you know it? Well, anyway, they had an auction house there, and we popped in, just for fun. They were auctioning off some items after the death of an elderly lady—mostly furniture and knickknacks, and then this! It was quite a bargain. I resolved to scour the auction houses a little more often. You never know *what* bargains you might find." She beams at Celia. "Now, look at me rambling on, and I haven't even gotten to my point. Fact is, I want you to have this."

"I beg your pardon?"

"Yes!" Mrs. Denton pushes the book toward Celia. "I want you to have this. I know how much you love these old books, and you really have been such a help, running this shop for me. I have leaned on you very heavily, Celia, these last months, and I don't want you to think I'm taking you for granted."

"But it's my job! I couldn't possibly take it." She stares at the book in disbelief. Is this to make up for the argument they had over the advertising? "It's too much. You could make an excellent profit if you sell it—"

"Nonsense." Mrs. Denton holds one hand aloft, nudging Celia with the book with the other. "I don't want you to think or worry about money, please, Celia. I am lucky to have had a good settlement from my ex-husband. All I want you to do is to keep doing what you are, and accept this as a token of my friendship and thanks."

Celia takes the book. She really isn't a big fan of Dickens, actually. Too long-winded and wordy. And all those perfect, simpering, angelic girls. Little Nell of *The Old Curiosity Shop* being the worst of the lot. If she'd had a bit of backbone, she probably wouldn't have wound up dead. But Celia can hardly refuse, can she? She smiles at Mrs. D. "Then, thank you. It's a wonderful gift, and I shall treasure it," she lies.

All of this piling onto the existing guilt at the knowledge she'll be leaving to work for the BBC in a matter of just a few months. But she can't worry about that yet.

"Mrs. D . . . was the friend you went to Dorking with Mr. Humphries by any chance?"

"It was." She looks coy. "He is wonderful company. He's just popped out for a walk. He'll be back soon."

"But . . . how well do you know him? I mean, I have a hunch he might not be too trustworthy."

She bites her lip. Did she say too much? Will she make Mrs. D angry at her interference? Instead, Mrs. D chuckles and pats Celia on the arm.

"Oh, Alfred is perfectly harmless. He fancies himself, of course, but what man doesn't? I assure you, I'm quite safe with him. Now *you* on the other hand, I want to warn you about young Septimus Nelson."

"Oh!" Celia is caught off guard. "Why?"

"Well, I know the two of you had lunch together, and a little bird tells me you are going on a date on Sunday."

"It isn't a date," Celia snaps. Are there no secrets around here? "He simply asked me to show him some of the less-well-known sights of London. I've made it very clear that I'm not in the market for a boyfriend."

"Weeell," she says, drawing out her vowels, "fact is, I know Mr. Nelson rather better than you do."

"Ah, yes. You knew him in America."

"From a young age," Mrs. D says, staring out the rain-splattered window as though outside lies her Californian past, not the Strand. "Quite the little rogue he used to be."

"How did you know him?"

"His mother," Mrs. Denton says. "We were acquaintances—neighbors, as it happens."

"What do you know of his past?"

Mrs. Denton tears her eyes from the window and back to Celia, as though searching her face for clues.

"Not much, really. Only that his father died when he was young, and his mother, a ballerina, had a tough time raising him on her own."

"Oh dear, I can imagine . . ."

"Yes . . . Very pretty lady, as I recall. Died of cancer, sadly, a few years back."

"But that's tragic! How awful for Septimus to have lost both of his parents."

Mrs. Denton's face reddens. "Oh dear. I probably said too much. But I felt sorry for the boy. So much tragedy in his young life. I suppose that's why he went a little off the rails."

"He did? He seems squarely back on them now. Strange he never mentioned any of this to me."

"Hmm. Perhaps I'm wrong about his mother," Mrs. Denton admits, looking stricken. "As I say, I didn't know her awfully well. I'd moved away and thought I heard about her death through the grapevine. But perhaps I'm confusing her with someone else." She pauses. "I rarely talk to Septimus about the past. He doesn't like it. It was a painful period of his life."

It's true. Septimus hasn't talked to her about his past either. But then, perhaps they don't know each other well enough to divulge such personal details. Still, now that she thinks about it, he always focuses his attention on *her*. She will gently ask him on Sunday. It might help him to talk about it.

"How old was Septimus when you moved away?"

"'Bout seventeen, I reckon. Already the Lothario even then, judging by the girls who used to visit their house."

"So . . . he's twenty-six now?" Celia avoids the pointed remark, thinking instead how Mrs. D seems quite oblivious to Alfred Humphries's roving eyes and aging Lothario behavior around Celia.

"Sounds about right."

"I'm surprised you recognized him."

"I didn't at first. He's changed, of course, in the last nine years, but he remembered me. By chance he read the announcement the previous owners for some reason decided to put in the *London Gazette* that the bookshop was under new ownership—mine—and he came in to say hello."

"Small world."

"It sure is. But, as I say, be careful. Take this as fair warning. Leopards, as the saying goes, don't change their spots and all."

"Are you telling me Septimus is dangerous in some way, Mrs. Denton?"

"Not *dangerous* as such. More . . . untrustworthy, shall we say, when it comes to the opposite sex." She pauses. "He likes to play the field, if you understand my meaning. I just want to protect your feelings from any hurt, that's all. You seem so . . . sweet and innocent."

Celia hates that phrase. She was always taught that a girl who is "too knowing" is *not nice*. But as she's gotten older, she is growing to realize that this "nice girls are innocent girls" illusion is simply a way to control women. An innocent girl must throw her entire well-being and safety into the hands of men, keeping the relationship as one of father and child, not equals, as men and women should be. All the innocence is for the man's benefit, not a woman's, she has decided, and fancies she would like to become all-knowing sooner rather than later. She forces herself to take a deep breath and not say anything she will regret.

"I am quite sure I will be fine, Mrs. Denton. I'm very much able to look after myself. Septimus and I are simply friends. Besides," she lies, "I am practically engaged to someone else already, and Septimus is not remotely interested in a romance with *me*. I assure you." And she smiles the most reassuring smile she can muster.

Chapter 22

Celia

When Celia arrives home from work one Saturday, two weeks on since the Revelation (her world now being divided, BR and AR), Mother is sitting alone in the front room, in the early stages of knitting a sweater, an odd occupation for a glorious day in early August.

"Why don't you turn it on?" Celia nods at the blank screen of the television. "It might provide entertainment while you knit."

"I don't need entertainment," Mother says, clashing her needles. "And I've got the radio if I need company."

"The radio's not company."

"Nor is the television. It's an eyesore."

Celia ignores the comment. She had been planning to have lunch with Mother, but she doesn't know what to say to her anymore. All Celia wants to do is ask question after question about her real mother. But that is the one subject Mother doesn't want to discuss. Celia finds increasingly she can't bear to be in the house. Can't bear the idea of sitting together at the kitchen table racking her brain for something to say on a subject she has no interest in. She can't bear that she wasn't really ever wanted here.

"I'm off out," she says from the doorway.

Mother pauses her needles and turns to look at her. "But you only just got in."

"Yes, well, I've got plans for the afternoon. With Daphne. I'll be back by five. I can help with supper."

"Suit yourself." Mother sniffs. "It's like a guesthouse here, the way you and André treat the place." She turns back to her knitting. "Don't worry about lunch, I'll eat on my own."

"I'm sorry."

She tries to imagine how it must be for Mother, all these years keeping this secret to herself, and being held responsible by Father for the terrible things that happened. That wasn't fair of him. Celia can see it has made Mother bitter, and the bitterness has nowhere to go but is oozing out of her like discharge from an infected wound.

She leaves anyway, knowing it will hurt Mother, but she hardens her heart. While a part of her pities her, another part is raging. Mother hadn't wanted her.

And Celia isn't ready to forgive her for that.

She grabs yesterday's *Evening Standard* that Father left on the hall table and takes it with her. She walks toward Waterloo, buying a cod and chips from the chippie on Waterloo Road and sitting on a bench to eat it outside the Royal Festival Hall on the South Bank. The billboard tells her Frank Sinatra is playing there. That would be quite something to see, but she could never afford tickets. She turns and looks out over the muddy waters of the Thames. Perhaps it's time to cut the apron strings, as Mother would say, and strike out on her own. She needs to get out of the poisonous atmosphere of home. And perhaps Mother and Father would be happier without her. Without the constant reminder of their dead daughter and her fall from grace. On Celia's increased salary, she might just be able to afford it. She scours the newspaper advertisements for rooms to let, boarding houses, and bedsits, then drops the newspaper in frustration.

It seems that after the night school fees and other expenses, she won't be able to afford anything but the cheapest, most basic accommodation.

She finishes the last of the chips and throws the empty wrappers into the bin. One day, she promises herself, as soon as she has a better job and can afford it, she'll leave 13 Copperfield Street and move into a place of her own. A place with no judgment or restrictions.

And best of all, she won't have to live where she isn't wanted.

"Tell me," Miss Clarke says, cocking her head to one side, "how are Mr. and Mrs. Duchesne after all these years? I know they took Jeannette's loss very badly. One never recovers from such a thing. Over time, one must find a way to learn to live with it, though." Celia finds Miss Clarke's references to *one* confusing. Does she mean herself, or other people? She isn't used to the affected way the woman speaks. Her aristocratic mannerisms. Chelsea, this flat, even the silky cover of the salmon-pink sofa could be in another country altogether. After finishing the chips, on a whim, Celia had made her way here, hoping she would find the woman in on a Saturday afternoon. Fortunately, she was, and seemed unperturbed by Celia turning up unannounced.

"The truth of it is, I don't think they have even come close to recovering from it."

"I'm awfully sorry to hear that."

"They refuse to talk to me about my mother . . ." The back of Celia's neck prickles. Somewhere across London, Maggie is giving her a fierce glare. *Don't you share our dirty laundry with a stranger.* She takes a breath. *This isn't a stranger; she knew my mother.* "That's why I'm here. I'd love to learn as much about her as I can. From someone who knew her. And apart from them, you are the only other person I know who did."

Miss Clarke's stiff posture almost imperceptibly softens. "That's perfectly understandable," she says, although Celia isn't sure if she means that Celia wants to learn more or her parents' refusal to discuss it. "So, my dear"—she crosses one long leg over the other—"where would you like to start?"

Celia has thought about this. She takes a deep breath. "I found out about my mother by pure accident. It so happens a friend of mine works for the same firm of solicitors who acted for my grandparents when they were trying to seek compensation from the War Office for Jeannette's death. She found an old file and passed it to me. Why were they seeking compensation? I suppose it would have helped with my upbringing?"

"That was an unfortunate business," Miss Clarke says, the composure in her features slipping for a moment. "However hard I worked for my agents—and believe me, I did—it could never be enough. Compensation, a pension—no monetary recompense was ever on the cards for agents' dependents. Not like those in the regular armed forces or official agencies. Agents of the Secret Operations Executive, or SOE, were civilians, you see. Civilians we handpicked for their special skills and abilities, who went voluntarily into the breach, so to speak. But that meant there was no protection for them under international law."

"Sorry, what do you mean, protection under international law?"

"If an agent was captured, unlike members of the armed forces who, if in uniform, should be taken prisoner, our agents were classed 'enemy civilians.' That meant the Nazis would do to them whatever they wished. Torture, execution. And after the war, well, they would have been forgotten, had I not fought tooth and nail to find out what happened to each and every one of them. I also made sure my agents were among those put forward for recognition for their bravery. I never had any children, Celia. My agents were as precious to me as any child would have been. I gathered the evidence that brought the perpetrators of the heinous crimes against them to justice."

Miss Clarke's eyes glaze over for a few silent minutes as she is lost in memory, and Celia senses she has said this not out of any need for thanks or congratulation but from a genuine passion and place of pain she doesn't get much opportunity to express.

"What I don't really understand," Celia says, breaking the moment of stillness, "and I really would like to, is how my mother was involved in the SOE at all. Surely, like me, she was just an ordinary girl. What was she supposed to do, up against the Nazis?"

"As I mentioned before, the SOE was a secret body, built up from scratch and staffed by amateurs, rather than established professionals. Well, you can imagine what the establishment— the regular army, the RAF, the likes of MI6—thought of it. Tried to undermine us at every turn. Anyway, the concept behind it was sabotage and guerrilla warfare. To build up, organize, and arm a resistance army within Nazi-occupied territories. Hitler's advance across Europe in 1940 seemed unstoppable, and Churchill was willing to fund anything, however crazy the idea seemed, to interfere with the enemy's advances."

"The SOE no longer exists?"

"Oh no. It was disbanded not long after the war was over. Like I said, we weren't popular among the establishment, who saw us as a bunch of incompetents." Miss Clarke's brow furrows.

"There were a few mistakes, it's true. But we also achieved extraordinary success. And they didn't like *that* either." She gives Celia a wan smile.

"With very little support, we hired staff for our HQ at 64 Baker Street."

The address on the letter. And Celia recalls the nondescript building she had stared up at that day.

"Our agents were recruited from all walks of life, any age, and from both sexes, people who would never have been eligible to serve in the regular forces. They were a hotchpotch, I tell you. But they had certain things in common. Excellent language skills, resourcefulness and intelligence, and above all, extraordinary bravery. So you see, your mother was anything but *ordinary.* We couldn't care less where someone came from, their class, their background; it was their qualities, their spirit, if you like, we were interested in."

She reaches into her pocket and pulls out a packet of cigarettes, offering it first to Celia, who shakes her head, then lights up, blows out a plume of smoke.

"War is a great leveler, you see. At the SOE, we were organized into country sections. I worked in the French section and assisted with the preparation of over four hundred secret agents who were dropped behind enemy lines into France." There is obvious pride in the woman's voice.

"Women were crucial, my dear, because they could move around the country more easily than men, without raising suspicion. The presence of an idle man could seem odd and questionable, especially when the available French labor force was sent en masse to Germany to work in weapons factories to aid their war effort. But a woman, a housewife, cycling around the countryside, visiting the local market, for example, would not have seemed

strange in the slightest. It was crucial for the resistance to *blend in*."
She takes a drag on her cigarette. Taps the ash into the ashtray
on the coffee table.

Celia tries not to cough. Unlike most of her friends, neither
Celia nor her parents—*grandparents*—are smokers. Father main-
tains that smoking ruins the tastebuds and seeks to protect his
like a piano player might his fingers. Mother finds the habit
altogether disgusting, as the smoke clings to clothes, however
often you wash them.

Miss Clarke seems to mistake the coughing for disbelief
about what she is telling her. "This was *war*, Celia. I understand
why you find this hard to comprehend in these peaceful times,
but in a war situation, normal rules are thrown out the window."

Celia's mind flutters to the nuclear arsenal being built up in
the Soviet Union, pointing their deadly noses at London, *right
now*, and wonders just how peaceful these times really are.
Would she be prepared to do the same as her mother in the
name of peace?

"Not only was Jeannette a fluent French speaker, but she
was also a shining star at Morse and wireless transmission,"
Miss Clarke is saying. "It was darned difficult to find good ones,
and we desperately needed them to keep the lines of commu-
nication between agents in the field and HQ in London open.

"There were those who said she shouldn't go. That she was
too young and naïve." Her dark eyes are clear and earnest. "But
I knew she could do it. She wanted *you* to grow up in a free and
safe country."

"But still. Women don't fight wars."

Miss Clarke laughs. "Physical strength is not the most important thing in war. Mental strength, living on your wits, out-
smarting the enemy. That's what matters most. Your statement

is a convenient narrative lots of men would have us believe." She pauses to take a long drag on her cigarette. "I don't agree. Everyone must do whatever they can to fight the enemy. Besides that, the truth is, many women were glad for the opportunity to shrug off the chains of domesticity. Afterward, though, the men didn't know what to do with us. There was a nostalgia for some version of the past. A past where the woman stayed home and devoted herself to the welfare of her husband and children. But it was just a narrative. It suited men for women to be homemakers, but I, and many like me, didn't fancy that."

Celia murmurs her understanding, although she thinks on balance, she would gladly swap the likely risk of death for a peaceful life of cooking and babies.

"In war," Miss Clarke goes on, "women are often the ones who suffer the most, but they can also, oddly, prosper."

"Not me," Celia interjects, "and certainly not my mother. She was dead by the time she was twenty-one, leaving me an orphan." Miss Clarke glances up at Celia's sharp tone.

"She knew the risks. And she chose to go."

"What happened to her?" Celia asks. "In the end. How did she get captured?"

Miss Clarke finishes the cigarette, stubs it out, and sits back in her chair, regarding Celia as though to decide how much she should reveal. "There was a betrayal," she says finally. "One of our agents turned out to be a traitor. He was responsible for the capture and execution of over one hundred of our agents, your mother among them. Had it not been for him, she may have come home safe after all."

Celia sits in silence, letting all she has heard sink in. In contrast to the words and the weight of their meaning, she is aware of the soft, comfortable sofa beneath her, the wealth contained in the room surrounding her. She stares at the patterns on the parquet floor, the whorls and lines, the different tones and colors, thinking of her mother's helpless end in a dark hell of a concentration camp, far from home and loved ones. She thinks of the faceless traitor, and anger flares, so sudden and intense that it catches her breath.

"What happened to him—the traitor?"

There is a movement in Miss Clarke's cheek. A flicker or twitch of a muscle beneath the skin. The only indication of any tension in her body.

"He's dead," she says in a flat tone. "He was tried for treason in Paris after the war, but he wasn't convicted. So, to our disgust, he walked out of court a free man. He took to drug trafficking and gold smuggling after that. Toward the end of 1954, his plane went down in the jungles of Laos carrying a cargo of gold bars. There were no survivors from the crash."

"Well, that's good, then, isn't it? I mean, he got what he deserved."

"I hope so."

"What do you mean?"

Miss Clarke inhales. Breathing out, she says, "No matter. It's all in the past. Now, my dear, tell me, what is it you do?"

"Me? Oh, I just work in a bookshop. Antiquarian, actually. H. J. Potts, on the Strand. Do you know it?"

"Ah, yes. That's the address you gave me. Why didn't you use your home address?"

"I didn't want to upset my parents. You know, dragging up the past and all that."

Miss Clarke watches her for a few moments before nodding her understanding. "So," she asks, "what is the dream then, Celia Duchesne?"

Celia shifts in her seat. "I'd love to work in television. If dreams could come true, then I'd be PA to the director general."

"Personal assistant? Nonsense, darling. You should be aiming at director general yourself!"

Celia laughs at that preposterous idea. "In all honesty, Miss Clarke, I'm not really the right sort to make it into the BBC at all. Not even the typing pool."

"And what *sort* is that?"

"I think it would help to be from Mayfair, not Southwark, if you know what I mean."

"Ah." Miss Clarke smiles. Then, leaning forward as though about to impart a delicious secret tidbit, she winks. "My dear, the solution to *that* is simple. People will believe any story about you that you want to portray, provided you do it convincingly. You simply act a part to become it. And trust me, Celia, I am the expert in *that*."

Chapter 23

Celia

Celia's alarm jolts her from a deep sleep. She is momentarily confused. It's Sunday, not a workday. Then she remembers. It's her first date with Septimus, and her heart leaps. No, it's not a date. She is doing a favor for a friend, that's it. She remembers Mrs. Denton's words of caution. She can see he might be a serial heartbreaker. And he is just the type to charm a girl into bed, and then what? She'd be no better than her mother and her life would be ruined. She must be firm if he dare try anything.

In the kitchen, she encounters Mother in her blue dressing gown, fresh from a bath, curlers in her hair, putting the kettle on. She spends more time getting herself looking nice for God on a Sunday than she does for herself any other day of the week.

"You're up early," Mother says, suspicion clouding her eyes.

"I'm meeting a friend."

"Which friend?"

"Just someone I met through work." Celia sighs. "Her name is . . . Susan."

"I see."

"She lives in Paddington. She's rather new to London, so I said I'd show her some of the sights."

"How very community-spirited of you."

"I'm sure you would do the same if it was someone who had just joined the church."

Mother sniffs, spooning sugar into her tea and stirring with unnecessary vigor.

"Perhaps you could try trusting me every now and then," Celia says. "I'm not Jeannie," she adds, regretting the words the moment they are out.

Mother blanches. "You mustn't say such things. Don't be flippant about Jeannie."

Mother picks up her tea and sweeps out of the kitchen, leaving Celia alone bar a bluebottle buzzing around the window. She watches it hurling itself repeatedly at the glass, unable to find a way outside through the invisible barrier.

If only she too could leave, move on, find a new way to *be*.

Yesterday evening, in desperation, she'd knocked on Sam's door, needing the company of a friend. But when he'd opened it, he'd not been alone. A fair-haired, green-eyed girl had been with him, a *friend* from the animal sanctuary. The girl was there for dinner, he'd explained, and to meet his mother. Cindy, or Mindy, or Lindy, or something. Celia hadn't quite caught it. But she *had* caught the energy between the two of them. The way they smiled at each other. The way they touched shoulders and finished each other's sentences. And there Celia had been, taking Sam for granted. Thinking he would always be there, the reliable friend.

The room swims as self-pitying tears she has no right to swell in her eyes.

Celia Duchesne, who even is she?

Celia has no idea.

What sort of man was her father? What sort of woman her mother? According to Miss Clarke, she was brave and clever; according to her parents, foolish and shameful. But how did she look first thing in the morning? What was her voice like? Did she like to sing or read or do the crossword? Was she serious or funny, introvert or extrovert? Did she long to be loved, like Celia? Is that why she fell for Harry's charms? Or was she wild and brash, careless and carefree?

Or perhaps she had simply fallen in love.

SEPTIMUS IS ALREADY waiting at the bottom of Nelson's statue in Trafalgar Square. He smiles in welcome, and his golden eyes are dangerous and hot, like the sun.

Damn.

"Good morning," he says, teeth flashing white. "I hope I didn't drag you out of bed too early."

"Not at all. I'm always up and about this time on a Sunday," she lies.

"So. Where are we going, tour guide?"

"You said you wanted to be off the tourist trail, so we're going to take an excursion around Brick Lane and the East End. It's real London," Celia says. "Crowded, dirty. Probably smelly."

"Excellent." He rubs his hands together. "Lead the way."

Bringing him there, Celia supposes, as they take the tube to Aldgate East, is her small act of rebellion against the wealth and privilege she imagines he has so far come across as assistant to the American ambassador. It's time to bring him back to earth from the heady heights of society parties with their champagne and finger food.

But if she had intended to shock him, it doesn't work.

Septimus sucks it all up like water in a desert. They wander the East End, crowded with multiple nationalities who have landed here in wave after wave of migration, from way back with the Huguenots, the Jews, the Russians, the Irish, to those from the African and Indian subcontinents. She watches Septimus weave his way through the crush and cacophony of Chrisp Street and Petticoat Lane Markets with their hotchpotch of cheap goods as though he has done this all before. He stops here and there, striking up conversation, laughing and joking with stall-holders, picking through the clothes, the kitchenware, boots and shoes, books, silverware, watches and clocks with fascination. He buys a thin silver chain with a tiny snake charm and gives it to Celia. Gently, he lifts her hair to one side and clips it around the back of her neck. The brush of his fingers brings goose bumps to her skin. *Payment for giving up the morning for me*, he says.

They stop for coffee and sip it as they wander the ruins of St. Dunstan-in-the-East. Nature is slowly reclaiming the site, saplings, weeds, and grasses pushing their way up into the light. Septimus removes his jacket, laying it on the ground for Celia to sit on. They lean their backs against a sun-warmed stone wall.

"What happened here?" Septimus asks, looking up at what remains of the soaring arches and steeple.

"Beautiful, isn't it? Even though it's just a ruin, it's one of my favorite spots. The church was built in the twelfth century, then got partially burned down in the Great Fire of 1666. It was patched up by Sir Christopher Wren, only for it to be bombed in the Blitz. Not sure what they'll do with it now." She sips at her hot, bitter coffee, wincing. She should have gotten tea.

"You sure know your history." Septimus smiles at her.

She shrugs. "Not really. I just happen to know this place. My mother used to bring me when I was small. Not sure why. Perhaps she felt closer to God here. I played among the piles of rubble while she contemplated the unfairness of the world."

"I gather you aren't very religious, then?"

"Nope. I had it forced down me as a child. I suppose I've rebelled. What about you?"

"The opposite. I was brought up without any religion at all."

"Lucky you."

Septimus looks relaxed, the coffee cupped in his hands, one long leg slung over the other.

"Maybe."

"Tell me about your family. And America. I want to hear all about California."

"There's not so much to tell. I was born in Canada. My mother and I moved to San Francisco when I was ten. My father was a scientist, a college professor, my mother a dancer. My father died suddenly when I was four, and I have only the barest of memories of him. My mother is now happily settled with someone else. After college, I joined the diplomatic service because I had the urge to travel. My first foreign posting was to Canada, and now London."

Celia takes a breath. "Septimus, you know, Mrs. Denton told me that your mother died of cancer years ago."

Septimus nearly chokes on his coffee.

"Why the hell would she say a thing like that?"

Celia shrugs. "She did then say she might be mistaken, but she thought she heard it through a mutual friend."

"Well, it's nonsense. My mother is alive. What an awful thing to say!"

"I'm sure it was an honest mistake . . ."

But Septimus has stiffened. He splutters a few expletives.

"Please, Septimus, don't be cross. She's muddled, I'm sure of it."

"Why were you even discussing my mother?"

"I think she was just trying to protect me. She told me how, when you were young, you had quite the roving eye . . ."

Septimus lets out a laugh and shakes his head, the tension releasing out of him as fast as it had risen. "Did she now. Well, what teenage boy doesn't?" Celia shrugs. "I'm not that boy anymore, Celia." Septimus fixes her with his startling eyes, flecked with gold in the sunshine, as though challenging her to believe him. It takes a huge effort to break her gaze, her stomach roiling as if she were on a stormy sea.

She breathes in deeply then exhales. "Although, to be honest, I think it's *her* who needs protection."

"Oh yeah? Who from?"

"She has a man friend. I don't exactly know what their relationship is. But he takes her out, on and off. They seem to spend quite a bit of time together."

"And what's wrong with that?"

"I think he's after her money. It's just a hunch. But he doesn't seem very trustworthy to me. In fact, he gives me the creeps." Celia shudders involuntarily, just thinking about him. "He's a bit . . . Well, you know."

Septimus shakes his head. "Not really—do explain!"

"A bit touchy-feely. Stares at my chest. Gets too close."

"Does he now . . . ?" Septimus tenses. "Who is this guy?"

"Alfred Humphries. Do you know him?"

Septimus nods slowly. "I do. The—" He clamps his mouth shut. "Don't worry about him. I'll have a word with him."

"How do you know him?"

"Through Vera." He turns toward Celia, head propped on his hand. "But you are right not to trust him."

"Why not?"

"He's a sleazebag."

"But what about Mrs. D?" Celia cries. "Haven't you warned her off him too?"

"Ha! She can look after herself, trust me. And besides, he won't be interested in her in *that* way. You, on the other hand . . ."

"I'm completely fine, thank you. As I told you, I'm almost engaged to someone, in a way."

"You did mention it. But, Celia, how can you be *in a way* engaged?"

"Oh. It's just not official yet."

"I see." Septimus stares moodily into the middle distance. "Anyway, make sure you stay away from that idiot Humphries." Septimus thumps his empty cup on the ground. "He always has an eye for a pretty young girl. And besides, if we are talking about trust . . ." He pinches his lips tight. "Now, I don't want to spend the rest of this lovely morning talking about that fool . . . I've been wondering, how much longer are you planning on working in that fusty old bookstore? Fond as I am of Vera, you could do much better. If I remember rightly, you are going to night school. What are you studying?"

"Just shorthand and typing. I mean, I love the shop and the books, but I've been there almost since I left school. I want a *career*. This is the 1960s, and things are changing, all over the world. You are lucky to be in a profession where you can travel. I would love to travel, to have an interesting job. To be able to make my own money and never have to rely on a man to support me. I don't want to be beholden to anyone. I mean, this should be a time of women's liberation, but I don't feel very liberated, that's all."

"What does liberated look like to you?" He cocks his head, eyes trained on her as though there is nothing and nobody else in all the world who is about to say anything more interesting.

Celia sweats beneath his gaze. "Liberated means, on a general level, that I want to live in a world without the threat of nuclear weapons. I want to know we have a future and that our entire planet won't simply be annihilated by some idiot in Moscow or Washington. On a more personal level, well, I'm nineteen, I still live at home with my parents and have never been farther afield than Littlehampton—that's on the south coast of England, and trust me, it is not a place you want to venture." She is tempted to add, *And my real mother was a World War II heroine, but she was executed by the Nazis. My grandparents have raised me as their own because she wasn't married, so they have wiped her memory from the earth and they have wished all my life that I didn't exist.*

Instead, she says, "I just need to get away from them. My parents, I mean. I'm going to night school so I can improve my chances of getting a better job. With luck I'll be able to earn enough to move out and find a little bedsit of my own."

Septimus wrinkles his nose. "Bedsit? That doesn't sound too glamorous."

"My ambition is to work in television."

"You should go into politics."

Celia snorts. "Don't be daft."

"Why not? You want to change the world. That's the way to do it, no?"

Politics! "I wouldn't have the first clue how to become a politician. And besides, they'd not want someone like me."

"Why not? You're smart. You could do anything you want. You could study a language if you want to travel. How about Russian? You could negotiate with Khrushchev himself then. To be honest, I think he'd be a bit scared of you."

"Don't mock me!" But she laughs all the same.

"Celia." Septimus leans closer, suddenly serious as he gazes into her eyes. "You talk as if all that you desire is an impossible dream. But what you want—it isn't that unusual in this day and age. I think you should set your mind to it, a higher goal than you even think possible, and just go for it. See where it all leads."

Celia sips her coffee, no longer tasting it.

"But you see, Septimus, I'm just an ordinary girl. Ordinary girls like me, we don't . . . we can't—"

"Ordinary people do extraordinary things *all the time*, Celia." He's said that before. So did Miss Clarke. "You just have to believe it. That's all." He pauses. "We are all ordinary. All men, all women are equal. It's just governments or society, or parents, or schools that try to tell you different."

Celia smiles at his enthusiasm. If only it were that easy. And suddenly she sees it. The gulf between the American *can-do* in him, the English in her. *Know your place. Don't step out of line. Don't dare have ideas above your station.* And for a stinging moment, she envies him his sex and his birthright.

"I wish I did believe it," she says finally. "But the reality just isn't like that. At least, not where I come from. And certainly not if you're female. Get married, have kids. Don't moan, be grateful for what you have."

Septimus studies her. "Things are going to change. And when they do, opportunities for women will be just the same as they are for men. And I believe in you. If nothing else, you make a damn good tour guide."

She laughs, he laughs, and he's leaning further toward her, and she thinks he will close the small gap between them and they will kiss. Her body throbs in anticipation, and she finds she is leaning toward him, too, but then he backs away, looks at his watch, and the moment is gone.

When they later say good-bye in Trafalgar Square, Celia

wonders if she hadn't told him about the almost-engagement whether he really would have tried to kiss her.

It's better this way.

But the more she gets to know Septimus, the more he surprises her. She touches the silver snake charm around her neck and smiles.

There is, it seems, much more to Septimus Nelson than just his handsome face.

Chapter 24

Septimus

Septimus clings to the last delicious vestiges of sleep before the shrill tone of his alarm fully penetrates and consciousness floods in. He throws out an arm and slams the palm of his hand on the top of the clock to shut the alarm off. Rolling over, the temptation to fall back to sleep is strong. He wants to return to the dream he was rudely dragged from. A sensuous, luxurious dream of which he can't recall the details, only the sensations of it. How *good* it made him feel. He closes his eyes and then jerks them open as the realization hits that the dream involved Celia. She was pulling him, he recalls. Pulling him away from something. It had been important, but they were laughing. He'd let her lead him away from a place he *should* be to somewhere, but he didn't know where.

Septimus sits up, squints at his clock. Rubs his face until his eyes clear. It's 5:52 in the morning.

Hell. He can't let this happen. It won't happen.

It's true he has come to enjoy their Sunday mornings together, look forward to them even . . . But the deal was, he isn't meant to get *attached*.

Septimus is not the type to form attachments. He's disciplined and single-minded. He is ruthless, and *this*, it's all he has ever wanted. This job, this life. He reminds himself how proud his mother, his real one, would be of what he has achieved. Reminds himself of the sacrifice *she* made for *him*. So that he could have all this. He wonders where she is now. If he can ever hope to find her again. The last time he saw her, he was ten years old, just a little boy. Would she even recognize him? He's made inquiries through his channels, of course, but has found nothing. She moved away from the village he grew up in only six months after he left so unexpectedly, sixteen years ago, and has seemingly vanished. But he is sure she is alive, and he will find her. One day.

Out in the cool fresh of the morning, he walks to the corner of the street, windmilling his arms and high stepping to warm up his muscles. He jogs across the main road then takes off at a faster clip toward the entrance to Kensington Gardens. He turns in the direction of Hyde Park.

The run is good. This stretch of nature, right in the heart of London, and so close to home and his place of work, is a balm. It's nothing like the vast wilds he still longs for, but the soft green expanse, the gentle shroud of overhanging trees helps to unravel his taut nerves. Beneath his shoes the crunch and crush of gravel, the ebb and flow of birdsong on the breeze.

The pounding of his feet on the hard ground reminds him what got him here. Discipline. Sacrifice. Ambition. His thoughts stray again to his mother, and the sacrifice *she* made, of him, which must have caused her so much pain. Of him and for him. He won't let her down.

He ignores the fatigue numbing his legs and pushes on, faster.

His mother, who he can still, after all these years, remember so very clearly. After his father died so suddenly, it was just the two of them. Out there, living deep in the wilderness so far from anywhere, it was as though the rest of the world didn't exist. It was, he thinks as he rounds the Serpentine, increasing his pace again, an idyllic childhood. Roaming the vast forest with his few friends from their tiny village school, swimming naked in the river, ice cold even in the height of summer, flowing as it did from the freezing north. The men away working for such long stretches at a time, making it a society of just women, children, and the elderly. When they came home for breaks—the husbands, the fathers—they felt like aliens, disturbing the peace and equilibrium of daily life until they went off again.

Septimus's breath is coming fast, his mouth wide open gasping air, chest burning. Despite the cool of the morning, sweat courses down his face, his back, and he contemplates diving into the water beside him. It's tempting, but he doesn't. He slows his pace a little, turning for home, still indulging in those long-ago memories.

He will never forget the day he turned ten years old and the government men arrived. The day his mother saw a chance of buying freedom for her only beloved son. And she snatched it with both hands.

But freedom is a strange concept. An ethereal, slippery, intangible thing men talk of without ever really understanding what it means. But they use it nonetheless, to drive revolutions, start wars, justify killings. Give up their children.

But what most people don't grasp, and certainly his mother could never have understood, is a truth he knows now only too well.

Freedom for ordinary people doesn't and never will truly exist.

SEPTIMUS THINKS HARD about the message before passing it to Shauna, the Big B's secretary, for onward transmission. It is safer, they all agree, if she handles the most sensitive matters, given the possible unwanted focus on Septimus. He confessed, in the end, his suspicions about being followed. It's taken until now, almost the end of August, for confirmation, but it turns out, he wasn't being paranoid after all.

Words matter, especially when you must use as few of them as possible. Accuracy, fact-checking, then checking and double-checking, was drummed into him right from the start until it became second nature. But what is accuracy? What are facts? Is there even such a thing as *correct* or *right* or *certain*? And do these things even matter, when it is *perception* that matters more in the end? He frowns and reads what he has written one last time.

> *Have it on good authority will be trouble ahead.*
> *Official at Soviet embassy, Eugene, has the inside*
> *track with Sec of State for War, John Profumo, with*
> *whom the Big B is also good friends. Girl, Keeler, is*
> *having relations with Profumo, Eugene, and possibly*
> *another friend, Stephen Ward, who introduced them.*
> *British agencies are watching and think they can*
> *turn Eugene. Huge scandal would ensue if Profumo*
> *sharing state secrets with official via Keeler. Ward*
> *may be useful in all this, Fox-Andrews believes.*
> *Source is reporter for gossip column of British society*
> *magazine. It is only a matter of time. Keeler may*
> *have loose tongue.*

He stares at it for a few more minutes. It is not his place to destroy anyone's career, but this cannot be a fruitful relationship. He knows for a fact the man, Eugene, hasn't been able to come up with any intelligence on the possible placement of nuclear weapons in Europe. Instead, he has gotten himself mixed up in a sordid business of prostitution, money, and corruption. Sharing a young girl might seem like the perfect way to gather intelligence, but Septimus hopes nothing more has been shared than bodily fluids. Miss Keeler, he thinks, is the same age—nineteen—as the sweet, innocent Miss Duchesne. Secretary of State for War Profumo is forty-six, old enough to be her father. Politics and the higher echelons of society are a murky, dirty world.

Power, as was so famously said by Lord Acton, corrupts, and from what Septimus sees in his new life, rubbing shoulders as he now does with the political and social elite, it seems it also results in a complete loss of morality. He wonders what Mother would think about that. All her efforts to help him to escape the poverty, the harsh day-to-day monotony of home for this world of one-upmanship, self-gratification, deceit, and distrust.

In the end, he supposes, it isn't power that corrupts; it's that people, or most of them anyway, are by nature corruptible, and the power, the money, simply gives them opportunity. He longs for the pure, the good, the altruistic. *Rosa.* But she was so long ago. His memory of her hazy, like a mirage.

He thinks of Celia and her mention of the British government's secret preparations for war. He tried to find out what else she knows, but she clammed up. She would do well in his own line of work. He wonders what other nuggets she might have. Intelligence doesn't always come from the top.

Don't mix business with pleasure.

He makes up his mind, folds the note, and places it in a plain white envelope, checks his watch. Just gone five. He passes Shauna's desk on his way out, dropping the envelope in front of

222 ~ Louise Fein

her. *For hand delivery.* She barely looks up from the letter she is typing, her fingers galloping across the keyboard. He wonders how they don't ache by the end of the day. Perhaps they do, like Septimus's brain.

Alfred Humphries is waiting, as arranged, at the edge of the Serpentine, lobbing chunks of a baguette at a group of mute swans. Septimus strolls alongside, hands in pockets, and stops as though to watch the majesty of the swans.

"Stay away from Celia Duchesne," he warns in a low voice, despite the fact there is nobody within a hundred yards. He doesn't want his voice to carry.

"Nice to see you too, Nelson." Alfred plucks another hunk of bread and tosses it to the birds. "Did nobody teach you any basic manners? A 'hello, how are you' wouldn't go amiss."

Septimus draws air deeply into his lungs. "I'm a busy man, Humphries. No time for niceties." There aren't many people who rile Septimus. But he holds a visceral dislike for this man; he certainly doesn't trust him. The feeling is undoubtedly mutual. Of all the places in the world two people who had rubbed their unfortunate noses together in San Francisco could land, it's here in London. They might have crossed paths before, but the two couldn't be from more different worlds. With what Celia told him and what he knows of the man's sordid past, Septimus feels a rising antipathy toward him. But he must temper it. Control it. One must never give in to one's baser emotions. Unfortunately, Alfred is a necessary part of this, and they are on the same side, so for now at least, he has to put up with him. Fact is, it's Septimus who is on the up. It is Septimus who is building this network, becoming valued and indispensable, and Alfred Humphries must hate that. He paints his most charming smile on his face.

"I'm merely warning you, keep your hands off Miss Duchesne . . ."

Humphries scowls. "Is that the reason you called me here? I do hope you aren't neglecting your duties, Nelson, getting distracted by a bit of skirt."

"Don't judge me by your own standards." *Steady now.* Septimus exhales his anger. "But no, it isn't the sole reason. Tell me, what do you know of the Committee of 100, or more specifically, the subgroup, the Spies for Peace?"

Alfred shrugs. "I've never heard of them. The Committee of 100, yes, but only what I've read in the papers. That's Bertrand Russell's lot, no?"

"That's it. Well, do some digging, then. I want to know what they know. Join them. Get the inside track."

Alfred squirms. He glances at Septimus.

"That's outside my remit," he says. "I'm already working my butt off at the Admiralty. I can't risk losing my job there by joining some clandestine group . . . You know how that would look. There must be someone else—"

"There isn't. And besides, as I understand it, it's your *bit of skirt* who is doing the leg work, so your being there is essentially superfluous. You are merely the middleman, Humphries, which makes you dispensable."

Septimus turns to look at the man, to make sure he knows just where he stands.

"Fine." Alfred speaks through clenched teeth. Their eyes meet before Septimus turns to leave. In that brief moment he sees the man's suppressed fury. It must be quite the comedown to have to take instruction from someone half his age. Septimus couldn't care less about that. A mercenary like Humphries gets what he deserves, in the end.

But as Septimus walks away, an unease settles in his stomach, where it sits, stubbornly, for the rest of the day.

THE FOLLOWING SUNDAY morning Septimus waits, picnic basket at his feet, outside Chalk Farm tube station. Anticipation at seeing Celia for a few hours bubbles like oxygen in his blood. Last week he'd taken delivery of a car, thanks to the powers that be agreeing it would be advantageous for him to be able to travel more easily out of town to visit his growing network, where necessary. He'd considered picking Celia up today, impressing her with the Morris Minor, but the thought of navigating the busy London streets on the wrong side of the road without sufficient practice made him leave the car at home.

She arrives wearing a sky-blue sleeveless shift dress that accentuates her long, slender neck. Her hair is tucked beneath a pale blue hat, dark fronds of her fringe peeking out, and she wears matching gloves that rise halfway up her forearms. She looks so young, so sweet, and it makes his heart ache.

"You're wasted in that bookstore, you know," he says as they make their way toward Primrose Hill. It was his idea, the picnic. A break from the touring, he had suggested last week, and a way to say thank-you. It might also make his shadows, as he has come to think of those who follow him, more convinced the two really are forming a relationship. A cozy picnic gives the impression of romance. He'd even bought a basket and blanket from Selfridges yesterday, filling it with delicacies from their food department to add authenticity to the idea.

"So you keep saying." Celia laughs. "But I've told you, I'm not quitting until I've finished my course. What would be the point? Besides, I'd feel guilty leaving Mrs. D in the lurch. I'll need to break my departure to her gently. Perhaps even help her to recruit someone new before I go. I couldn't possibly leave now."

Septimus grunts. "How much longer?"

"I could have a new job by Christmas, if the right opportunity comes along."

"That's a long time."

"It really isn't. Just three or four months. And anyway, why are you so interested?"

"Because I think you could do much better."

"Well, it's sweet you care so much."

They find a spot near the top of the hill, and Septimus spreads out the picnic blanket. It's still early, and there are few other people on the slope as yet, despite the un-London-like balmy weather. He had prayed for no rain, and fortunately the weather gods had been listening.

"This is lovely." Celia beams, arranging herself on the soft fabric, legs tucked neatly to the side. She takes off her gloves and removes her hat. She finds a pair of sunglasses in her handbag and slips them on. "Thank you for suggesting it."

"You are welcome." He pulls out a thermos of coffee and another of tea, making Celia squeal in delight. "Hope I've made it to your satisfaction," he says, pouring it into the cup. He unpacks the pastries, cold boiled eggs, slices of ham, and buttered slices of bread, plus apples and bananas.

"What a strange mix." Celia laughs. "But it looks delicious."

"I'm not used to packing picnics," Septimus admits, staring at the spread before them and wondering if he should have packed wine too. He'd thought that might have been a bit much for breakfast, but now thinks he was being too cautious.

"Well, I think you have done marvelously for a first attempt," Celia says, biting into a Danish pastry.

"So . . ." Septimus relaxes back onto his elbows to watch her. "What does this almost-fiancé of yours think about our little Sunday outings?"

"Nothing."

"And why is that?"

She gives a little flick of her head and carries on chewing. Even behind her sunglasses he can tell she isn't meeting his eyes.

"Might it be because he doesn't know?"

Celia sighs and finishes her mouthful. "All right. No, he doesn't know. He volunteers at an animal rescue sanctuary on Sunday mornings. He's very kindhearted."

"Sounds like he might not make the ideal husband."

"What's that supposed to mean?"

Septimus shrugs, suppressing a smile. "I don't mean anything. *Animal* sanctuary? Perhaps . . . Oh, it doesn't matter."

"No, it does." Celia straightens. "Explain, please."

"Only that a soppy guy like that might . . . Well, he *could* have other preferences."

"What do you mean, *other preferences*?"

"I shan't spell it out if you don't understand."

Celia doesn't reply. Septimus sees her face flush hot, whether that is with indignation for herself or for her so-called fiancé, he can't be sure. But he suspects she understands more than she is letting on. She looks out over the green slope, dotted with trees, down toward the spread of London in the distance.

"Or perhaps," he adds to lift the mood, "it's because I'm jealous and I'm trying to pick holes in the guy . . ."

"It's all rather more complicated than that," Celia says softly, as though she has given in to some internal dilemma. "Sam is . . . Sam is lovely, but the truth is, we are just friends. And besides, he has a girlfriend, and she isn't me."

Septimus can't suppress his smile at that. "Then why did you tell me you were practically engaged?"

"It's a useful defense sometimes," Celia says, "to fend off unwelcome advances."

"Me?"

"Not you. You haven't made any advances."

"And you haven't welcomed them."

She laughs, and for the first time, Septimus wonders if maybe, *maybe* there could be a way. He sits up and pours himself a coffee, his pulse notching up, and there is something like a stirring of hope in his belly.

Celia lies flat on her back, hands behind her head, and smiles up into the hazy blue.

"It's almost possible to imagine oneself on the beach in Saint-Tropez, this weather is so good." She smiles, and behind her glasses, Septimus sees her eyes flicker closed. He imagines how it would be if he leaned over, just now, and brushed away the hair that has fallen across her cheek. How it would feel to run his fingers down her neck, across to where the snake charm he gave her glints at her throat. Down to the place her skin meets the top of that dress.

"Do you ever wonder," she says, eyes still shut, "if you would do things differently, were our life span like a mayfly's at just one day? Or, maybe the other extreme—if we were like a yew tree and lived to be more than a thousand years old. How would that change things?"

"Um, no, I can't say I have ever thought about either of those possibilities. But I guess those different perspectives would certainly vastly change things. Especially if my life was going to expire this evening."

He watches Celia, the gentle rise and fall of her chest, the faint smile on her lips. The shape of her, lying so relaxed on the blanket, hands resting on her stomach, one leg crossed over the other, her hair in a tousled pool around her head. His heart lurches, and he knows in that moment the fight has gone out of him. His battle for self-control dissolves like sugar in warm water.

Celia opens her eyes and sits up, taking off her sunglasses. "Oh yes. What would you do differently?"

"Well," Septimus says, "I wouldn't bother with cleaning my flat or working. But most importantly, I would kiss you, Celia Duchesne, and not wait a moment longer for the right opportunity to arise."

And without giving himself or her the chance to back out, he closes the gap between them, his lips on hers, arms encircling her waist. For a few heavenly minutes, she melts against him, an invisible force drawing them together, heat rising between them, until suddenly, she stiffens and breaks away, hair falling over her face, refusing to meet his eyes as she scrambles for her shoes and straightens her clothes.

"Celia . . . What is it? What's wrong?"

"Nothing. Everything's fine. I just . . ." She checks her watch, gives him a weak smile. "I'm sorry, I have to go."

"Please don't . . ."

But she gathers her jacket and her bag, and he is powerless to stop her. He watches, dismay and disappointment settling inside like soured milk as she hastens away from him.

Part IV

Chapter 25

Jeannie

Paris
Autumn 1943

Paris was a sight to see at sundown. The metropolis stretched into the far distance, fingers of pale gray bleeding into patchworks of dark forest. The best time of day to be airborne, Capt. Albert told her, the grime of the city invisible from up here. And it was true. The view from the cockpit *was* Godlike, the land laid out below like a pristine model. Grids of buildings erected in the city's heyday, crisscrossed by valleys of streets, broken here and there by dark patches of woods and gardens.

The engine throbbed as Maurice Albert banked the plane gently, following the curve of the broad, black line of the Seine, which sliced Paris in two. The last low rays of sun reflected off the gleaming surface of the river as it slipped, snakelike, through the city center, sliding beneath bridges, curving out into the suburbs. They passed the blinking lights of the Tour Eiffel at the steady cruising speed of 162 miles per hour, and Jeannie could barely believe she was actually here. She, the disgraced waitress with a baby born out of wedlock, here, flying above Paris in the service of her country, in the service of France, in the service of freedom. Who would have believed it? She suddenly glimpsed Harry's smiling face and hoped she was making him proud. Then Father's voice echoing from the long-ago past, calling her his *coeur de lion*. Perhaps one day he would say those words to her again. Better to focus on that than allow her mind to slip into thinking about the very real dangers lurking down there on the streets she would soon be walking.

"The Musée d'Orsay," Maurice shouted to her above the rattling noise of the engine of the Caudron Simoun he was so at ease flying. He pointed at the hulking shape of a building far below, then another. "Musée du Louvre." There was no doubt about it, he was a very accomplished pilot. The man oozed confidence in everything he did. From the moment Jeannie met him that first day at the SOE training camp, he had left a lasting impression on her.

They had been on a journey together during the five months of training after that initial selection weekend where they'd been judged physically and psychologically suitable. A month of basic military training was followed by six freezing weeks at Special Training School 21, Arisaig House, up in the wilds of the Scottish Highlands. There they were rigorously trained in sabotage, close combat, silent killing. They were taught how to cross minefields, barbed wire, impassable rivers, and mountain topography. They learned to build and disguise explosives, set booby traps, mines, and shoot. Two shots, always, from the hip. They learned the art of escape, to hide in plain sight, to confuse and blindside the enemy. The instructors were looking for not only the physically fit, but for those with initiative, risk takers, innovators. They were put under constant stress and psychological pressure and watched closely to see how they solved puzzles, tackled problems and physical hardship; tested for memory, speed, endurance. They were never given feedback, so they had no idea of their progress. Jeannie thanked her father silently, every day, for the early training she had had on her camping trips as a child. Little did she know the value of those, the way he had taught her to be tough, to work things out for herself, to think on her feet. Never to be squeamish.

And somewhere deep inside, she held her lost baby, Celia, close. It was as though she were doing all this for her too. Somehow it made all of it easier to bear.

After Arisaig, they were moved to STS 51b, Fulshaw Hall, in Cheshire, for parachute training; then Jeannie went to STS 54a, Fawley Court, in Henley-on-Thames, for Morse code, coding, and wireless transmission. Finally, they were reunited back at finishing school in Beaulieu, Hampshire. They had watched other trainees fail to make the cut, either physically or mentally, with those who knew too much ending up in the Cooler, a remote country house in the Scottish Highlands with all creature comforts provided, bar the freedom to leave, so they couldn't give away anything about this most secret of organizations. Somehow, she, Maurice, and a handful of others had made it through. Jeannie, it turned out, excelled at coding and wireless transmission. Maurice, already a pilot and a native Parisian, was judged by the SOE to be vital to the resistance in several ways. And now here they were, no longer pretending.

Maurice banked away from the river and headed northeast, past the towers of the Sacré-Coeur and, dropping the plane a few hundred feet, began the descent into the airfield at Le Bourget.

Behind them, in the body of the four-seater plane, lay the mail sacks it was Maurice's job as a pilot for Air Bleu to fly all across France. His job was the perfect cover for a resistance worker whose clandestine job was to transport agents and secret messages across France, too, as well as across the English Channel. Maurice's intimate knowledge of the topography of the country from the air, of the landing strips and locations of the watching Nazi eyes was also vital for the SOE, who needed to know the safest places to drop their agents and to pick them up. But Maurice Albert had promised Jeannie he would make sure she knew the location of the safe houses in Paris, who to trust, the best spots to transmit her scheduled messages to London from. How to avoid suspicion. Her gut instinct was that she should rely on her own wits, not someone else's. Wasn't that what she had been taught? But then again, this was his city, and they were both on the same side.

Maurice expertly landed the plane, sharply applying the brakes, for the landing strip was short. They bounced before coming to a halt in front of the long, low mail building. Jeannie glanced at Maurice's profile as he switched off the engines and thought, as she had so many times before, how easy it might be to fall for this good-looking man. But she sensed he was part wild thing; likely he would never be fully tamed. There was a streak of something ruthless about him. She suspected somewhere there may be a wife, plus almost certainly other girlfriends. And besides, Jeannie reminded herself, she wasn't in the market for love.

She simply wanted to live.

Behind the airfield, Maurice collected his battered old Citroën and drove them on bald tires into central Paris. By the time they arrived, the gas tank perilously empty, darkness had fallen. At the sight of the German soldiers, the checkpoints, the Nazi flags flying, Jeannie's guts contorted. No amount of mental preparation could prevent the pure adrenaline-fueled terror as they slowed to have their papers checked to enter the city.

"You'll get used to it," Maurice said, glancing at her as they waited their turn. "Just stay calm. They have no reason to be suspicious. If asked, you are my girlfriend and we have been away for a dirty weekend, okay?"

Jeannie nodded, mute. Surely they would see the fear in her eyes, smell the sour sweat on her body. But when their turn came, a bored-looking soldier took in the Air Bleu insignia on Maurice's flying suit and waved them through without so much as a glance at Jeannie. She exhaled and wondered as she stared at her shaking hands if Miss Clarke, Peter Berkley, and Arthur Royston had made a dreadful mistake about her. That she would let everyone down.

Get a grip, she instructed herself. *You will do this, and you will survive. For Celia.*

You, Jeannie, have the heart of a lion.

The drive through the nighttime, blacked-out streets of Paris felt fraught with danger, with just the pale gaze of the moon to light their way. There were barely any cars on the road—*Fuel shortages*, Maurice explained—and several times he almost ran into bicycles, impossible to see in the dark. But even through the gloom, the Nazis were ever present. Road and building signs in German, soldiers on the streets. Bar the iconic buildings, central Paris could have been any city in Germany itself. In the sixteenth arrondissement, Maurice stopped abruptly outside the elegant façade of 53 Rue Pergolèse.

"Come," he said. "There are people you need to meet." He led her up four flights of stairs to the top floor of the building, tapping quietly on the door opposite. She wondered fleetingly at the trust she was putting in this total stranger, but what choice did she have? Besides, Mr. Berkley had vouched for Maurice completely. They'd been great pals before the war, apparently, when Mr. Berkley had worked for Reuters. *A jolly good chap. Best sort, and damned good pilot too. You're in safe hands with him, my dear*, he had pronounced at her debrief before she left.

"Julienne runs a safe house here," Maurice was saying in a low, soft voice as they waited for the door to open. "But you should know we are just meters away from the home of the Sicherheitsdienst, the SD—the local intelligence agency for the Gestapo in Paris—whose headquarters are at number 84 Avenue Foch. Fact is, they pay very little attention to what is right beneath their noses."

The door opened, and Maurice hustled Jeannie into a sparsely furnished flat. This would once have been the preserve of servants when this building was a single grand house. Julienne was skin and bones, like everyone in starving Paris. She was tall and had a long face, her bony shoulders poking through the thin material of her tatty dress. The whole ensemble creating an impression of extreme deprivation. A scarf was tied around her head, covering her fair hair, and she held a wooden spoon aloft, apparently in the midst of cooking an evening meal.

"Welcome to Paris, Anya," Julienne said, a smile lighting up her face. She shut the door and ushered them toward the tiny, narrow kitchen. "It's vegetable stew," she said, pointing to the pot on the stove. "Mostly turnip and carrot. We have no meat, I'm afraid."

"It's so kind of you to put me up," Jeannie said, conscious of being another mouth to feed.

"Well . . ." Julienne tilted her head to one side as though to assess Jeannie better. "We should be thanking you. Risking everything to come here, to help the resistance."

"It's what allies do. And I would rather be doing something than sitting at home doing nothing."

Julienne smiled and nodded. "Pour her some wine, Maurice, will you?"

Maurice was leaning over the pot and wrinkled his nose. "Julienne is a shockingly bad cook," he told Jeannie, which earned him a whack with the wooden spoon.

"I can cook if I have something half decent to cook with."

Maurice poured three glasses of red wine from an unlabeled bottle. Jeannie took a sip and winced. It was so sour and rough it stung the back of her throat.

Maurice watched her and laughed. "It gets better the more you drink, but it's not kind to the head in the morning."

Jeannie took one more sip then put the glass down. She needed to keep her wits.

"Madeleine will be here soon." Julienne turned to Jeannie. "She is very keen to meet you. She often has urgent material to inform London of, but we are so short of wireless transmitters in the Paris region. She is not in your circuit, but that can't be helped. It's too important."

"Of course. That's what I'm here for," Jeannie said, her heart beginning to thrum faster. Security for the SOE was a prime concern. If agents were captured, it was very likely they would be tortured for information about the rest of their clandestine operation. By organizing agents into limited circuits, usually of three members—a leader, a courier, and a wireless transmitter operator—there would be limited damage if anyone was captured and caved under torture. The crossing over of personnel from circuits, or the sending of messages on behalf of other circuits, was against the security protocols. And here she was, on her very first day, agreeing to send messages on behalf of another circuit.

"Look," Maurice said, "I must go. Finkel is waiting for me."

Julienne exchanged a look with him, and her face darkened. She turned back to the stove.

Jeannie followed Maurice into the hallway. She wasn't expecting him to leave, not so soon.

"Who is Finkel?" she asked, watching him pull his coat back on.

"Fritz Finkel is the head of the SD. I've known him a long time. We were friends long before the war. In fact"—he paused— "we went to school together. It's important I keep abreast of what they know. What they are thinking, you understand?"

Jeannie blinked in surprise.

"Julienne didn't seem too pleased."

He looked at her. A long, searching look. "She doesn't trust me not to let anything slip." He laughed and shook his head. "I say we have no choice *but* to trust, right, Anya?"

She nodded. She wanted to trust him. She really did. But something held her back. Something about the exchange with Julienne felt off.

He took a step closer, and for a moment Jeannie thought he was going to try to kiss her. Instead, he reached out a hand and placed it on her shoulder.

"I'll see you around, Anya."

DAYS FLOWED INTO weeks. Time became an abstract thing. The now was all that mattered. That and the time for Jeannie's "skeds"—her scheduled times for sending messages back to London. Jeannie was a nomad, constantly on the move, staying only one or two nights at various safe houses in the Paris area. Less chance of being caught that way.

A bearded, rough-looking man who went by the name Arnaud

was the head of Jeannie's circuit, code-named Onion. He would leave hidden messages for her that needed to be sent back to London, not risking too many meetings. Her contacts became her trusted friends. Maurice, Julienne, Madeleine. Jeannie liked Madeleine immensely from the moment she met her. It would be hard not to. A local girl, petite, pretty, and oozing charm, Madeleine was everyone's darling. Together, they navigated Paris as much as possible. Rules or no rules, despite being in different circuits, they needed each other.

Madeleine's job was information gathering. She was, apart from being young, beautiful, and charming, blessed with a photographic memory, a talent for languages, and a ferocious intellect. She was also an excellent actress. Fluent in German as well as French and English, Madeleine was employed as an interpreter by a French industrial company apparently seeking to do business with their German occupiers. Her job brought her into contact with senior Nazi officers. She floated about their favorite bars, listening in on their conversations, always smiling and jolly. With her big, innocent eyes and affable demeanor, the German officers completely underestimated her. They had no idea their plans and discussions, which they held quite openly in front of her, were being passed on to London via Jeannie's coded messages.

But the most dangerous job of all was Jeannie's. Nazi vans were always out on patrol, picking up the clandestine messages via radio waves. It was a race to get her messages sent before the Germans could track her down. As much as she could, she varied her locations and asked for her skeds to be at different times of the day.

Jeannie wondered what Madeleine's real name was. What she must have been before the war. She longed to talk to her about their true lives, their true selves, but it was too dangerous. Every agent had been so painstakingly prepared with a full backstory along with their new name that had to be memorized in every detail until they almost believed in it themselves. They were clothed in continental cloth with the correct provincial stitching, seams, collar and buttonhole detail. In Jeannie's case, these had been carefully replicated by refugees from close to the Belgian border who knew the local styles. Everything, from their underwear, glasses, cigarettes, shoes, laces, belts, money, hairstyles, even their teeth fillings, were supplied and replaced with authentic items from where they were supposed to have originated. Any amateur mistake—for example, an English zipper—could be enough to cost a life.

Like all the others, Jeannie had come to Paris equipped with everyday items that, if found on her, would not seem suspect but could be used to change her appearance in case a sudden getaway was needed. Boot polish, sponge, chalk, razor, scissors could all be used to alter her facial features, hair, and coloring. But the battered, rectangular case containing her heavy SOE-issue wireless transmitter was much harder to disguise. If she was caught with it, that would be disastrous. Her instructions, therefore, were to bury or hide it if she were being pursued. And to kill, of course. They must always kill, ruthlessly, swiftly, silently. Again, she offered silent thanks to Father for teaching her not to be afraid to kill. Always better to kill than to be killed.

JEANNIE HAD BEEN in Paris for eight intense weeks when she was back at Julienne's for a couple of nights. Exhaustion made her eyelids heavy, but the bite of the cold night, and the lack of coal to burn, kept them open. She huddled around the stove, helping Julienne sort the completely rotten potatoes from the ones potentially salvageable. Three sharp taps at the door. They both paused, stared at each other. Nobody was expected this evening. Tensions were running high among the occupiers. There were chinks in the invincibility of the German military superiority. Perhaps, went the word on the street, they were spreading themselves too thin. The Soviet victory at Stalingrad at the beginning of the year. Now the Afrika Korps had surrendered to the British Eighth Army, and there had been a distinct increase in bombing raids from the Allied air forces across Europe these last weeks. The Allies were weakening German strategic targets: airfields around Paris; an aircraft factory at Nantes; shipyards at Kiel; submarine works at Wilhelmshaven; a tire plant at Hanover. The list went on.

And of course, the ever-present rumors of a big Allied invasion into France soon. The Germans were intent on finding out where and when. It made them increasingly nervous, and nervous Germans made for dangerous ones. Julienne wiped her hands on her apron and went to the door.

It was Madeleine. "Dear *God*, we thought you were the Nazis." Jeannie hugged her tight, but Madeleine wriggled away.

"Anya, I have something really big. You need to send a message back to London, *right* away. It can't wait. And I have something, too, which will need to go in plain text, but I don't know how. Will you help?"

"Of course. What is it, Madeleine, what do you have?"

The three women left the dinner preparation and gathered around the table, supplying Madeleine with the pen and paper she requested.

"As usual I was hanging around in the bar of Hotel Majestic," Madeleine began, still short of breath from her fast cycle through the streets of Paris. "Some of the officers invited me back to a small gathering at a house on Avenue Hoche."

"Did you *go*?" Julienne's eyes widened.

"Of course I did! It was too good an opportunity to miss!"

"But weren't you afraid of what they might do to you?"

Madeleine giggled. "Not for a moment. These officers know I would never sleep with them. It's clear what sort of girl I am, so I'm quite safe. Now they simply set out to impress me. Anyway, at the house there was a jovial sort of atmosphere, so of course I did my usual silly girl act, which they *always* fall for." She rolled her eyes. "Anyway, it didn't take long. They were full of brag and bravado about a devastating new weapon they are developing. It flies unmanned and faster than any airplane. They said they are going to use it to bomb cities in Great Britain out of existence. They were awfully pleased with themselves." She took a deep breath.

Julienne rose and fetched the wine bottle and glasses, pouring them each a glass of the rough red wine Jeannie had become used to.

"Anyway," Madeleine continued, "I used all my usual tricks, telling them what they were saying couldn't possibly be true and where was the factory and so on . . . Well, of course they told me exactly where it is." Madeleine scribbled the name of the factory and the German town on a sheet of paper. "So I decided to push for more. I said I just couldn't believe such a thing could exist, and I certainly couldn't see how it would work and fly all by itself and at such speeds. A kindly officer obliged me by drawing a detailed plan and pointing out all the technical details to me. So I oohed and aahed as much as I could and smiled and thanked him, and as fast as I could, I got away. Now," she said, leaning over the paper, "I'm going to draw the plan so that you can warn

London. We need to send the drawing urgently—it must go to someone who can understand it. I hope they bomb the hell out of this bloody rocket factory."

Madeleine set to work drawing the plan of the rocket that she had memorized. Jeannie watched in fascination. Madeleine was, without a doubt, the cleverest person she had ever met. And those German soldiers the most stupid she'd had the good fortune not to meet, for not realizing it.

While Madeleine was busy drawing, Jeannie considered giving the plans to Maurice to carry back to London with the next batch of plain text messages he always carried, along with SOE agents during his frequent trips across the Channel. But something in her gut warned her against it. She remembered, suddenly, sitting in a park with Harry watching the fat pigeons pecking at crumbs from their sandwiches and how Harry had admired them for carrying messages during times of war. She pictured the sleek silver wings of a racing pigeon flying low over the choppy waters of the English Channel, Madeleine's plan rolled tightly into a tube at the pigeon's belly. She shook her head to rid it of the absurd idea. She would find another way to get the drawing back, through Arnaud, and in the meantime, she would send a coded message to London about the rockets, the factory, and the plans that would follow. Whatever the danger, she would do this right away, thinking about the countless lives Madeleine was going to save. Lives that may well include those of Celia and her parents.

It was late. The streets teeming with Nazis. The women agreed it would be less of a risk to send the message at this hour from the attic of 53 Rue Pergolèse.

Quietly, Jeannie and Madeleine climbed the ladder into the loft. Moonlight from two dormer windows in the roof sliced through the darkness. Madeleine held a flashlight while Jeannie, with nimble fingers, set up the radio transmitter. She used an adapted car battery as there was no electricity up here. She made the transmission as swiftly as she could. But in what felt like less than a minute after transmission, there was a ferocious rapping on the front door of the apartment block. Jeannie and Madeleine stared at each other for a few stretched and horrified moments, frozen in fear as the sound of metal-tipped boots rang up the stairwell.

"Quick! Get out!" Jeannie urged Madeleine as she shoved the radio equipment back in the case and pushed it behind an old, broken wardrobe. Jeannie darted to one of the dormer windows and shoved up the stiff bottom sash. From downstairs they could hear the pounding of fists on doors, echoing shouts. "There's no time," Jeannie shrieked, and Madeleine slipped through the gap, crouching on the rooftop just as they had practiced in their imaginations a hundred times before.

"Come on," Madeleine urged from her position, clinging onto the tiles, almost five stories above street level.

"No." Jeannie shook her head. "We need to split. It's best you get away—you are the most valuable. I'll distract them—here." She reached out the window and passed the drawing of the rocket back to Madeleine. "Get this to Arnaud. He'll find the safest way to pass it to London. Now go!"

For a moment their eyes connected, and Jeannie could see the battle going on inside. But they both knew the truth of it. Madeleine's safety was paramount. Of the two, her connections, her ability to extract material from the Nazis would make the biggest difference to the war effort. Jeannie was merely the messenger, and at that moment, the most dispensable.

The sounds from the stairwell grew louder, and there was no

time to argue. Madeleine nodded once. "Take care," she whispered, and then she was gone, crawling spiderlike on hands and feet across the dark slate roof, disappearing around the chimney breast of the next-door property.

Jeannie shoved the window closed and wiped her sleeve across the frame to rid it of fingerprints. She backed out of the attic space, around the pile of old mattresses, the moth-eaten linen and junk, praying the Gestapo wouldn't see stray footprints in the dust or the wiped-clean windowframe. Her body weak with terror, mouth dry as the desert, Jeannie checked the top-floor corridor was still clear. Heavy boots sounded on the floor below. She quickly let herself out through the hatch, sliding the cover into place, and tiptoed back down the corridor to Julienne's door, thinking about all the pointless disguises she had practiced applying during her training. There was no time. Instead, she pictured Madeleine's getaway over their rehearsed route, down the black iron zigzag of the fire escape that snaked its way from behind the next-door property to the back of the buildings. By now she would have jumped over the back wall onto the path behind the buildings, out onto the road, and, God willing, to safety.

Julienne was waiting, ashen-faced, at her door. She wasn't alone. Behind her, an elderly, senior-looking officer of the SD police. And next to him, Maurice Albert.

Escape or kill, never risk capture. Her trained brain assessed the situation. It was impossible. Maurice had made sure of that. Her pistol (two shots, always, from the hip), useless, somewhere in the apartment. Her knife in its sheath, tucked inside her sleeve, even more so when there were tens of Nazis on the floor below and the SD officer had his gun trained at her head.

Maurice, the snake, who didn't, or couldn't, meet her eye.

Maurice, who nodded to the officer she knew had to be Fritz Finkel. Finkel stepped forward and took her arm.

Jeannie's vision blurred. Through the darkness folding inward, all she could see was Celia. That bundle, the dangling foot as she was carried away.

Chapter 26

Celia

It's the early hours of Monday morning, and Celia tosses and turns in bed. She's managed to dodge Septimus over the past week when he called twice at the shop, and she failed to turn up for their usual Sunday rendezvous yesterday morning. He will no doubt be wondering why, linking it to the disastrous kiss. She cringes each time she thinks of it. At first, how wonderful it felt to finally be kissed by him, the press of his body against hers. How they seemed to fit together, like two pieces in a jigsaw puzzle. The intoxicating smell of his skin. The growing need to have more of him.

But then a memory had poked at her as his warm and electric hands had slipped down her body, making her react in strange and terrifying ways. Had made her gather her things, face red with shame, making her excuses to leave the picnic in such a rush.

It was a memory of the girls at school in their final year, aged fifteen, heads bent together at breaktime, discussing *the sexual act*.

"A man has no control," Jemima had proclaimed to the rest of the group—the Ignorants. She, an authority on all things *sex*, having both a boyfriend *and* an older sister, recently married, dropped crumbs of knowledge for her rapt audience like she was feeding bread to hungry ducks. Celia, as desperate to know as the others, had listened with eager ears. "It's always up to the woman to say no," Jemima had told them with a flick of her hair, "and to stop him from reaching *the point of no return*."

"What's the point of no return?" Celia had blurted out.

Jemima had granted her a disdainful look.

"The man," Jemima had continued to her riveted audience, "is *programmed* to do the deed at *any* given opportunity. He can't help himself. If a girl flashes him with her tantalizing flesh, well, he can't be blamed, but the consequences for her could be *dire*."

Celia had opened her mouth to inquire about the dire consequences and just *why* the man is so helpless in such circumstances but had thought better of it and shut it again.

"Egging him on, encouraging him *in any way*, might tip him over *the point of no return*. And no girl wants to be a slag and end up *up the duff*, does she?" She'd trained her disparaging blue eyes on Celia and said in an exaggerated slow voice, "That means *with a bun in the oven*, for those who don't quite follow." How ironic that neither Jemima nor Celia at the time had known she was addressing one of those many little shunned and unfortunate buns.

That day at the picnic, with Septimus's exploratory hands on her, Jemima's words had echoed around her brain like the warning bells of doom. *Do not let him reach the Point of No Return!*

What's wrong? he'd asked as she'd pulled away from him, his color high, face bunched in confusion. *What did I do?*

Nothing. She'd avoided his eyes as she'd slipped on her shoes and readjusted her clothes. *I just need to go. Didn't realize the time.*

Septimus was silent and in the sudden discomfort between them, where before there was warm ease, Celia wondered if she'd mistakenly let him get too carried away. Should she have stopped him sooner, at the early stages of the kiss? Before the wet slip of his tongue and the travel of his hands? Was it her fault, and now he was angry and disappointed? Had she, inadvertently, allowed him to hover dangerously near to the Point of No Return without even realizing it?

Just like your mother, prods a nasal, accusatory voice. She squeezes her eyes shut. *Loose. Dirty. Slut. Conceived up against a wall in a back alley somewhere.* The voice has morphed into Mother's, and her eyes ping open, her heart banging in her chest.

Celia gives up on sleep and gets up. She'll have to face Septimus sometime, give him some sort of explanation. It will be better once that's done, and today is as good a day as any.

Later, at work, she is jumpy, staring at the shop door each time it opens, hoping it won't be him. But as though she has willed him there, at half past ten the doorbell jangles, and he is stepping over the threshold, removing his hat and making her heart flutter like a trapped butterfly.

"You didn't come yesterday." There is hurt in his eyes and a lack of preamble.

"I'm sorry, Septimus. I couldn't make it. If I had had your phone number, I could have let you know."

He shifts from one foot to the other. "I should have given it to you." He turns his hat slowly, round and round, in his hands. "It's only that . . . last week . . . it all seemed to be going so well between us, and then you ran away. I wasn't sure what I'd done." He takes a deep breath. "Fact is, I really like you, Celia, and I thought you felt the same way. Did I get it wrong?"

Celia's mouth is dry, and she longs for a glass of water. She is not good at this, and Septimus, usually so full of easy grace and confidence, is awkward this morning, and it's all her fault.

Celia takes a deep inhale of breath and tries to summon her inner Daphne, who is always so at ease around the opposite sex.

"Look, you haven't done anything wrong, Septimus. I like you. Very much, actually, but things are a bit complicated right now. I'm not in a good frame of mind for having any sort of boyfriend." A rash of heat spreads upward from her chest. She plows on. "I wasn't expecting the kiss. It was a bit sudden. Sorry."

"Why didn't you say? We could have talked about—"

"Like I say, it's complicated."

"Are you okay?"

She summons a smile. "Completely fine."

"I'm not so sure."

"I will be. Soon."

"Please let me help."

Celia shakes her head, swallows the lump in her throat. He's being so kind. *Don't cry.*

"I'd really like to try." Septimus checks the time. "Look," he says, "I can't stay, I have a meeting in half an hour. But how about dinner tonight? I know there is no class this evening. Sounds like you could do with a sympathetic ear."

He is right. And she has no wish to hurry back to Copperfield Street after work, the way things are at the moment. Besides, she could do with some company. But is he taking advantage because she is in a vulnerable situation? Has she said too much?

Father's warnings sound in her head. She ignores them.

"All right. But I have to be home by ten P.M. or Mother'll send out a search party."

"Splendid. I'll pick you up outside the shop at six, and I promise to have you back long before curfew!"

Septimus's usual smile is back, and the world is suddenly a little brighter.

At twelve, Celia is tidying the shelves in the poetry section following some new additions to the collection when Mrs. Denton returns, Alfred Humphries in tow. He seems more rugged than usual, unshaven and apparently rattled by something.

"I swear to God it's her," he is saying loudly as they come into the shop. "What the hell is she doing snooping around, I ask you?"

"You are being paranoid, Alfred."

"I tell you, *moya dorogaya*, I never forget a face."

Celia stops, book held in midair before the shelf. *What the hell language is that?* They don't know she's here, hidden as she is behind the floor-to-ceiling shelves. Something tells her to keep silent.

"Stop it!" Mrs. Denton's voice is sharp.

"Stop what?" There are some muffled words, as though he might be holding Mrs. D close and speaking into her hair. That foreign word again, *dorogaya*, or something.

"*Alfred* . . ." He sniggers, and Celia wonders if they are embracing—what should she do? She can't hide behind the bookshelf for the rest of the day.

Humphries again says something so quietly she doesn't catch it.

"Give it to me." Mrs. Denton's voice is firm. Then it becomes softer, quieter, so she can't hear what she's saying either. Celia holds her breath, strains her ears. "I'll look after it . . . Not going anywhere until Christmas . . ."

There is a moment of silence.

"You would do that for me?" His voice is wheedling, then ends in a chuckle.

"Stop messing about, Alfred . . ."

The crinkle of something, an envelope or package perhaps?

Celia's heart is thudding so hard, she wonders if they can hear it. She stays absolutely still, arm aching slightly from holding the book in the air.

Mrs. Denton's heels clack toward the flat door. "I'll put this away and make some coffee. Want some?"

"Where's the girl?" Humphries asks, and the door behind the counter creaks.

She doesn't catch Mrs. D's reply as her voice comes from inside the flat. Celia holds her breath. A sigh and more footsteps toward the door. Silence. Celia lets a few moments go by. It seems she is alone. She exhales and checks that the coast is clear, both of them now in the flat, the black door standing wide open. She darts down the cellar steps, returning several minutes later, clattering up the stairs with maximum noise, a second box of poetry books in her arms. Mr. Humphries and Mrs. Denton are back in the shop, cups of black coffee in hand, standing at the counter.

"Hello—you're back," Celia says brightly.

Mrs. Denton smiles at Celia. "All okay here?"

"Absolutely," Celia says. "Very quiet, as usual, so I decided to sort the poetry boxes."

"Vera—"

"Shush."

"Why don't you hop out for your lunch, dear," Mrs. Denton says. "Mr. Humphries and I have some . . . business to discuss."

"I brought sandwiches and a book today," Celia says, desperate to know what's going on, what Mrs. Denton is looking after for Mr. Humphries. "I thought I'd just eat them here, if that's okay with you?"

Mr. Humphries and Mrs. Denton exchange a glance. Their silence speaks volumes.

"But it's a nice day, so on second thought, I'll eat in the park."

"The fresh air will do you a world of good." Mrs. Denton beams.

Celia grabs her bag with her corned beef sandwich, apple, and copy of *The Pale Horse*, which she has nearly finished. She's thinking about the exchange she heard between the two of them. Alfred Humphries is odd, she decides, as she makes her way down toward Temple Gardens and the river, where she will find a bench to eat her lunch. The scar, the way he saunters in and out with his overnight bag. Mrs. Denton keeping stuff for him. Those foreign words. He seems furtive and full of secrets. Could it be drugs? Or maybe Mrs. D has no idea what is in the package? Perhaps Alfred is a serial killer and Mrs. D loves him so much she is covering for him, hiding all the evidence he carries to the flat in that overnight bag of his and then cleaning it up. But *why* would she be helping him?

None of it makes sense.

Stop it, Celia. Clearly, she has been reading too much Agatha Christie, and she makes a mental note to read one of the classics next. There is probably a perfectly innocuous explanation for all of it.

AT SEVEN THAT evening, Celia is sitting in a cozy little French bistro on the edge of Mayfair with Septimus, his face lit by flickering candlelight; the half-drawn blood-red blinds, plush cushions, and low lighting make the place feel intimate, romantic even. Two glasses of Mateus Rosé are softening Celia's edges. Septimus is drawing her out of herself, and in spite of the promises she made to Mother and Father, the truth spills out into Septimus's sympathetic ears. She tells him everything, from the finding of the file, to Miss Clarke, and all that her grandparents have revealed.

He's a good listener. He nods encouragement, those mesmerizing lion eyes fixed on her, concentrating intently. From time to time, he reaches for Celia's hand and gives it a sympathetic squeeze. Celia talks as her wine glass empties, is refilled, and empties again. They eat wafer-thin round pieces of toast with paté, followed by chicken and perfectly cooked vegetables. Celia doesn't taste any of it.

"What a terrible shock for you," Septimus says. "No wonder you need some space." He strokes a thumb across the back of her hand, sending shivers up her spine. "I'm glad you told me."

"You don't hate me, now you know my real mother wasn't married? Now you know she only knew my father for a few weeks?"

"I couldn't give a damn, Celia. Besides, it makes you half American, so . . . That's a bonus."

"I'd not thought of it that way." Celia smiles.

"Listen, the people who judge this stuff? They're the hypocrites who don't want change. Those who want to keep things the same for their own benefit. Seriously, what difference does it make? Marriage, like religion or having to wear a suit to work, is simply a construct of a patriarchal, unfair society. The aim is always to control, to box in, and to place people in a hierarchy. Those at the top with an overinflated opinion of their own self-worth, usually carrying around the idea they don't have to comply with the rules they set for everyone else, and those at the bottom with a deflated opinion of *their* own self-worth."

"Is that really what you believe?" Celia has never, ever met anyone, especially a man, who speaks like this.

"Sure, it is."

"I'd have thought, what with you working in the diplomatic service, you would be very, well, conventional."

Septimus winks and says nothing. They drink a little more.

Something heavy swells in Celia's chest, filling her lungs, closing her throat.

After they've eaten, Septimus orders coffee for him, tea for her, which arrive with a little plate of petit fours.

"I've been wondering what my mother might make of me," Celia says. "I'd like to do something that would make her proud. Working at a bookshop, shorthand and typing . . . It's not much, is it, compared to being in the SOE?"

"But she did what she did during a time of war. I'm sure she'd be proud of you—you march for peace. You *are* using your voice to speak out."

"It's not enough, though. And in spite of all the shouting about it, everyone is still oblivious." Septimus tilts his head, his expression serious. What a drug he is, this man. "All I've done," she continues, "is protest and march and type a few leaflets . . . It's so little. What more can I do?"

He stares into her eyes for what feels like a full minute. She can't read the expression on his face. Uncertainty? Dilemma? Perhaps deciding how much he can divulge to her?

Finally, he says, "I think, Celia Duchesne, our ideologies are more aligned than you realize. Fact is, we—I mean, myself and my compatriots—do what we must for the good of our nations. Unfortunately, countries, governments, are run by people, and people are flawed and make mistakes and sometimes do terrible things. There is a whole unseen, uncelebrated army of minions, though, like me, just doing our best to make sure nobody messes up too much, to repair damage, to smooth over cracks. And we listen, and we learn, and we persuade. That's where we can make a difference, if you follow me?"

Celia isn't sure she does, but she finds she doesn't care. Her head is feeling pleasantly muzzy from the wine, and whatever Septimus says is so interesting, but even if it wasn't, she wouldn't much care, because just being here with him is enough.

"Perhaps you and me, together, we could make a pretty good team . . . Make a difference . . ."

She nods and smiles, still not sure of his meaning, but she likes the sound of him and her being a team.

"You know," he continues, "the most likely thing that will cause nuclear annihilation of the human race?"

She shakes her head.

"Human error."

"Really?"

"Really. Now, that could be error of judgment on the part of the politicians or the generals, or error of those pilots or submarine officers or operators who handle the weapons. So, by that token, just having them exist is the worst threat of all, right?"

"Right."

"See, the decision-makers invariably look at the big picture." Septimus draws a large circle with his hands above the table. "Thinking that it's *their* decisions that will change policy and direct world events. But in fact, out there"—Septimus points toward the window, where darkness gathers around the edges of the pulled blinds—"it's chaos. Nobody really has control over it, because there is always unpredictability, the unexpected, and the power of momentum when forces are released." He drums his fingers on the table. "You see, there is perception, and then there is reality. Often, they are so far apart that the one has no relation to the other. And at the end of the day, it's *perception* that matters most." Septimus is talking in riddles. "I'll give you an example." He lowers his voice. "We all feel relatively safe because everyone thinks that there is a balance in the nuclear capabilities of both superpowers. But what if, in reality, that wasn't true? What if there was a huge gap between the nuclear capabilities of the USA and the Soviets?"

"Well," Celia says slowly, "I suppose if one was significantly weaker than the other, the weaker might be less bellicose toward the stronger?"

"Exactly. Or they might feel threatened and cornered and lash out. But the reality doesn't matter. If they both *think* something, whether it is true or not, it is irrelevant."

"I think I see," Celia says, feeling distinctly befuddled. "Is that really the case, then? Does America have much greater nuclear firepower?"

Septimus laughs. "Like I said, Celia, I'm just a minion doing my job. Now—" He looks at his watch. Something, Celia has noticed, he does a good deal. Time, and keeping it, seems to be important to him. "It's almost nine. I should get you home. We don't want you turning into a pumpkin, now do we?" He winks again, sending a wild swoosh through her insides.

Out on the street, they walk slowly, arm in arm. She would be fine getting back to Copperfield Street on her own. She doesn't need an escort, and she certainly doesn't want to risk an encounter between Septimus and her parents. But she says nothing, because being with Septimus is like finding a raft to cling to in a choppy, lonely sea, and she doesn't want to let go.

Septimus asks her again about what she knows of the British government's secret war plans. But his probing is uncomfortable.

258 ~ Louise Fein

She tells him she doesn't know much, no details, no names. Even if they are on the same side, her instinct is to say nothing.

"Would you come with me?" Celia asks, changing the subject suddenly, without the thought properly formulating in her head. "To see Miss Clarke about my mother? She's away house-hunting during September, apparently on the South Coast, but I've arranged to see her again in October. It would be nice to have someone with me."

"Well, of course I'll come with you, Celia."

They walk on, pushing through the crowds at Piccadilly Circus, ducking down toward Trafalgar Square and on to the river Thames.

"You know," Septimus says as a thought apparently strikes him, "the American ambassador, David Bruce, or the Big B, as I call him, lived here in London for a period of time during the war too. All through the Blitz, I believe, and then he came back again, from 1942 onward." Septimus pulls a pack of cigarettes from his pocket, offers one to Celia, which she refuses.

"What was he doing here?" Celia asks.

"Intelligence," Septimus replies as he strides ahead, leaving Celia to jog a few paces to keep up. "He headed up the Office of Strategic Services, the OSS—the precursor to the CIA." He smiles. "You British led the way, of course. It was *our* version of your Special Operations Executive. But they worked very closely together during the war. I wonder if he knew your Miss Clarke?" he asks. "There's a good chance, I suppose. We can ask her when we see her."

"That would be such a coincidence . . . It feels like everything always leads me back to my mother, somehow." They walk on in reflective silence. At the top of Copperfield Street. Celia stops and tells Septimus to go, using the excuse that Mother mustn't spot her with a man.

"Well, all right, if you are sure," he says, pulling her close. "But I'm not leaving until you give me a kiss good night."

She snuggles into his arms. "If I really have to," she says, tilting her face toward his.

"I'm afraid you do."

His lips meet hers, and, determined not to ruin things this time, she allows her eyes to drift shut, cutting out the proximity of Copperfield Street, cutting out the rest of the world. She presses herself closer, allowing herself, finally, to let go.

Later, lying in bed as she waits for sleep to come, she realizes she has divulged her greatest secrets to Septimus, and yet, she still knows almost nothing of him.

Chapter 27

Celia

Celia's arm, pinned between Septimus's solid shoulder and the stiff leather of the back seat of his Morris Minor, is becoming alarmingly numb. As much as she admires his muscled torso, Septimus is not an insignificant weight.

She can feel his heart banging against his rib cage, pressed up against hers, and she imagines his passion building and rising inside him like steam in a pressure cooker, just as he groans, "Oh, Celia, I want you so *bad* . . ."

He *knows* she won't go all the way. Surely he does, knowing now the sordid story of her own beginnings? It's been two weeks since she told him the whole of it, and things between them have quickly progressed to a new level of intimacy. Perhaps, deep down, he knows it's in her genes to be *easy*.

Like mother, like daughter.

Celia's breath comes quick and fast, and her heart pounds strong and rhythmic in her own chest like the beat of a drum. Her skin, her thighs, her very blood is tingling and alive with what she and Septimus are doing. Half of her, the bad, slutty half, wants to give in to herself, surrender to the delicious feelings and urges and to Septimus's wanting her, to reach whatever pinnacle of wrongness and points of no return he wishes to take her to. But the other half, the good, sensible half, is horrified at herself.

Good girl. Bad girl.

Conceived up against a wall in a back alley somewhere . . .

"Stop! Septimus, *stop!*" Celia shrieks, and thumps her fists against him. Septimus springs away, hands raised as though she is holding a gun to his head.

"I'm sorry! I was getting carried away. I didn't mean to . . ."

"It's okay." Celia wriggles out from under him, pulling her skirt firmly down, fumbling to do up the two top buttons on her blouse she hadn't even realized were undone.

She glances at him, running his hands through his hair. He is breathing heavily. Even in the darkness she can see his face is flushed.

"I'm sorry," she says. "I was afraid you wouldn't stop."

"I was always going to stop," Septimus says in a low voice. "I would never do anything to hurt you. I admit, I got a little carried away. I'm sorry." He reaches for her hand and gives it a light kiss.

They sit in silence for a few moments, clasping hands and staring out through the front windshield at the quiet street. They are parked behind the Astoria, on a side street off the Old Kent Road. The building looms, a vast and solid silhouette against the starlit night sky, rising above the surrounding low tiled roofs of the terraced two-up two-downs, reminding Celia of a Victorian cotton mill rearing above workers' cottages. Inside, though, are not downtrodden girls in ragged dresses with delicate fingers trapped in vicious machinery, but canoodling couples in the warmth of the auditorium watching Robert Preston star in *The Music Man*. It had been her idea to see the film, but somehow, they never made it out of the car.

Septimus turns to her. He rubs a hand across his face, and she thinks she hears him swear under his breath.

"Septimus, what's wrong?" Celia asks him. "You look perplexed."

"I . . . I think . . . Well, Celia, I think I'm falling for you. What I mean is, I've never felt this way about anyone else. You're like a drug I can't get enough of . . ."

Her blood pumps hot. Can he mean it? Or are these the words to get her into bed?

He threads his fingers through her hair, pulling her face close, his eyes gleaming in the dark. "Please tell me you feel something for me too, Celia. Please?"

She draws back, laughs. "But you know I do!"

"I don't." He shakes his head, takes a deep breath. "Celia . . ." His voice cracks. "See . . . I think I'm falling in love with you . . ."

She *does* see it then, a vulnerability in his expression she's not seen before. He's exposed his true feelings. Finally, she thinks, there is a hint of the real Septimus. The one hiding behind that suave, educated, polished exterior. *That's* the Septimus she wants more of.

She takes his face between her hands. "You have to trust me, Sep . . . There is nobody else I'd rather be with than you. But I need to figure out who I am first before I can fall in love. I hope you can understand that. Just . . . give me a little time. Please?"

MOTHER IS WAITING for Celia in the sitting room when she arrives home just after nine the same evening.

"Hello, Mother."

"Celia . . ." Mother rises stiffly from the sofa, sits down again. Something about her movements sends alarm bells ringing.

"What is it?" Celia asks, coming into the room, seating herself in Father's armchair opposite the sofa. Mother's face is grim, her lips pinched. The air in the room thickens.

"We need to talk."

"What do you mean?" Celia's mouth is dry. Did Mother see her with Septimus? Could she have been waiting at the sitting room window and spied her getting out of his car?

"There's something you should know." Mother seems to be having some sort of internal battle. Her fists are clenched, her face red. "I found this in your room," she finally exhales, and fishes an envelope from her pocket, holding it out for Celia to see. It's the reply she received from Miss Clarke to her request to visit again and suggesting the date in October. She'd brought it back from the bookshop and must have forgotten to hide it.

"Why were you looking through my things?"

"I wasn't. I was putting some washing away, and there it was, lying on top of your bookshelf for all to see. I need to know . . . Why are you writing to *that woman*?" The venom in Mother's voice takes Celia by surprise.

"Why do you hate her so much?"

"I told you to leave this all alone. And now I find out you've been going behind my back and writing letters to all and sundry—"

"Mother! I've not been writing to anyone except Miss Clarke. Try and understand from my perspective, finding out you and Father aren't my parents at all—it's been a shock. I want—no, *need*—to know more about my mother. You've made your opinion about what she did crystal clear, and that overshadows everything. Father won't talk about her, and Miss Clarke is the only other person I've found who knew her. If I want to ask her questions, I have every right, and you can't stop me."

Her words are harsh, and Mother shrinks beneath the weight of them, suddenly looking as fragile as a browned, curled leaf tossed on the autumn breeze, and Celia softens. All this, she can see, is breaking her unbreakable grandmother.

Mother swallows hard. Stares at the envelope in her hands.

"We've only ever wanted to keep you safe, see, Celia, but now, after everything, I realize we went about it the wrong way. We smothered you, tried to hold on to you. But you can't *keep* a person, can you? Not against their will."

Celia shakes her head. "I—"

Her grandmother holds up a hand. "Please, let me finish what I want to say. Then you can say your bit." She looks away, then trains her sad eyes on Celia. "We made mistakes, Celia, like I say. I'm not making excuses, but I want you to know *why* . . . I've never been any good at emotional stuff. Saying what I feel or touching and all that. It's not that I don't *feel*. It's just me. Our generation, I suppose. But thing is, Celia, I've *always* loved you." Her voice falters on the words. "And so has André. We couldn't have loved you more—that's the truth—granddaughter or daughter. But you can't know that, because I never told you. André didn't want you at the beginning, it's true. Or at least the idea of you, not to start. But that's 'cause he was thinking of Jeannie and what was best for her. Once he had no choice, once he got to know *you*, well, he grew to love you just as much. We did what we could to save you from other people's harsh judging. Because they do judge. Rightly or wrongly. Do you see, Celia? We didn't tell you any of it because we thought we were protecting you. André, well, he could never accept the loss of Jeannie. And he blamed me for it. Which isn't fair, but he was just hurting so much, he had to blame someone, or something. I was there and the easiest thing to blame. You never get over the loss of a child . . . Everyone deals with their grief in a different way. I had God, he had me."

Celia nods, but she can't speak. A lump the size of an apple is wedged in her throat.

Mother reaches into her other pocket and pulls out the journal Celia recognizes from the box in the loft.

"I know you want to learn more of your mother. I realize that now. And, I suppose, it's only natural and right that you should. It's all been buried so long, in here"—she places her fist on her chest—"that when you started asking questions, I didn't think I could deal with the pain. But that's not fair to you. You were right to push me." She stares at the book in her hand. "I kept this silly journal during the war. When Jeannie went away, I'd no idea what sort of danger she was in. She told me it was translating, but it was so hush-hush, and she was gone so long, I knew it was something more than that. I'd never have guessed she was really in France. Our only contact was Miss Clarke. And she never let on." Mother's face hardens. "I'll come back to her. Still, all that time with Jeannie gone, with André away, too, I had nothing to take my mind off thinking about you. When I found out you were still in the orphanage, that no one had yet come forward to adopt you, it felt like a sign from God. You weren't *meant* to be given up. I went to see you, and, oh, once I'd set eyes on you, that was that." She pauses. "As soon as I'd signed all the paperwork, I wrote to Jeannie, gave the letter to Miss Clarke to pass on. I knew she'd return, for you. I just knew it. And don't go thinking that was the only reason I adopted you. It wasn't. I'd have done it anyway, whether Jeannie came home or not."

Mother blows her nose. "But Jeannie never did come back, and never knew I'd fetched you home, because that *evil* Miss Clarke never passed the letter to her."

With a stab to the heart, Celia remembers the torn letter. Miss Clarke never mentioned this when Celia visited her.

Mother holds the journal out for Celia to take. "I know it's not much. But it's a start. You see, it was so strange. I somehow knew when Jeannie had been caught. I knew, too, when she was no more. I wrote it all in here at the time, and then when that *Miss Clarke*"—she pulls a face as if she's bitten a chili—"came and told us what had happened to our Jeannie, she confirmed all the dates. I was right. I'd known it in my bones, in the depths of my soul, that her end was bad. I thought it was God telling me. But perhaps I'm wrong about that too. I don't know." She involuntarily shudders, then seems to gather herself. "So if there is anything you want to know about our Jeannie, I'll do my best to tell you. I can't promise André will open up. He's damaged to the roots of himself. But I'll try to answer all your questions, Celia. I owe you that."

The tears win their battle and begin to flow. On impulse, Celia snatches at Mother's hand and gives it a squeeze. "*Thank you . . .*"

They sit for a moment, both contemplating the little book in Celia's hands, Mother's expression reflecting little of the anguish Celia knows she is carrying inside.

And suddenly, Celia sees her as she has never in her life seen her before. No longer the fierce, undemonstrative, impossible-to-please matriarch, but a frail, vulnerable, fallible human being who makes mistakes and gets things wrong and hates herself for it but can never admit it for fear, or pride, or heaven knows what. And a different version of her remembered past blows through her mind like a soft breeze.

Mother making nutritious meals, regardless of how tired she was after a long day of working. Mother washing, mending, sewing Celia's clothes with intricate care, often late into the night. Mother fretting when Celia was late home. Mother indulging Celia's desire for a pet or listening quietly to her endless prattle.

Mother's presence, always, when Celia was upset, needed help, had something to share. Her love was never demonstrated by hugs or words or pride or indulgences but had been there all the time in plain sight: an ever-present, fierce dedication to practical and physical care that Celia had never even noticed.

Mother is the first to break the silence.

"Anyway, fact is, I need to warn you. I know I shouldn't have snooped, but I can see from this letter you're going back to see Miss Clarke. But, Celia, you mustn't get mixed up with her. She's not to be trusted."

"Why ever not?"

"That woman and all that lot should have been locked up and the key thrown into the Thames." Mother's voice is shaky with emotion. "Like I said, she never passed on the news about you. I suppose she was worried they would lose one of their prize agents. That and the negligent way they ran that SOE operation. They were amateurs. They let the man responsible for your mother's capture, Claude Beaumont, into their old boys' network, because he was a former school friend of one of theirs. But they *knew* he was also a long-time friend of the head of the Nazis' secret police in Paris. Didn't they think that might be a security risk? They said they cared about their agents. But it was just talk. They were arrogant and stupid, and it was *that* which resulted in your mother's death. And many more deaths besides."

"What? Slow down, what do you mean?"

Mother takes a deep breath. "Did you know how she was betrayed?"

"Yes, Miss Clarke told me about it. She didn't mention his name . . . Only that the man got off the treason trial and died in a plane crash a few years ago."

"Claude Beaumont, alias Captain Maurice Albert." Mother

spits the name as though it tastes like rotting meat. "And I'll bet she didn't tell you that if *she* had bothered to give evidence at that trial, he would have been convicted for sure?"

"No. But that can't be true. Surely—"

"Oh, I blame *her*, all right. For seducing our Jeannie in the first place into thinking it was okay to send a young, traumatized woman off to an almost certain death in France. Then not telling her we'd brought her daughter home. And finally for allowing her betrayer to walk out of his trial scot-free. And now she's selling *you* a pack of lies into the bargain!"

"I don't understand—how could it have been Miss Clarke's fault that Claude Beaumont got away with it? Surely it was the judge's fault?"

"Miss Clarke"—Mother exhales slowly—"had gathered more than sufficient evidence to prove the man was a double agent and that he had turned more than one hundred of the SOE agents over to the Nazis. But for a reason nobody understands, she didn't appear at the trial. This meant all the evidence she had gathered was inadmissible. Ask yourself, why would she have gone to all that bother to painstakingly interview dozens of people, trek around all the concentration camps of Europe to track down survivors and Nazi officers, and then not give evidence at the trial? More to the point, what's-his-name—oh yes, *Peter Berkley*—gave evidence that Beaumont was entirely trustworthy and that he had instructed Beaumont to maintain contact with the Germans. Well, after that, the trial collapsed."

"How do you even know all this?"

"*I was there!* At the trial," Mother hisses.

"You went to France?" Celia stares at her in utter shock. This is a woman for whom straying farther than the boundaries of Southwark constitutes a major expedition.

"This was my daughter's nemesis. I needed to see him pay for what he did to her. For the awful, agonizing end she must have suffered because of him." A tear leaks from one eye. "But she was denied even that."

Celia sits back and stares at Mother. Perhaps there *is* more to all of this than Miss Clarke has let on. Perhaps she shouldn't trust her, after all.

LATER, LYING IN bed, the conversation with Mother circulates around Celia's head. She trusted Miss Clarke. Jeannie trusted Miss Clarke. She appears to be a trustworthy person. And yet, it turns out, she wasn't. And what of this man who betrayed Jeannie? He had probably appeared trustworthy too. Why would Miss Clarke allow him to go free, if all she said about caring for her agents like her own children was true?

She thinks of Mother and Father. She's known *them* all her life and never knew what they really were either. Just as she thought she knew herself. The Celia she thought she was is an illusion, a facsimile. The real her, the essence of Celia, she holds hidden deep inside, not round and wholesome but rough edged, with pits and imperfections.

Then there's Septimus, as impenetrable as ever. His declaration of love. Can she believe him? But maybe tonight she saw a sliver of the real him. What do people ever know of each other? Perhaps it *is* better they know only a little, at the beginning. Peeling back all the layers is a risk. You just have to hope you like what you find beneath.

Chapter 28

Celia

Daphne is waiting for Celia outside the entrance to the beautiful circular building that forms the British Museum Library in Bloomsbury. As ever, Daphne is dressed head to foot in primary colors and attracting far too much attention for a Wednesday afternoon.

"Thank you so much for this, Daph. I really owe you," Celia says, kissing her friend's cheek.

"Listen, darling," Daphne says, flashing her freshly painted crimson nails at her friend, "you owe me plenty. A holiday in the Riviera, I should say. I had to lie through my teeth to beg an afternoon off. Dying relatives and everything. I just need to remember to be suitably somber tomorrow. Right, shall we go in?"

Celia hooks her arm through Daphne's. "Yes, let's. And I promise, I *shall* one day treat you to a holiday in the Riviera, just as soon as I've landed that job as PA to the director general of the BBC. And to cement the promise in the meantime, how about fish and chips after? I'm afraid that's as far as my H. J. Potts salary will stretch . . ."

Daphne grins. "That will do perfectly nicely," she says. "What excuse did you give for not being at work?"

"Oh, I just asked for the afternoon off. Mrs. Denton is very obliging."

Daphne groans. "You are so lucky. Now, do tell, what on earth is this mysterious errand all about?"

As they find their way to the Reading Room, Celia fills Daphne in on the surprising conversation with Mother and her warning that Miss Clarke wasn't to be trusted, as well as the possible thawing of relations between them. She finishes with the small matter of Septimus declaring his love.

"I am not forgiving you for *that*," Daphne says, tugging at Celia's arm. "Oh, Celia. How can you start going steady with a man working for the American government when I thought we were prioritizing saving the world?"

"I've not stopped, Daph," Celia insists. "For your information, I've been going to Pitman's every day after work this week typing out those leaflets for the Spies for Peace. D'you know, the boys managed to break into one of the bunkers? They have proper proof now . . . Anyway, you'd be surprised about Septimus. He isn't what you think he is."

"Look, Celia, this is serious. He could be a spy."

"Don't be daft."

"I'm not! Our government *and* the Americans hate the CND. They think we are all communist traitors. Does he ask you questions? Has he asked to come on marches?"

"Not really," Celia says slowly. She fingers the snake charm he gave her, dangling as it always does at her throat. Now she comes to think of it, he *has* asked her questions. About the Committee of 100 and the Spies for Peace. Oh God. What did she say? She tries to remember. Not much. But anyway, he was just showing an interest.

"What do you mean, *not really*?"

"I mean, apart from general chitchat. And he hasn't asked to come on marches."

Daphne frowns. "It still feels wrong."

"Daph, I really think you have Septimus wrong. He is just as against nuclear proliferation as we are. You simply need to get to know him better, then you'll see. But listen, today is all about Miss Clarke. I—" As they enter the enormous circular Reading Room, a chorus of shushing stops her midsentence.

They find their way to Newspapers and Periodicals and engage the help of a stern-faced librarian who turns out to be most helpful. While she searches in a back room for the newspapers Celia has asked her for, Celia tells Daphne why her mother warned her not to trust Miss Clarke.

"So," Celia explains, "I've decided to do a little research of my own before I next visit her. Forewarned is forearmed and all that."

The librarian comes back with a trolley loaded with newspapers dating from the end of the war running through to 1948. Celia grimaces at the task. It will take them hours, days even, to search all these.

"Never fear," Daphne whispers. "I've got a great method for this I learned at work when searching through documents. We need a few keywords or phrases, and then we simply scan the headlines of all the articles searching for them. I promise it won't be as bad as you think."

They set to work, splitting the tasks so that Celia searches for anything relating to Miss Muriel Clarke, and Daphne anything relating to the traitor, Claude Beaumont.

There are plenty of glowing references for Miss Clarke's work with the Secret Operations Executive, and after the war for her tireless searching for what happened to all of her missing agents. Miss Clarke, in order to carry out her duties, was made a squadron leader of the Women's Auxiliary Air Force when the SOE was disbanded, so she could continue her investigations. These went on for a long time, Miss Clarke spending many months in Germany, trailing around the concentration camps, interviewing former Nazis who ran them, gathering evidence of war crimes. Celia can only imagine what terrible things she must have learned. Despite what Mother told her, she can't help admiring the woman. Celia reads that not only did Miss Clarke trace what happened to every single one of the missing agents, but she was also instrumental in obtaining mentions in dispatches and medals for the agents, who would otherwise have undoubtedly sunk from collective memory and whose bravery and achievements in the most difficult of circumstances would have been forgotten.

So far, Miss Clarke seems to be everything she claimed to be. Perhaps Mother was wrong about her. So warped by her grief that she struck out and blamed the only link to Jeannie she had. That would be quite understandable.

"Let's call it a day," she whispers as her friend looks up, finger marking her place on the page of small print. "I'm starving and there's nothing here. Mother's clearly deluded."

"Wait, I think I've found something, look."

Celia leans over Daphne's shoulder to read. The article in the *Daily Mirror* is dated November 29, 1946:

Claude Beaumont, alias Capt. Maurice Albert, of the Secret Service is held as a Traitor

David Welk, Paris, Friday

A French pilot who worked for the British Secret Service during the war was arrested here today as a traitor to France and Britain. Claude Beaumont (36), acting as Capt. Albert, dropped British and French agents in France and then told the Gestapo where to find them. He was first arrested by Scotland Yard in Croydon in April this year and, after a trial in which he pleaded guilty, paid a heavy fine (£300) for smuggling platinum and gold worth £10,000 from London. He claimed that a member of the SOE was building a new underground organization and asked if he could help. He said it needed money, of which there was plenty in England but none in France. He was not expecting any personal gain from the transaction, other than being able to retain £100 of the funds. He was later deported once the fine had been paid. Beaumont has, since his arrest in Paris, been subjected to intensive questioning, as a result of which, it is said, he has confessed.

"Okay," Celia whispers, "but apart from the arrest and fine in London, we knew all of this. And Miss Clarke told me he smuggled drugs and gold after the war."

"True," Daphne agrees, "but now look at this." She moves the copy of the *Daily Mirror* to reveal a copy of the *London Evening Echo* of June 27, 1948. Daphne pushes the paper closer to Celia for her to read the Opinion essay about the trial and Claude Beaumont's acquittal. It finishes with:

This is a story of deception and rivalry between two of Britain's wartime secret agencies, the SIS and the SOE. At the center is the enigmatic figure of Claude Beaumont, the SOE's air operations officer in Occupied France who gave away vital information to the Gestapo, which directly cost many lives. He was acquitted in the French trial after the war for want of evidence from London, specifically from WAAF officer Miss Muriel Clarke, who spent months painstakingly gathering evidence against him. Miss Clarke was not, however, called as a witness.

The writer of the article then went on to speculate as to the reason:

It would be of no great surprise to me if the reason for the omission of Miss Clarke from this pantomime trial was because those in the great British establishment wished to avoid the extreme public embarrassment that bringing this woman to the stand may unearth for the British secret services. Miss Muriel Clarke occupied a position of great importance within the Secret Operations Executive. A position she should not have been given, for the simple fact that our Miss Clarke was herself a Romanian Jewish refugee.

Upon arrival in the country in 1937, she changed her name by deed poll to the English-sounding Miss Muriel Clarke but was not naturalized as a British subject until February 1944. As an alien at the time she was granted her pivotal role in the SOE, she should, by rights, have been interned, but instead she was handling matters of state of a top secret nature. Had this become known to the enemy at the time, imagine the bargaining position they might have obtained? Indeed, given the duplicitous situation of M. Beaumont, one has to wonder, exactly who knew what? Because the plot thickens. Top secret papers from an unspecified source also reveal that Miss Clarke went on a secret mission to Europe in the early days of the war. Nobody knew the reasons for this mission, but it has since come to light that it was a private one that involved paying a large sum of money to the Nazis.

It is this writer's belief that this awkward situation is the reason for the lack of appearance by Miss Clarke at the trial, and the astonishing acquittal of the traitor, M. Beaumont. She had, in her months of investigation and interviews, gathered more than sufficient evidence for his conviction. Unfortunately, of the other witnesses, that is, the Gestapo officers who ran M. Beaumont, none have survived execution following their own trials at Nuremburg, hence Miss Clarke's evidence was vital.

The appointment of M. Beaumont in the first place as an agent was highly controversial, given his long-term links and friendships with high-ranking Nazis. Not only that, but other members of the SOE also had similar highly questionable friendships, including Peter Berkley, who, incidentally, was called by the British to give support for the *acquittal* of M. Beaumont. Is it any wonder that the SOE was dismantled so soon after the end of the war? Those involved are very happy to talk only of its successes, but let's not bury the controversies and the failures. Many of our brave men and women lost their lives as a result of these. That we should never forget.

Celia sits back and stares at the newspaper, the print swimming before her eyes. She looks up at Daphne.

"My God. Mother *was* right. But I don't understand. Why did Miss Clarke seem so pleased to see me?" Celia thinks of her posh, affected Englishness. She had been so certain she was some sort of minor aristocrat. But it's all an act! The woman is a refugee, just like her own grandfather, the same as the rest of them. The only difference being, those like her grandfather are at least honest and up front about it. Why hide it? She shakes her head in disbelief. Then she remembers what Miss Clarke had said to her at the end of their last conversation, something about how you had to act a part to become it. *And trust me, Celia,* she recalls her saying, *I am the expert in that.*

Celia looks back at the newspaper. She squints and leans in, focusing on a headshot of a man slotted just next to the beginning of the article. The caption reads, *Claude Beaumont, "Capt. Albert," acquitted this afternoon at his trial in Paris for treason against France and Britain.* She peers closer. This was the man who betrayed her mother. The back of her neck prickles.

Then her blood runs cold.

"*Christ!*" she exclaims, and jumps in her seat.

"What is it?" Daphne asks, ignoring the round of angry shushing from those sitting close by. She stares at the photo.

"I'm not sure . . ." Celia pulls the paper closer. There it is. Despite the poor quality of the photo, she is certain she can see the line of a scar running from the center of the man's forehead diagonally down to just above his eye, slicing through his eyebrow. He looks younger, handsomer, but the photo was taken at least fourteen years ago. The likeness is there, all the same. "I *know* this man," she says in a low voice in Daphne's ear. "I swear this is Alfred Humphries, friend of Mrs. Denton and regular visitor to the bookshop!"

Daphne squints at the photo, then gapes at Celia. "It can't be! What would he be doing in London of all places? You must be mistaken."

"He has a scar exactly like that." Celia taps the photo. "He's not aged well, to be fair, but he carries echoes of someone who may once have been good-looking."

"I thought you said Claude Beaumont died in an airplane crash?"

"That's what Miss Clarke told me . . . But what if she was lying?" Celia looks at her watch. It's already past seven. "I understand if you've had enough. I need to keep going—see if I can find anything covering the airplane crash."

"Are you kidding? Just as it's getting interesting? We should stay until the library closes."

They go in search of articles from the autumn of 1954, the year she remembers Claude Beaumont was supposed to have died. It takes less than an hour. The article is short, unsentimental, and to the point.

November 23, 1954

News has been received of the crash two days ago of an Air Laos commercial plane, a twin-engine Beech 18, into thick rainforest near a long-disused airfield approximately seventy kilometers from Sayaboury, Laos. Early investigators on the scene reported that four bodies have been found among the wreckage, in addition to a quantity of gold bars being carried on board. The body of the pilot, however, a French citizen, Monsieur Claude Beaumont, has not yet been found, but it is believed he too died in the crash. The cause of the accident appears to be due to fuel starvation. Monsieur Beaumont was a controversial figure, having been an agent for the British during the war, aiding the French resistance effort. He was, however, tried for treason in June 1948, having been accused by the British of being a double agent and allegedly handing information to the Nazis. He was acquitted, but suspicion over his role in the capturing of various other agents during the war never left him. He was long separated from his wife and spent much of his time in the Far East as a pilot for Air Laos. The search for his body continues.

Celia and Daphne stare at each other. *A body was never found.*

Chapter 29

Septimus

If Septimus is honest with himself, Celia Duchesne is surplus to requirements. His reason for keeping her close—to avoid suspicion over his frequent visits to H. J. Potts—has worked. He has not noticed any tails for some time, which means his efforts with Celia are convincing. Further, his involving Shauna as an additional funnel of information has spread out the risk.

But the problem with honesty is he also has to face the fact that Celia is of far greater importance to him than as simply a convenient foil. The better he gets to know her, the more he wants. She is so young, so innocent, so vulnerable. All he wants to do is protect her. Keep her safe and make her happy. And besides, he thinks she has potential to be so much more, to him and to the cause they are both so passionate about.

His operation has grown, and he is busier than ever, keeping tabs on his recruits while continuing to ensure his own brief is fulfilled, making sure in among it all he doesn't let anything slip. It's enough to keep any man busy without the added complication of falling in love. Can the impervious Septimus really be in love? The only girl he thought he would ever love was Rosa. But that wasn't real. It was merely a childish infatuation.

Celia, though, is a drug he can't get enough of. And like any drug, it has messed with his equilibrium. His usual self-discipline has faltered. He can't sleep for thinking about her. It isn't about sex, which is definitely not on the cards with Celia, not yet, not this way. Perhaps it's *because* she is the forbidden fruit. Or perhaps it's because Celia is good and pure to the very core of her being. Whatever it is, he can't shake her out of his system.

Slightly problematic is her mission to find out about her mother and dragging him along to visit some retired old bird from the British secret service. He shouldn't have mentioned a possible link between Miss Clarke and the Big B. For someone who never allows himself to make a mistake, it was sloppy. But, then again, it's pretty unlikely they knew each other. And besides, thinking about her mother's history, perhaps intelligence is in Celia's blood?

At six, Septimus gives up on sleep and pulls on his tracksuit. An extra-long run will help. The way things are going, he *needs* a calm and clear head.

It has rained overnight, and it's still dark. The air outside is cool and damp. He allows the park to absorb him. The palest dawn light, the dripping trees, the smell of wet grass reminding him of those long-ago childhood mornings before he was sent to California to live with his mother's sister. He remembers summer days spent playing with Alexander and his sister, Rosa. Alexander, of course, hadn't wanted her there, but for Septimus, an only child who had always had an empty ache in his soul for a sibling, Rosa was perfection. To ten-year-old Septimus, thirteen-year-old Rosa was a goddess. No girl in all the world could ever match her beauty, her purity, or goodness. She was so kind to him, patient. He remembers the soaring feeling when something he said evoked a tinkle of laughter from her.

He'd ignored Alexander's grumbling and eye-rolling, always inviting her to accompany them into the forest. More often than not, she declined, but now and then she indulged them. The day

Septimus held her hand, helping her across the stepping stones in the fast-flowing river, then again as they scrambled down the steep sides of the ravine, was the day he became a man.

He lost Rosa, but he won't let Celia slip through his fingers too. But first he must deal with more pressing matters.

The job he was given in June—to direct attention onto Berlin—has been an overwhelming success. The entire summer, Kennedy, his foreign policy unit, and of course the American ambassador to Great Britain have been obsessed with Berlin, just as Septimus had been instructed to ensure. Now it's late September, and, with the midterm elections on the horizon in early November, Septimus can see how this could play in Kennedy's favor. The people want a strong president. One who will stand up to a Soviet Union agitating for war over Berlin, which Kennedy has predicted will break out before the end of the year. It is in everyone's interest that the American people retain the impression he is that man.

But there is a niggling worry. With all the attention on Berlin, America has barely given a passing thought to the island of Cuba, and Septimus has heard that ship after ship from the Soviet Union has arrived on the island largely unnoticed. Has this direction of American attention onto Berlin been a decoy?

Even the press reports of increased shipping traffic to the island from the Soviet Union seems to have failed to attract Kennedy's attention. The CIA, the Big B's old outfit, are confidently reporting that Soviet military equipment and personnel on Cuba are merely defensive. Septimus shakes his head as he runs. There is a sickening churning in his guts. Something inside tells him it's much more than that. But how could he be right and the entire US intelligence network be wrong? The CIA reported on September 19, just ten days ago, that they are confident there are only around four thousand defensive Soviet troops in Cuba, and that the Soviet presence is merely to assist their Cuban brethren in defending the island from what they perceive to be a possible threat of American invasion.

Unless . . . Unless Khrushchev is making supreme efforts to keep these shipments secret. And there could only be one reason for that. That the Soviet Union is putting *nuclear* weapons on Cuba, right on the doorstep of America. If so, it would either be a work of genius or idiocy, Septimus isn't entirely sure which. Idiocy, probably. And something inside tells him his hunch is more likely correct than not. The American threat of invasion of Cuba is real enough, and Khrushchev must be anxious to re-balance the nuclear threat between East and West. He must also be anxious to protect and spread the communist brotherhood around the world, without giving Chairman Mao of China any opportunity to seize leadership of this mission.

If it's true, Septimus thinks, the world feels a lot less safe than it did a couple of months ago. On the one hand, he can see why Khrushchev might have done it. The Soviet Union has had to put up with American Jupiter nuclear weapons on *its* doorstep, just over their borders in Turkey and Italy, with the capability of reaching Moscow and Leningrad. On top of that, there are the American Thor missiles aimed at the USSR from Britain. It's hardly surprising that Khrushchev will want to show the Americans how it feels to have nuclear weapons only ninety miles from its own coast. But if they find out, which surely will only be a matter of time now that they have resumed their U-2 reconnaissance flights over Cuba, then hell really could break loose.

Septimus wonders what America will do if they find nuclear weapons on the island. With elections looming, Kennedy can't risk his government looking any weaker than it's already reputed to be. Will they bomb the missile sites? Invade Cuba and seize them?

But Septimus knows something else, of which perhaps Khrushchev himself isn't yet aware. The trouble with the business of intelligence is that it isn't the *knowledge* itself that matters. It's who knows it, and what they do with it. Somewhere deep within the Soviet shadowy network of illegals is a mole, a double agent, who Septimus, for his sins, knows well. This mole has passed information to America. Information that, contrary to what America had previously thought, there *is* a gaping void between the American and Soviet nuclear capabilities. The balance of power they thought was there isn't. If the information about possible Soviet nuclear missiles on Cuba reaches the Americans, they are far more likely to invade quickly than not. And if they do, and if the Soviets retaliate, the result will *have* to be nuclear war.

The thought makes Septimus numb.

But what on earth can he do?

Nothing, he concludes, but watch and wait. And hope he has got it all wrong.

No wonder Septimus can't sleep.

Septimus thinks of Celia and Daphne and their protests and marches and desire to rid the world of nuclear weapons. Just as the mysterious Spies for Peace have predicted, London *is* likely to be the first target of the Soviets. Information gathered by Alfred Humphries has confirmed what Celia learned is true. The British government *is* preparing for war, building underground bunkers in the regions but keeping the population ignorant for fear of inducing panic. It has certainly induced panic in Alfred. Septimus knows from Fox-Andrews, too, that the British government also has plans to move priceless artworks out of London to save them from a nuclear attack. Never mind the people, so long as the art is safe.

Septimus eases down to a walk as he nears the park gates. He looks behind him at the expanse of green, then toward the yawning mouth of the gates and the traffic out on the main road beyond. He is quite alone. At the bench closest to the entrance, he stops and performs some stretching exercises. Leaning down to touch his toes, he reaches with one hand to feel beneath the seat of the bench. There, tucked under a slat, is the edge of a folded piece of paper. He grasps it with his finger and thumb, careful not to tear the thin sheet. Sliding it out, he slips it quickly into his shorts pocket. He performs a few more stretches, then leaves the dead drop, surreptitiously checking there are no watching eyes.

Back in his flat, he smooths out the wafer-thin sheets left the night before by Molly Barton—probably not her real name—who works as a secretary at the British Non-Ferrous Metals Research Association, gathering for Septimus all the latest developments in British nuclear weaponry for him to pass on to his Soviet bosses. The need for the nuclear capability gap to be closed is more urgent than ever before. There are other Mollys and Shaunas elsewhere in London and across the southeast, working diligently as lowly secretaries, quietly passing state secrets to Septimus. People like Alfred's *bit of skirt* (poor girl) working at the Admiralty Underwater Weapons Establishment whom nobody pays any attention to because they are so ordinary. And yet, here they are, taking extraordinary risks, usually for no personal gain other than being driven by the knowledge that what they are doing is fundamentally right.

Septimus reminds himself that this is why *he* is doing this, too, not only for his country, but for *all* of mankind. He thinks of his years of education in California. Not the school he went to, but the special training he received from his long-time mentor, Lena. She taught him not only the art of working in deep cover, but his morals and his politics. Of the need to defend a system that gives ordinary people a decent life, a good education, health, and plentiful food. He is doing all this not for the misnomer that is *freedom*—that fantasy, he has seen for himself, exists for no one—but for *fairness*. One day, he hopes, he will be able to go back to the Soviet Union, possibly as a hero, to live with the girl he has fallen in love with and experience the promised land, his utopia, the place he has been working for since the tender age of ten, for himself.

THE FOLLOWING WEEK, Septimus waits in weak autumn sunshine on a different bench in a different park. Sir Reginald Fox-Andrews arrives in a haze of cigar smoke and with a deep-throated, phlegmy cough. He stops in front of Septimus, tipping his hat with one hand, holding his cigar aloft in the other.

"Hullo, my man," he says in that affected, gruff voice that grates on Septimus's ears like nails down a blackboard. "Mind if I join?"

"Please. Be my guest." Septimus shifts to make room for Fox-Andrews's ample behind.

They sit for a moment and survey the scene. The curve of the duck pond, the trees, the flat expanse of grass. The sound of traffic on Horse Guards Road. Not a soul within listening distance. Not a soul with any idea that war and oblivion hang in the balance, their fate resting on the unstable judgments of a few egotistical men relying on incomplete and insufficient evidence of what may or may not be a fact in the world.

Fox-Andrews's breathing is labored. Undoubtedly on account of the back-to-back cigars and his vast, rotund belly, evidence of forty years of good living.

"I hear you want to tie the knot." Fox-Andrews gets straight to the point. Neither of them wants to sit here longer than they have to. "Who is she?"

"She's just an ordinary girl," Septimus responds, echoing Celia's words.

"Then why don't you just enjoy her company while you are here?"

"She's not that sort of girl."

"Then find one who is."

Septimus sighs. "I've done enough of that. This one's different. I want to keep her."

Fox-Andrews is silent. He takes a puff on his cigar. Narrows his eyes.

"What does she know?"

"Nothing. I swear, she is a total innocent in every sense of the word, and I intend to keep it that way. For now, at least. But I believe she is sympathetic. She's a member of CND and has, let's say, *leanings*. Give me time, and she will become part of our team."

"They won't like it, you know. If you marry her, it will limit future options for a more . . . fruitful match," he says.

"I know." Septimus keeps his voice calm and level. "But equally, it can be seen as an advantage. She will provide excellent cover, as well as the fact being married to her will make me a very happy man."

Fox-Andrews grunts. "Your happiness is hardly their concern."

"As you will know from past experience, unhappiness can cause problems too. People going astray, for example."

The man gives Septimus a sharp look. "And we all know how that will end." He pauses. "We've run some checks. She seems clean enough."

"Like I said, she is a complete innocent. She will remain one hundred percent uninvolved until the time is right. You have to take my word for that."

She *will* remain uninvolved for now, but Septimus feels it with growing certainty that he will be able to recruit her to the cause. Septimus is very used to bringing people into the fold, and abandoned, lonely, deep-thinking Celia is ripe for recruitment. As a couple, a *real* couple, they will be a force to be reckoned with.

"How will you manage it?"

"Trust me. I've had a lifetime of training. It won't be hard."

Fox-Andrews grunts again. He smokes some more, resting his elbow on the arm of the bench as he thinks.

"You're set on this?" He turns to look at Septimus, little gray eyes sharp beneath hooded lids.

Septimus nods. Fox-Andrews stares for a few minutes, then seems to make up his mind.

"All right. I'll put in a recommendation," he says briskly, "but I'm not making any promises."

"Right," Septimus concedes. He hardly, as ever, has a choice. His life was planned out for him a very long time ago by others; nobody consulted him. It is only of late that he has begun to think this in any way bothersome.

Choice, like freedom, he reminds himself, is an illusion.

Fox-Andrews heaves himself off the bench. "I'll be in touch," he says. Then, turning to face Septimus, he adds, "You are doing a great job, Nelson. You have a bright future. Don't screw it up."

"I won't, sir," Septimus says, never meaning it more. He stands to face Fox-Andrews, fixing him with a steady gaze. "I absolutely give you my word on that."

Chapter 30

Celia

Celia's night is punctuated by strange and vivid dreams, most involving Alfred Humphries's scarred face, lips curled up into a sneering smile, looming ominously over her. *I made sure your mother was caught*, he tells her in one of them, *and now I shall make sure you see an untimely end too. You are a bastard child and have no right to live* . . . She snaps awake again. Switches on her light. Her bedside clock tells her it's 3:30 A.M.

The room is too warm, the air still and silent as if a storm is about to break. It's a labor to breathe, as though there isn't enough oxygen in the room. Celia leaves her bed and goes to the window, pushing up the sash, letting in the cool, damp October night air. She has no idea what to make of everything. Could it be possible Miss Clarke and Alfred Humphries are in cahoots?

And what of Mrs. Denton? Celia thinks of her diminutive size, her tinkle of laughter, and her kindness to Celia. She must be innocent in all this. Could Humphries be a danger to them both? Or is he just a washed-up old crook? Or maybe this whole thing is just a product of her fevered imagination.

She gives up on sleep, wraps herself in her dressing gown, and goes downstairs, lights the stove, takes a half pint of milk from the refrigerator, and pours it into a pan. She spoons cocoa and sugar into a mug, and as she waits for the milk to simmer, Bartholomew wakes in his basket, stretching and arching his back. He winds his way toward her, chirruping a greeting as though her presence in the kitchen in the middle of the night is a pleasurable thing.

She pictures Mother's drawn face as she confronted her about the letter Celia had written to Miss Clarke. How she had apologized for everything that had happened, how she and Father had tried to do the right thing by her. She looked so beaten down, and there is a pulse of guilt that it was Celia's reaction to it all that has caused Mother this latest pain. She's already suffered so much, in silence, Celia could see. A wave of gratitude and love sweeps through her. Mother *had* kept her, even after Jeannie didn't come back. She had raised her in the only way she knew how, by keeping her safe and close. Because, Celia realizes with a dart of pain deep inside, she loves her. Mother loves her in a way that Celia, only now, as if viewing the world through a clearing fog, is coming to see.

The milk begins to simmer, and Celia switches off the gas. Bartholomew is mewing at the back door, and she opens it, the cat slinking off into the darkness, no doubt in search of a mouse or two. She carries the mug of cocoa back upstairs and sips it in bed, curling her hands around its warmth.

As soon as she can, she will tell Mother what she and Daphne found out in the library. Tell her about Septimus. Tell her she regrets doubting her. It's time to make amends with Mother and Father, she realizes, and a germ of an idea is forming as to just how she might go about doing so. They all need to learn to trust each other again.

A sense of peace settles inside now that her mind is made up.

She places her empty mug on the bedside table, switches off her light, and settles down to wait for the oblivion of sleep to take her.

LATER THAT MORNING, when Celia wakes at seven, Mother has already left for work, and she encounters Father alone in the kitchen.

"You're up early," she says, peering into his face. He looks gray with exhaustion, his hair tousled, eyes red-rimmed.

"I couldn't sleep," he says, lowering himself into a chair as though he has suddenly become an old man.

"You and me both. Here," she says, remembering her vow to make amends. "I'll make us some tea."

"In a minute, love . . . I know Maggie's spoken to you. But there's things I need to say too. Sit down, just for a moment."

She does as he asks.

He swallows, his Adam's apple moving in his throat. "I'm not good with words, Celia. You know that. But it doesn't mean I don't *feel*."

She nods, a fresh swell of tears forming behind her eyes. "I know, Father."

"Thing is"—he waves a hand helplessly toward her, then lets it drop onto the table—"I was wrong about a lot of things. I can't make it better with Jeannie, and I'll never forgive myself for that, but with you, there's still time . . ."

His voice falters, and Celia reaches across the table to take his hand.

"Actually, Father, I've had an idea. Not for now, but maybe soon. Something difficult, but I think which might help us all . . ."

AN HOUR LATER, stepping outside, she notices the temperature has markedly dropped, and Celia wraps her scarf tighter around her neck. It's only the seventeenth of October, but winter is already in the air. A brisk northerly wind blows fallen leaves in eddies around her feet. The only other person on the street is the postman, dropping the morning mail through letter boxes. He nods a greeting to Celia and goes on his way.

The door of Number 11 suddenly opens and Sam appears, bending to pick up the milk bottles left there earlier this morning by the milkman. He hasn't noticed Celia on the pavement, and she pauses a moment, taking in his floppy unbrushed hair, untied navy-blue dressing gown, bare chest, and red-striped pajama bottoms beneath. She ought to look away. It's too intimate, voyeuristic even, watching him in a state of undress. But she can't.

Bartholomew emerges from the house behind him, tail in the air, and Celia smiles. Not mouse-hunting after all, but somehow finding his way inside his second home. She hears him mew and Sam say, "All right, you cheeky ol' thing? I know what you want. Mother'll kill me, but I'm a soft touch, so here you go." He is crouching down, stroking the cat, then pushing down on the silver milk bottle top, pouring the creamy top of the milk into a saucer he places on the doorstep. Sam loves that cat with the same passion as she does. Her heart wilts as she watches him rub Mew's shining striped coat.

"All right, Sam?" she calls, hating to break the spell but knowing it would be worse if he caught her watching. She shrugs her handbag straps across her shoulder and steps closer to face him.

He jumps at the sound of her voice, peering round at her through his thick, disheveled hair.

"Celia!" He leaps to his feet, hugging his dressing gown around his naked torso, hastily tying the cord, grinning from ear to ear. "'Scuse my state of undress, but it's a bit early. I was on lates last night."

"Don't know how you cope with shift work, all those different sleep hours."

Sam shrugs cheerfully. "Y'get used to it, I suppose, and it pays the bills, eh?"

"I'll take your word for it . . ."

Sam is still smiling, eyes glistening. He turns to look back at Bartholomew, crouched low, eyes closed in bliss as he laps at the cream, his front paws planted on either side of the saucer. "Hope you don't mind. He waits for me every morning," Sam says. "Gives me the giant pleading eyes, like you never feed the poor creature."

Celia laughs. "Don't you believe him. You're spoiling him rotten. He'll never want to come home again."

"Oh, he will." Sam gives her a long look, pulling her gaze into his.

"How have you been?" Celia asks as they stand awkwardly facing each other. "Not seen you around in a while." She wonders if he's still with the girl with the freckles and has a sudden urge to reach out and touch him. She shoves her hands into her pockets.

"Oh." He shrugs. "You know."

"Same as?"

"Same as."

"How's . . . Lindy, is it? Or Mindy? Sorry. I forget . . ."

"It's Ginny."

"Of course. Ginny."

"Ah, well." He scratches his head. Wrinkles his nose. "It didn't really work out."

"Oh no. I'm sorry."

"Actually, I'd been thinking of paying you a visit, Celia."

"Oh, really?"

"I've some news. I'm moving to Yorkshire."

"*Yorkshire?*" There's a plummeting in her belly. "Why? But that's so far away!"

Sam laughs. "It's not Mongolia. It's a promotion. The gas board is offering me a management position. It was too good an opportunity to turn down."

"But . . . don't they have gas board managers in the North of England? Why do they have to steal you?"

"Congratulations are normally in order when someone gets a promotion." Sam gives her a sideways look.

"Sorry. Congratulations."

"And yes, of course they do. But the job was advertised. I thought, why the heck not, and applied on a whim. Never expected to get it, but I did. I fancy a new adventure. Will you miss me?"

"Of course I will, you idiot." She swallows. "So will Bartholomew." She really would. They both look down at the cat. "When are you leaving?"

"Not till January. You'll have to put up with me till then."

"You'd better get a haircut before you go."

He laughs and tugs at his unruly hair. "You're probably right."

Celia shifts. "Look, I'd better get going to work . . ."

"Yeah, and I'd better get washed before breakfast. See you later—let's go for a drink soon."

She nods as he closes the door behind him, leaving Celia alone with Bartholomew. How can Sam be leaving Southwark, and she still be here? This isn't how it's supposed to go. It's impossible to imagine living at Copperfield Street without him. She shakes her head and bends to greet Bartholomew. He chirrups and purrs loudly as she rubs his face.

"All right, old boy? I've a feeling it's going to be a busy day."

THERE ARE THREE boxes of books on the doorstep of H. J. Potts when Celia arrives. She spends the first hour of the day sorting through them. At every sound outside she looks up, wondering if Alfred Humphries will appear, either from the flat or at the shop door. Without Mrs. Denton, and in the absence of any customers, she's all alone, and this is suddenly a terrifying prospect. But that's ridiculous. How many times in the past has she been alone when that man has come in? True, he *has* made her feel uncomfortable, but he's never *done* anything. If she were to scream, Mrs. D would be bound to hear her from the flat.

But Mr. Humphries doesn't appear. When Mrs. Denton eventually comes down, Celia offers to cart the boxes to the nearby home for stray cats, which holds charity sales every now and then. Mrs. Denton agrees this would be best, as all the books were deemed worthless.

As Celia walks to and from the cat home, she wonders how best to quiz her employer about Mr. Humphries. She considers asking her outright or telling her what she read in the papers, but if she *has* gotten the wrong end of the stick, she'll look a right fool. Mrs. D might react angrily. Celia could unwittingly spoil their excellent relationship. She needs this job just a little longer. Her time at Pitman's will be drawing to a close in only a few weeks, and she needs to hang on to it at least until then.

She suddenly remembers the odd exchange she witnessed between Mrs. Denton and Mr. Humphries when she was hidden behind the bookshelves. How Mrs. Denton had offered to keep something safe for Mr. Humphries. She had said something about not going anywhere, *at least until Christmas*. At the time, Celia had thought that Mrs. Denton was being her usual kind self, helping him out without really knowing what sort of person he is. But what if she is somehow *in league* with him? He's a criminal with convictions for drug trafficking and smuggling. If Mrs. D is really in love with him, perhaps she is knowingly covering up for him. Celia feels a wave of nausea. It would explain the seemingly plentiful supply of money, despite the lack of customers in the shop. And besides, what if some of those browsers who never buy anything are surreptitiously slipping packets of drugs to Mrs. Denton and receiving envelopes of money in return?

She stops in her tracks.

Is she in the middle of a crime racket? Should she go to the police station at Charing Cross? They'd laugh at her. She doesn't have evidence of anything *wrong*. Just a grainy photograph and an article from a newspaper about a man who is meant to be dead, and the rest exists only in her head. The most likely outcome would be her landing in the loony bin. Perhaps Mother is right. Reading is giving her an overactive imagination.

She exhales and continues her walk back to the shop, deciding to talk it over with Daphne.

"Quiet for a Wednesday, isn't it?" Celia says, when she's back.

"Is it? Yes, I suppose so. Off to see your beau tonight, are you?" Mrs. D asks with a wink. She opens the till, surveys its contents.

"Oh, no. Not this evening."

"Keeping Septimus dangling, eh?"

"Not at all." Celia sees her chance. "And what about you and Mr. Humphries?"

Mrs. D looks momentarily startled at the mention of his name, but she covers it with a laugh.

"I mean, how well do you really know him, Mrs. Denton?"

"As I said before, he's an old pal of mine. From way back."

"From your San Francisco days?"

"Exactly!"

"Quite a coincidence that not one but *two* old friends from San Francisco ended up right here in London with you, no?"

Mrs. Denton gives her a long look. "Mr. Humphries doesn't live in London, as it happens. He lives in Dorset—Weymouth—but his heart is in London. He enjoys culture, just as I do, and there isn't much of it down there. So I provide him with a base, a place he can keep a few bits and pieces, and he can stay over if he so chooses. In the spare room, obviously."

Celia feels her face flush hot. She can't hold Mrs. Denton's gaze. "I didn't mean to . . ."

"Didn't mean to what, exactly, Celia?"

Celia stares at her shoes.

"Pry?"

"No!"

"Good, because whom I choose to entertain in my own home is really nobody's business but my own."

Celia looks up at Mrs. Denton. The woman is glaring at her, her jaw set hard. Celia's insides squirm. "You are quite right. I'm truly sorry. I just, well, I suppose I thought we were friends, and I didn't want to see you taken advantage of, or anything. But it was silly of me—of course it's none of my business."

There is a beat of silence.

"Please forgive me, Mrs. Denton."

Her employer's expression softens. She sighs. "I know you mean well, Celia, but I can look after myself, I assure you. Mr. Humphries leads rather a lonely existence, I'm afraid, down there on the coast. Some dull job working for the Admiralty, I believe. I feel sorry for him, that's all. His visits to London are a welcome break to the otherwise unbroken tedium of his life."

Celia studies her face. She looks so kindly, so genuine. How could Celia possibly think this poor woman is in league with a criminal? No, Mr. Humphries is taking advantage of Mrs. Denton's sweet and generous nature. Some women do seem to attract the worst sort of men, and perhaps Mrs. Denton is one of them, when she thinks about the ex-husband too. But Celia can't save her if she isn't prepared to save herself.

"Oh . . . Yes, I'm sure he must look forward to his visits." She doesn't wish to offend her any further.

"Now," Mrs. Denton says, turning away, "I really must get on with some paperwork." She turns the handle to the flat, but it's locked. "Damn, I've left my keys inside!" She flicks a smile at Celia and takes the spare keys from the hook where they have lived ever since Celia has worked at the shop, beneath the counter. "I'll pop them back later. Do feel free to shut the shop if it's quiet and you want to get off early tonight. All right, dear?"

"Thank you, I will."

As soon as Mrs. D is gone, Celia lets out a groan and collapses onto the counter, her head cradled in her arms. How wrong could she be? How could she embarrass Mrs. Denton like that?

The remainder of the afternoon crawls slowly by, the conversation with Mrs. D circulating round and round her head. Everything she said made sense. Mr. Humphries being bored and lonely down there on the South Coast. But if Humphries *is* Beaumont, she is sure he has duped Mrs. D, leading her to believe he is someone he is not. He has duped enough people before. Celia feels a stab of pity for her. Imagine finding out that the person you thought was interested in you is simply using you for his own nefarious purposes.

And suddenly she longs to be away from the shop. She checks her watch. Four forty. Nobody will come in now. She's in no hurry to go home. She can go to Pitman's for an hour and type up another few leaflets for the cause.

She deadbolts the door, top and bottom, tucks the keys into her handbag, and pulls on her gloves. Outside, the brisk breeze has blown itself into a bitter northeast wind. Gun-metal clouds race thick and low over the city. October is too early for snow, but Celia senses it coming, stinging the inside of her nostrils, needling the exposed skin on her face and hands.

If Celia is going to bring Alfred Humphries down—assuming he is Claude Beaumont—she is going to need hard evidence to prove he is one and the same man. And where on earth, she wonders, will she be able to find that?

Chapter 31

Celia

Celia stands outside H. J. Potts and hesitates. Turn right and she will go to Pitman's for leaflet typing, left and she can head to the American embassy unannounced and ask to see Septimus. Something she has never done before. And with no guarantee that he will be free to see her. But these are exceptional circumstances and that calls for exceptional action.

Celia turns left. She walks fast, descending the busy stairs of the tube station, dodging the slow walkers, the tourists, and the loitering schoolkids. A train is standing on the platform, and she elbows her way through into a full carriage, the closing doors squeezing her in tight against the solid back of a fellow passenger. She has a couple of hours before she will need to head back to Copperfield Street.

The tube lurches to a halt at Green Park. Celia walks briskly to the magnificent embassy building in Grosvenor Square, a rush of pride as she looks up at the rows of lighted windows, wondering which Septimus is working behind.

After several wasted minutes of being passed through a security check—"Apologies for the wait, ma'am, but we can't be too careful these days with the protests"—Celia is shown to an empty waiting room while a receptionist calls up to Septimus's office. *He has his own office?* The waiting lasts forever. She picks up a discarded newspaper from the seat beside her. *Tuesday,*

October 16, 1962: Drama as Siamese Twins Die. She puts it down again. How long can it possibly take to get hold of Septimus?

Finally, he arrives, punching his way through a set of double doors, the color high in his cheeks, lips tight with worry.

"Celia? Good God, whatever has happened? Are you okay?" His fingers grip her upper arms, eyes imploring.

"I'm fine! I'm sorry, Septimus, I didn't mean to scare you."

He stares at her. "Nothing is wrong?"

"No! Nothing terrible, I promise."

He exhales. "Thank God for that." He sinks down onto a chair beside her.

She notices he is breathing hard, as though he has been running. His cheeks are pinched, and the flesh beneath his eyes is puffed and purple.

"Septimus, are you okay? You look so tired. I've not seen you for days . . ."

"I'm sorry, Celia. We're working such long hours, and I'm not sleeping well. Things are pretty stressful at work."

"Oh, Septimus." She touches his cheek with her fingertips. "I would never normally dare come here, but . . . there is something I need to talk to you about—it really can't wait—is there any chance you could slip out for a bit?"

"Is it really that important, Celia? There's a lot going on down here right now," he says quietly, moving closer to her ear. "But if you need me to, of course I'll come."

She bites her lip. "It really is. Thank you. And besides, what with you being so busy . . . I've missed you, Septimus."

His expression softens. "And I you."

They get up and leave the building, Septimus walking decisively, her arm tucked into his. He leads her onto North Audley

Street and into a café, asking a bemused-looking waitress for a quick order.

"So, what's this all about?" Septimus asks.

"I wanted to ask you how well you *really* know Alfred Humphries."

"What?" Septimus wrinkles his brow in confusion. "You came all the way here to ask me about *Humphries*?" He shakes his head and puffs out his cheeks. "Do you have any idea what's going on right now?"

"No, I—"

"Of course you don't." He says it like it's her fault.

"How could I if you haven't told me!"

"No. And I can't, for obvious reasons." There is an awkward silence. Then a little more kindly: "Not well. I don't like the way he looks at you. Why the sudden interest in Humphries?"

"The thing is—" Celia speaks in a rush. She needs to make him understand why she came. Once he knows, he'll forgive her. "I don't think his name is Alfred Humphries at all. I think he is Claude Beaumont, a double agent who worked for the British secret services during the war, the SOE, like my mother, like your ambassador worked for the American equivalent . . . But Beaumont was also working for the Nazis. He was the one who betrayed my mother. It's *his* fault she is dead. And now he is right here, in London, pretending to be Alfred Humphries."

Septimus snorts. He stares at Celia as though she's sprouted horns and a forked tongue. "This is madness, Celia." He taps his fingertips on the table, glancing round the room for the waitress. He catches her eye, and she nods. Moments later she comes over with the tray, unloading the coffee, pot of tea, milk and sugar, apologizing for keeping Septimus waiting. Once she is gone, he leans across the table, speaking in an exaggerated whisper. "How on earth could you have dreamed up such nonsense? What could make you think they are the same person? And even if they were, what would he be doing here, in London, where he would presumably be a wanted man?" Septimus's voice is hard. So different to his usual light sweetness.

"I haven't dreamed it up." She pours a cup of weak tea. She is messing this all up. Making Septimus angry with her. "I found a picture of Claude Beaumont in an old newspaper, and honestly, the likeness is there," she tries. "He even has the same scar across his forehead."

Septimus is staring at her in astonishment. "Is that it? You have based your theory on an old photograph that must have been taken years ago?"

He's right. Now that she's saying it out loud, it sounds preposterous. The image was poor. Perhaps it wasn't a scar in the picture, merely a mark that happened to be in the same place as Mr. Humphries's scar.

"I thought you were smart, Celia," he continues. "Right now, you are sounding crazy. And anyway, didn't you tell me the traitor was dead?"

"I did tell you that. And he was supposed to be dead, but, Septimus, there is more. I read the article about the plane crash he was involved in. It said no *actual* body was found. He was the pilot, and the other passengers' bodies were all found, just not his. And then a man who bears more than a passing resemblance to him shows up years later in London. Don't you think that's weird?" Celia leans back and takes another sip of tea.

Septimus shakes his head. "You must have spent hours researching all this. Where did the plane come down?"

"In Laos."

"Right. In the middle of the rainforest?"

She nods.

"Don't you think there might be another explanation that this man's body wasn't found? Other than that, somehow, he miraculously survived the crash that killed everyone else, found his way out of the jungle, all the way to California, where he met Mrs. D, followed her to London, and persuaded her to buy the very bookshop the daughter of the woman he betrayed works in?"

Celia is silent. Wretched. She is such a fool. What on earth was she thinking, coming here? Septimus seems off, but it's no surprise, her showing up at his workplace unannounced. He clearly thought something terrible had happened, and now she has taken him away from some important matters of state on a silly suspicion that likely has no basis. If only she could wind back the clock. Turn right, not left. At this moment, she could be at Pitman's honing her typing skills, doing something for the good of the nation, not leading Septimus to think she is deranged.

"I'm sorry. You're right. I'm being silly."

"I think so." Septimus is red-cheeked and bristling with anger.

"I'm so sorry, Septimus. I took you from your work, and I had no right . . ."

"Ah, Celia." He snatches her hand, gives it a tight squeeze. "It's okay. You've been through a lot, learning all that stuff about your mother. I guess it's no surprise your imagination is working overtime."

"Will you forgive me?"

He smiles. "Of course. Always." He lifts her hand and kisses it. The tension eases, and the old Septimus is back.

"Look, I really have to go." Septimus checks his watch. "There is some awful *real* drama brewing over the island of Cuba."

He lowers his voice, leans closer to her. "The Americans have found evidence that the Soviets have nuclear weapons there. The president was informed this morning. I think they will invade Cuba . . . This really *could* be nuclear war."

"Oh, Septimus . . . *No?*" Celia's guts contract.

"Yes. Really. It means I can't come and meet your Miss Clarke this weekend. I'm sorry, but I'm going to be working crazy hours for the foreseeable. I'll try and snatch some time with you when I can."

"Of course. Should we . . . should we be scared?"

He looks grave. "I think so, yes."

She lets her face sink into her hands. "And here I am whittling on about the most ridiculous nonsense, and you . . . you are dealing with *this*."

Septimus laughs. "It's okay. Really." He leans across the table and kisses her on the lips. "But I must go." He removes a pound note from his wallet and puts it on the table. "Ask for the bill, will you?"

"Of course. And, Septimus, I need to repair things with Mother and Father. When relations are better between us, I would love you to meet them. I've not told them about you. But I will. I think they'll like you."

"I'd like that, Celia. Let's hope there is a world left for it to be possible."

"You'd better go and save it, then."

He gives her a weak smile. "If only I had the power. Still, I'll do my best."

"Bye, Septimus."

She watches him leave, weaving his way through the tables and out into the night.

LATER, BACK IN Copperfield Street, with Father out working at the restaurant, Celia and Mother are alone together.

"I've got rather used to the television," Mother confesses as they clear up the supper things. "It's good company when you and André are both out in the evenings."

They fall, without speaking, into their natural routine, Celia washing up, Mother drying and putting away. She thinks back to her conversation with Septimus and how she would like to introduce him to her parents, but even as she thinks the thought, she knows the time is not yet right. It is far too early. The thaw has only just begun, and the most delicate shoots of trust have sprung up between them. She can't risk trampling on them yet. Instead, she wonders if she should mention her investigations into Miss Clarke and Claude Beaumont. How she thought he could be the same person as the man who visits Mrs. Denton in the bookshop. But she doesn't want to say anything until she is sure and decides to wait until she has seen Miss Clarke, as they have already arranged, on Sunday, and has a chance to quiz her.

No, right now she needs to focus on rebuilding their relationship, on getting Mother to open up. "Mother, may I ask you something?"

"'Course."

"Why didn't you have more children," Celia asks, "after Jeannie?"

Mother sighs. "Truth is, I'm not good at it, mothering. I'm not a natural, not like other women. My own mother, what, with nine kids, she was worn to shreds. My father was an invalid after the Great War. Never earned another penny, so it was down to my mother. She had three jobs, waiting tables.

Breakfast, lunchtime, and evening, plus all the cooking, cleaning, caring for Father—it was down to her. She was permanently exhausted. We kids had to pull our weight. As soon as we were old enough, we had to go out and earn money too. But 'cause I was the eldest, I had to look after the younger kids. I loathed it. I promised myself, if I ever had children, I'd stop at one. That way, the eldest would never have to look after their siblings."

"Go on," Celia whispers, and hands Mother the clean oven tray. The clock ticks behind them. Celia picks up a dirty saucepan and dips it into the washing-up water.

"We were dirt poor. My mother could barely afford the rent. As I've told you, we were often thrown out on the street with all our things." She smiles a sad smile. "But the neighbors took us in until we were back on our feet. We did the same for them. We looked out for one another, you know? Then along came André, and I was married at eighteen. He felt like a way out. Back then, a chef, a foreigner, made him exotic, wonderful. But I was so inexperienced. He was the first and only man I ever knew in *that* way. Then, of course, I fell pregnant almost immediately and along came Jeannie. I was smitten. But André understood what kind of life I wanted for her, so we stopped at one. I suppose, in truth, he would have loved a son, but he never said. He poured all his love into Jeannie. Taught her French, taught her to swim, to ride a bike, take care of herself. But then, when she got herself into trouble . . ."

Mother gives Celia a sad smile as she hands over the saucepan. "But we've been through all that. You know," she says, "Celia was the name Jeannie gave you, just after you were born. She would have been so happy to know that's the name I gave you when I brought you home."

Jeannie named me. She stops cleaning the plate she is holding and stares at Mother for a long moment, feeling the prick of tears once more at the backs of her eyes.

They finish the last of the washing up in silence. But it is a companionable one, so unlike the tense, prickling silence that has existed in the house since the Revelation.

"Shall we go and watch a little television now?" Mother says, laying the wet tea towel over the range to dry.

"Yes, why not," Celia agrees.

Outside in the street, the temperature is dropping. The cold slips through the thin panes of glass in the sitting room bay window, making Celia shiver.

On Granada TV, a music program is playing.

"Let's not watch the news," Mother says, peering at the screen. "It's too depressing, with all that talk of war and nuclear threats. This will be much cheerier."

Celia remembers what Septimus had said, how worried he had been. The helplessness of it all is overwhelming. The demonstrations, the sit-ins, the search for the truth about the British government's plans—in the end they are meaningless. What can any of them do against the might and madness of the Soviet Union and the Americans?

"I think you're right," Celia agrees. "Watching it will only be upsetting."

They settle themselves on the sofa. The announcer tells them a new band, the Beatles, will be playing on television for the very first time. "Now watch these four young men," he says. "They are on the up, and I have a hunch we'll be seeing a great deal more of them!" Mother and Celia watch as they sing their own song, "Love Me Do," followed by a cover of "Some Other Guy." Celia finds herself nodding along to the music and tapping her feet.

310 ~ Louise Fein

Mother watches the band in open-mouthed astonishment.

"What is the world coming to?" she says, shaking her head. "What a load of old rubbish this is. I have a hunch we *won't* see this lot again. Perhaps we should have watched the news after all . . ."

"Oh no, leave it," Celia says. "I think they are rather good."

The telephone rings shrill and sudden in the hallway. Celia steps out of the room to answer it.

"We need to up our efforts." Daphne's voice is urgent down the line. "It seems the Soviets have put nuclear weapons on Cuba, and the Americans are likely to retaliate. We are starting a round-the-clock vigil outside the American embassy. Are you in, Celia?"

Chapter 32

Celia

It's Sunday, the twenty-first of October, and Celia finds herself, as arranged, back outside Miss Clarke's flat in Chelsea. She almost didn't come. She should be with Daphne, begging for a future, waving her banner for peace, the trajectory of which can still be altered, rather than being concerned with the past, which cannot. But she can't help herself, her burning desire to know why Miss Clarke never passed on her grandmother's news about her own adoption, and why Miss Clarke didn't give evidence at the trial of Claude Beaumont. What does she know of what really happened to him afterward? Celia can invent theories, and the woman might not be trusted, but Celia needs to pose the question to her face and see her reaction.

Nerves flutter in her belly as she hears a buzz and a click and then the front door releases. She shuts the door behind her, taking in the smell of wood polish, the shined marble floor, the elegant hall table with its cut crystal vase of fresh flowers, and climbs the stairs.

Miss Clarke flings open the door to her flat with a flourish. "Celia, my dear, it *is* good of you to visit again." She leads Celia into the pristine sitting room, where a fire burns cheerfully in the grate. "What can I get you?" Celia opens her mouth to say tea, but before she has a chance, Miss Clarke says, "White wine, claret, or gin? It is after midday, so we are quite permitted."

"Oh, well, a white wine would be nice then, thank you."

While the woman disappears into the kitchen, Celia walks over to the French doors and looks out over the Juliette balcony. In the gardens, the last of the dying leaves cling to twigs and branches, reaching out like skeletal fingers beneath the press of a low, heavy sky.

Miss Clarke returns and places on the table two wine glasses and a bowl of salted peanuts. She settles herself into the same armchair she sat in the last time Celia was here, lifts her wine glass in a toast, and says, "Chin-chin."

"Well. Isn't this nice?"

Celia smiles and lifts her glass. The wine is smooth and cool.

"Your timing is excellent, dear Celia," she says. "After several weeks of searching, I've found the most perfect cottage in Winchelsea. Once the sale has gone through, and I've spruced it up a bit, I'll be moving in, hopefully early in the New Year. I rather fancy living by the sea. But I *shall* keep this flat. It will be useful to have a London base, even though I'll be spending most of my time in East Sussex."

Celia thinks of the crisis over Cuba and wonders if she, too, might be safer on the South Coast, and whether there is any chance she could persuade her parents to move. "How nice for you to be getting out of London." She swallows another mouthful of wine, considering how to steer the conversation toward what she really wants to ask.

Miss Clarke cocks one elegant eyebrow. "Now, my dear, you wrote and asked to see me again, so, how can I help you?"

Celia puts her glass down and takes a deep breath.

"My grandmother told me that after she adopted me, she specifically asked you to pass a message to my mother, telling her the news. But you held the information back. Why?"

Miss Clarke sighs. Places her glass on the table and threads her long fingers through each other, flexing her knuckles. "Oh, my dear. How to explain such a thing. You see, your mother was working in conditions of extreme stress and constant danger in Nazi-occupied Paris. I planned, of course, to tell her once she was safely home. But I couldn't risk sending such news to her at that time. She needed to keep her head. I was doing it partly for her own protection, and partly because she was there for reasons greater than any single individual interest. I know that is difficult to understand, and you may think a little cruel. But it's the truth."

"So you think, then, that acting for the greater good of freedom, for your country, should come above personal interests, Miss Clarke?"

"That's it in a nutshell."

"In that case, why did *you* risk going into Nazi-occupied territory to pay them a vast sum of money? Was that for personal gain, or the good of your nation? Indeed, which nation, Britain or Romania?"

Miss Clarke's eyes widen.

"I read some old newspaper reports . . ." Celia continues as Miss Clarke remains silent. "I found an article that talked about you and asked some interesting questions. How you weren't even English and were a refugee. How you shouldn't have been working for the SOE at all and that was an embarrassment to the powers that be, and *that* was why you didn't give evidence at Beaumont's trial."

Miss Clarke lets out a low whistle. "Well, my dear, that *is* good work. It would have taken some doing to find *that* article. In fact, it made it into just that one obscure newspaper, thanks to one of my detractors—there were several—tipping off a journalist, but after some rapid phone calls to editors by, as you call them, the powers that be, it was not permitted to be repeated in any other newspaper."

She looks Celia directly in the eye. "I'm sorry I didn't pass that message on to your mother. But the truth of it is, it wouldn't have made any difference as to her safe return. Your mother put her trust in a traitor, and that is the reason for her capture. As for me, yes, I was a refugee, and yes, many people, despite the fact I was willing to do anything to help this country fight the Nazis, did not want me to gain a right to be here. Yes, I did pay an unscrupulous bastard"—Celia winces at the word—"to rescue my cousin from certain death and bring him here. But, I ask you, which person, given the chance, would not do anything to save a loved one?"

Celia shakes her head. She does have a point.

"As for the *trial*, well. The matter is complicated, but I would have done my duty for my country and given evidence against that hateful man if it had been up to me. Claude Beaumont was *directly* responsible for so many agents' deaths, including your mother's. He gave information for their capture often the moment they landed in France, before they had even had the chance to say *bonjour*. But I was prevented from giving evidence. I can only hazard guesses as to why. We are never given reasons for these things. 'Ours is not to reason why, ours is but to do or die,' to misquote Lord Tennyson." She sighs. "In truth, it is probably to protect the reputation of someone higher up the ranks. Sometimes that is worth sacrificing others for." She turns and looks out the window at the darkening sky.

Standing suddenly, she says, "Actually, I have something for you. I found it when I was packing up my things for the move." She disappears for a few moments, returning with a battered rectangular leather briefcase. She holds it out for Celia to take.

"It belonged to your mother," she says, and that velvet tone to her voice is back. "And I think it only right you should have it."

Celia takes the handle, a lump forming in her throat.

Something that belonged to her mother. Now it will be hers.

The case is surprisingly heavy. Celia hefts it onto her lap and runs her fingers across it. All those years ago, her mother touched the very same case, in very different circumstances. If only Celia could have known her. Loss snatches at her insides like the pulse of physical pain.

"Open it." Miss Clarke's voice cuts through Celia's jumbled thoughts. She perches on the edge of her seat to watch.

Celia opens the catches with trembling fingers. Inside is a radio set. She stares at it, at the flat black surface of the set, at the coiled red and brown wires, at the knobs: fix key, aerial matching, and anode tuning, waveband, meter selector, grid tuning, volume. At the headphone ports and the battery/mains plug sockets. Her pulse quickens as she visualizes her mother, that bright-eyed young woman from the photographs, tuning this very set, headphones pressed to her ears, tapping out Morse code messages with heart-thudding urgency, while Nazi soldiers hunted her down. Closing in on her as she transmitted vital secrets to London. What a woman she must have been.

"Was it really hers?" Celia asks finally, looking into Miss Clarke's cool, steady eyes. "I mean, how do you know that?"

"The Nazis, apart from being vile and brutal, also happened to be great record keepers. This was seized in the winter of 1943 during a raid on a Paris safe house when a number of SOE agents, your mother included, were rounded up. Transmitting messages via short band radio waves is not silent—there's the static and the beeps of the Morse code as the agent taps out the encrypted messages. Similar methods of transmission are still used today. The Nazis constantly policed radio waves for clandestine messages, and Jeannie had been heard sending an urgent message through to London from the attic of the safe house."

They both stare at the radio on Celia's lap.

"The Nazis used this set," Miss Clarke goes on, "impersonating your mother, to send messages to London out of Gestapo headquarters on Avenue Foche, Paris, while Jeannie herself was locked up in Karlsruhe prison. But your mother was strong. She never gave away a single secret, and I know that for a fact. I interviewed the men responsible for extracting information from her. But, at the time, the Germans fooled us into thinking it was her we were communicating with. I'm ashamed to say, despite warning signals, we continued to believe it was your mother, not the Germans, we were corresponding with for a year."

"A *year*?" Celia stares down at the set, now seeing the pale, perfectly manicured fingers of a sly Nazi on the knobs, in place of her mother's. "How on earth did they get away with it?"

Miss Clarke inhales deeply.

"It was certainly not our finest hour. The Gestapo called it the English Game. Some of the girls in Signals *did* have their suspicions, including me. But Arthur Royston, the head of the French section, refused to believe it. He was determined to make the SOE a success, partly because he so desperately wanted to help free France, but partly to push back against what the other agencies thought of us."

"Other agencies?"

"MI5, MI6, et cetera . . . They thought we were amateurs, wanted us disbanded." Miss Clarke takes out her cigarette case, offers one to Celia. She declines like last time, and Miss Clarke lights her own cigarette.

"In late summer and autumn of 1943," Miss Clarke continues, "some of the Signals Room staff began to raise concerns about missing or incorrect security codes. They were worried that many of the circuits operating both in France and the Netherlands were blown. But Royston refused to believe such a catastrophic breach could have happened. He decided that agents were simply being sloppy. When concerns were raised about your mother's messages, he instructed the Signals team to send back a message telling her not to forget to use her double security, which had been missing from her messages."

"What happened?"

"The operator sent the message as requested, and Jeannette's reply came back apologizing and explaining that she had forgotten what these were." Miss Clarke hangs her head. "Of course, we should have known better. We played right into the Gestapo's hands and sent back a message informing them what they needed to do to pass the security checks. After that, all her messages came in perfect. The Gestapo were delighted with us, of course."

"But why did you go along with it, if you thought something was wrong?"

"Ah." Miss Clarke shifts in her seat. "We, the Signals Room girls and I, were all women, for a start. That is a disadvantage when it comes to being listened to. Secondly . . . well, as you now know, my own position as an alien was tenuous. I desperately wanted to be naturalized. I needed Arthur Royston's support. He was one of the few to speak up for me. My naturalization came through in 1944. If I had my time again . . . Anyway, the fact was, by then, your mother had been captured, so what we did and didn't believe wouldn't have helped her much, but it may have helped many, many others." Her expression is grim.

Celia shuts the lid to the radio, unsure whether she really wants to keep hold of it now, knowing its full treacherous history.

"Celia, I am sorry for what happened to your mother. For any part I played in the negligence that may have contributed to her capture. They were desperate, chaotic, sleep-deprived days when all we could do was our best in terribly difficult circumstances. But what I will say is that whatever *our* faults were in the SOE, the true responsibility lies with Hitler and the Nazis. In particular that lowlife double-agent Beaumont, who only cared about saving his own skin."

Celia can see the turmoil in Miss Clarke's face. She senses the woman is telling the truth, that although flawed, she cannot have been, or be, in league with Beaumont. Celia leans forward on impulse, grabs both of her hands. "I understand you did your best, and that is all anyone can do. But I've come here about something else too. Something maybe you can shed some light on. You see, Miss Clarke, I don't think Claude Beaumont *did* perish in a plane crash. Preposterous though it might sound, I believe he is still alive, and indeed, I believe he is right here in London."

Miss Clarke lets out a noise somewhere between a laugh and a gasp.

"I know you probably don't believe me, and I'm quite possibly deluded . . ."

"On the contrary, Celia. I don't think there is anything deluded about you. You have done nothing but impress me since I've met you. You said *part of it*—what is the other part?"

"Do you think you could top up our wine glasses, Miss Clarke? This might take some time."

Chapter 33

Septimus

Septimus lies on his back in the early hours of Friday morning, October twenty-sixth, wondering if London will survive long enough to see November. He throbs with exhaustion, but he cannot sleep and he needs time to think, something he has had precious little of during the long panic-filled days of the past week. In a strange mirroring of his personal life, things are spiraling out of control as both he and the American and Soviet governments are losing their grip on events. He hasn't seen Celia since their snatched tea ten days ago and now he longs for her. Did they leave things on bad terms? He can barely remember, so much has happened in between.

That same day he saw Celia, the Americans finally deduced from photographic evidence by a U-2 spy plane overflight of Cuba, together with updated intelligence, that the Soviets had, contrary to their previous estimates of four thousand troops, accumulated over *forty* thousand troops on the island, as well as medium-range and intermediate-range ballistic missiles. The medium-range missiles could reach Washington, the intermediate almost the whole of the United States. Septimus was secretly pleased to see the panic this evoked. In their arrogance, the American imperialists had considered themselves invincible. Now they discover they are not. Besides, it is equally pleasing to see not only the spectacular failure of their own intelligence, but how they're receiving a dose of their own medicine.

On Monday, Kennedy made a speech to the nation, advising the American population (and the rest of the world) of the threat to peace by the shocking, clandestine, and cavalier decision by the Soviet Union to conduct this mission in secret and how such action could not be tolerated. He had droned on about the lessons from the 1930s, how the Americans have been patient and restrained and how they will not, despite this, shrink from having to face war, a nuclear one if necessary. They then announced a blockade of all Soviet ships of any kind bound for Cuba, such that any containing military equipment or personnel would be turned away.

Septimus had seen a transcript of the speech. Seen the power of the president's words, the call to arms, the skewed message to the world of how peace-loving, gentle America is on the side of "right." That big bad Russia is at it again.

How can people not see they are being taken in by his imperialist rhetoric? How can they not understand they are being fed a narrative no less corrupt, no less manipulative, no less truth-stretching than that of Chairman Khrushchev? Kennedy talks of peace and freedom. That nebulous quality again. But freedom from what and for whom? Perhaps those big guns with all the money and the power and the influence. Perhaps they feel free. But what about the rest? How free are they, Mr. President? How much peace do they have in their day-to-day lives?

Niggling at the back of Septimus's mind is the worry, as Fox-Andrews recently pointed out, that London will be first in Moscow's sights as a target for *their* nuclear strikes, should things escalate. The city is within their reach. Moscow will be banking on the fact that a strike on London would be devastating enough to shock the Americans into backing down.

Septimus has had his network of underground agents working

around the clock to gather information, not only on anything he can glean from the Americans, but on the intentions, too, of the British government. Thus far, he has seen fear on all sides. So much so, the British have put in place Operation Methodical, whereby eleven large vans will take the most valued works of art from the Royal Collection and London's top museums and galleries to quarries in the countryside for safekeeping. Despite the best intentions of the Spies for Peace, the plan has been kept top secret, for fear of causing panic to the population of London were this to get out. More alarming still, as Septimus learned from intercepted minute notes from a meeting between MacMillan and his top military brass, is that the British prime minister, within the next day or so, will order forty RAF Vulcan bombers to be loaded with nuclear missiles at four airfields around the country, engines primed, pilots to be at their sides and on fifteen-minute standby, ready to drop their nuclear payloads on the heart of the Soviet Union.

How warped are the values of the capitalists to be intent on saving works of art over people? Still, Septimus doesn't have time to worry about this right now. Right now he must do his best for the greater good.

These are extraordinary times, which call for extraordinary action. He switches on his light and goes to his desk. There is a way, he realizes, that Moscow can benefit from the US's and Britain's reticence to start a war. If Moscow can hold its nerve, it can use this advantage to press for a better deal. He carefully composes the message.

> *Despite putting RAF Vulcan bombers on state of high alert, British PM is urging caution. Through ambassador, he has offered Kennedy to give up the*

*60 nuclear Thor weapons on British soil in exchange
for removal of nuclear sites on Cuba that he thinks
would help Chairman Kh. "save face." Macmillan
has serious doubts about Kennedy's ability to handle
crisis, and does not support blockade, bombing, or
invasion of Cuba. Kennedy, according to Ambassador
B, remains under pressure from generals to invade
island/bomb installations at minimum, but he himself
is not keen. Nerves here high. From all information
gathered, suggest this puts Moscow in position of
strength and gives advantage to capitalize on Western
reticence. USSR should insist on withdrawal of
medium-range missiles from Turkey at minimum,
although could include British Thor too, as well as
assurances of non-invasion of Cuba before agreeing to
withdraw. Advise further action.*

As Septimus seals the message in a plain manila envelope, his mind strays to Celia. A complication in his life he set out to avoid, but now that she is in it, he cannot undo his feelings. He will do what it takes to keep her safe. He has neglected her this past week, but with the danger ratcheting up, day by day, hour by hour, he needs to get her to safety.

A plan begins to formulate in his mind. He rolls it around a few times. He begins to like it. It might be short-lived. It might not even work. But then, they might all be dead in a few days anyway. He thinks back to the conversation he and Celia had at that picnic, the first time he kissed her, when Celia had posed the question of how one's perspective would change if one had a different life expectancy, for instance, just a day like a mayfly, or a thousand years like a tree. It appears his life expectancy is shortening drastically, and it has shifted the balance of what's important in his mind. He will not die regretting he didn't take this chance.

The decision made, a sense of peace descends. Septimus stumbles back to his bed, curls onto his side, and pulls his eiderdown over himself. He closes his eyes, finally descending into the blessed oblivion of sleep.

SEPTIMUS IS WAITING for Celia when she steps off the bus on the Strand at five minutes to nine later the same morning. He hooks his arm through hers and marches her in the opposite direction.

"Septimus! What on earth?"

"Shh," Septimus cautions, checking behind him before guiding Celia quickly across the road as the lights change. He walks her at a fast clip down toward the river and into Middle Temple Garden.

"Septimus, I'm happy to see you, but I have to get to work!" Celia protests.

"Please. This won't take long. But keep your voice down."

"Why? What's going on?"

Septimus puts a finger to his lips. Once he is certain they haven't been followed, he slows his pace. He stops and drops to one knee. It feels faintly ridiculous in the circumstances, but he wants to do it right. Keeping hold of her left hand, he looks up into her face.

"Septimus, what—?"

"Celia, you know I love you, and I think, I *hope* that you love me too." She opens her mouth, but before she can respond, he gushes on. "Look, maybe this is coming sooner than we both thought, but there isn't much time. I have to leave London, unexpectedly, and I can't imagine going without you. Leaving you here . . . Please, Celia, come with me. I think we should get married."

The answer to the message he sent to Moscow a couple of hours ago was received by return with his orders. This is the only way to get Celia out of harm's way.

There is a beat of silence while she stares down at him, her mouth still open.

"I know I should be taking you to some swanky restaurant, presenting you with a diamond ring, doing it all properly, but, well, time is of the essence here, and I couldn't wait . . ."

Celia glances around. "Stand up, Septimus, please. The grass is wet and your trousers will be soaked."

He gets to his feet.

"Come here." He pulls her toward him, wrapping his arms tight around her back. He breathes in the faint floral scent of her perfume, the shampoo in her hair, and beneath it all, her own intoxicating smell. He tips up her chin. Kisses her, long and slow.

"I've missed you. I'm sorry I've been so busy. And I'm sorry about the last time we saw each other. I stand by what I said about Humphries, but, well, I felt like I handled it badly, and I want to apologize for that."

She pushes him gently away to look into his eyes. "It's okay. I was being silly, and you are under so much stress. I mean, with all that's going on, don't you want to wait until things calm down?"

"But they might not, Celia! Don't you see?" He grips her arms and only just stops himself from giving her a shake.

"Okay, okay, I get it." She is silent for a moment as they gaze at each other. "Septimus, I care for you, truly, but . . . this is all a bit sudden." She lets out a nervous laugh. "You've not even met my parents yet." She speaks gently, as though not to rattle him. "But I'm only nineteen. You see, in England, until I reach the age of twenty-one, I can't marry unless they grant their approval."

Damn. He hadn't thought of that. This will all take too long. *Think, think.*

"All right," he says. "But, Celia, you need to understand just how grave things are over Cuba. You heard Kennedy's speech?"

"Of course. It is frightening, but . . . surely they will come to some agreement? The blockade seems to be working. They said on the news that the Russian vessels have stopped or are turning around."

Septimus shakes his head. "The news is being controlled, just like your Spies for Peace have been warning. They don't want people to panic. Fact is, everything rests on a knife-edge. I *believe* Kennedy and Khrushchev do not want a war, but events around them are spiraling out of control. Anything could happen. Russian submarines are patrolling the seas around Cuba, armed with nuclear weapons. The British and American armies are on the highest military alert. In fact, the American forces are mobilizing as we speak, with the air force making sure nuclear armed fighter planes are *constantly* in the air."

"How do you know all this?"

"Does it matter?"

"Maybe not, but you probably shouldn't be telling me."

"Too right I shouldn't."

"Then why are you?"

"Isn't it obvious? One wrong move from either side, and it will all be over. Nuclear oblivion."

"Well, then we shall all be dead, so we won't know anything about it . . ."

"It's no laughing matter."

"I'm not laughing."

Septimus takes a deep breath. "Fact is, London is likely to be the first target for a nuclear strike if war breaks out."

"Why not America? What's the point of all the weapons in Cuba?"

"That's not to say the Soviets won't use those. But London is within strike distance of Moscow. Besides, Khrushchev will know that Britain will be the first to back the US and that the Thor missiles stationed here will be used against them. It would be mad not to."

"I don't understand, Septimus . . . Are you trying to frighten me? How is this meant to convince me to marry you?"

"Oh, Celia, I'm handling this so badly. It's just . . ." Shit, this is going so wrong. He hasn't had time to properly think it all through. He knows he is coming across as desperate. Which he is. The more she is the voice of sense and caution, the more certain he is that she must come with him. He *wants* her. That's all there is to it. And Septimus is accustomed to getting what he wants. "With all this going on, I'm now worried it will be too late. Nuclear war will not be like any previous war. The first strike is all that matters. It will determine the winner and the loser."

Celia scratches her arm and looks at him with a mix of suspicion and amusement.

Septimus clenches his teeth in frustration. "I'm really not overestimating this. There is *intelligence* confirming it." He couldn't expect her just to *believe* what he says. He knows she is too smart for that. But even so, at this very moment in time, it would be extremely helpful if she would just take his word for it.

In the background, beyond the gardens and the elegant buildings of the Middle Temple, the sounds of London life rumble on regardless. The roar of an engine, faint sounds of chatter and laughter rising from the pathway near the buildings. It all sounds so run-of-the-mill, so ordinary. Septimus suddenly feels inexplicable sadness that soon all of this may be obliterated.

"I want you—us—to get out of London," Septimus says, his voice cracking. "We can get away from here. Go to Scotland. We can get married there, with *or* without your parents' permission. Let's run away together."

"Run away?" Celia laughs, a look of incredulity spreading over her face.

Septimus grabs both of her hands. "We are mayflies, Celia . . . We mustn't wait," he says, the urgency back in his voice. "We have no idea how long we have . . . I can find us a remote cottage on the west coast of Scotland. Right up north. On an island. I don't care. We can keep sheep, live a quiet life. Together, just us. Safe. Away from all this." He flaps a hand at the invisible threat.

"Septimus . . ." Celia strokes the backs of his hands with her thumbs. "I think this has all gotten to you. This stress, lack of sleep, too, probably. I can't just run away, not now, just as things are getting better with my parents—it would destroy them. And besides, if the threat really is that great, how can I leave them?"

"We'll take them with us," Septimus says in growing desperation. Although he knows this is impossible. They will need to travel with speed and agility. They will need to change identity, shake off those who will be certain to pursue him, assuming war isn't inevitable. If it is, well, they will have bigger things to think about than him. He can plan everything in twenty-four hours. She just needs to agree.

"They will *never* agree to that. They haven't even met you! And there is Bartholomew to think about too."

"Who the hell is Bartholomew?"

"My cat. How can I leave him?"

"For God's sake, Celia! All right, we'll take the cat as well."

Celia smiles and falls against him, pressing her ear to his chest. "And that, Septimus, is why I think I might love you. The fact you will save the cat too. All right, I'll think about it."

"Please don't think too long. Time is running out." Septimus speaks into the top of her head. "I'll need an answer tomorrow night, at the latest. So we can be away first thing Sunday."

"Okay," she says, and a bubble of hope rises inside him.

"Thank you," he whispers, closing his eyes and saying a silent prayer to a deity he doesn't believe in.

Chapter 34

Celia

Septimus insisted on accompanying Celia to H. J. Potts. She'd be late for work, and he had said he would explain to Mrs. Denton it was all his fault, not hers. They agreed, however, to keep his marriage proposal to themselves. The possible elopement too. *Who would tell anyone they are planning to elope?* Celia had wondered.

Mrs. Denton, of course, as Celia had predicted, had not yet materialized from the flat when they arrived at nine thirty, so his journey there had been completely unnecessary. Fishing the keys from beneath the counter, he'd darted into the flat in any case, just to say a quick hello and good-bye. Was there anyone who didn't know the hiding place of the spare set of keys? By the time Celia had removed her coat and hat and was smoothing back her hair, Septimus was back.

"Until tomorrow evening," he'd whispered, kissing her on the neck and slipping her a card with his address. "Come to my flat at seven?"

"I promise, Septimus. I'll be there." She'd smiled into his eyes and squeezed his hand, trying to reassure him, even though her own stomach was doing somersaults.

Now, alone again, her hands refuse to stop trembling as she tries to focus on the usual morning tasks. *Septimus asked me to marry him! To elope!* What should she do, how should she feel? She knows she loves being in Septimus's company, the way he looks at her, his interest in her, how interesting *he* is. And she is definitely attracted to him. But is this enough? And is she *in love* with him? And, more importantly, how well does she even truly know him? Even after all this time, Septimus Nelson still feels like an enigma.

All morning, Celia's head feels fuzzy and odd, her stomach distinctly upset by the cocktail of emotions, the terror at impending nuclear annihilation, and Septimus's answer to it all. Working seems superfluous to everything, and she wonders over and over what she is doing here, why she isn't rushing back home to Mother and Father, cuddling Bartholomew, and working out, together, what they should all do.

At midday, Mrs. Denton dispatches Celia to the bank with the contents of the till. As she hurries along the pavement through a light drizzle, a tap on her shoulder makes her jump. She spins around to find Miss Clarke of all people, wrapped in an elegant navy coat with brass buttons, face almost completely obscured by a large-brimmed felt hat.

"Miss Clarke!" she exclaims. "What are you—?"

Miss Clarke puts her finger to her lips in exactly the same manner as Septimus had this morning. Can the day turn any more peculiar?

"I'm glad I caught you." Miss Clarke speaks softly as she threads her arm through Celia's, and they continue walking toward Lloyds Bank. "I didn't want to call you at home, for fear of upsetting your grandparents, and I certainly didn't want to come into the shop. I knew you'd emerge at some point for your lunch break. As we discussed when you were at my flat on Sunday, I promised to look into things, and I've been doing some digging over the last few days. What I have to tell you is rather interesting. But what we *need* is evidence. Do you have time for a cup of tea, Celia dear?"

"Oh, yes!" Celia says, suddenly impossibly relieved to see Miss Clarke. "I've had quite the morning and could do with a friendly ear."

THAT EVENING, CELIA meets Sam and Daphne at the Horse and Groom for a drink.

"What's up with you?" Daphne asks as Celia downs her third glass of Babycham.

"Nothing, why?"

"Sweetie, you are drinking like a fish. That's not you. And besides, you've not heard a single word Sam or I have said in the last half hour, have you?"

"'Course I have!"

"What have we been talking about, then?"

But Celia can only shrug helplessly. It's true. She has no idea.

Daphne puts a hand on Celia's arm. "C'mon, spill the beans. What's going on?"

Celia takes a deep breath. She checks nobody is listening in, then tells them everything. Well, almost everything. She leaves Septimus and his suggested elopement out of it. She knows exactly what they will have to say about that, and as far as Septimus is concerned, only *she* can decide if he is worth leaving Southwark for. She has wanted to get away for so long, and here it is, the possibility of just that, with the gorgeous Septimus by her side.

Instead, she focuses on her theory that Alfred Humphries is, in fact, Claude Beaumont, the man who betrayed her mother.

She explains to Sam what she and Daphne uncovered in the library, then tells them how Miss Clarke agrees that it is, although unlikely, a possibility. That Beaumont could have sold himself to the highest bidder—that is, the Soviets—faked his own death, and is now an agent for them. They would have provided him with a new identity and dispatched him on a new mission. After all, he switched sides before. It is not impossible that a man like him switched again.

But Miss Clarke also said that if they are to move forward, they will need evidence. Over tea earlier, she told Celia to be patient and to wait while she tries to convince the Services, whoever they may be, to set up a tail to follow him. But Celia doesn't have time. And she has a hunch she can find the proof they need. Humphries, she tells a riveted Sam and Daphne, regularly stays over at Mrs. D's flat; not only that, but a month ago, she overheard Mrs. Denton offer to keep a parcel or package of something safely in her flat for him. That she'd said something about not going anywhere until Christmas, so it must still be there. Surely it is incriminating, if only she can find the hiding place. It's a risk, but one she has to take, for her mother's sake, for hers, and, if it really is true, to save Mrs. Denton from being associated with this traitor.

An hour later, with the help of her friends, Celia has a plan.

"Are you *positive* you want to do this?" Daphne asks, grabbing Celia's hands. "Surely there must be another way?"

"I'm one hundred percent sure," Celia replies, stomach clenching in protest.

"And you're equally sure I can't come too?" Daphne pleads again. "I can help!"

"No way. I won't let you put yourself in any danger. And Sam will be right outside." She turns to him. "But, are *you* sure about this, Sam?" She searches his earnest brown eyes for any sign of hesitation.

"Too bloody right I am." He takes a sip of his drink. "Anything for you, Celia, you know that." He smiles and gives her a reassuring wink, which sets unexpected butterflies fluttering in her belly.

AT NOON SHARP the following day, Celia finishes her half-day shift at the shop. She says good-bye to Mrs. Denton, who tells her she'll be closing the shop at lunchtime as she wants to rest before getting ready to go with Alfred Humphries to the Princes Theatre to see *Gentlemen Prefer Blondes* that evening. Celia hurries to the bus stop, jittery with nerves. She hopes that the preparations Sam agreed to be part of last night are going to work. She has only until seven this evening, then she must give Septimus her answer to his proposal.

Back at 13 Copperfield Street, all is quiet. It's Saturday, and Father is working the day shift, Mother at the deli. She kisses Bartholomew and rushes upstairs to change and packs what she needs into a bag. She wonders if she should leave a note for Mother. Probably best. She scrawls one quickly:

Dear Mother, I'm out helping Sam at the animal sanctuary this afternoon. I'll probably have supper at Daphne's house. Don't wait up. Love, Celia.

She leaves it propped against the kettle. She'd love to turn on the news and see what she can glean about developments in Cuba. Since Kennedy made his speech, all media eyes are suddenly trained on that little island off the coast of America. But there is no time.

She picks up the bag and leaves the house.

Next door, Sam, dressed in his work overalls, is waiting for her.

"Ready?" she asks.

He grins.

She and Sam walk together to his brightly colored van.

"I'll miss you," she says, "when you go to Yorkshire. I want you to know that, just in case things go . . . unexpectedly today."

"Everything will be fine! And, nah. You won't miss me. Seems to me your life is full of excitement. Still, thanks for the compliment, Celia. I'll miss you too."

"And I really appreciate this. I know it's a risk for you. Using the van like this."

Sam gives her a wink, and they climb into the cab. "You're right," he says, "I shouldn't. But like I said last night, I'd do anything to help you."

They fall silent, each lost in their own thoughts as Sam drives over Southwark Bridge, the water of the Thames flowing, liquid umber, beneath.

"Right," Celia says, once they are close enough to H. J. Potts. "Here will do."

Sam pulls over and lets her out of the van.

"I'll wait here," Celia says, "just out of sight. Once the coast is clear, I'll go in, have a look around the flat, and be back out as fast as I can."

"Don't worry," Sam says. "Any hint of trouble, I'm coming in."

"No, you mustn't. If I don't come out, call the police, and Miss Clarke." She hands Sam a piece of paper with her number written on it. "She'll know what to do, and she'll be able to explain to the police why I've broken into someone's flat. Now go. Good luck."

Celia watches Sam's van slide out into the traffic, then pull over again next to H. J. Potts. The shop is shut, and even from this distance, Celia can see the shape of the white Closed sign hanging inside the door window. Adrenaline pumps through her body. Sam walks up to the door between H. J. Potts and the shop next door that sells barristers wigs and gowns. The door leads to a set of stairs for the little-used separate entrances to Mrs. Denton's flat and the flat above the barristers attire shop. He rings both bells, stepping back to wait, glancing around. She wills him to look casual.

Time creeps slowly. What if Mrs. D is having her afternoon nap and doesn't hear the bell? And what about the neighbors? Perhaps they are out. Maybe they're ignoring the doorbell. Then suddenly, miraculously, the door swings open and Mrs. Denton appears in the doorway of the flat patting her hair, adjusting her cardigan, head cocked as she listens to Sam speak.

Moments later, the door of the adjacent flat opens, and a middle-aged couple appear. Celia smiles a little as she watches them crowd around Sam. Last night they had debated whether to involve next door. She was against it, but Sam said it would be more authentic if they did. Now she sees that he is right. He pulls out some paperwork, which he shows them. There are a few gesticulations. Celia imagines the conversation.

I'm afraid we have had reports of a gas leak. We have traced it to the pipe running in front of your properties, and I need to carry out some emergency work. It is a delicate operation and I must evacuate you while I take care of the problem. No, it shouldn't take too long. Give me an hour, tops. If there are no complications, you can go right

*back inside. Your safety is paramount, sir, madams. I shouldn't need
access to your property, no, but I'll update you on your return.*

Or at least, words to that effect, although Sam will no doubt
be more convincing with the technical details. She watches as
he points at a manhole cover in the pavement outside the shop.
Sam has done his homework and checked the network of gas
pipes last night. Celia feels a stab of gratitude. He is risking his
job, his promotion, his move to Yorkshire, for her. And he's not
hesitated for even a moment. She watches as all three disappear
back into their respective flats for a few moments, while Sam
opens his van and cordons off a section of the pavement, hanging
signs announcing gasworks at each end. The couple are the first
to reappear in hats and coats. After a quick word with Sam, they
head in the direction of Embankment.

Celia bites her fingernails. What if Mrs. D doesn't buy it?
What if she refuses to leave? But then, there she is, bundled into
her long woolen fuchsia coat, her large black handbag dangling
at her elbow. She hesitates for a moment, then sets off in the
opposite direction to the couple. Celia suspects she will buy a
magazine and sit in the comfortable lounge at the Strand Palace
Hotel and have a drink. At least, that is what she hopes. She
makes herself wait five long minutes to make sure Mrs. Denton
hasn't forgotten anything, and then, with a deep breath, she is
running across the road toward the shop.

Sam has opened the manhole and is pulling tools from the
back of his van.

"Right," he says, not looking up at her. "In you go quick. I'll
busy myself out here"—he jerks his head toward the gaping hole
in the pavement—"and keep watch. I'll fiddle with the pipes a
bit. No one will be any the wiser. Any hint of trouble and I'll

bang this hammer very loudly on a pipe three times in a row. You should have no problem hearing that from inside, right? If I do, you get the hell out of there. I'll try and keep them here, at the back of the van with the paperwork, for as long as possible, if necessary. Okay?"

"Got it," Celia says with more conviction than she feels. "I'm going in. As soon as I find that package belonging to Mr. Humphries, I'll be out. I just hope it's *something*." Enough, she hopes, to prove she is right—that Humphries and Claude Beaumont, the man who betrayed her mother, are one and the same. Celia slips through the shop door. She fumbles under the counter for the spare keys to the flat. Relief floods through her as her fingers make contact with them. Thank heavens they're still there.

It's completely dark inside the flat, and Celia fumbles for a light switch. Finding it, a single bare bulb flickers on over-head and she climbs the stairs, every muscle in her body tense. What on earth is she doing? Breaking into her employer's flat is a criminal offence. The risk, the madness of this whole crazy mission driven by her desperate desire to seek justice for Jeannie. But whatever it was Celia witnessed Mr. Humphries handing over to Mrs. Denton for safekeeping might no longer be here. And what if it's innocuous? Her step falters. She could just turn around and leave, no damage done. But she's here now. And time is running out. If she doesn't do this now, she won't get another chance. She continues her climb. She stands a moment at the top of the stairs, orienting herself. To her left is a small galley kitchen. The first thing that strikes her is the mess. There are unwashed pans by the sink. Dirty cups, plates, old food left on the side. It smells rancid, and Celia notices the overflowing bin just inside the door. This is not at all what she expected from the pristine, neat Mrs. Denton with her twin sets and gleaming pearls. And all that vacuuming. Definitely odd.

Don't get distracted.

She makes her way out of the kitchen, every sense heightened. She hears her own breath, her skin prickling with fear. Her ears strain for the sound of someone coming, eyes search the gloom of the poorly lit landing. To the right, through an open door, a sitting room. Not there. Straight ahead is a bedroom and a bathroom. The bedroom is immaculately tidy and her heart sinks. It looks completely unused. She checks the cupboard and the chest of drawers, but they are empty. Back on the landing, Celia sees there is another, narrower flight of stairs heading to the second floor. She takes them two at a time. At the top, another bedroom. This one holds the lingering scent of Mrs. Denton's perfume. One of her cardigans hangs over the back of a chair, and there is a flowery bedspread laid over the bed. Beside the window is a dressing table on which lies a jumble of jewelry, makeup, and discarded rollers and hairpins. She glances out the window where the narrow iron steps of a fire escape zigzag down the wall to a small backyard with several bins and a square patch of weeds in the middle.

Celia doubts the package would be in here, and she goes to leave, but then, what if Mrs. Denton and Mr. Humphries's relationship is more intimate than she's been led to believe? She walks farther into the room, pulls open the chest of drawers, lifting neatly folded sweaters, underwear, a cotton nightgown, running her hands beneath. It feels awful to be going through her employer's things. Intrusive and wrong.

Miss Clarke's words from their recent meeting ring in her

ears. *I need more than your hunch and a grainy photographic likeness to go on, Celia. We will need firm evidence.*

What sort of evidence? She doesn't even know what she is looking for, except the rustling package or envelope Mrs. D promised to look after for him.

She returns to the sitting room, looking around with increasing desperation. There is nothing here. What if she's imagined this whole thing, just like Septimus told her she had? She's dragged Sam into it, too, and now she's broken into a flat, risking them both getting caught, and for what? A hunch? It was a terrible, stupid thing to do. She should have listened to Miss Clarke and waited for the professionals to gather what they need.

She runs down the stairs to the ground floor in a last hope of finding something in Mrs. Denton's study. The room, unlike the kitchen and bedroom, is perfectly well organized and tidy. The desktop is empty; the desk drawers contain only a blank letter pad, envelopes, a fountain pen, and ink. On the shelves above the desk are Mrs. Denton's ledgers and a row of black files, probably, she thinks, created by the Blythes. *Invoices Sent, Invoices Paid, Creditors, Bills Received, Bills Paid, Ledgers 1960– 1961, Ledgers 1961–1962*, et cetera. On the back wall there is a bookcase filled with old leather volumes, a few paperbacks, some hardbacks, and more files. But no sign of the mysterious package belonging to Humphries. Damn, damn! If only there was something, *anything* to make this crazy venture worthwhile.

Celia sighs and climbs back up the stairs to the first-floor landing, glancing around one more time before she leaves. Then she notices something she missed earlier, before her eyes had adjusted to the gloom. There is another door off the landing. Smaller, narrower, it opens into a closet beneath the stairs to the second floor. The closet is full of cleaning equipment, the vacuum Celia has heard so much of taking up the space in the middle. Her eyes drift past to a mop and bucket and an ironing board propped against the back wall, and two shelves. The lower one is stacked with sponges, feather duster, iron. The usual. But on the top shelf, she sees a leather case. She stares at it, almost not believing what she is seeing. Celia's heart bangs hard in her chest.

It cannot be.

She pulls it down. It's heavy.

Celia lays it on the floor, clicks open the hinges with shaking fingers. Her breath stops.

Inside is a wireless transmitter, perhaps more modern, but not unlike the one Miss Clarke gifted her, the one that once belonged to her mother.

Celia sits back on her heels. She remembers what Miss Clarke had said about the noise of transmitting, and something clicks into place in Celia's brain. All that hoovering. Covering up the noises of the transmitter. Ice fills her veins as the truth slowly dawns.

It's Mrs. Denton.

She's *not* the innocent.

She's a . . . spy? Is it possible? She remembers the foreign words Humphries had used when she overheard that conversation between them. Could they have been *Russian*? She must be using this radio set to transmit messages. No wonder the woman shows no interest in the bookshop. It's all a front!

Mrs. Denton hasn't been duped by Humphries: she's in league with him.

A wave of dizziness strikes as the danger she could be in sinks in. Her ears strain for sound. She needs to get out. Find Sam, get away before Mrs. Denton comes back. As soon as she's safe, she'll call Miss Clarke. She'll know what to do.

She shuts the radio set back inside its case and scrambles to her feet. Her head swims, and she forces herself to take slow, deep breaths. In and out. In and out. Is this enough evidence? Does it implicate Humphries or Denton? What if they deny knowledge of it and say it was already here when Mrs. Denton moved in?

She hesitates. There is no sound on the stairs. No loud bangs from Sam outside to suggest anyone is coming. Perhaps there is more, and she hasn't yet come across that package.

She stands on tiptoes and reaches her fingers along the top shelf. They brush against a lumpy folder. Is this it? On the front she reads, *Invoices Received*. She fumbles to open it, and several passports tumble onto the floor. She picks them up, flicking through the first few. There are Mr. Humphries's and Mrs. Denton's pictures, but with names she doesn't know, and passports belonging to another two men whom she recognizes as "customers" of the bookshop. Riffling through the folder, she finds blank paper. A cigarette lighter. An envelope full of strange scraps of paper with tiny square blobs she cannot decipher. A pad containing pages of the alphabet, set out in groups of five letters, which, after her meetings with Miss Clarke, she supposes is a cypher for encryption of messages. She stares at the haul in front of her, hardly daring to believe it's true. Vindication, mixed with heart-thumping fear.

She needs to get out of here.

As she begins to shove the items back in the folder, there's a creak, and she freezes. Then a voice.

"So, I see you have discovered my little hiding place."

Celia whirls around, dropping the folder, the contents spilling out around her feet. Mrs. Denton! Where the hell was Sam's warning? Or didn't she hear it? It's only then she notices the woman is holding a gun, almost discreetly, at her waist, and it's pointed at Celia.

Celia's breath is caught in her throat. She's unable to speak, her mind darting in crazy directions, trying to work out what to say, how to escape.

"And don't even think of trying to escape," Mrs. Denton says, as though she can read Celia's mind. Her voice is hard, so different to the fluffy tone she normally uses. "There is no way out. The door to the shop is locked and bolted, and Alfred is coming up the outside stairs as we speak. This pistol is loaded, in case you were wondering. Now, young lady, it's time you confessed. Just who, exactly, are you working for?"

Part V

Chapter 35

Jeannie

Natzweiler-Struthof Concentration Camp
July 1944

The mountain air was crisp, cooling fast as the Volkswagen climbed higher, engine straining against the incline of the rough mountain road. The windows were rolled down, and Jeannie closed her eyes for a moment, transporting herself to a different time and place, a time when she was young, just her and her father on a weekend expedition, tent, fishing tackle, waterproofs, their heavy rucksacks, as they bounced along the country roads in the old Green Line buses. She recalled so vividly the mixture of pure, childish joy and excitement, the weekend stretching ahead, just the two of them, with no idea of what adventures might be before them. She smiled as she remembered how they passed the long evenings, the fire lit, singing a mix of old French songs and the odd silly sea shanty her father had been taught at school, "Hey Ho and Up She Rises" and "Blow the Man Down."

The car lurched around a steep bend, almost on two wheels, snapping Jeannie's eyes open, back to the reality of being captive alongside three other women, Julienne, Simone, and Celine, in the custody of a Nazi officer, his gun in his lap, his watchful eyes flickering between them, on constant alert as though worried they may leap from the moving car at any moment.

Jeannie had no idea what awaited them. All she knew was that she was glad to see the back of the hellhole that was Karlsruhe prison. After Jeannie's capture in Paris late last year, her perspective, her motivation over the freezing, long weeks had shrunk to just one thing: survival. Her own survival and that of her fellow agents. Clinging to the faint hope that one day, when this war was over, she may see England again. See her beloved mother and father again. She fantasized, too, about finding her daughter. It had been thoughts of Celia and an iron resolution fueled by her visceral, violent anger at Maurice Albert, the man who had orchestrated her and her companions' capture, which had kept her from giving away a single morsel of information that might help the Nazis. The worse her treatment, the firmer her resolve became. Torture and death were likely coming for her anyway, so she would never, ever give them what they wanted.

She resisted the Gestapo at Avenue Foch. She resisted them at Fresnes prison, and she resisted them in Karlsruhe, despite the solitary confinement, the shackling, the pain, the loneliness, the starvation. Whatever lay ahead, she could not imagine it could be any worse. Indeed, just being here, seeing the mountains and the sky, the trees, the grass, the fresh air, it seemed as though she may have, after all, been granted a second chance at life. Perhaps they really *had* given up on her. Perhaps she, and the others, were now being taken somewhere quiet, somewhere benign, to see out the rest of the war. They'd been told they were going to a labor camp. That didn't bother her. She could work hard. If she could just stay fit and healthy enough, useful enough, then she had a chance.

The car rolled to a halt outside the main gate of Natzweiler-Struthof concentration camp. Jeannie and the other women climbed out of the car, stretching their stiff limbs, blinking into the bright light, clutching their few possessions at their sides.

A guard led them through the gates of the camp. The wooden watchtower and entrance looked hastily constructed, reminiscent in their rough construction to that of medieval fortifications. But the miles of vicious-toothed barbed-wire fencing, the watchtowers and huts stretching out as far as the eye could see, were reminder enough that this was a prison camp.

The camp fell away, down the steep hillside, down toward a green canopy of trees that curved and folded into distant shimmering layers of amaranthine hills. In the late afternoon haze, an indifferent sun sunk slowly west, drenching the Alsace-Lorraine countryside in rose-gold light. Away from the stench and misery of a cold, damp prison, this place filled Jeannie with renewed hope. She hooked arms with Julienne and together they walked through those camp gates with light footsteps.

Guards led them down the hill toward the main part of the camp. To each side of the track, prisoners—all men—pressed their faces to the fences, silently watching as the women walked by two by two, heads down so as not to meet the haunted and hungry men's eyes. News of the women's arrival seemed to buzz like electricity through the camp, pulling them in straggling crowds toward the fences to watch, tens deep.

They reached the central block and entered the crematorium building, which stood in the middle of it all, herded together into one of the cells to wait. An argument broke out among the SS commanders. Simone, fluent in German, translated for the rest in urgent whispers.

"It's a bloody problem. Yours to solve, Ernst."

"Why me?"

"Because here we seem to have four dangerous women, alone among thousands of male inmates. What on earth are we to do with them?"

Simone looked at the others with nervous eyes as she listened for what came next.

"But these are *night and fog* prisoners," the man called Ernst replied. "They are not my responsibility."

"They are nobody's responsibility," hissed the first man. "That is the bloody point.

"These prisoners are so special and so secret that we have been told, verbally, we are to do with them what we want. Paperwork is expressly forbidden, for no trail as to their whereabouts can be left."

Jeannie caught the hands of the other women, and they instinctively moved closer to one another. She peered through the bars of their cell. From the surrounding cells, the gleam of many other eyes too.

Hushed discussions continued, which Jeannie and the other women could no longer make out. At one point, orders were barked that the prisoners in neighboring cells must stay away from doors and windows, with the threat of immediate execution for those who disobeyed.

Finally, it seemed, a solution had been reached. The commandant sent for the camp doctors and for the fire stoker, who was ordered to stoke the fires of the crematorium.

The women huddled closer still.

The doctors arrived, and there were more urgent discussions, some violent shaking of the doctors' heads, apparent anger among the SS officers, and all the while, the fire stoker shoveled coal into the arched hatches of the crematorium, the roar and the heat inside growing by the second.

"There is only enough dose for *three* of the women, not *four*," one of the doctors was heard to say.

"It is the best option," the camp commandant yelled at the doctors. "Make it work, and fast. I don't care how you divide up the dose. Just do it. That's a command." The doctors nodded their assent, and they all left, leaving the fire stoker alone in his work.

Jeannie tried to summon words of comfort to offer the other women. But she couldn't find any. So, like them, she sank to her haunches on the floor and waited.

Some minutes later, with a clatter of footsteps and ragged breaths, one of the doctors returned. His face was gray. Sweat beaded across his brow; his hands shook. He disappeared into a room that Jeannie discerned must be the medical room. After some minutes, he returned and called each of the women in turn.

"Typhus injection," the doctor explained in English when it was Jeannie's turn. She was the last to be fetched from the cell. As she had waited and the others hadn't returned, her anxiety grew, twisting and churning inside her empty guts, a growing pressure in her chest like the crushing grasp of an iron hand.

Be brave, she commanded herself. *It will soon be over.*

"Routine for all newcomers," the doctor was explaining, apology in his voice.

"Please," said the doctor, with great politeness, "strip to your underclothes."

"Why?" Jeannie asked, unable to help herself.

"To receive your injection," the doctor replied with a show of patience. She wondered about the dose they apparently didn't have enough of. Had they found more? Or were they each being given one-quarter less than they should be? "Then you will take a seat beside the guard on the bench outside the room, and we will fetch you some prison garments to wear." He bowed, then turned away from her as though to show good manners in not watching her undress.

As Jeannie slowly removed her dress, she took in his shaking hands, the sweat that was rolling down the back of his neck.

She folded her dress and placed it on the chair just as the doctor picked up the vial, resolutely, as though he had suddenly made his decision. She knew what was coming even though she still refused to believe it. Couldn't.

Out of the corner of her eye, the shadow of Celia was there. Smiling, holding out her arms.

Mummy. It's okay, Mummy. I'm right here with you.

The needle slid into the soft flesh of Jeannie's thigh, the cold rush of liquid beneath her skin. She stepped outside and sank down onto the bench, aware of the eyes from the surrounding cells still gleaming as they watched through the gloom. It didn't take long. Her head began to whirl; nausea rose. It worsened, and Jeannie felt consciousness slipping away. That's when terror gripped her, resisting against the pull of oblivion. This was no typhus injection. The realization hit in her final seconds before the dose triumphed and darkness swept her under. There was a dull sensation of being hauled across the floor. She wanted to stop. Not go where they were taking her. But she had no strength. Blackness folded in and out. She heard a voice, hers, call out as though from a great distance. *Pourquoi?* Why?

There was a flash of white light and violent heat.

Her father's voice: *My coeur de lion. My lionheart.*

Her last thought was how she was to disappear without a trace.

Dispatched silently and mysteriously into the foggy night.

OUTSIDE, AGAINST A darkening sky, the prisoners watched in silence as flames and sparks leaped high, up and out of the tall crematorium chimney; one, two, three, and for a final fourth time, before shrinking and retreating once more.

The silence between the men stretched long, as all around, birds sang their twilight songs and leaves rustled in the breeze. Slowly, the sun sank below the horizon, spreading blood-red streaks above distant rolling hills, the uneven lines of trees standing stark black, sentinels, against a vibrant sky.

Chapter 36

Celia

"You," Celia cries. "I work for you!"

"Don't play the fool with me, girl." Mrs. Denton's face grows red. She jerks the gun. "You know exactly what I mean. Who is it?" she barks. "MI5? The CIA?"

"Honestly, Mrs. D, I don't work for anyone except you. This is all a big mix-up. I can explain . . ."

"Well, if you won't tell me, Alfred will get it out of your accomplice down there."

Her heart stops.

"Sam has nothing to do with it. Please! What have you done with him?" Celia's voice comes out in a croak.

Mrs. Denton stands, blocking Celia's way to the other set of stairs. "I told Alfred," she says, ignoring Celia's pleas. "I warned him, after you bothered me with all those questions. 'Alfred,' I said, 'that one, she's not so stupid. Been asking too many questions—we should get rid of her.' But he told me you were just a pretty face and a necessary front for the shop . . ."

There is a loud banging that sounds as though it is coming from inside the shop. Mrs. Denton's attention is diverted, and in that split second, Celia makes a sudden dash around and flicks off the light switch, plunging them into darkness. She clatters down the stairs toward the shop on jelly legs, almost tripping, somehow staying upright. But when she tries to wrench open the shop door, it's locked.

She's trapped. The light snaps back on, and Mrs. Denton's silhouette appears at the top of the stairs.

"There's no getting out that way," she says. "Now come back up here before I lose my patience and use this thing."

Celia walks slowly back up, numb. Strangely, her terror has melted away, now that she knows there is no escape.

"What has happened to my friend?" she asks. "He's innocent and has nothing to do with this. If you let him go, I'll explain."

Footsteps pound up the outside stairs.

The outer door bangs open, and seconds later, a red-faced Alfred Humphries appears. Celia presses herself against the wall as he lunges for her, grabbing her arm and making her squeal. But as she stares into the face of the man who betrayed her mother, flames of fury erupt, pumping a fierce energy around her body. She is immune to fear.

"I know what you did, you hateful, vile man!" She struggles against his grip, writhing and twisting, striking at his face with her free hand. "You killed my mother!"

Her hand makes contact with his jaw, and Humphries growls. He manages to grab her other hand and within moments has her spun around, her wrists pinned in a viselike grip behind her back. Of course, he is a trained, silent killer, and she just a girl with shorthand and typing skills. Not a fair match, even if she has the age advantage.

Mrs. Denton and Celia stare at each other. Mrs. Denton lowers the gun.

"Get me some rope," Humphries orders, "so I can secure this little bitch. Stronger than she looks."

Mrs. Denton ignores him.

"What do you mean?" Mrs. Denton asks Celia. "About him killing your mother?"

Celia's arms are twisted at a horrible angle, forcing her to bend to ease the pressure for fear a bone might break. Her armpits, her back, her neck are slick with sweat, her clothes sticking to her skin. She draws a breath, keeps eye contact with her employer. They've a relationship. They've worked together; they are both women in an unforgiving man's world.

"Look," she says, "Mrs. Denton, I'm sorry, I have no idea who you are, or what you are doing here in the shop, and I'm not sure I care. I've worked here for years. I love books and that's all. But since you've been here, and *this man* has been coming in, I've found out, by pure accident, that he isn't who he says he is. I believe that Mr. Alfred Humphries is really a Frenchman called—"

"Oi! Shut it, you!" Alfred jerks Celia's arms, causing her to cry out in pain.

Mrs. D raises a hand to Alfred, holding Celia's desperate gaze. "Oh no, do continue, Miss Duchesne. *I* would like to hear this . . ." Alfred grunts, but releases a little pressure on Celia's twisted arms.

Celia takes a breath. "A Frenchman called Claude Beaumont, alias Captain Albert, who was a traitor to this country and who gave my mother up to the Nazis. They executed her when she was only twenty-one years old. I can't imagine what he is doing here now, or why—it's almost like the universe intervened, isn't it? But you should know he is completely untrustworthy. I wanted to see if I could find any evidence, anything at all, to prove who he really is, and to make him pay for what he did back then."

Mrs. Denton's jaw drops, and she clasps the banister. Clearly this was not what she had been expecting. She looks over the top of Celia's head.

"Is it true, Alfred?"

He suddenly drops Celia's wrists, clasps her shoulders, and spins her around, gaping at her face.

"I see it," he says, staring at her, eyes wide in shock. "Anya. You are Anya's child . . ." he breathes. "I see the likeness. I always thought there was something familiar about you . . ."

Celia feels his hands begin to tremble on her shoulders; then his expression changes and he gasps.

"I *knew* I'd seen her! It was that Clarke woman, wasn't it? I *told* you I thought I'd spotted that dangerous bitch, Vera, hanging around here, and you told me I was seeing things. But I *never* forget a face . . ."

Celia stares into the eyes of the man who betrayed her mother. The man in whom an innocent young woman put her trust in the most dangerous of circumstances. Tears blur her vision and from the depth of her being rises a fury, the force of which she has never experienced before.

"It was *your* fault she was murdered," Celia screams, lurching toward him, struggling against his grip. "You betrayed her!"

"I was acquitted of that; it wasn't true—" He shoves her against the wall. "Now *shut up*, and tell us who you—"

"*Alfred*, we don't have time for this," Mrs. Denton interrupts. "We need to get out of here."

"Yes, Vera, I know but—"

"That's an order!" she barks. "Secure her with the boy. I'm going to grab my things."

Mrs. Denton spins on her heels and makes for the stairs. So much for female solidarity. Tears course down Celia's cheeks. She's helpless.

Humphries gives Mrs. Denton's back a look of pure hatred but says nothing. He pulls Celia roughly toward the stairs. She understands in that moment that he plans to lock her and Sam in the basement and for he and Mrs. Denton to make their getaway. Using every ounce of strength, she struggles against him, wrenching her arms free, but he manages to grab one again, and, gripping hard, yanks her downstairs.

He shoves her into the shop, past the counter, and toward the cellar door, from where she can hear Sam shouting and banging. She should never have involved him.

As Humphries reaches out to unlock the door, Celia's free hand swings wide, hitting a book lying on the countertop. Without hesitating, her fingers wrap around its thick leather spine, and then she is swinging it in a wide arc with all her might, smashing it into the unsuspecting side of Alfred Humphries's head. Her aim is perfect, and the heavy book makes contact with his temple. He cries out, releases her other arm, and stumbles. Celia lunges at him just as he loses his balance and falls sideways, his head smacking hard against the edge of the glass-topped counter. There is a crack, and his eyes roll backward as he crumples to the floor.

Dropping the book, Celia turns the key that's stuck in the lock of the cellar door, and Sam springs out.

"*Thank God you are okay!*" he exclaims, and then his arms are around her, pulling her close.

"Oh, Sam, I'm so sorry."

Sam stares at Humphries's body, sprawled out cold on the floor. Releasing Celia, he picks up the book. "*War and Peace,*" he says. "How apt."

Celia turns the key to the flat door, still blessedly there from earlier, locking Mrs. Denton in. She removes it and hands the set to Sam. "The second key locks the outside door. Quick, go round, lock it, and leave it jammed in the lock so Mrs. D can't unlock it from the inside. I'll call the police." She lifts the receiver and dials 999. "There is another way out, down the fire escape, but Mrs. Denton has a gun, so . . . Let's hope they can get here fast."

Sam nods and runs to the door. "Keep hold of that book, Celia. Any sign of life and give the bugger another bash on the head. Hard as you did the first time."

A crisp voice at the end of the line asks if she needs police, fire, or ambulance. "Police," she says. "Come quick, please. There is a man and a woman with a gun . . ." Her voice trembles as she gives the address of the shop.

Once the police are on their way, she telephones Miss Clarke, watching Alfred Humphries the whole time for signs he is coming round. "You need to come to the shop," she tells her. "I've got all the evidence you need."

Chapter 37

Celia

Celia rides the number 18 bus toward Paddington. The events of earlier replay in her mind, over and over. *They got him!* The police arrived within minutes of the 999 call. They swiftly cuffed Humphries and apprehended Mrs. Denton halfway down the fire escape at the back of the building. Celia had given her name and address to the officer in charge, and left Sam and Miss Clarke to await the special team from Scotland Yard. She wonders now if they have arrived yet, the euphoria at catching her mother's betrayer seeping away as she stares out the window into the late October darkness, her spirits falling with every turn of the wheels.

An inner argument she knows she will lose begins to rage inside.

It isn't too late. I don't have to go through with this.

But I do.

She wonders at the fact that, as the bus stops and starts, maneuvering its bulk in and out of the traffic, right at this moment, the president of the United States and the chairman of the Presidium of the Soviet Union must trust in *their* own judgments, making decisions on what should happen next, the future of the world—not just their own lives—hanging in the balance. How they must have listened to hours upon hours of conflicting opinions from all their advisors. How they have hopefully listened to their populations, who simply want to live their lives in peace and not be obliterated because one government or the other has been backed into some untenable political corner. She hopes that one of them will be man enough (perhaps that should be woman enough?) to back down and admit that peace comes before ego and winning.

Because with nuclear war, there can be no winners.

The bus pulls up at the stop before Lancaster Gate, and Celia climbs down the steep, winding stairs from the top deck and out into the night. There is a blustery wind, fat with rain. She wraps her scarf tighter around her neck and walks north along Westbourne Street, the dark expanse of Hyde Park behind her. Her stomach growls, reminding her that all she has eaten since this morning is a couple of rich tea biscuits. She follows Septimus's instructions on how to get to his flat, wondering at the fact that she has never been there before in all the time she has known him. There is so little she really knows about him.

She reaches a redbrick Georgian block, six stories high, halfway along Sussex Gardens. She presses the bell. From close by, the strangled sound of a fox's bark. An answering call comes from farther away. There's a click as Septimus opens the door, and then there he is, smiling at her, eyes drifting for a moment over her head, flickering left to right.

"I'm so glad you came," he says, once she is inside, his voice warm with relief. "I was so afraid you wouldn't." He leads her up two flights of stairs to his flat, which looks out over the street. It is surprisingly spacious, filled with comfortable sofas, a modern fitted kitchen, and one bedroom with a double bed, the covers rumpled and unmade. A suitcase lies half-packed on the floor. A box in the lounge is filled with Septimus's personal effects, a few books, a framed photograph stacked inside. His life, the sum of it, fitting into a suitcase and a box.

She fights the lump in her throat, the growing ache in her chest.

"Septimus . . . I don't want to raise your hopes. I'm here to tell you . . . I've thought long and hard. I'm not leaving."

His eyes don't blink. Reflected in the amber lighting of the room, they are tawnier, more leonine than ever.

"I'll get us a drink," he says after a beat, finally tearing his eyes away, moving to the kitchen. He pulls two bottles of beer from the fridge. "These are all I have, I'm afraid. Since I'd been planning we would leave first thing tomorrow . . ."

"Septimus," Celia says slowly, taking the beer from him. She doesn't drink beer, it's disgusting, but she takes a long slug anyway, barely tasting it. "I can't elope with you. I'm sorry."

Septimus presses her to sit on one of the sofas beside him. He pulls her in close, puts his arm around her shoulders.

She pulls back. "I can't come with you, Septimus," she repeats, meeting his gaze, trying to resist the magnetic pull of his beautiful eyes. "Because I know the truth. You aren't really Septimus Nelson."

She sees the shock of her words in his face, watches his pupils dilate, feels the jolt run through his body.

"Septimus Nelson," she presses on, "was a boy born in Canada in 1936. He died when he was just five years old in 1941, sadly, of pneumonia, following a case of flu. You brought him back to life sometime before you came to London by adopting his identity."

Septimus shakes his head in disbelief, puffing out air, shrinking away from her. "How the hell did you find out?"

Celia shrugs. "I did some digging. Or at least, Miss Clarke did some digging on my behalf."

"But why? You never seemed suspicious." He is staring at her. Recalibrating.

"Why," Celia says, putting her now empty bottle down on the table, "do men perpetually underestimate the ability of women to be in the least bit perceptive, or to own the smallest iota of intelligence?"

Septimus lets his head sink into his hands. "How could I be so stupid?" he says, his voice muffled. "What did I miss?"

"From the moment I met you, I wondered about your visits to the bookshop. True, I thought you *might* be interested in me, but I thought it highly unlikely I was the real reason you came so often. Besides, your story and Mrs. Denton's never really quite tied up. You never seemed to want to talk about your past. You got fidgety when I brought up California, shrugging off my questions, always changing the subject. But the clincher came when I began to be suspicious of Alfred Humphries's identity, and you ridiculed me. There had to be a reason for you to put me off the scent, and that's when I knew I was onto something.

"I told Miss Clarke everything," Celia continues while Septimus remains mute. "Although she is retired, she still has so many connections through her old friend David Bruce, the ambassador, and the CIA, as well as within MI5. They took me seriously enough, unlike Mrs. Denton and Mr. Humphries, who thought me naïve and silly, and you, who thought me blinded by love. Anyway, over the last week, Miss Clarke was able to connect with the right people in Canada and America, and tonight, I've finally learned the truth. That Vera Denton and Alfred Humphries—or should I call them by their true names, Maria Kirova and Claude Beaumont?—were, just like you, given new identities in America. Then they were briefed and sent to England on a special secret mission, with you. Indeed, you were sent to mastermind the setting up of a new network operation of resident illegal spies, without the protection of the Soviet embassy, to extract American and British nuclear weapons secrets to share with your masters in Moscow. The aim being to close the gap in nuclear capability between the USSR and America. Mrs. Denton was to serve you as the communications conduit to Moscow, under the cover of the bookshop. It was most unfortunate for all of you that she picked the one I worked in and kept me on as her shopgirl. But I can't take all the credit. It turns out, the network and the shop were already of interest to the British and American secret services. But they had no idea about you, the extent of the network, or the organization you had running."

Septimus shakes his head as though still fighting his disbelief. "Well, you have certainly done your homework."

"But what really intrigues me, Septimus, is what you planned to do with me if I had agreed to run away with you tomorrow. Why even take me? I would only slow you down. Mess it all up. Surely you would be quicker on your own. You could slip away unnoticed. Get another identity. Become someone new, find somewhere else to carry on the good work. Or did you simply plan to *get rid of me*?"

Septimus recoils as though he has been slapped.

"Never! Celia, whatever else I might be, I didn't lie to you about my feelings. I have only ever cared for you. You mean everything to me. You have to believe me."

"How could I possibly believe you after all this?"

"Surely you must know my feelings are genuine? How could I tell you . . . ? Celia, I only want to keep you safe. You knowing nothing about who I really am, I thought, was the most assured way to do that." Septimus turns toward her, and it is only then that she sees tears in his eyes, rolling freely down his cheeks. That is a stab to the heart. Maybe he really does feel something for her.

"All right," he says, "so far you know some of the truth. But I'm going to tell you all of it. Then maybe you will understand. My real name is Vasili Petrov. I am from a small village in Siberia, in the middle of the most beautiful, wild, and untamed countryside in all the world. The closest city to where I lived, Krasnoyarsk, was hours away from my village. My father was a scientist. He worked, like most of the men, in the huge aluminum plant there, leaving home for weeks at a time, returning for a few days, then off again. But he died suddenly when I was very young. My mother always said—privately only, of course—under mysterious circumstances.

"I don't know how true that was. But I do know he was involved with the KGB, hence their interest in me. I did well at school. I was bright and disciplined, excelling in math and science. I was happy. Of course, we were poor, but so was everyone else, so there was nothing to long for. I had all a child could need—the wilderness, friends, school. But then, when I was ten, the KGB paid my mother a visit. They made her an offer she was not permitted to refuse. They would send me to America, give me a new identity. I would assimilate into American culture, learn how to live like them, without ever forgetting who I really was. I was to live with my aunt, my mother's sister Sylvie. Sylvie was a beautiful ballerina who had escaped to the West while on a ballet tour, marrying an American military man who ended up beating her and then abandoning her. The KGB gave Sylvie and me new identities, a house, and a life in California. Sylvie was to raise me as her son, but I was to belong to the KGB. They visited our house in San Francisco often. I was groomed from the age of ten, after school, during the weekends, the school holidays. A procession of nameless, faceless men, some of whom slept with my aunt, willingly or not, some of whom didn't. I was introduced to Maria Kirova when I was seventeen. She, like me, was being educated for deep cover in the West."

Septimus (how can she think of him as Vasili?) pauses, searching her face for her reaction. It is tragic, all this he is telling her. Somehow, she knows it is the truth, however preposterous it sounds. For the first time, she sees Septimus's armor of self-confidence and bravado, of sophistication and higher knowledge, fall away, revealing something of his true, muddled self. Watching him, she sees the acute discomfort in his telling a truth he can have admitted to almost no one since he was just a child. A *child*! What sort of government recruits *children* to do its bidding?

What can she say in response to such a thing?

"I'm . . . I'm so sorry, Septimus. How your life has been stolen from you . . . It's unspeakably awful."

Septimus shakes his head, becomes agitated. "No. You don't understand. It's not awful. My work is vital to the advancement of mankind! Especially since I secured such a crucial position at the American embassy. I've been able to pass on vital information about American thinking, the advice the British are giving them. All of it helping the Soviet government's decision-making. I'm just one of many important sources who help drive their policy, can't you see? Above all"—he reaches out suddenly, grabs her hands—"everything I do is to help preserve peace. We want the same thing, you and I, don't we?" He smiles, eyes imploring. "Whatever I do, if it helps communism triumph in the end, then my own self-sacrifice is worth it . . . I think, although you don't know it yet, because you have been taught to fear it, really, you want the same thing as me. A society of equals, where everyone has enough to eat, where everyone has an education, a job, a decent life. For men *and* women."

"Septimus . . ." She is momentarily lost for words. The tumult of thoughts in her head whirling too fast, too churned up to construct into meaningful sentences. But there is so little time. She needs to push him. "What did you think we would do? Run away to Siberia? Were you even going to *tell* me your plans? And why run away, since everything is going so well for you here? I don't think I understand . . ."

Sweat is glistening on Septimus's forehead. His palms are clammy against hers.

"Problem is," he says, shuffling closer to her again, "events have rather taken over. I can't see how war can be avoided now—an American U-2 plane has been shot down in Cuba. Another has strayed over Russian territory in the north, and last thing I heard, MiG fighter jets have been scrambled to intercept it. There are four nuclear submarines being hunted down by the US Navy in the Atlantic as we speak—they will probably think World War Three has broken out already. Do you know how hard it is to communicate with subs, ships, planes while they are out there? Impossible, mostly. They will probably have their orders to fire their nuclear weapons in defense if they are attacked. And men, as we know, orders or no orders, when deprived of sleep or under immense strain or fear, behave unpredictably. It only takes that one mistake. That one shot, and that will be it."

"Sorry, Septimus, you aren't making sense."

"What I mean, Celia," he says, swallowing hard, the sweat now pooling at his hairline, crawling down his cheeks, "is there is nothing more any of us can do. We have to hope for the best and do what we can to protect our loved ones. In the meantime, I've received orders to leave London. Tonight, not to wait until morning. They have word—now I realize, thanks to your digging—that they think my network is compromised. I will travel to Scotland tonight, with or without you. They will fly me elsewhere first thing tomorrow, assuming the world still exists. There will be a regrouping. A new identity. Come with me. Please, Celia. I don't want to go without you. I love you, I mean it. And I do think you should be my wife. We would make a great team. Now you know it all, there really is no choice. You have to come."

They are both silent for a moment. He is watching her face, waiting.

"It's impossible . . ." she begins. "I—look, Septimus, I believe you really do think you love me. And I admit, I did think I was falling in love with you too. But I was falling for the Septimus I thought you were. Not *Vasili Petrov*, or whatever your name really is, the spy. And I don't think you quite understand me, not like you think you do. Septimus, I feel wretchedly sorry for all that you have been through, the man they have made you, because I think, deep down, you are a good, caring, gentle, and loving person. You are intelligent and kind, but what you are working for, all the 'good' you're doing—it's . . . it's a fantasy they've brainwashed you into believing. This promised land— it doesn't exist. But listen . . ." Celia hears a noise on the road. The changing note of an engine, a reminder of life outside this flat, of time tick-ticking away. "It isn't too late. You could change sides." She shakes his hands, urging him. Knowing there isn't enough time.

"If you did . . . they would be lenient. It happens, doesn't it? You could still have a good life, Septimus. I feel dreadfully sorry for you. I can see none of this is your fault. Perhaps over time you'll be able to see . . ." Her eyes are filling with tears now, just as she hears the noise from downstairs, the feet on the stairs.

Septimus hears it too. For a moment confusion clouds his eyes, then realization leaks through and his face changes. It twists in pain and shock. His hands fly to his head as horror takes hold.

"No . . . No, no, no, no, Celia, *how could you!*" He's on his feet, looking wildly around the flat for something. His wallet—he grabs it off the kitchen worktop, and he is flying to the entrance, grabbing his coat off the hook as he goes, flinging open the front door. The police, a dozen of them, are on the stairs, in the hallway, mere feet away from him. He makes a dash to go up, not down, but it's too late. They have him. Three of them wrestle him to the floor, twist his arms behind his back. There is a flash of silver and a click as the handcuffs are secured in place.

Celia watches, choking on her own tears.

The last she sees of him as he glances back at her are his eyes. The pain, the resignation in them. Her magnificent lion. Caught.

"Tell them! Tell them all of it," she yells after him as they lead him downstairs to the waiting police cars outside. "Think about what I said. They will listen."

Then her knees give way, and she sinks to the floor, listening to the opening and closing of the car doors. The engines spitting into life, then the sirens receding into the distance.

HALF AN HOUR later, one of the policemen drives her home. Celia is numb, saying nothing as the police car drops her back on Copperfield Street.

"I think she'll be needing a good strong brew with lots of sugar in it," the female officer says, handing Celia over to Father at the front door. He has his coat on, and she dimly realizes he is probably on his way out again to work, having popped home for his break. She's lost all track of time. When she was last home, writing that note, feels like days ago. Weeks.

"Good Lord, whatever's happened?" He blanches seeing Celia's tear-streaked face in the hall light. "Are you hurt?"

"I'm fine," she says, and only as he wraps his long arms around her does she notice she is trembling.

"Come indoors, out of the cold," he says. "Maggie! Put the kettle on, will you? Our Celia looks like she's been through the ringer. I'll telephone the restaurant, tell them I'll be late."

He rubs her upper arms with his big hands. A comforting gesture that makes her want to cry again. But she's spent all her tears for now. She just wants to sit down and let the whole thing out.

"Thanks," she says, as he helps her off with her coat. "I've got so much to tell you both."

Chapter 38

Septimus

It was always going to come to this. He should have known, not fooled himself into thinking otherwise. It was why he had always kept such tight control over his own emotions as well as his actions, his thoughts. He'd been slack. Let himself fall in love, and that was the beginning of his downfall. Not only that, but he'd allowed himself to become panicked by external events that seemed to have been irrevocably spiraling out of control toward what seemed like an inevitable nuclear attack on London. *Always remain calm in a crisis.* He'd forgotten the absolute basics of his training. And, of course, they are still here. Everyone, in the end, backed down. The only thing he has gleaned from catching a snippet of news from a radio playing nearby was that yesterday, Sunday, Nikita Khrushchev announced on Radio Moscow that he would dismantle the Soviet missiles in Cuba. There was no mention of his demand that the United States promise not to invade, or that they remove their nuclear arsenal from Turkey. Which meant either the Soviet Union chairman was the better man, or that the US had made a secret deal that they did not want made public, to save their own embarrassment and their own necks with NATO. He suspects he knows which of those is true.

Septimus lies rigid on his side on the narrow bed in a high-security custody cell. The springs poke through the mattress, reminding him that he is alive and hasn't—not yet, at least—descended into some sort of hinterland between life and everlasting hell. It's been two days since his arrest and now his back is against the wall, physically and metaphorically, and he stares at the opposite one, painted the color of vomit. Alfred and Vera are being held here, too, as well as two others from his network. The Special Branch officers must be patting themselves on the back. Quite a coup they have here. But they haven't gotten them all. They haven't gotten Fox-Andrews or Shauna. Nobody in this network but him knows about them, so he reckons they are safe, for now at least.

Septimus tries not to think of his mother. How disappointed she might be that he has thrown away all his promise, all his hard work because of a girl. A girl who, despite everything, he cannot help loving. How he misses her, aches for her. And in between the aching, the missing, he rages at her so viscerally he physically shakes.

As the waves of conflicting emotions wash through him over the passing days, he comes to realize that the Celia he fell in love with, the Celia he *thought* he was in love with, or at least the girl he wanted her to be, was a mere fabrication. An illusion. The pure, sweet, innocent is a fantasy all his own, and is as false as his memories undoubtedly are of his perfect mother and of Rosa, his past life and even of the motherland. The real, breathing, living Celia, the flesh-and-blood one, has thoughts and opinions of her own. She is smart and ruthless. And prepared to sacrifice him.

As it has ever been since the dawn of time, he realizes. He has made the same mistake as countless men before him. He has woefully underestimated his woman.

Footsteps sound outside, echoing along the corridor. There is a jangle of keys. Doors unlocking. Voices.

By the time they reach his cell, he is on his feet, jacket and shoes on, ready to go. He'd been expecting them, waiting for this day. He knows the likely outcome, but even so, his guts churn and there is the tiny glimmer of hope that *somehow*, he will have gotten away with it. Somehow, one of his comrades— Fox-Andrews—high up in the British establishment, will find a way to get him out of this mess. He holds out his arms for the officers to cuff him.

The journey in the armored vehicle to Bow Street Magistrates' Court is silent and short. All five keep their eyes on their shoes, straying every now and then to the small, barred windows and the glimpses of buildings and bare-limbed trees outside. Pulling up outside the court building, there are armed police and journalists jostling to get closer; cameras click, flashbulbs blind them as they are bundled inside the building. This is a high-profile case.

It doesn't take long. In turn, all five stand and are charged with espionage. The trial will be in January 1963.

There is no late reprieve for Septimus. No Fox-Andrews coming to the rescue.

He is on his own, just as he always knew he would be.

He thinks ahead to his trial. Thinks about offering to turn himself over to the other side, like Celia urged him to do. But he can't bring himself to do it. Even if he wanted to, his own side, the KGB, would hunt him down. They will find him, however many new identities he adopts, or to whatever obscure part of the world he vanishes. They will use him as an example, a warning never to stray from the path he was allotted to follow.

Septimus thinks about simply confessing the full truth of

it, asking for leniency, seeing how he was given little choice as to his profession. But who will believe him anyway? Because he understands that truth, like freedom, is a nebulous thing, muddied by memory and motivation and is never the same for everyone.

Whichever way he turns, he is finished.

And so he resigns himself to his fate, whatever that may be.

Chapter 39

Celia

Natzweiler-Struthof, France
December 1962

They almost didn't come, with such bad weather forecast. But if they didn't do this now, Celia had reasoned, they might have to wait months—until the spring. Celia has been planning this for weeks, with her parents' approval, and feels sure this is the right thing to do. To go before Christmas. And before she starts her new job in January.

They had all been dreading it, but at the same time, they all, in their own way, know this visit is needed if they are to make any sort of peace with the past and begin to take steps toward a new way of being.

Just before leaving, Special Branch confirmed that Claude Beaumont will face a second, albeit different, treason trial. This one, they told Celia, thanks to the evidence she managed to uncover in the flat above H. J. Potts, Booksellers, is sure to result in a conviction. Beaumont, it seems, is, quite simply, a mercenary, offering his services to whoever suits him most. The British, the Nazis, the Soviets, never caring about those, like her mother, he sacrifices along the way. He clearly has no morals, and she hopes that this time, justice will be done.

Celia stares out the window of the train as they make their way from Strasbourg to Rothau, the final leg of their journey.

374 ~ Louise Fein

Seated across from her are her grandparents and next to her is Miss Clarke, the woman whom Mother and Father are slowly coming to forgive and of whom Celia is becoming increasingly fond.

She thinks as she sits on the cushioned seat how different things could have been just a few weeks ago as the world teetered so precariously on the edge of nuclear Armageddon. In the end, perhaps more by accident than by design, they were pulled back from the brink. Celia wonders just how much of that really was to do with Septimus and his information-sharing with the Soviet leadership. Whether what he told her about the near misses on that terrifying Saturday really were true, and that they came as close to war as he said.

What she does know from Miss Clarke is that Khrushchev agreed to withdraw the Soviet Union's weapons from Cuba, but only if the United States agreed to remove the Jupiter missiles deployed across its border in Turkey and not to invade Cuba. But the American agreement to these terms has to be kept secret, because the Americans can't be seen, Miss Clarke said, by their NATO allies to be making resolutions without them. So who, Celia muses, is the winner in this game of secret information and secret deals? Perhaps America in the public's eye, or Russia in reality, or Cuba, whose sovereignty is now to be guaranteed? Or perhaps more so, the world, who can breathe a temporary sigh of relief, and hope that the test ban treaty will now be signed, and nature once again sleep easy. But how long that relief lasts depends on the decisions of a handful of men in the future. Now that these weapons have been invented, they can never be uninvented, and the safety of the world will forever be reliant on good leaders, and sense, and no accidents, and the good alignment of the stars. She wonders how much a part Septimus played in it all. How he, like she, had only ever wanted peace.

Septimus. Her mind gets stuck on him, as it very frequently does. She reaches up to touch the snake charm he gave her back in the summer, where it nestles, still, at her throat. She thinks about how Special Branch permitted her to visit him. How, despite her pleading with him, and after his discussions with various senior personnel in the CIA and MI6, they resolved that he would never be turned. All that he is, so ingrained in every fiber of his being since childhood, is a lost cause.

She shakes thoughts of Septimus away. Somehow, she needs to move on.

Their train pulls into the Rothau station, and then they get into a taxi, which slowly, on chained tires, brings them up into the snowcapped mountains, Miss Clarke explaining as they go how the area had been of interest to the Nazis in the early 1940s for its pink granite. They wanted this special stone for the prestigious buildings they planned to erect to wow the world with their might and wealth. To mine it, they erected a concentration camp up here; to gather a large workforce of political prisoners, male only, who could do the hard labor needed to extract the rock from the mountains. This would serve two purposes—free labor and a way to work the prisoners to death—thereby ridding the Nazis of the inconvenient problem of having people under their rule who didn't agree with them. The Nazis liked efficiency in all areas. Over time, she tells them, the camp increasingly became a place of cruelty, torture, and executions.

They follow the elegant stride of Miss Clarke toward the high wooden gates of the concentration camp. The snow is thick up here, the air bitingly cold. Celia is finding it hard to breathe.

The Nazis certainly picked a beautiful location, set high on top of an expansive hill, with views all around the surrounding mountains, to put the hellish encampment of Natzweiler-Struthof. Beyond the vast wooden structure around the gate, Celia can see the body of the camp spreading down the steep slope where terraces have been built into the hillside. On some, wooden huts remain, but the rest are gone, leaving exposed concrete floors, partly hidden by snow blown into drifts. A high, vicious barbed-wire fence, several layers thick, extends around the whole camp, with watchtowers protruding at regular intervals. Celia imagines a guard placed in each one, others patrolling the area, rifles trained and at the ready. Escape must have been impossible.

As she walks over the snow-covered earth, she pictures her mother's neat lace-ups, the ones she was wearing in the photograph Celia has studied over and over in minute detail, stepping on the same ground. Could she have known her fate as she strode this path? Was she already damaged, in pain, hungry, tired, cold?

An icy wind tears across the hillside, and Celia raises her face to the sky, fighting to inhale air into lungs that feel as though they are being crushed. She stops, closes her eyes. *I got him for you, Mummy*, she tells her. *I got him, and he will be punished this time.* She sees, from the corner of her eye, Father reach out and clasp Mother's hand. The gesture moves something inside her. She hopes that this pilgrimage to the spot where her mother met her untimely end will bring Jeannie peace, too, knowing her parents and daughter are reconciled.

Miss Clarke says something and the caretaker nods. They wait in silence for him to fetch the keys and grant them access. Miss Clarke's former status still garners favors, it seems.

Nausea stirs like eels swimming in Celia's belly. The wriggling of the eels intensifies as the man shoves the gate wide enough for them to pass through.

Miss Clarke beckons them over. "This is Monsieur Bernard." She raises her voice above the roar of the wind. "He can answer your questions and will show you everything you want to see." The man stands before them, his head hanging, expression glum. Celia wonders if he knew the place when it was a camp.

Mother and Father have barely said anything since they boarded the train this morning. It's the fear of what they are about to see, Celia supposes. Facing up to something you dread takes guts.

They walk in silent, single file through the gate of the camp, down the slippery steep slope, past the remaining huts and the empty concrete of the long-gone huts on the terraces, down toward the buildings at the base of the camp. Snow lies in deep drifts, and Celia shudders inside her warm coat, imagining how frozen the ill-clad inmates must have been. She aches at the thought of her mother's agony, her horror as she walked this very path, knowing, as she was sure she did, that her life was soon to be so cruelly snuffed out. How terrified and alone she must have felt.

Celia glances at her grandparents, who lean together as though, without the other, their grief would topple them. Tears streak down Mother's face, and Father's cheeks are pinched, his mouth pressed as though to keep inside his torment. He clings to Mother's hand with both of his own. Miss Clarke translates the caretaker's words in a low monotone for Mother and Celia.

"The gentleman says that in the winter the prisoners only had a thin striped uniform and would be lucky to have had shoes. They were starved, beaten, tortured. The four girls, in one sense, were lucky that they didn't have long to spend here. At least their end was mercifully swift."

Celia is certain she can feel the suffering of all those who endured this hell. It is imprinted on the mountainside, stamped for all eternity into soil and rock; infused on the wind. Celia feels it, keenly, intensely.

"They were taken straight in there." The man points to the building out of which a tall, blackened, narrow chimney extends into clear mountain air. Celia can almost see the vile smoke from burning human flesh pouring out of the chimney, polluting the air. "The four women were taken to the medical room, given a lethal injection, and then they were cremated."

The little group stands in silence and stares up at it, imagining the unimaginable.

"The lethal injection," Miss Clarke continues, "was the very kindest way to go. They would have known nothing of it. It was swift and painless. The women had the comfort of each other. They stayed true, brave and strong right to the very end. Not one of them broke and gave away a single secret. Not one."

She falls into silence, and Celia knows her words of the swift and painless death are not true. She has told them this lie out of kindness. An attempt to save them from the pain of knowing the truth. Because in the end, what use is their suffering? Didn't her mother do enough of that for all of them? She died so that others like Celia could live and love to the fullest. And she will do that with all her heart.

"We should go," Father says, tears now falling down his own cheeks, red-raw from the cold. He glances at Mother, her face contorted as though in physical pain. She nods. "We needed to come, to see this. But now we wish to leave."

Miss Clarke nods, and they make their slow way back up the hill and out of the gate, the caretaker locking it behind them.

Before they step back into the car, Celia, wiping away her own tears with a sodden handkerchief, turns and glances out over the camp one last time.

Good-bye, Mummy. I am so sorry you suffered, but now you are free. I will do my best to make you proud. I know you live inside me, and you always will.

You may rest easy.

SNOW IS FALLING thick and with intent to continue all night when their train pulls into Victoria station. Thankfully, their ferry docked before the snow really hit, before it has a chance to clog up the railways and the roads, which it seems certain to do. There are dire predictions for this winter to be worse than any in living memory.

They bundle into a taxi, too exhausted and cold to consider the Underground, followed by a bus and then a walk home.

"I hope Bartholomew hasn't frozen to death," Celia comments, staring out the window at the blanket of falling snow.

"Cats are sensible creatures," Father comments. "He'll find somewhere to shelter. Most likely he'll be curled up next to Ursula Bancroft's fire. Sam wouldn't let him out in this weather, the soppy sod."

Celia smiles, looking forward to having her purring companion back. He doesn't make up for the loss of Septimus, but he helps. As do Daphne and Sam and their cheery support. The trip to France has helped. Thinking about something, *anything*, other than him helps.

It will be better when she can work again. The new job, at least, will utilize her mind. Since Mrs. Denton was arrested and taken away for interrogation by the Scotland Yard team, the bookshop, of course, has been closed. She has no idea what will happen to it. The stock sold, the space leased to someone else, she supposes. The trial will be in the new year, and, for Septimus, she is dreading it. Fearing the outcome, whatever it is.

In the meantime, she tries to think about things that aren't him. But it's hard. Everything seems to remind her of him. She longs to discuss things with him. Misses his wisdom, his affection. It will get easier, she tells herself. And it's true—it already has, thanks to certain developments in her life.

She brings to mind the conversation she had with Miss Clarke a couple of weeks before they left for France.

"Now, Celia, my dear," Miss Clarke had said in a conspiratorial tone, "what are your plans after all this? Jobwise, I mean."

"I suppose, now that I've passed my Pitman's exams, I shall apply to the BBC like I always wanted. I'll see if they have any openings in their typing pool."

Miss Clarke had given her a quizzical look. "Do I detect a tiny reluctance?"

Celia sighed. "It was always the dream," she said, "but I suppose I have learned a thing or two about myself over the last few months, and now . . ."

"And now?"

"Well, being a secretary is great, and I know it's a dream job for lots of girls, but I suppose, after all that excitement, I want something more . . ." As soon as the words were out, she had wished she could take them back. She sounded so ungrateful, so *demanding*. "Interesting," she finished in a small voice.

"Well, I am delighted to hear that, Celia. I rather hoped you might feel that way."

"I'm sorry?"

"Don't be. A bright girl like you shouldn't go to waste, if you don't mind me saying."

Celia's jaw had dropped in surprise.

"Look, I'll say this rather quickly, as I don't know how it will go down with your grandparents, but after your sterling work, I think you would do extremely well if you fancied joining MI6. I could have a word for you. I don't doubt they would be interested. Now, I'm not for a minute suggesting you would be doing anything dangerous like your mother, but to me, you seem well-suited to the secret service. And trust me, Celia, we need good people more than ever at this moment in time. The Cuban crisis might be over, but threats do not go away. Think about it. Write to me, or telephone and let me know if you would like to have a chat at least."

Celia had almost fallen over in shock.

"But what would I tell my grandparents? What would I say about where I work?"

"You would simply tell them you work for a government department. As soon as you tell people you work for, say, the Ministry of Transport, you'll see their eyes glaze over and they won't ask any further questions." She gave Celia a wink.

"Well, I—"

"Don't give me your answer now." Miss Clarke had patted her arm. "Think about it."

She didn't need to think about it. There really had been only one possible answer she could give to Miss Clarke.

It was the answer, she knows for sure, that would make her mother proud.

MUCH LATER, REFRESHED after a bath and an early supper, Celia removes the snake charm necklace and places it in a box at the back of her bedside table. It is time, she thinks. She slides on her coat, hat, and scarf. After Daphne—and she happens to be busy tonight—there is only one person she wants to see right now. One person she can share all this with, who will quietly listen, without judgment. A person who, since the night of the arrests, she has come to see in a different light.

Sam.

Why does this have to happen, when there is barely a month left before he is due to start his new job in Yorkshire?

We can write, he has told her, whenever she raises his imminent departure. *And it'll only be for a couple of years. After that, I'm sure I can get a transfer back.*

Sometimes, what you want is right there in front of you all along. You have gotten so used to seeing it that you simply don't notice it at all. Until it is gone.

When the knock comes on the front door, she says a quick good-bye to her grandparents, letting them know she's going for a quiet drink with Sam. She opens the door to find him leaning against the doorframe, all tight T-shirt and leather jacket, hair quaffed like James Dean.

"There you are," he says, smiling, moving toward her, reaching out for her hand.

"Here I am," she says, taking his, and they step out together into the night.

Epilogue

Celia

November 1964

Celia collects her post from the cubbyhole in reception. It's still early, and as always, she is one of the first to arrive in the building.

Miss Taylor, the receptionist, sits down with a sigh behind the impressively large and shiny mahogany reception desk.

"Getting chilly out there in the mornings now," Miss Taylor says conversationally as Celia flicks through the several envelopes that have arrived in the first post, awaiting Celia's attention. Miss Taylor pulls a mirror from her bag, checks her reflection, reapplies her lipstick. "I'll make you a cuppa if you like," she says to Celia, putting her makeup away and shoving her handbag beneath the desk. "I know how busy you are—barely ever see you in the kitchen."

It's true. But then, Celia has no interest in standing around in the kitchen, gossiping with the others while the kettle boils. She adores her work, and anyway, gossip is for *after* work, in her opinion. *She's a dark horse*, she hears the others whisper when she fails to volunteer information about her love life, or lack of it. She smiles to herself, keeping secret the knowledge that, in less than a month, Sam will be back in the Big Smoke. He's finally got his transfer and will be heading up a team in Battersea.

What will happen between them, she has no idea, but she has an inkling that it will be fun finding out. No expectations, no promises, but whenever she thinks of him, her heart races. It is the 1960s, after all.

"That would be lovely, Miss Taylor, thank you," Celia says. "No sugar, though, I've given up."

"Sweet enough, are ya?" She cackles at her own joke.

Celia smiles politely and escapes along the long passageway to the ground-floor office she shares with the other three who make up Internal Security. The job of her secretive team within MI6 is to sniff out moles not only within the service, but those who hide in the other agencies and in government. Celia loves the thrill of her work, the meaningfulness.

She opens the door to the office, sighing with pleasure at the sight of the empty room. The peace of it. An hour or so to herself before the clatter and activity, the phones ringing, the noisy bustle. She enjoys that, too, and the camaraderie with her colleagues, but this precious morning hour is worth the early alarm.

She sits down at her desk and continues sorting the post, stopping at the sight of a plain manila envelope with familiar writing. Miss Clarke. She smiles. Miss Clarke is now living almost all year down in Winchelsea, which she describes in her letters as quite the idyll.

Celia fingers the slim envelope before opening it. There is something lumpy inside. She slices the envelope open with the paper knife Father gave her, a "congratulations on the new job in the civil service" present.

The lump turns out to be a paper clip holding together a cutting from a Russian newspaper and a neatly typed English translation. There is a sentence at the bottom in Miss Clarke's handwriting.

Dearest Celia, I thought you would want to see this. I can imagine how you will feel. Call me when you would like to talk it over. Best wishes, Muriel

Celia unclips the translation from the article, lays the two pieces of paper flat, side by side, on her desk. She almost doesn't want to read. Doesn't want to know what is written here. Her stomach clenches.

She knows the article will be about Septimus. Dear, sweet, misguided Septimus. The man with the beautiful face, the lion eyes. A part of her still misses him. Still wishes things could have been different, but that was never really a possibility. Because whatever Celia did or didn't do, fate would always have parted them in the end. They were two lost souls, from two such different worlds, caught for a moment in time somewhere in the void between, connecting, holding each other up, until, inevitably, they were swept apart once more.

She smooths the sheets with her hands, gathering courage. Remembering. With evidence from MI5, the CIA, and the Royal Canadian Mounted Police, it hadn't taken long for Septimus Nelson, Vera Denton, Alfred Humphries (she will never be able to think of them by their real names), and the two other spies to be convicted at their trial for espionage at the Old Bailey in January 1963. Septimus had been successfully running an entire network of Soviet agents, all of whom were in "deep cover." It is likely there are more, yet to be uncovered, but the apprehension of Septimus and the breaking up of this network was a huge coup for the British security forces. It was all over the papers. But there was no mention of Celia or Miss Clarke in the story. *It's better that way, trust me*, Miss Clarke had told her with a knowing wink. Vera and Alfred were sentenced to twenty years each, Septimus to twenty-five.

At the beginning of December 1962, Septimus was moved to a prison in Birmingham to await his trial. Celia had visited him only once before he was moved, just after he'd been charged. She had promised to visit again. But she never did. It wasn't a good idea on so many levels, and besides, the weather was a good enough excuse. From December 1962 until February 1963, the coldest winter for two hundred years kept them all snowed in for months. Even the Thames froze solid enough to drive a car over. She promised herself she would visit in the spring.

But before she found the opportunity, suddenly, quietly, Septimus was sent back to the Soviet Union in exchange for a British spy.

Celia takes a deep breath. Forces herself to read the article.

October 3, 1964—Moscow

News has been received of the sad and unexpectedly early death of Vasili Petrov, the renowned Soviet Agent who was returned a hero to his motherland over a year ago. Friend and neighbor Oleg Golubev described Petrov as a quiet, polite man who kept to himself. He never talked about his foreign exploits and played down his hero status. During the time the men lived as neighbors, they came to be friends. They had a common love of nature and would go for expeditions into the country-

side. Mr. Golubev was shocked by the sudden and unexpected death of Mr. Petrov, who, he said, appeared
to be a healthy man when he returned from Britain.
Mr. Petrov's body was found by a local man walking his
dog in a suburban forest outside Moscow. It is believed
Mr. Petrov had been on a mushroom-picking expedition.
A postmortem confirms he died of a stroke. Mr. Petrov was
twenty-eight years old. A spokesman for the pathologist
explained that while strokes in young men are unusual,
they are not unheard of, and it is likely Mr. Petrov had
some undiagnosed pathological weakness or disease that
caused his untimely death.

Celia stares at the page until the ink blurs. Nausea rises, and
she slaps a hand over her mouth, wondering if she needs to make
a run for the ladies'. The feeling recedes, and she stares with
unseeing eyes out the window onto the still-dark street. This
was no natural death. Septimus was young, fit. But he feared his
own side more than the enemy. When she visited him before the
trial, he told her he would be relieved to be given a long sentence
in a British prison. At least there, he might be safe.

Poor, dear Septimus. What a horrible, hateful end he didn't
deserve. Or did he? He could have changed sides. He could have
simply stopped. Disappeared. Made different choices. But even
as Celia thinks those thoughts, she knows it isn't that simple.
Life, events, wars, or avoiding them are all a series of accidents,
of unplanned disorder that simply happens, however in control
anyone thinks they actually are of the world around them. Septimus was both master of his fate and victim of it. Like he
always used to say, he was merely a cog in a wheel, playing his

tiny part in a much bigger whole, just as her mother did, just as she is doing now.

Miss Taylor bustles into the room with the tea.

Celia looks up at her with a grateful smile. "Thank you, Miss Taylor," she says. "Do you know, on second thought, I think I might like that sugar, after all."

Author's Note

Life, politics, and events are as much story as fact. This is also true of history and the retelling of it. Read several nonfiction books on a single event—for example, the Cuban Missile Crisis—and you will always learn something a little different. Each source I read on all the subject matters explored in this novel varied according to the author's knowledge at the time of writing, facts available, opinion, slant. As a novelist, I have taken various liberties in the writing of this fictional story, inspired by real events, people, and places.

The majority of *The London Bookshop Affair* is set in 1962, culminating in the two weeks of October 1962 surrounding the Cuban Missile Crisis. The crisis was, to a significant degree, caused by aggressive American policy toward Cuba. Many of Kennedy's decisions over the crisis were politically motivated rather than driven by security concerns. There was a spectacular failure on the part of US intelligence to ascertain the buildup of Soviet troops and the arrival of the nuclear arsenal during the summer of 1962. The ending of the crisis, resulting in the withdrawal of Soviet missiles from Cuba, and American removal of the Jupiter missiles from Turkey, was a deal made in complete secrecy.

On Saturday, October 27, at the height of the crisis, several mishaps occurred, each of which alone almost triggered a war. Newly translated accounts of the events sixty years ago show just how terrifyingly close a B-59 Russian submarine came to firing its nuclear-tipped torpedo as a result of the overly aggressive tactics of American submarine hunters. Another near miss occurred when an American U-2 spy plane accidentally strayed over Siberia, resulting in the scrambling of F-102 fighter jets to protect it. Unbeknownst to the chiefs of staff who gave the orders, the jets had already been armed with nuclear missiles as a result of the raising of the alert to DEFCON 2. Such errors can happen anyplace, anytime, and the avoidance of catastrophe is as much to do with luck as with sensible decision-making. A recent example of a similar mistake took place in September 2022 when a Russian fighter jet "malfunctioned" and released a missile, narrowly missing a British surveillance plane in international airspace.

If war had taken place in 1962, Britain would have been the launchpad for the sixty American Thor missiles that were secretly kept on British soil (Project Emily). Forty of Britain's RAF Vulcan bombers were on fifteen-minute standby at four airfields, their pilots and crew sleeping with their aircraft, waiting for the cue to unleash nuclear weapons on the heart of the Soviet Union. While Campaign for Nuclear Disarmament protestors massed in London and families went about their day as usual: the general public was completely unaware that London was likely to have been the first place to face a nuclear attack by the Soviet Union.

As mentioned in the novel, London was closer to Moscow than Washington, DC, and because of the now-infamous Soviet spy rings operating in London, Khrushchev was well aware of the plans to launch American weapons from Britain. A few days before Kennedy's televised speech to the nation, he had given advance notice of the escalating crisis to the United Kingdom (four hours before the other European powers), which included a copy of the speech he planned to make, photos of the missile sites, and a briefing from the CIA. This was delivered to the UK via the American ambassador. I have used this channel as Septimus's method to gain his information to pass on to the Soviets. Septimus, as a Soviet agent at the embassy, and in his position as aide-de-camp to the ambassador, is entirely fictional.

From the Second World War, and extending well into the 1960s and '70s, the growing tension between the Soviet Union and the West resulted in Soviet spy networks springing up in the UK. Spies were recruited at all levels of society, many, infamously, from the higher echelons, the Cambridge Five and the Portland Spy Ring being examples. The inspiration for Septimus's network of spies for this story is the Portland network. This network was operative in the late 1950s and early 1960s and passed information relating to the UK's submarine fleet to the Soviets, enabling the manufacture of a new generation of Soviet submarines. The real Portland Spy Ring was operational only until their arrests in 1961, but for the purposes of this story, I have pushed the timeline of their operations to include the Cuban crisis in 1962. The Soviets preferred to target lower-level employees, such as secretaries, to gain access to material. The Portland network were deep cover "illegals" who had no diplomatic cover. They were living in the cold, under false names and identities. My fictional Mrs. Denton is very loosely based on a couple, Peter and Helen Kroger (real names Morris and Lona Cohen, American-born KGB illegals), who, prior to operating within the Portland network, passed on top secret intelligence on US atomic research from agents including Julius and Ethel Rosenberg. The Cohens were spirited out of the United States in 1952 and arrived two years later in the UK with New Zealand passports. They used radio equipment to pass secrets back to Moscow from their house in Ruislip, a quiet suburb of London, acting as a funnel for information gathered by other spies in the network. Their cover was running an antiquarian bookshop on the Strand, until the breaking of the network in early 1961 and their arrests and trials.

For the purposes of this story, I have my fictional Mrs. Denton operating out of the bookshop itself, and the information obtained includes not only that gathered by Alfred Humphries from his *bit of skirt* at the Admiralty Underwater Weapons Establishment (AUWE), but the secret discussions that took place between British Prime Minister Macmillan and President Kennedy. Details of these discussions are now available in declassified records. In reality, the Soviets probably did know about the plans to launch nuclear weapons from the UK through information passed from Soviet spy Anthony Blunt. He was the curator of the queen's art collection, and at around this time, the decision was made that priceless artwork should be moved out of London to save it from possible nuclear war.

Alfred Humphries himself is an amalgamation of real-life spy Harry Houghton, who worked at the AUWE, and the WWII double agent Henri Déricourt (see further below). Houghton became involved with a filing clerk, Ethel Gee, who handed top secret documents to Houghton to pass on.

The rally attended by Celia and Daphne in the early summer of 1962 was based on a real speech given by Sir Bertrand Russell in the summer of 1959 in Manchester. He gave various speeches in Trafalgar Square in the early 1960s, but I have used the content of this one, as it most served the purposes of the story, despite being incorrect in terms of place and time. The content of the speech, however, was equally relevant, if not more so, by 1962.

The Spies for Peace was a real group of antiwar activists associated with the Committee of 100 who actually did break into a
secret government bunker, but not until 1963. Until their rev-
elations in the pamphlet they published and distributed to the
national press, politicians, and peace activists—*Danger! Official
Secret*—the British public had been virtually unaware that the
government was planning for the aftermath of a nuclear attack.
None of the "spies" behind the group were ever caught.

The inspiration for Septimus Nelson was Konon Molody, aka
Gordon Lonsdale. He posed as a Canadian businessman and
was the mastermind behind the Portland Spy Ring. He never,
however, worked at the American embassy. The real Gordon
Lonsdale was born in Canada and died when he was a young
man. Konon Molody was born in Moscow, and his scientist
father died when he was young. The NKVD helped his mother
get him a foreign passport when he was twelve, and he went to
live with his aunt in California, where he attended school and
became familiar with American culture. He returned to Moscow
and after the war traveled to Canada, where he adopted the
identity of Gordon Lonsdale. After his capture and conviction,
in 1964 he was sent back to the Soviet Union as part of a spy
swap. In 1970, at the age of forty-eight, he died of a stroke on
a mushroom-picking expedition. Another retired KGB agent
claimed Molody had been healthy but was receiving injections
for high blood pressure from KGB doctors.

I have used the Special Operations Executive (SOE) as
inspiration for Jeannie's storyline. It was established in 1940
to conduct espionage and sabotage missions and to support
local resistance movements in occupied Europe. SOE was
also known as Churchill's Secret Army or the Ministry of
Ungentlemanly Warfare, with its headquarters, named the

Inter-Services Research Bureau, situated on Baker Street. Its existence at the time was top secret. More than thirteen thousand people, of whom more than three thousand were women, were involved in the SOE until it was formally ended shortly after the war. Much has been written about the SOE, its brave agents being portrayed widely in films and novels. Less has been written about the disastrous infiltration of some key SOE circuits by the Germans, which went largely undetected, or at least unbelieved, by the senior SOE figures in London.

Four women—Diana Rowden, Sonia Olschanezky, Vera Leigh, and Andrée Borrel—were executed at Natzweiler-Struthof concentration camp on July 6, 1944. They were all given a lethal injection, but according to prisoner and Gestapo evidence, there was not enough of the lethal dose for all four women. It is believed they were put into the crematorium ovens alive, the first three women unconscious, but the fourth, Diana Rowden, was likely conscious. Other female agents were beaten, tortured, and executed at different concentration camps. They included Violette Szabo, a young widow and mother to a baby daughter, Tania, executed at Ravensbrück; a talented young wireless operator, Noor Inayat Khan, died at Dachau. As civilians, not military personnel, they were afforded none of the protections granted by the Geneva Conventions for prisoners of war. My fictional agent, Jeannie, is very loosely based on Violette, Noor, and the four women executed at Natzweiler—she is a compilation of all these incredible women and the horror they experienced.

My character Madeleine is based on the real-life Jeannie Rousseau, a truly incredible woman, code-named Amniarix. Portraying herself as a "silly girl," she managed to coax out of Nazi officers extraordinary details of the German's secret work on V-1 rockets, which led to the British raids on Peenemünde, where the V-1 and V-2 rockets were under development, resulting in delays and saving thousands of lives. Contrary to the Nazis' impression of Rousseau, she was of great intellect and had a photographic memory, which she used to replicate the intricate drawings of the rockets, which were then sent to Allied intelligence. She was eventually captured and sent to three concentration camps, none of which could break her. She survived and lived to the age of ninety-eight.

As mentioned earlier, Alfred Humphries is in part loosely based on Henri Déricourt, an SOE agent from 1943 to 1944. A talented pilot, Déricourt was the leader of the Farrier circuit, and with his unparalleled knowledge of French airspace, he found landing fields for dropping agents, and coordinated the arrival and departure of agents between England and France. But Déricourt was almost certainly a double agent working for Karl Bömelburg, head of the Gestapo in France. Déricourt had been friends with both Bömelburg and British journalist Nicolas Bodington (in the novel, my character Peter Berkley) in Paris before the war. Bodington went on to become second in command to the head of the French section of the SOE in London, Maurice Buckmaster (in the novel, Arthur Royston). Although MI5 said they were unable to guarantee Déricourt's reliability, his old friend Bodington enthusiastically endorsed him, and in November 1942, he was recruited as coordinator of the air operations for SOE. It is thought that Déricourt's treachery led to the capture of more than one hundred agents.

The Nazis, using a captured wireless set, began communicating with the SOE in London, engaging in "the English Game," assuming the identity of the captured agents to gain intelligence from London. Despite rumors from the field about Déricourt, and that agents and wirelesses had been captured, as well as the suspicions of the women in the Signals Department that there was a change in agents' "fists"—that is, the individual pace and style of each agent's Morse code transmissions—the French section leader, Buckmaster, refused to believe any of it.

The truth finally emerged in 1946 when Vera Atkins (on whom my character Miss Clarke is loosely based) began to track down what happened to her missing agents. This included her interviewing the Gestapo who had worked with Déricourt. Atkins herself had worked for Buckmaster but had not acted on her own suspicions about Déricourt due to her compromised position as a Jewish refugee from Romania working inside a British spy agency, without British citizenship until 1944. As for Atkins herself and her activities after the war, she was intensely secretive and is a little shrouded in mystery. While outwardly she worked for an educational establishment sponsored by UNESCO, there were rumors of her doing paid work for the CIA, but also of her being sympathetic to communist ideas, and to the Soviets. Indeed, establishments such as those she worked for were sometimes front organizations for the Soviets.

At the 1948 treason trial of Déricourt in Paris, no British SOE personnel gave evidence against him; indeed, Nicolas Bodington, his old friend, gave evidence that he had known and approved of his contact with the Germans and that he had total trust in him. Why Atkins never gave evidence is unknown, but her biographer, Sarah Helm, gave one reason to be the idea that her own compromised position in the SOE should not risk being outed.

Déricourt was acquitted, but his reputation was destroyed. He became involved in drug trafficking and the smuggling of gold bars. In November 1962, Déricourt flew four passengers and a load of gold into Laos. The plane crashed due to fuel starvation. There were no survivors, but Déricourt's body was never recovered. Although it seems unlikely, there were rumors that Déricourt's death was faked to allow him to assume a new identity and operate elsewhere. There was an alleged sighting of him once in New York, and suggestions that he may have been spying for the Soviets. Certainly there are cases of other faked deaths, for example Horst Kopkow, who was a senior counter-intelligence officer for the Reich Security Main Office during the Nazi era. He was arrested and held in British custody in 1946, and, after being considered "helpful," in 1948 his death from natural causes was faked so he could work for British and American intelligence.

Finally, the idea for Jeannie's baby being taken away from her because she was an unmarried mother was sadly a reality for countless women. A damning report was published in the UK in July 2022 by the Joint Committee on Human Rights that estimated that 185,000 children were taken from their mothers between 1949 and 1976. It blamed the government, state institutions, and their employees for the lifelong pain and suffering caused. The stigma and shame poured on women and girls for becoming pregnant out of wedlock meant they were wrongly perceived as having voluntarily given up their babies. Many were placed in mother and baby homes for the last weeks of their pregnancies, where they were treated with inhumanity, forced to scrub floors, and often physically punished for their "crime" of becoming unmarried mothers.

In creating *The London Bookshop Affair*, I have taken liberties with the real facts behind it, moving time frames and making connections between people that did not exist. I have therefore changed the names of all the real people from whom I have taken inspiration, bar those historical figures who make only a minor appearance in the novel. The characters of Celia, Maggie, and André are entirely invented. There is also no public record of any Soviet spies within the United States Embassy in London.

Apart from the original source materials from the National Archives, the JFK Library, the British Library, and the King's College London archive collection, I am greatly indebted to the following authors, whose books have, at least in part, informed the factual background for this novel:

A Life in Secrets: Vera Atkins and the Missing Agents of WWII, Sarah Helm

Between Silk and Cyanide: A Codemaker's War, 1941–1945, Leo Marks

They Fought Alone: The Story of British Agents in France, Maurice Buckmaster

The Women Who Lived for Danger: Behind Enemy Lines During WWII, Marcus Binney

Six Faces of Courage, M.R.D. Foot

SOE Syllabus: Lessons in Ungentlemanly Warfare, World War II

The German Penetration of SOE: France 1941–1944, Jean Overton Fuller

Ambassador to Sixties London: The Diaries of David Bruce, 1961–1969, edited by Raj Roy and John W. Young

One Minute to Midnight: Kennedy, Khrushchev, and Castro on the Brink of Nuclear War, Michael Dobbs

Nuclear Folly: A New History of the Cuban Missile Crisis, Serhii Plokhy

The Likes of Us: An Official Biography of the White Working Class, Michael Collins

Acknowledgments

A novel has the author's name on the cover, but in truth, publishing a book is a massive group effort. My eternal thanks, firstly, to my agent, Caroline Hardman, for being such a champion of my writing and writing career, for discussing ideas and challenging me to strive to be better. My thanks also to the entire team at Hardman & Swainson for your hard work and advice, whether that be in seeking translation rights, negotiating contracts, or a myriad other tasks. My very grateful thanks, too, to my wonderful editor, Liz Stein. It has been an absolute joy to collaborate with you on making this book the best it can be. Your astute, insightful input has been utterly invaluable. Thank you to brilliant copy editor Kathleen Cook for your incredible attention to detail and for spotting my (many) errors and inconsistencies. Indeed, my most grateful thanks go to the whole team at William Morrow, including Ariana Sinclair, Jeanie Lee, and Mumtaz Mustafa, for the fabulous cover design. There is so much that goes on behind the scenes in producing a book— my thanks to everyone involved.

I am so grateful to all my author friends, who keep me sane on a daily basis. Being an author would be a lonely life without you all. Special thanks to Nikki Smith, Nicola Gill, Polly Crosby, Zoë Sommerville, and Frances Quinn for variously brainstorming ideas, reading early drafts, discussing titles, sharing writing retreats, and just generally being there. Thank you to all my nonwriting friends for putting up with me endlessly talking books and disappearing into my writing shed for long intervals, as well as for being so generous and kind as to say nice things about my books. You are the best.

I'm forever grateful to all my family not only for giving me the space and time to write but also for being endlessly supportive, understanding, and encouraging, especially when I'm having doubts and confidence crises, which in truth, is rather often. I couldn't do this without you.

Enormous thanks to all those involved in spreading the word about not only this book but all books, from reviewers and bloggers to booksellers, librarians, and book groups.

Special thanks must go to Laurie Alexander of Ohio for naming Bartholomew the cat in this book. I ran a competition in my newsletter, and this was the perfect name for him! I am also most grateful to wonderful reader Robert Elmore from Oregon, retired from working with the US Air Force, and with whom I consulted about possible roles Septimus might have had that would have brought him close to the action with the American ambassador in London. Bob—I have enjoyed our correspondence and am most grateful for all your kind and thoughtful advice.

Last, but most definitely not least, my eternal thanks to all my readers. I am touched that so many of you have been so kind as to take the time to get in touch and let me know how much you have enjoyed reading my books. This means the world to me.

About the Author

LOUISE FEIN is the author of *Daughter of the Reich*, which has been published in thirteen territories, and the international bestseller *The Hidden Child*. She holds an MA in creative writing from St. Mary's University. She lives in Surrey, UK, with her family.

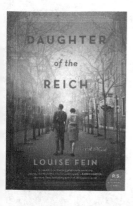